PRAISE FOR PATRICIA POTTER'S NOVELS

"A gripping reading experience. Don't miss this excellent tale of heartbreak and innocence in the Old West."
—*Rendezvous* on DIABLO

"An action-packed . . . western romance whose lead characters are superb, and the supporting cast is first rate."
—*Affaire de Coeur* on DEFIANT

"Another wondrous read from this master craftsman."
—*Romantic Times* on WANTED

"Save a space on the keeper shelf for RELENTLESS."
—*The Talisman* on RELENTLESS

"Absorbing, powerful. This is definitely a book you will keep."
—*Rendezvous* on NOTORIOUS

"Patricia Potter has brought much pleasure with this Gold 5 offering."
—*Heartland Critiques* on RENEGADE

"A stunning achievement."
—*Romantic Times* on LAWLESS

"A delightful adventure, full of twists and turns and the passions of the time."
—*Rendezvous* on RAINBOW

Bantam Books by Patricia Potter
Ask your bookseller for titles
you may have missed

THE MARSHAL AND THE HEIRESS
DIABLO
DEFIANT
WANTED
RELENTLESS
NOTORIOUS
RENEGADE
LIGHTNING
LAWLESS
RAINBOW

THE
Marshal
AND THE
Heiress

PATRICIA POTTER

Bantam Books
New York Toronto London Sydney Auckland

THE
Marshal
AND THE
Heiress

Prologue

1868

How do you tell a four-year-old girl that her mother is dead?

U.S. Marshal Ben Masters worried over the question as he stood on the porch of Mrs. Henrietta Culworthy's small house. Then, squaring his shoulders, he knocked. He wished he really believed he was doing the right thing. What in God's name did a man like him, a man who'd lived with guns and violence for the past eight years, have to offer an orphaned child?

Mary May believed in you. The thought raked through his heart. He felt partially responsible for her death. He had stirred a pot without considering the consequences. In bringing an end to an infamous outlaw hideout, he had been oblivious to those caught in the cross fire. The fact that Mary May had been involved with the outlaws didn't assuage his feelings of guilt.

"Sarah. Promise you'll take care of Sarah." He would never forget Mary May's last faltering words.

Ben rapped again on the door of the house. Mrs. Culworthy should be expecting him. She had been looking after Sarah Ann for the past three years, but now she had to return east to care for a brother. She had already postponed her trip once, agreeing to wait until Ben had wiped out the last remnants of an outlaw band and fulfilled a promise to a former renegade named Diablo.

The door opened. Mrs. Culworthy's wrinkled face appeared, sagging slightly with relief. Had she worried that he would not return? He sure as hell had thought about it. He'd thought about a lot of things, like where he might find another home for Sarah Ann. But then he would never be sure she was safe. By God, he owed Mary May.

"Sarah Ann?" he asked Mrs. Culworthy.

"In her room." The woman eyed him hopefully. "You *are* going to take her."

He nodded.

"What about your job?"

"I'm resigning. I used to be a lawyer. Thought I would hang up my shingle in Denver."

A smile spread across Mrs. Culworthy's face. "Thank heaven for you. I love that little girl. I would take her if I could, but—"

"I know you would," he said gently. "But she'll be safe with me." He hoped that was true. He hesitated. "She doesn't know yet, does she? About her mother?"

Mrs. Culworthy shook her head.

Just then, a small head adorned with reddish curls and green eyes peered around the door. Excitement lit the gamin face. "Mama's here!"

Pain thrust through Ben. Of course, Sarah Ann would think her mother had arrived. Mary May had been here with him just a few weeks ago.

"Uncle Ben," the child said, "where's Mama?"

He wished Mrs. Culworthy had already told her. He was sick of being the bearer of bad news, and never more so than now.

He dropped to one knee and held out a hand to the little girl. "She's gone to heaven," Ben said.

She approached slowly, her face wrinkling in puzzlement; then she looked questioningly at Mrs. Culworthy. The woman dissolved into tears. Ben didn't know whether Sarah Ann understood what was being said, but she obviously sensed that something was very wrong. The smile disappeared and her lower lip started to quiver.

Ben's heart quaked. He had guarded that battered part of him these past years, but there were no defenses high enough, or thick enough, to withstand a child's tears.

He held out his arms, not sure Sarah Ann knew him well enough to accept his comfort. But she walked into his embrace, and he hugged her, stiffly at first. Unsure. Then her need overtook his uncertainty, and his grip tightened.

"You asked me once if I were your papa," he said. "Would you like me to be?"

Sarah Ann looked up at him. "Isn't Mama coming back?"

He shook his head. "She can't, but she loved you so much she asked me to take care of you. If that's all right with you?"

Sarah Ann turned to Mrs. Culworthy. "I want to stay with you, Cully."

"You can't, pumpkin," Mrs. Culworthy said tenderly. "I have to go east, but Mr. Masters will take good care of you. Your mother thought so, too."

"Where is heaven? Can't I go, too?"

"Someday," Ben said slowly. "And she'll be waiting for you, but right now I need you. I need someone to take care of me, too, and your mama thought we could take care of each other."

It was true, he suddenly realized. He did need someone to love. His life had been empty for so long.

Sarah Ann probably had much to offer him.

But what did he have to offer her?

Sarah Ann put her hand to his cheek. The tiny fingers were incredibly soft—softer than anything he'd ever felt—and gentle. She had lost everything, yet she was comforting him.

He hugged her close for a moment, and then he stood. Sarah Ann's hand crept into his. Trustingly. And Ben knew he would die before ever letting anything bad happen to her again.

Chapter One

ABOARD THE LADY MARY ON THE
ATLANTIC OCEAN
1868

"Annabelle!"

Ben tried to keep the irritation from his voice as he stuck his head under the lifeboat. The shirt he had grabbed and thrown on without buttoning flapped in the wind.

Damn, but it was cold. He'd known cold before, but not like this; the icy ocean wind seeped through his bones. It didn't help his bad leg, either, which had stiffened during the voyage.

"Annabelle, come on, now. Come out of there," he cajoled in the soothing voice he'd used many times before to try to lure his prey from hiding. Unfortunately, the present outlaw wasn't responding one bit better than those in the past.

"Mr. Masters?"

He pulled his head out and squinted up at Mrs.

Franklin T. Faulkner. The dowager, who had sat at the captain's table with him the night before, had her mouth pursed in disapproval.

If only his fellow marshals could see him now. They would laugh themselves silly.

"I'm looking for my daughter's cat," he explained curtly, then turned back to his mission, digging deeper under the lifeboat. Sarah Ann would be inconsolable if she lost the half-grown calico cat they'd rescued off the streets of Boston before boarding the ship. The cat, though, had been irritatingly ungrateful. Once adopted and feeling safe, she delighted in scampering out the cabin door to antagonize the ship's rat-catching cats. Apprehending her tested every one of Ben's hunting skills.

"A cat?" Mrs. Faulkner said.

"A cat," Ben confirmed, his hand stretching toward the ragged bundle of fur.

"Annabelle?" she added in a disbelieving tone.

Ben didn't answer. He wished the woman would scurry away as quickly as Annabelle had escaped his cabin minutes ago. The thought amused him. The hefty Mrs. Faulkner couldn't scurry if her life depended on it.

"Mr. Masters!" The voice was indignant.

He cursed audibly and heard a shocked gasp in response. He clenched his teeth. He was used to being on his own or with men as rough as himself. He would have to temper his speech as well as his actions for the next few months. But for the moment, politeness be damned.

He almost snatched Annabelle, but she reached out and raked his arm with her claws. He grabbed one of her paws and started dragging her out. "Gotcha," he said with as much satisfaction as if he'd bagged a killer after months of hunting.

Annabelle suddenly feigned docility, though he didn't trust it, not one bit. She snuggled against him, purring contentedly. Ben swore vengeance silently, though he would never take it. Except on occasion, Annabelle wound him around her little claws almost as securely as Sarah Ann had twisted him around her small fingers. Something about babies did that to him, he was discovering.

Prior to meeting Sarah Ann, he'd never experienced wet baby kisses or rough kitten-tongue swipes across his cheek. There was something rather endearing about both, though he wouldn't have admitted it out loud. So he just simply glowered at Mrs. Faulkner after he slowly, awkwardly, emerged from under the lifeboat with his trophy clutched tightly against his chest.

Mrs. Faulkner's gaze went to his bare chest, then drifted upward to his half-shaven face. He knew soap still clung to parts of it. He hastily buttoned his shirt with one hand.

"My apologies for the state of undress," he said stiffly.

Six months ago, he wouldn't have cared how anyone saw him; after weeks, sometimes months on the trail of an outlaw, his clothes and beard would be in a sorry state, and it wouldn't have mattered. But Sarah Ann's future, her acceptance as a peeress, might well depend on him and his actions. He still couldn't quite believe the events of the past month, the news that was now sending him to Scotland.

Mrs. Faulkner looked at him oddly. "Your child's a dear little soul, but she doesn't favor you at all."

Ben loathed the woman's curiosity, even as he felt strangely satisfied by her words. Sarah Ann was lovely with her red curls and green eyes, a tiny replica of her mother.

"You don't think so?" he said, forcing disappointment into his voice. He wanted to be rid of Mrs. Franklin T. Faulkner and her thinly veiled questions. He suspected she had ulterior motives, principally her unmarried daughter. If she knew some of the things he'd done, she wouldn't be so eager to consider him son-in-law material.

He had been circumspect about sharing with other passengers information regarding Sarah Ann or himself, saying only that he was an attorney traveling with his

daughter. He was, by nature, a cautious man. A lawman
had to be.

Besides, there were still too many unanswered questions for him to reveal more. If Sarah Ann found a new
home in Scotland—a family who would care for her—he
would return to America. It would . . . crack his heart,
but a family of her own would be far better for her than a
man who knew more about hunting outlaws than drying
tears. And if all didn't work out to his satisfaction, well,
then, the two of them would come back together and he
would return to his original plan.

He had taken precautions, though. He had officially
adopted the child. A great deal of money apparently was
part of Sarah Ann's potential inheritance, and it was his
experience that money corrupted. The greater the amount
at stake, the greater the corruption.

"Poor motherless child." Mrs. Faulkner obviously
wasn't going to give up. "You should marry again." Her
eyes were avaricious on behalf of her daughter.

"Sarah Ann's mother died just a few months ago," he
said abruptly, trying to end the conversation.

"Still, she needs a mother's hands."

"She needs Annabelle right now," he said. "Please
excuse me."

A loud "humph" followed him as he headed for the
stairs, then, "What a doting father."

Ben grinned. He decided he and Sarah Ann would
take their meal in their cabin tonight rather than risk
sitting at the captain's table again with Mrs. Faulkner and
her marriageable daughter.

In the cabin, he found Sarah Ann standing in the
middle of the small room, her wide eyes anxious, her
lower lip trembling.

"You found her," she exclaimed happily, and Ben felt
ten feet tall. A lot taller than when he'd brought in a man
to hang.

As she took the kitten from him, she saw his bleeding
hand and scolded Annabelle.

"Bad cat," she said, but there was no bite to her words. The cat licked her cheek with apparent satisfaction rather than remorse. Sarah Ann put Annabelle in her basket and shut the top, then touched Ben's bloody scratch.

"Doth it hurt?" she lisped with concern.

Ever since he had said he needed her, she'd taken the role of caretaker very seriously. Sometimes she even seemed like a tiny mother, very grown-up in some ways, yet very much a child in others.

He smiled. A cat scratch was nothing compared to the wounds he'd suffered. "No, Sugarplum," he said. "It doesn't hurt at all, but we'll have to be more careful to keep Annabelle inside the room."

Sarah Ann looked remorseful but pleaded to be allowed to "fix" his hand. She carefully washed it as he had done with her small cuts.

"Tell me 'bout my new fam bly," she demanded.

He'd already told her repeatedly, but she never tired of hearing it, which was just as well because he wasn't very good at fairy tales.

"Well," he said, drawing the word out, "there are two Ladies Calholm. There's Lisbeth Hamilton and there's Barbara Hamilton. They were married to your uncles, Hamish and Jamie."

"My papa's brothers," Sarah Ann coached him. She had never known her papa. He'd died at a poker table before her birth, leaving Mary May the pregnant widow of a known crooked gambler. Alone with a baby daughter to support, Mary May had turned saloon girl and confidante to outlaws, not the best of heritages.

But now there was another heritage, a brighter one, Ben hoped. For it seemed that her scapegrace father had been the third son of a Scottish marquess, and with all three sons dead and no other grandchildren, Sarah Ann was heiress to a title and a vast estate. The notion had seemed more fanciful than real to Ben, but Silas Martin, the U.S. attorney acting on behalf of the Hamiltons'

Scottish solicitor, had convinced him that it was all true. Despite his own personal feelings and plans—and even a temptation to ignore the summons to Scotland—he couldn't deny Sarah Ann the knowledge of her heritage and the chance to know her real family. So, having been her guardian for only a few months, he'd closed his newly opened law practice in Denver, packed a few belongings, and here they were—on a ship bound for Scotland. "That's right," he said. "They are your aunts."

"Who else is there?" Sarah Ann asked eagerly.

"There's your cousin Hugh," Ben continued. He tried to hide his anger. Silas Martin had said that Hugh Hamilton, who stood to inherit the title behind Sarah Ann, had tried to bribe him not to search too aggressively for Sarah Ann's father. Ben wondered just how far the would-be heir's ambition would drive him.

Already, an unusual number of deaths had occurred in the family, and Ben had never trusted coincidence. The Hamiltons seemed prone to tragedy, which looked like a recipe for disaster to Ben. He didn't believe in curses, but if he did, surely one had been visited upon the Hamilton family.

It was up to him to see that the curse—or whatever it was—didn't extend to Sarah Ann. And God help anyone who tried to interfere.

He let nothing of his concern show in his face, though, as he spun a tale of magic castles and Scottish lakes. And princesses.

"Am I a princess?"

"No, but I think you'll be a lady."

That always made her giggle. He had tried to explain about titles—about lords and ladies and marquesses. His own knowledge was incomplete, possibly wrong, but she loved hearing about them anyway.

"And I get to curtsy?"

"Yes, indeed," he said, "just as Cully taught you. She must have secretly known you were a real lady." He had been enchanted the first time Mary May had taken him to meet her daughter, and Sarah Ann had performed a perfect curtsy for him. She had won his heart then and there.

"Will they like me?" she asked with anxiety.

"Of course." He hoped to God it was true. But how could anyone not adore her, with those wide eyes and wistful smile and tumbling red curls? And her eagerness to like and be liked.

"And will they like Annabelle and Suzanna?" Suzanna was her doll, her inseparable companion. She clung to it as she did to the scarf she presently wore around her neck—the last presents her mother had given her. She wore the scarf even in her sleep, claiming it kept away the "bears," her name for nightmares. But it didn't always work. Too often, he woke to her whimperings and knew the night demons remained with her.

In answer to her question, he nodded and she threw her arms around his neck. "I love you, Papa," she said. "So does Annabelle."

His heart clutched at the overwhelming tenderness he felt. Tenderness that almost squeezed out the foreboding that chilled his bones.

❖❖❖

Ben stood on deck, holding Sarah Ann so she could see over the crowd lining the railing of the ship. The wind was cold and damp; it always seemed to be that way in this corner of the world. The ship was approaching the Glasgow docks, and Sarah Ann wriggled with excitement.

The port—like those all over the world—was dirty and teeming with people. Dockworkers and finely dressed citizens waited on the pier as the ship maneuvered between other craft, some steam, some elegant sailing vessels.

Ben wondered if anyone would be there to meet them, then discarded the idea. It wasn't as if they were really welcome. Just the opposite if Martin's warning about Hugh Hamilton were true.

Still, Martin had sent advance word to the Hamiltons

that he had located the daughter of the late Ian Hamilton and that the child and her guardian were booked on a ship to Glasgow. Ben wasn't sure whether he'd specified the name of the ship. And Ben had delayed an earlier departure to ensure the legality of his guardianship.

Sarah Ann wriggled again in his arms, and he hugged her to him. With each passing day, he was coming to feel more and more like a father, although many times a befuddled one. He was even growing used to her calling him Papa. At first, the term had been more than a little disconcerting—strange—but he'd known how she hungered for a parent all of her own, and now he relished the sound.

He loved her smile, so rare in the weeks after her mother's death but appearing ever more frequently, and that endearing grown-up pose. At times she seemed old beyond her years, a tiny wise person who continually surprised him. She could already read a bit and count to fifty, and she had infinite curiosity. He was always answering "why." Her questions made him look at things differently, made him rethink old assumptions and simple facts, made him devise reasons for the sky being blue. She was vastly expanding his imagination.

Now the great unknown facing them brought a torrent of endless questions from Sarah Ann.

"Where are we? When can we leave? When will I get a pony?" He had promised both a pony and new clothes when they reached Scotland, though she'd shown little interest in the latter.

The great unknown also brought out some of her fear. She snuggled even closer against him.

"Don't ever go away," she whispered for the hundredth time in as many days. The frequency of the demand always pained him because it indicated that she still didn't feel safe.

"You'll always be safe," he swore. "I promise you that."

The answer seemed to satisfy her. Then her gaze went

to the horses lined up on the street beyond the dock. "Can we get a pony here?" she asked.

"When we get to Calholm."

"How long?" she wheedled.

He grinned. According to his information, it was twenty miles by coach to Calholm. Soon enough, Sugarplum," he said. "For now, we'll find a hotel and get some good hot baths, then we'll see about a coach tomorrow."

"Perhaps I can be of assistance. I know Glasgow well."

Ben turned and recognized Andrew Cameron. Cameron had seemed to single them out on shipboard, charming Sarah Ann with several magic tricks. His curiosity had not ingratiated him to Ben.

Andrew Cameron was a gambler and a Scottish lord of some kind. He was a charmer with an easy smile and a gentle way with Sarah Ann, though he was said to be deadly in a card game. Some other passengers had claimed he'd cheated, and the captain had ended the games a few days ago and told him he wasn't welcome on any of his ships.

Ben withheld judgment. Cameron was a puzzle. He was likable on the surface, but there was also a dark, brooding side to the man that put Ben on guard. Hell, he had his own dark, brooding moments, but still . . . Cameron had asked too many questions, particularly when he'd heard Ben was heading toward Calholm.

So Ben merely nodded his thanks at Cameron's offer of help. "The name of a good hotel would be welcome."

"How long will you be staying?"

"Only until we can catch the coach to Edinburgh. I understand it goes near Calholm."

"It does," Cameron said. "It passes a small village called Duneagle, and you can rent a coach there to take you by Calholm."

He spoke of the estate with easy familiarity. Which prompted Ben to ask, "You've been to Calholm?"

"I know the family." Then, without elaboration, he

changed the subject. "As for an inn tonight, you might try the Four Horses. It's small, but the food's very good and it's clean. And it's close to the Edinburgh stage." He grinned suddenly. "It's usually too respectable for me, but I think you'll find it suitable for you and the young lass."

Ben nodded again. "We'll try it, then. Thank you."

" 'Tis a real pleasure to assist such a bonny lass," Cameron replied. He was tall with light brown hair and hazel eyes. His smile was infectious, and Sarah Ann favored him with a delighted smile of her own.

Cameron grinned. "Maybe we'll meet again. I'm going to Edinburgh myself, now that I'm banned from the Blankenship line." The words were carelessly tossed out, without rancor or concern. Ben wondered whether being "banned" was a frequent occurrence for him.

Sarah Ann was gazing at Cameron with open adoration, and he leaned down and plucked something from behind her ear, then turned it over in his hand. A coin. "You're the only lassie I know who keeps her money behind her ear," he teased.

Sarah Ann giggled as she took the offered pence.

"Papa's going to get me a pony," she told him.

"That's grand," he said. "It will find Calholm a good home, and so will you. It's a bonny place . . ." He trailed off for a moment, then, seeming to return from a distant place, added, "The hills are as green as the lass's eyes."

A faint warning note sounded in Ben's mind. But then why shouldn't Andrew Cameron know Calholm, especially if he was a member of the peerage. Had he known Sarah Ann's father, Ian Hamilton? Was cheating at cards an interest shared by both men? He had hardly tamped that thought when Cameron spoke again, this time quietly to him.

"Be careful. The docks in Glasgow can be a dangerous place so watch yourself and the wee one."

Wearing city clothes—a suit of fine wool he had purchased in Boston and a heavy, flowing topcoat—Ben knew he looked more like an American businessman than a western marshal, and he wanted to keep it that way.

"How long do you plan to stay at Calholm?" Cameron asked him.

Ben shrugged, annoyed at the man's persistent questions. "I'm not sure," he said and glowered. He was usually good at that, but his look didn't seem to faze Andrew Cameron.

"I have rel'tives there," Sarah Ann offered, continuing a conversation Ben wanted to end.

"Ah, that sounds fine," Cameron said. He looked at Ben again, a smile still hovering around his mouth.

Ben sighed, realizing Cameron wasn't one to take a hint. Nor was Sarah Ann. And he questioned whether he wasn't being too suspicious. He had become a loner, first shaped into one by the war, then by his chosen occupation. His job as a U.S. marshal had precluded friendships with anyone except his peers. And even those had been few. "Trust" was a word he'd all but forgotten.

His attention shifted from the Scotsman to the shore. The ship had docked and the gangplank was being lowered. Passengers surged toward it; at the same time, a man from shore pushed against the arrivals to gain the deck. He stopped to speak with the purser. Ben was about to turn away when he saw both men turn toward him, then away. He thought for a moment that the men might be talking about him, but their glances were so fleeting, he couldn't credit the idea.

The man from shore—a burly figure with a pugilist's battered face—continued to gaze around, his eyes studying other passengers as he gave the purser a package. Then he moved down the gangplank, disappearing into the milling crowd.

Ben turned toward Cameron. "Perhaps we'll meet again," he said, then took Sarah Ann's hand and headed toward the purser.

The officer was talking to several other passengers, warning them to be careful on the docks, offering the services of crew men to help take luggage to hired carriages lining the street.

Ben asked him about their luggage.

"I'll have a seaman take care of it," the officer said. "And where are you and the young miss staying?"

"Mr. Cameron suggested the Four Horses. Do you know it?"

"Lord Kinloch?" the man asked, obviously surprised. "Aye, indeed. It's a good inn, though I'm surprised Kinloch mentioned it." The purser scowled. "His taste usually runs to the more, uh, shady."

"Kinloch?"

"That's Cameron's title, though he's shamed it enough."

Despite the purser's contempt for Andrew Cameron, his endorsement of the inn convinced Ben to give it a try.

A number of hawkers shouted the quality of their wares as Ben and Sarah Ann walked along the pier toward the carriages for hire. The bags, the purser said, would be with them shortly. Keeping Sarah Ann's hand firmly in his, Ben reached the end of the pier and had just started down a path between stacks of crates when he heard a familiar voice shout behind him.

"Look out!"

At the same time Cameron's warning reached him, Ben heard the creak of moving crates, his well-honed instincts instantly sounding his internal alarm: *danger*. Ben shoved Sarah Ann ahead of him, just as one of the crates came crashing down on top of him, and everything went black.

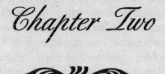

Chapter Two

CALHOLM

Lisbeth Hamilton tried without success to eat her dinner as her sister-in-law, Barbara, and cousin, Hugh, argued about the impending arrival of Calholm's new heiress. Lisbeth hated discord, having grown up surrounded by it. At the moment, however, she had some appreciation for her dinner companions' frayed nerves.

The trustee for Calholm, John Alistair, had informed them a month ago that an heir had been located, then sent word last week that the child—and her guardian—should be arriving in Glasgow any day. He had not mentioned an exact date. The news had been met with varying reactions: anger on Hugh's part, curiosity on Barbara's—and on her own part, hope.

"Ben Masters," said Hugh contemptuously. "Sounds like an American ruffian. No doubt he's latched onto our little cousin for the money."

Lisbeth privately agreed that was most likely the case. Still, she wondered what the American would think of this household, whether he would find it as unsettling as she did. Through various wills and trusts, both she and Barbara, as widows of successive marquesses, had lifetime rights to live in the house. After her husband Jamie's death, Hugh had come to live with them as the heir presumptive, taking over some of the sheep-farming aspects of the estate. John Alistair, though, had refused to petition parliament to designate Hugh as heir and had launched a search for Ian, scapegrace though he had been.

No one had expected Ian to be found. But after a year, the search had yielded not Ian himself but his daughter—and heir.

The news had squashed Hugh's hopes and spurred her own. She and Hugh had long been at odds over the future of Calholm's breeding of horses. She was as committed to it as the old Marquess. John Hamilton had harbored a lifelong dream to establish a stable second to none in the British empire. The goal was to produce a champion for the Grand National, the most respected steeplechase in the British Isles.

And they now had a prospect: Shadow, a five-year-old stallion who'd been born the day Lisbeth had come to Calholm as a bride. She had always felt linked to the great gray horse. She had helped train him, had spent hours currying and talking to him; and when Jamie died—two years after his father's death and one year after his older brother, Hamish—she'd assumed their quest. She would give Calholm its champion.

Lisbeth lived for that goal. But then Hugh had arrived, equally determined to sell the horses and take Calholm in a different direction: sheep farming.

There was also the matter of the twenty tenant families, another bone of contention between herself and Hugh. John Hamilton had been committed to the descendants of the men who had fought with his father, the original marquess, during the Napoleonic wars. The men who had helped the first Marquess distinguish himself, thus winning the King's favor, a title, and the land. Those families wasted land better used as sheep pasture, Hugh argued. But she wouldn't allow the tenants to be put off the land, not as long as she still drew breath, not as long as even a sliver of hope remained.

Now, with the discovery of Calholm's heiress, Hugh appeared to have lost everything. So did Barbara, who'd tied her future to Hugh's. Their fates, and Lisbeth's, seemed to be in the hands of the American who held guardianship over Ian's daughter. And none of them knew what to expect, or even if the claim was valid. Perhaps there was no proof that the girl was, indeed, a Hamilton.

The burning question was: would the American and the little girl bring about Calholm's salvation or its ruination?

"They have no right," Hugh said bitterly at the table, stabbing at the meat on his plate. "The letter said the child's mother was an entertainer. An *entertainer*, of all things!"

"I thought you liked entertainers—particularly actresses," Lisbeth said, unable to keep sarcasm from her voice. Hugh was a notorious rake who had accumulated a ton of debts on the expectation that he would inherit Calholm.

He glared at her. He was aware that she had eagerly supported the search for another heir.

"You would rather have an American opportunist claim Calholm?" Hugh inquired, one eyebrow raised.

"At least he may not gamble it away," Lisbeth said, unable to rein in her impatience with him. "John Hamilton would whirl in his grave if he knew your plans for what he so carefully built."

"You care about those damn nags more than people," Hugh shot back. "And you know I've stopped gambling."

"No, I don't," Lisbeth said. "Your creditors cut you off when it appeared you might not inherit."

"Just wait," he said. "The American will sell those bloody horses of yours. It's the only thing that makes any sense. And he'll bloody well kick off those tenants with a hell of a lot less than I would. He's obviously after money, and he won't be feeling any need to give it away to a bunch of poor farmers—family loyalty be damned."

"He can't destroy Calholm any faster than you would," Lisbeth retorted, feeling sick inside. Hugh was right. Her cause was probably hopeless. Still, she had to believe—for Jamie's sake, for the sake of all the families who depended upon Calholm to survive.

She had sufficient funds to maintain herself in a comfortable if not lavish manner. Jamie had left some money in trust. And her lifelong tenancy in the Calholm home was secured, though she doubted she would want to remain here if Hugh had control of the estate. Remaining would not mean much to her then, not if she couldn't keep her promises to Jamie and Jamie's father.

"I wonder what he's like," Barbara mused. "I haven't met any Americans."

Lisbeth noted Hugh's swift glance toward Barbara, and she almost felt sorry for him. He thought Barbara was his; indeed, Lisbeth knew the two of them had been carrying on a liaison almost from the moment Hugh had arrived at Calholm. Had they been two other people, Lisbeth might have believed it was a matter of love at first sight. But Hugh had a long and honestly won reputation as a rake, and Barbara an equally well earned image as a flirt. A gleam already sparkled in her eyes at the thought of a new man at Calholm.

And the American would be susceptible. Every man was. Barbara was a great beauty and had the charm to match. If she didn't use these assets for all the wrong reasons, Lisbeth probably would have liked her. In many ways, Barbara was like a child: pleasant and happy as long as she got what she wanted.

It was early November, but Barbara had already depleted her year's allowance—*more* than her year's allowance. Lisbeth knew she would never again see the money she had lent Barbara, and she'd refused to lend her more, despite Barbara's continued requests. Everything Lisbeth had was needed for the horses, their training and feed—a fact that Barbara resented.

Hugh glared at Barbara. "He's probably an old rustic. Not your type at all." Then he added slyly, "He might prefer Lisbeth."

Lisbeth didn't much care for Barbara's amused smile, even though she knew she wasn't a beauty. She'd never even tried to be, considering the expenditure of the time it required a waste.

"Or perhaps he has a wife," Lisbeth countered, although Mr. Alistair hadn't mentioned one. Or he might be old and rickety, as Hugh suggested. Old and rickety probably wouldn't stop Barbara, though, not if she could get her hands on Calholm.

Suddenly Lisbeth lost her appetite. Too much depended on Ben Masters—and his integrity. Unfortunately, with the exception of Jamie, most men she'd met lacked that quality. And even Jamie had been unable to deny Barbara anything she really wanted.

"He'll be short and fat," Hugh was saying, knowing that Barbara preferred handsome men. And Hugh *was* handsome.

Barbara gave him an infuriatingly smug look.

"If you—" he started to threaten, and Lisbeth could bear no more.

She rose from the table, and her dog, Henry the Eighth, who had been lying next to her chair, rose with her.

"Do you have to bring that beast into the dining room?" Barbara asked. "I don't imagine the Yankee will approve."

Henry the Eighth, a huge, wooly beast, stretched, ignoring Barbara as he always did. He didn't care for Hugh or Barbara any more than his mistress did.

His tail hit Barbara's chair with a resounding thump, and she jumped slightly. Henry wagged it again in utter defiance, and Lisbeth had to grin. Henry was a continuing bone of contention in the household, but he went every place she did, and the American would simply have to live with that. She would fight for three things: Calholm's tenants, her dog, and her horses.

"Mayhap the American will not." She shrugged. "And mayhap he likes dogs."

"Not that great ugly dog," Barbara said and shuddered.

"He's not ugly," Lisbeth protested on Henry's behalf, not that Henry cared. She did, though. He was her best friend. Her only friend. She had always been an onlooker, often an unwilling one. She was that now, in this home. Calholm had never really been hers, not even for the brief time when she was its official mistress.

She soon would no longer have even nominal control. The new heiress—a mere child—would have the estate in entitlement until she gave birth to a son. That, at least, was the most prevalent interpretation of the mishmash of wills and entitlements.

If only Jamie had lived . . .

"The American might even sell that scruffy animal of yours," Barbara baited.

"Or make *you* live on your allowance," Lisbeth retorted. Angry at herself for rising to the bait, weary of the conflict and speculation, she started for the door. "I'm going to take Shadow out."

"You shouldn't ride by yourself," Hugh protested with rare concern.

Lisbeth looked at him suspiciously but saw no guile in his eyes.

"Remember what happened to Jamie," he added.

How could she ever forget? That day would always be clear in her memory: Black Jack, Jamie's favorite horse, limping home during a hunt; the search for Jamie, and finally the discovery of Jamie's body; the magistrate's conclusion that he had fallen. She had never fully accepted it. Jamie had been a superb rider.

"I won't," she said bitingly. "I saddle my own horse now." The implication hung like a sword over them.

She'd never directly accused anyone, but she'd expressed doubts about the verdict of accidental death.

God's toothache, but she needed fresh air. It was still an hour before dark, and Lisbeth hurried upstairs, changed to a pair of boy's britches and a shirt, and ran down the back stairs to the stable. She didn't want to encounter Hugh's and Barbara's disapproving expressions over her attire, but she'd discovered long ago that these clothes were much more effective while training and jumping horses. But she was careful about when and where she wore them.

Shadow was eager. She quickly cinched the light racing saddle. Callum Trapp, Calholm's trainer, and the grooms had apparently retired for the day, and she was thankful. She wanted to be alone. She wanted freedom.

She gave the horse his head and allowed him to race down the road as the cold fall wind pummeled her. A familiar exhilaration filled her, the pure joy of the moment. She wouldn't think about tomorrow or the next day, about the impending arrival of her niece and the American and what it might mean for Calholm, for her own dreams.

She could only hope that the man wasn't an opportunist who would drain the estate's assets. She couldn't quite suffocate that thread of fear, though. Mr. Alistair said the guardian was a solicitor, and her experience with solicitors—with the exception of Mr. Alistair—had proved them to be money suckers and only slightly above criminals.

Lisbeth turned Shadow toward a fence. Elation surged through her as the great stallion lifted and soared over the barrier without shying. On landing, she slowly pulled the gray to a halt, then leaned over his neck, stroking him and murmuring endearments. Shadow arched his neck as if to say he could do it any time he wanted.

"You're a big fraud," she muttered.

Henry the Eighth barked from behind the fence. It was a decidedly disgruntled bark, and Lisbeth shook her head. Henry was probably big enough to make the fence himself, but he was disgustingly lazy. He would be as fat as his namesake if he didn't get more exercise.

Lisbeth turned Shadow back toward the fence. Once more, he took it easily, snorting with well-earned arrogance as they returned to the stable, Henry running happily alongside, his tongue lolling out the side of his mouth. Lisbeth's elation at Shadow's jumps faded as she approached the grand stone manor of Calholm. A few more days and the horses might all be gone and the only contentment she'd ever known gone with them.

She was living from day to day. Tomorrow she would take Shadow over the jumps again. If Ben Masters could see him jump, he would understand the potential of Calholm's stable. She had to believe that.

❖❖❖

The rickety coach bumped along the rutted road until Ben thought every bone in his body had been shaken out of place. The jarring movements certainly weren't doing any good to the livid bruises on the right side of his body. Those and the bump on his head were, fortunately, the only injuries he'd suffered when the crates fell on top of him.

Nagging doubts about this trip deepened. The falling crates could have been a simple accident, most likely it was, but he'd always found coincidences suspicious.

Cameron had seen nothing suspicious, nor had anyone else. Ben had accepted Cameron's offer to accompany them to the Four Horses, where they all took rooms. Even Cameron decided to stay, saying he too planned to catch the Edinburgh coach the following morning.

That had been two days ago, and he and Sarah Ann were now finally approaching Calholm, having left the main coach at a village and hired this old vehicle for the final leg of the journey. The damned thing groaned as it took a corner, tilting for a moment before settling back on all wheels.

Sarah Ann's eyes blinked open. She'd slept much of the way. She'd had nightmares the night before and had awakened screaming. The "bears" were back, she'd told him in a tiny, frightened voice. She was alone in a dark room with no doors, and the room kept getting smaller and smaller. She kept crying but no one answered.

And she'd had no Andrew Cameron today, not since Duneagle, to amuse her with stories and magic tricks.

"We're neara there, sirrah," the coachman said.

Sarah Ann stirred and moved closer to Ben.

"We're almost there, Sugarplum," he said.

She gave him a sleepy smile, then picked up Annabelle's basket and opened the top. "You see, Annabelle. We *did* get here."

Annabelle answered with a plaintive meow, and Sarah Ann plucked her from the basket. In the past weeks, Annabelle had grown substantially. So had her claws. In addition to bruises, he now had several vivid scratches.

But Annabelle seemed happy enough just to be out of the basket, and she plumped herself into Sarah Ann's lap, accepting Sarah Ann's crooning noises as her due.

Ben peered out the window. A stately structure loomed in the distance, and his premonitions returned. What business did he have in a place like this, in a country not his own?

At that moment, a horse, with a rider stretched low on its back, appeared out of nowhere in front of them. The coach lurched, the driver reining in the horses to prevent a collision. But the abrupt movement caused the lumbersome vehicle to tilt and in the next instant, it keeled over.

Ben just had time to grab Sarah Ann before the carriage crashed. Annabelle screeched and promptly disappeared out a window. Ben heard curses outside the coach as he tried to straighten, his body complaining bitterly.

"Sarah Ann," he asked, holding her tight. "Are you all right?"

"Annabelle," she whispered. "Annabelle's gone."

"We'll find her," he soothed, wondering what mad-man had been riding like a fiend down a public road.

The door, now located above them where the roof should be, jerked open, and a voice said, "Anyone hurt in there?"

Despite Sarah Ann's presence, Ben swore and set her upright. Whoever had opened the door was gone, and he stood, poking his head out of the opening. The coachman was standing in the road, dusting himself off, which brought Ben to the conclusion that the voice he'd just heard had come from the slender, carelessly dressed youth perched on the wheel. He was evidently the same person who had caused the disaster because a riderless gray horse now stamped nervously nearby. The boy was clothed in loose-fitting cotton trousers, a shapeless tweed coat with a cap drawn low over the face.

"Of all the damned carelessness . . ." Ben began.

"We weren't expecting anyone," the youth said, more in accusation than apology. He took off the cap, and as a long auburn braid fell down the slender back, Ben realized the boy was not a boy at all but a woman.

"Shadow could have been hurt," she added, frowning.

Ben barely suppressed a roar of anger. "Dammit, any fool should know better than to race down a public road."

"This isn't a public road. It belongs to Calholm," the woman started angrily, but then Ben lifted Sarah Ann so that she could be seen, and the woman's voice trailed off. She moved closer. "She isn't hurt, is she?"

Obviously his own injuries were irrelevant, but at least she was acknowledging that her actions might have harmed a child.

"No thanks to you," he said.

She ignored him, her gaze scrutinizing Sarah Ann, who was now sitting on the edge of the door opening. The woman's eyes suddenly widened with apprehension. "You're not—"

At that moment, Sarah Ann wailed. "I want Annabelle."

Ben flinched. Sarah Ann seldom wailed. In fact, he had worried about that. He expected a child to cry more than she did; but except for a very few tears, she'd endured all her upheavals with stoicism.

The woman, still perched on the wheel, spoke softly to Sarah Ann. "Who's Annabelle?"

Sarah Ann sniffed. "My kitten. I want to get down and find her."

The woman grinned suddenly. "I think your Annabelle is just fine. She's busy chasing *my* dog."

Humor danced in her eyes, and Ben realized she was prettier than he'd first believed. He also realized he was still standing in the carriage, his head sticking out like the fool he'd called her, and he couldn't boost himself out with Sarah Ann clinging to the side. "Can you lift her down?" he asked.

"Aye." She leaned forward and took Sarah Ann with ease. She was stronger than she looked, but then she would have to be strong to control that giant of a stallion she had been riding.

Once Sarah Ann was safely on the ground, Ben lifted himself through the door and slowly, painfully, slid to the ground. His left leg, which always gave him some trouble, was stiffer than usual, and his body was sore all over.

Sarah Ann was looking frantically for Annabelle.

The woman knelt, her expression softening. "I saw your kitten jump out the door and go after Henry the Eighth. He's a great fraud, he is, and easily involved in games."

"Henry the Eighth?" Ben asked.

"My dog." Then at Sarah Ann's stricken face, she added, "Henry wouldn't hurt a mouse. That's why I have him. He absolutely refused to have anything to do with chasing foxes or pointing quail, and my neighbor was going to put him down. He thought Henry was cowardly. I think he's tenderhearted. But I'll send some people out looking for your Annabelle."

Sarah Ann was not pacified. Her face slowly began to crumple.

"I think we'd better look now," Ben said, more curtly than he intended. He was tired of accidents, pure or manufactured, and he was sore and frustrated. He'd never had much patience with irresponsibility, and he had none at all if it affected Sarah Ann.

He wasn't sure who the woman was. Maybe a servant stealing a ride on one of the estate horses. She surely didn't belong to the Hamilton family. He'd heard about the proper English gentry and had assumed the Scots would be similar.

Whoever she was, she looked taken aback by his tone, but she merely nodded. Just then, a great barking erupted from a distant copse of trees on the other side of the stone wall to the right of the road.

"Henry!" the woman exclaimed, and without another word, she easily mounted the large horse, backed him a number of yards down the road and flew over the wall as if it were two feet high instead of five.

Ben wanted to go after her. Dammit all, it had been years since he'd had to stand back and allow someone else to do his hunting, much less this slight figure of a woman with no more sense than a goose.

He made sure the coach driver was all right, along with the horses, which were still in their traces. Then he went over to Sarah Ann and checked her again for injuries. She'd sustained a few bruises—nothing of note. She stood there looking hopefully toward the wall.

Feeling helpless, Ben lifted her, then walked over and set her atop the wall. He vaulted up next to her.

"Who is she?" Sarah Ann asked. He could only shrug.

"Why is she wearing pants?"

That was a harder question to answer. He'd known only one woman who'd worn pants, and she had been an outlaw's daughter in the Indian Territory. Such behavior was daring even in the freedom-loving American west. God knows what it was considered here.

He tried to see through the copse of trees but couldn't. He heard barking, a screeching meow, and then a howl. Suddenly, what looked like a small pony came galloping out of the woods rushing straight for them. It veered, disappearing through an invisible opening in the wall, reappearing on the other side only to collapse several feet away from them. Putting a great, hairy head on his paws, tongue lolling thirstily from one side of his mouth, he eyed Ben and Sarah Ann cautiously. Minutes later, the woman appeared from the woods; she was carrying something gingerly in her arms.

"She has Annabelle!" Sarah Ann said.

"It appears so." Ben wondered what the kitten had done to the cowed dog—and the woman, who was eyeing Annabelle so warily.

Her careful approach gave Ben several moments to study her. She was not, by any stretch of the imagination, beautiful. Her features were ordinary and her face unfashionably freckled, something she'd made no effort to hide with powders. Her eyes, though, were quite remarkable. They were hazel, a mixture of amber gold, soft greens, and gray. They should, he thought, appear serene. They didn't. He saw cautiousness and suspicion in them instead—and hot, quick anger had ignited them when he'd accused her of recklessness. They were eyes that had learned to protect, to conceal, and in Ben's experience that was unusual in a woman.

Who in the hell was she?

She finally arrived beside their perch on the stone wall, and she gingerly handed the kitten to Sarah Ann, who instantly clutched the animal tightly to her chest.

"Thank you," Sarah Ann said politely, and Ben knew if she'd been on her feet she would have managed a perfect curtsy.

"You're welcome," the woman replied. The horse

pranced beneath her, and Ben noted the blood dripping from a scratch on her hand. Her gaze turned to him, and he saw the silent appraisal in those wide eyes. "You must be the solicitor from America." Her voice was husky, low, but there was no mistaking its femininity—nor the Scottish burr. "And," she added, moving her gaze back to Sarah Ann and allowing a hint of amusement to creep into her tone, "you must be the newest Lady of Calholm."

Sarah Ann looked puzzled and turned her face to Ben in question. "Papa told me all about that," she said, "but I still think I'm just a girl."

"Aye, that, too, and a bonny one as well," the woman said, and Sarah Ann beamed with pleasure.

Ben decided it was time to learn who the stranger was. "And whom do we have . . . the, uh, honor of addressing?"

"Or the misfortune?" she retorted quickly, a smile on her lips. Ben found himself liking her spirit.

"You redeemed yourself by finding Annabelle," he said.

"And how does Annabelle redeem herself?"

"She doesn't feel the need," he said.

"I see," the woman said, the smile widening. "I'm Lisbeth Hamilton, another . . . lady of sorts." Humor sparkled in her eyes, making her rather plain face appealing. "There are three of us in the household now. My sister-in-law, Barbara, is also the Dowager Marchioness—though I wouldn't call her that unless you want a glass thrown at you."

Ben was surprised. She looked more like a stable lad than a member of the peerage. "You're Lisbeth Hamilton?"

"The fool," she said, reminding him of his first utterance. "I really am sorry about the accident, but usually there's no traffic on this road, and I've been jumping Shadow—"

"That's *your* horse?" Sarah Ann asked eagerly.

"Yes," she said. "I'm training him."

"Can I ride him?"

"He's a little big for you."

"Papa promised me a pony," Sarah Ann confided.

"Did he now?" she said, then looked at Ben. "You're planning to stay, then?"

"Did you think not?"

"We know very little," she said. "Mayhap I can help you with that pony."

Though the offer was gracious, there was a sudden wariness in her that kept him at a distance. The smile had disappeared.

"Mayhap," Ben mocked slightly. "But now we would like to get to Calholm. We were beginning to think it didn't exist."

"It exists," she assured him. "Just over yon."

Ben slid from the wall, helped Sarah Ann down, then limped to the coach.

"You were hurt?" Lisbeth Hamilton said. Ben saw concern replace the reserve in her face, a reserve that raised his curiosity. He wouldn't have expected it of a woman who wore men's clothes and raced like the devil.

"An old injury," he said curtly. *And a new one in Glasgow,* he added silently.

"I'll ride back to Calholm and have our carriage brought for you and some men to right the coach," she told him. "I hope the rest of your trip was less . . . eventful."

He didn't reply, but he couldn't help but ponder the immediate question that popped into his mind: had she anything to do with the accident in Glasgow? Would she benefit if the new heiress disappeared—or died?

❖❖❖

Lisbeth pondered the meeting with the heiress and her guardian as she rode back to Calholm. No doubt about it, Sarah Ann was a delight. A beautiful child and well mannered, even under the worst of circumstances.

The American was another story—he was far more complex.

Ben Masters was reticent, which Lisbeth expected of a solicitor. But he certainly wasn't rickety or old or fat, as Hugh had hoped. She pictured him in her mind again, wearing that unfashionable sheepskin jacket. It made his shoulders look enormous. His feet had been encased in the strangest pair of boots she'd ever seen: brown leather tooled with a simple design. They had a slightly elevated heel that made him look taller than he already was, which was very tall, indeed. He was almost startling in his great size.

She was certain that Barbara would be on him like a leech. Would Barbara find him as easy to manipulate as others?

Lisbeth doubted it. Indeed, recalling the alert, cautious look in his eyes and his distinct lack of response to her attempts at humor, she knew he was not a man to be easily influenced.

What he was was interesting-looking. Not handsome—his face was too rough-hewn for that, with intriguing lines that inched out from his eyes and carved trails across his cheeks. She didn't think they had been made by laughter. His skin was bronze, as if it had been permanently colored from long hours in the sun, which was more than a little unusual for a solicitor. His light brown hair was colored with gold, and his eyes—a startling light blue—were suspicious and watchful.

He hadn't smiled, but then why should he, given the circumstances of their meeting. She had not made a good first impression, which didn't bode well for her winning him to her side. *A reckless fool.* That's what he'd called her, and her capture of the cat—even she couldn't call it a rescue—didn't seem to have helped.

He certainly didn't look like an opportunist. But then, how did one look? And what did he want from Calholm? Money was the logical answer.

But perhaps she was misjudging him. Perhaps he

would turn out to be the answer to her prayers, rather than her worst nightmare. Much to her distress, she didn't have a clue as to which it would be.

With a heavy sigh, Lisbeth spurred Shadow to a faster pace. Ben Masters was waiting and she had to tell her sister-in-law and cousin that the newest Hamilton had arrived at Calholm.

Chapter Three

Ben glanced at his pocket watch. It had been nearly an hour since Lisbeth Hamilton had ridden off, more than enough time for her to have alerted the household. He wondered if she would send a carriage at all.

At that moment, he saw a rather worn carriage approach. He had already helped the coachman lift their luggage to the ground, and Sarah Ann was sitting on one substantial piece, her hands firmly holding the top down on Annabelle's basket. She wasn't taking any more chances.

Their rescuer was little more than a lad himself. He doffed his cap as he pulled up, slammed it back on his head, and jumped down, going straight for their luggage. Three men rode behind him, and they immediately set about righting the coach.

"I'm Geordie," the boy said. "Me ma's Fiona the cook, best one in the county. I help in the stable and round 'bout." He leaned down, his hands on his waist as he winked at Sarah Ann. "And ye must be the new grand lassie."

"I'm Sarah Ann Hamilton Masters," she corrected him in her best grown-up manner.

The boy grinned. "Well, I'm verra pleased to meet ye, Sarah Ann Hamilton Masters." He looked up to Ben's face. "And ye be Mr. Masters?"

Ben nodded.

" 'Tis sorry we all are ye had this trouble, but we'll have ye hoome straightaway."

Almost effortlessly he started tossing the luggage on the back of the carriage as Sarah Ann watched admiringly. Ben helped, and in minutes they were inside and rolling along the road. The driver of the overturned coach remained behind, directing the efforts of the three men from Calholm.

"I like that boy, but I don't understand all he says," Sarah Ann said worriedly, patting her precious basket and stretching so she could look out the window.

"Me, either," Ben confided. He too had struggled through the thick Scots brogue. He wasn't surprised that she liked Geordie. Sarah Ann liked everyone. Sometimes he worried that she was altogether too indiscriminate, and much too trusting. Andrew Cameron came quickly to mind.

Ben thrust aside the worrying thought and gazed out at the manor ahead. As guardian of the heiress, he would become responsible for the estate. But his training in American law and his experience as a soldier and U.S. marshal left him poorly prepared for his newest role. He wondered whether there was an estate manager.

Hell, he felt like a bull mixed among horses—or, more likely, sheep. God knows he and Sarah Ann had seen plenty of sheep from the coaches. The few cattle in evidence were unlike any he'd seen in America—shaggy beasts with as much hair as a buffalo.

The carriage moved into a circular drive and stopped in front of the manor. It was enormous and as stately as a palace. His boyhood home in Chicago would fit into it twenty times over. How could anyone feel at home there—particularly Sarah Ann, who'd spent her first few years in a small cottage?

Her hand crept into his and squeezed tightly, clearly seeking assurance. He wished he knew whether he was doing the right thing. He'd wanted to give Sarah Ann a family, feeling she deserved more than a cynical bachelor who'd disdained ties for years. He'd hoped that her Scottish relatives wouldn't be able to help falling in love with her—as he had. If only he was certain . . .

As the carriage pulled to a stop, the door of the manor opened and Lisbeth Hamilton appeared in the entryway. She'd used the time to good advantage, he noted, exchanging her masculine clothing for a simple light gray dress that fell, without bustles, gracefully to the floor. Her only decoration was a length of red and blue plaid attached at the waist and draped over her shoulder where it was fastened by a plain brooch. Her auburn hair had been brushed and pulled back in a blue ribbon. She would have looked serene and gracious had it not been for the challenging gleam in her eyes. Ben had the impression of an actress about to play a part she deemed dreadful.

She stepped from the door toward the carriage just as another woman appeared. Her dress was much more elaborate than Lisbeth's, and for a moment Ben couldn't take his eyes from her. She was the most beautiful woman he'd ever seen.

She must be the second widow, Barbara Hamilton, Dowager Marchioness of Calholm. Her eyes were a deep violet, a color he'd never seen before. Her hair was raven-black and her face exquisitely formed.

Ben stepped down from the vehicle and swung Sarah Ann to the ground. In one hand she clutched the kitten's basket. The other hand clutched tightly to Ben's.

Barbara Hamilton glided, rather than walked, toward him, holding out her hand. She introduced herself in a voice as perfect as her appearance. "Welcome to Calholm."

Ben's free hand took hers, and he couldn't help noticing its softness. "Ben Masters," he said. "And this is your niece, Sarah Ann."

"You're pretty," Sarah Ann observed guilelessly.

Ben, who'd guarded his words as long as he could remember, was always amused at her complete openness. It was only one of many things that enchanted—and startled—him about his young charge.

"Thank you," Barbara Hamilton said prettily. "Lisbeth told us about your accident. I've warned her about riding around the countryside like a barbarian. You must be tired. The servants have prepared rooms and some food."

Ben glanced at Lisbeth, who had also approached but who stood several feet behind her sister-in-law. At the mention of rooms and food, she had raised an eyebrow, and the corner of her mouth twitched. Ben knew suddenly that it had been Lisbeth who had made the preparations, not Barbara.

He felt the antagonism between the two women. It reverberated in the air, was evident in the way Barbara Hamilton ignored her sister-in-law, and in Lisbeth Hamilton's expression of mild amusement. He sensed that he was the cause of her amusement and he knew why. She must be well used to the reaction her sister-in-law aroused.

It was, he thought wryly, nigh onto impossible not to stare at Barbara Hamilton, as impossible as it would be not to stare at a great painting.

"My thanks to you both," he said. "Sarah Ann is tired, and the two of us could use a bath."

Lisbeth looked startled, and Barbara disconcerted that he had included Lisbeth in his appreciation. Undoubtedly, Barbara was used to getting all the attention. But he was familiar—too familiar—with beautiful women.

He might enjoy looking at them, but he sure didn't trust them.

"Hugh will be devastated that he isn't here to greet you," Barbara said.

Hugh, Ben remembered, was the one who had tried to bribe Silas Martin not to find the heir.

"He had to go to the village on business," Barbara explained. "He's been running the estate until you . . . she . . . ah . . ." She stopped in mid-sentence, obviously at a loss.

"That's not exactly true," Lisbeth Hamilton interjected.

"Well, he *would* be running it if you didn't continually interfere," Barbara shot back.

The hostile currents grew stronger, and Ben watched with interest. He would have to tread carefully, trying to determine hard ground from quicksand. Some of his unease must have reflected in his expression, for Barbara's face took on a bright smile again.

"I've had cook make some scones for you," she said. "Come along and we'll give you a good Scottish welcome."

She turned toward the door, clearly expecting Ben to follow. He looked at Lisbeth Hamilton.

"Yes," she said, a little too sweetly. "Go along. Geordie will take your bags to your room, and I'll have water heated for baths."

A battle simmered between the two—that much was obvious—and Ben was oddly surprised that Lisbeth Hamilton participated in a blatant game of one-upmanship. She didn't seem the type. But it also appeared her heart was not in the game, and he suspected she thought her sister-in-law had scored the first victory.

He wondered about the game. He hadn't known what to expect on his arrival. Hostility toward him and Sarah Ann had seemed most likely. But it appeared the occupants of Calholm intended to court and indulge them both. What prizes were the Hamiltons after?

Ben smiled wryly. It might be an interesting adventure after all.

❖❖❖

Lisbeth was considering evening wear when a light knock came at her door. She opened it to a deeply perturbed butler.

Duncan MacCormick was really too old to still be in service, but he resisted all encouragement to retire. And Lisbeth hadn't the heart to force him to leave. Duncan didn't hear very well, had a habit of dropping things, and couldn't remember much. But he had been a family retainer since Jamie's father was young, and he took great pride in Calholm and his role as head butler. Every time she suggested retiring, great tears ran down his cheeks. The Hamiltons, such as they were, were his family, all he had.

At the moment, he looked as if he'd swallowed a raw eel—shocked and deeply offended. "The . . . American," he stuttered, "doesna like the rooms."

Lisbeth felt a growing anger. She had chosen the bloody man's room carefully. It was the finest in the house, aside from the master's bedroom, and there were few suitable alternatives—none at all in the west wing, which was where she wanted him, far away from Hugh's and Barbara's rooms in the east wing. Lisbeth thought it best not to put temptation so close to Barbara's path. The child, of course, would stay in the nursery.

"No doubt he wants the master's bedroom," she said.

"Nay." Duncan shook his head, distress written all over the ancient face. He knew, like all the other servants and tenants at Calholm, that the newcomer meant change and, most likely, trouble. They all trembled for their jobs. "He wants the small lass nearby," the butler continued. "He said the nursery wouldna do at all."

It was not the answer Lisbeth expected and, in fact, it puzzled her. Children *always* stayed in a nursery, usually with a nurse or governess to tend them. It had been her place of safety as a child, a haven from the violence that was always ready to erupt in the Campbell household. She had planned, first thing on the morrow, to inquire in the nearby village for a nursemaid—Barbara, of course, having completely ignored, as usual, any of the practical problems presented by the situation. It seemed, however, that Ben Masters wasn't willing to wait for Lisbeth to solve the problem.

❖❖❖

Ben had few reservations about changing the rooms assigned to Sarah Ann and himself. If Silas Martin was correct, he had the controlling hand and could sleep where he damned well wanted.

He hadn't wanted to assert his power. He'd never liked bullies or arrogance. But it had been a long time since he'd felt like anyone's puppet, and he had no intention of ever being one again.

Sarah Ann had been placed on a floor overhead, a far distance from his own assigned chamber. The nursery was the only proper place for a child, the old butler had proclaimed, obviously horrified and distressed that Ben had found the arrangement unsuitable. Looking around, he had to admit the room was pretty and filled with toys, including a rocking horse. But Sarah Ann, upon learning she was expected to stay there alone, had started wailing.

It had all been too much for her—the loss of her mother, of Mrs. Culworthy, the long, seemingly endless trip, and now all these new people. She probably also detected some of the tension in the household; she was too sensitive to moods not to have noticed.

So he'd balked at the separation. The stiff, elderly butler, saying he would have to consult with Lady Lisbeth, had stalked off.

Ben looked down at Sarah Ann. She'd stopped crying, but she still had a death grip on Annabelle's basket and her doll. When she tilted her head and looked at him, his heart nearly broke at the lost look in her eyes.

"Come over here with me," he said, giving her a wink as he tempted her toward the window. It offered a view of what lay behind the house. "Look," he said, lifting Sarah Ann so she could see the heather-covered hills beyond the house and, in the distance, a lake shimmering in the late afternoon sun.

It was a far cry from the dry, gray winter of Texas.

The scene drew an "ahhh" from Sarah Ann. "Can we go on a picnic?" she asked longingly. "Like the ones Mama took me on."

"It's a bit cold for that," Ben said, "but we will go exploring." He would see about obtaining a horse for himself and a pony for Sarah Ann. He also wanted to go to Edinburgh fairly soon and talk to the estate trustee. But Sarah Ann needed a few days to rest and get settled, and he needed some time to discover the politics of Calholm.

Suddenly she turned from the window and hugged him tightly. Annabelle's basket, still in her hand, was flung around his neck. He wasn't sure whether he would ever get used to those hugs, to the trust and sweetness inherent in them.

"You won't go away?" she whispered.

"No, Sugarplum," he whispered back, shifting her into his arms. "You're stuck with me."

She giggled, but her arms didn't relax their hold, and he felt the insecurity, the fear, that still haunted her. His own hands tightened around her. He still couldn't believe the richness she had brought to his life, wondered how he could exist without it. He had survived readily enough before simply because he hadn't known what he was missing. His mother had died when he was very young and his father had been a taciturn man consumed with his law practice. He'd seldom smiled and never touched or, God forbid, kissed his child. There had only been duty.

"Mr. Masters."

The sound of his name caused Ben to whirl around.

Lisbeth Hamilton stood in the doorway, her head tilted slightly as if she were curious about something. He swung Sarah Ann to the floor, keeping her small hand in his.

"Mrs. Hamilton," he acknowledged. The various titles confused him, and even if they didn't, he was uncomfortable with them. "I'm not quite sure of the proper address."

"Barbara and I are both formally Lady Calholm," she said. "But the servants—and many of our acquaintances—call us Lady Lisbeth and Lady Barbara. Otherwise it would get terribly muddled."

"Lady Lisbeth, then?"

"In the family, we dispense with all that. Lisbeth will do."

"Lisbeth, then," he said, searching her face. Despite the words that were almost friendly, her eyes reflected something else.

"I understand you are displeased with your accommodations," she said abruptly.

"Not having seen mine, I have no reason to complain about them. But I do understand the nursery is on the third floor and that my room is on the second. I would prefer to be closer to Sarah Ann." He watched her carefully as he spoke. "She's just turned four and is too young to be this far away from anyone."

"I thought we might try to find a nursemaid," Lisbeth Hamilton said. "It's customary—"

"I don't give a damn about 'customary.' "

The tiniest glimpse of a smile played across her lips and her eyes widened with surprise—whether because of his vehemence or the apparent impropriety of his demand, he didn't know.

"Would a room next to yours be close enough?" she asked.

He hesitated. Sarah Ann had been in his cabin on the ship and in the inns along the way. He had become very adept at stringing curtains between them while he dressed.

"I want to stay with Papa," Sarah Ann whispered almost desperately.

"And so you shall," Lisbeth Hamilton said, then added, "To bloody hell with convention." Ben was reminded of the masculine clothing she'd worn earlier and how she'd soared over a five-foot stone wall astride a stallion few men could handle.

"There's another room in the west wing," she continued. "It's not so fine as the one I intended for you, but it connects to a smaller room."

"I don't need fine," Ben replied. "I've often slept on the ground."

One of her eyebrows lifted in question, but he offered no explanation.

"I'll have Duncan show you the room. He's hovering somewhere in the hallway." With a soft smile, she added, "He's rather set in his ways."

Ben thought her manner toward the servant more suited to an indulgent daughter than to the mistress of a grand estate.

"I'm afraid the room needs airing and dusting," she said. "Perhaps Sarah Ann could eat her supper in the kitchen while we have dinner." She turned to go.

"Ah . . ."

Lisbeth stopped.

"Sarah Ann and I eat together."

She turned around again, and this time a real smile curved her lips. It lit her face.

"I'll inform Barbara," she said. "She and Hugh will be delighted to have you both at the table."

From the mischief in her voice, he gathered Barbara and Hugh would be no such thing. He felt a powerful urge to smile back at her, but he wasn't ready to take sides in what appeared to be a royal family row.

"I'm glad we'll be welcome," he said dryly, and her grin spread. He had the strangest notion that she realized exactly what he was thinking.

"Tonight, then." She turned to say a few words to Duncan, who was waiting outside, then left.

Duncan was at least seventy and probably more like eighty, Ben figured. No wonder the butler didn't like changes. The man should have retired years ago—an observation that did little for his opinion of Lisbeth Hamilton. He'd heard about loyal family retainers but this was ridiculous. Depending on what kind of power he would have, he would try to see to the servant's retirement as soon as possible.

Ben and Sarah Ann followed the ancient down a flight of stairs, Ben wondering all the way whether the man would make it. They passed through a long hallway until, near the end, the butler opened a door. The room was large and obviously unused. It smelled of dust, and the furniture was old, the fabrics faded. But it had a large window that looked over the lake. Compared to the hotels and barracks he'd used, Ben thought it was rather grand. He opened one of the inner doors and saw that it led into a small room that once might have been a sitting area. It too had a large window overlooking the lake.

Duncan was sniffing disapprovingly. "It needs an airing."

"It's beautiful, and awful *big*," Sarah Ann said, peering out the window.

The butler's stiff face relaxed slightly. "Geordie will bring the horse and other toys down when he finishes fetching your luggage. Effie will bring some water and air out the rooms during dinner."

Sarah Ann released Ben's hand and tried the bed. Ben and Duncan watched as she climbed up—it was very high—and bounced happily. Not thirty seconds had passed, though, before she had stopped bouncing and was spread out within the folds of a great comforter, her eyes closing despite her obvious attempts not to let them.

"She's a bonny wee lass," the butler said wistfully.

"Aye, she is," Ben agreed, automatically using the Scottish term he'd heard so much in the past few days.

"Calholm has not been a happy house since young Ian left, and the old Marquess died," Duncan said softly. "Perhaps she can bring some life back to it."

Ben only nodded. He wasn't sure whether she could. The atmosphere was so stifling, the tensions so high, and that only reinforced his misgivings about the wisdom of this venture.

He looked at Sarah Ann, who was nearly invisible in the great bed. She was smiling in her sleep. He had discovered that small things would make her do that. A wink. A kitten. Now a cozy bed.

He leaned down and took Annabelle from her basket and tucked her under Sarah Ann's arm. Surprisingly enough, the kitten stayed there. She too was probably tired from her great adventure, though he felt sure she had no fear in her. Annabelle thought she could lick the world, both figuratively and literally.

He wished he felt as certain about his own abilities in this misty green country. He was more used to directness than subtlety, to open hostility than concealed distrust, to declared outlaws than people who hid behind titles and fine clothes. Ben had sensed in the few hours he'd been at Calholm that with every step he took, he would be walking between charges of dynamite, never quite sure when one would explode.

Chapter Four

Currents raged around the Calholm library as predinner sherry was poured and sipped. And "raged" was the word, Ben thought, his gaze flickering among the three adult members of the Hamilton family. The small room, with its leather sofa and huge walnut desk and lingering, civilized smell of brandy and cigars, could hardly contain the swelling of hot emotions bouncing off the book-lined walls.

With Sarah Ann at his side on the sofa, Ben continued his deceptively casual perusal of the others. Barbara was being openly seductive; the cousin, Hugh appeared hostile; and Lisbeth merely watchful. Warmth was a distinctly missing ingredient. Only Sarah Ann's tentative smile provided a small glow.

Hugh eyed him with disdain. "Ben? What kind of name is that?" he said with scornful superiority. "Surely it must be Benjamin or—"

"No," Ben replied with a shrug. "Just plain Ben. My

father had no use for fancy monikers." It was a lie. His real name was Bennett Sebastian Masters, but he felt no inclination to divulge that information. A choking noise behind him made Ben turn. Lisbeth was coughing, or more likely, hiding a chuckle. He couldn't be sure whether she was amused at his feigning to be lazy and not very bright or at Hugh's ready acceptance of it.

Hugh, who had introduced himself as Hugh George Alexander Hamilton, looked briefly startled, then his features settled back into their previous self-satisfied smirk. Ben could read his mind. *The American is a country bumpkin, a man easy to sway and use.* It was exactly what he wanted the man to think.

"Ben is such . . . a straightforward name," Barbara said in the silence that followed. "And how do you and little Sarah Ann like Calholm?"

Sarah Ann, who was hanging on to his left hand, moved a little closer to him.

"It's . . . impressive," Ben responded.

Just then Henry the Eighth announced his arrival with a loud bark. He ambled in, yawned loudly, and went over to Sarah Ann, reaching out his giant tongue to lick a finger; then emboldened by that success, he started slobbering happily all over her. Sarah Ann giggled and reached out to pet him. She loved all animals and had no fear of them.

Barbara's face paled. "I warned Lisbeth not to allow the dog in here tonight."

"It's not your place to warn me of anything," Lisbeth said mildly. "This is Henry's home, too."

Barbara looked at Ben pleadingly. "It's unhealthy for the child."

Everyone was suddenly looking at him, as if waiting for Moses to come down from Mount Sinai. The first test, he realized. They all waited for his judgment: Lisbeth leery; Barbara expectant; Hugh gloating; and Sarah Ann pleading. At least, he knew what *she* wanted.

He shrugged. "After sharing close quarters with the

devil's own cat, I doubt Henry can do any harm." His gaze went to Lisbeth. Approval flickered in her eyes.

Ben turned back to Barbara. Her violet eyes had widened with something close to astonishment, but she recovered quickly.

"I was just thinking of the child," she said. "I should hate for her to become ill, and animals carry all kinds of diseases."

"So do people," Lisbeth inserted quietly. "How is the kitten doing?"

Sarah Ann's face lit like a candle. "Papa said I had to leave her upstairs, but she likes the bed. Someone brought her some milk, and she's very happy. But I don't think she likes Henry." She frowned. "Do you think they will be friends?"

"After they get to know one another, perhaps," Lisbeth hedged diplomatically.

The devil cat and the huge, friendly beast of a dog? Ben had to smile. So far, Annabelle only liked Sarah Ann, and he doubted whether Henry would join that short list anytime soon.

"However, Sarah Ann," Ben said, "I think you've had a sufficient bath for the moment." He guided her out of the reach of Henry's tongue and looked toward Lisbeth, who obviously took the hint.

"I think it's time for dinner," she announced, moving toward another room. Ben followed with Sarah Ann, leaving Barbara and Hugh to follow. They entered a large room, dominated by an enormous table that would easily seat thirty people. Five places were set at the far end of the table: the one at the head was flanked by two settings on either side. One of the chairs on the left side held a big plump pillow.

He looked toward Lisbeth. "Sarah Ann's?"

"Unless you want it," she said with an enigmatic smile. She was the greatest mystery of the three, full of contradictions: sometimes hostile, sometimes amused, sometimes simply watchful. He wished he could read her mind.

He helped Sarah Ann onto her chair, then waited to see who would take the seat at the head of the table. Hugh pulled out the chair across from Sarah Ann for Barbara and the one next to it for Lisbeth. Then Hugh took the chair at the head of the table.

The heir presumptive. As such, apparently Hugh had assumed nominal authority over the newest, and therefore more powerful, widow, Lisbeth. But who really ruled the roost here?

Ben took the seat beside Sarah Ann and helped her spread her napkin in her lap. She stared at the array of utensils in front of her. "There's so many," she whispered to him in a voice that everyone could hear.

Ben grinned. There *were* a lot of knives and forks and such. He might be out of practice, but he'd been to enough dinner parties as a young attorney to decipher them. "You only need one at a time," he whispered back.

Hugh frowned. "If you plan to stay, the child will need some instruction. Perhaps you do, too."

"Oh, we plan to stay," Ben said easily. "And I do think instruction is badly needed in this house, particularly in good manners, if not in how to handle forks."

Hugh's face went red, Barbara gasped, and appreciation played across Lisbeth's face. Ben felt a slow anger starting to fester inside of him. He could understand Hugh Hamilton's resentment, even his anger, after being denied what he thought was his. But enough was enough.

Ben looked lazily across the table at Hugh, making no attempt to hide his perusal. Hamilton was tall, and he sat straight. Women would probably call him handsome, but dissatisfaction in his eyes and a bitterness around his mouth detracted from what otherwise would have been a fine-looking face. His hair was sandy colored, his eyes dark blue.

"Hugh meant no offense," Barbara interceded. "He

only meant to say that some of our . . . customs will be new, and we want you to enjoy Calholm."

An obvious lie, though presented prettily. Ben saw the warning glance she sent to Hugh, and he realized that there was something between the two, something more than a distant kinship.

Hugh looked sullen and made no apology.

Barbara turned all her attention to Ben, and gifted him with a brilliant smile. "Did you have a good journey?"

"Good enough," Ben said.

"And how do you find Scotland?"

"Interesting," he replied unhelpfully as bowls of steaming soup were placed in front of them by a young serving girl.

"America's very impressive, I've heard." Barbara was trying valiantly. Ben had to give her that. She leaned forward, showing no annoyance at his brief replies. Lovely black lashes frequently swept those large violet eyes. She was flirting, and she was obviously so used to success that it didn't occur to her that he might be immune.

"Impressive," he repeated with a polite smile.

"I've never met an American."

She made it sound like an honor. Hugh cleared his throat in annoyance. Lisbeth raised an eyebrow, aware, Ben knew, of what Barbara was doing.

"I have so many questions," Barbara went on, fairly bubbling with enthusiasm. "America must be wonderful."

"Wonderful," Lisbeth echoed dryly. "But I think our guest might like to eat."

Ben grinned. "I do believe Sarah Ann must be hungry." He quickly found a spoon from the assortment of silver and handed it to her. Sarah Ann gave him that tremulous smile, and he realized she sensed the antagonism in the room.

She took a sip, tasted carefully, then took another sip. She had never been a fussy eater, thanks, probably, to Mrs. Culworthy.

He took several sips himself, then asked, "Tell me more about Calholm. How large is it? What about the crops?"

"Our main income comes from sheep," Barbara said. "We could double the income if Lisbeth would agree to certain changes. I'm sure you would approve."

"If he has any say at all," Hugh growled. "My solicitor doesn't agree there's a valid claim."

"Mr. Alistair disagrees," Lisbeth said mildly. She turned to Ben. "My husband's father started breeding horses for steeplechase racing, and my husband continued the tradition. We have some of the finest horses in Scotland and one—Robbie's Shadow—will run in the Grand National in England next year. If he wins, we can command exceptional prices—"

"*If* he wins," Hugh cut her off. "And in the meantime those bloody horses and the taxes are draining Calholm. There won't be anything left by the time that bloody stallion earns back even a fraction of the cost of those stables."

"The Marquess spent his life building that bloodline," Lisbeth said with no little passion. "You know he dreamed of a Grand National champion."

"And that dream killed your husband," Barbara interrupted. "I don't see how you can have anything to do with those horses."

Lisbeth looked stricken for a moment, then struggled to regain her composure. Ignoring Barbara's comment, she turned to Ben. "Do you ride, Mr. Masters?"

"A little," Ben said. Lisbeth looked slightly disappointed with his less than positive reply. At the same time, Barbara's face took on a tiny glow of victory.

"I understand you're from the west. I thought all westerners were . . . what do they call them? . . . cowboys," Hugh interjected.

"Not all," Ben said. "We do a few other things."

"Mr. Alistair said you were a solicitor?" Barbara adroitly changed the subject.

"By training." He felt no need to add that he hadn't practiced law in the past eight years. He'd been doing more deadly work.

"Were you in the Southern fight for independence?" Hugh asked.

Ben knew many Brits—including the Scots—had favored the Rebel side. He also had a feeling that Hugh Hamilton was only too aware of his lack of Southern accent.

"The rebellion, you mean?" he said. "I understand you had a few of your own. Should I ask which side your ancestors favored?"

"In other words, Hugh, mind your own business," Lisbeth said.

"Calholm *is* my business," Hugh retorted, sparks flying again across the table.

Ben wondered whether this battle was for his benefit or whether argument was a nightly custom.

"Hugh was merely curious," Barbara said softly. "We don't see many Americans." She leveled her violet gaze at him. "Have you seen any Indians?"

"A few," he replied cautiously. "More than I would have liked." That was true enough. Unless the Indians were renegades, he'd developed a policy of live and let live. He'd never understood the hatred most whites had against Indians.

"Do they really scalp people?" Barbara's mouth was pursed in an attractive little O.

Ben looked toward Lisbeth to see whether she shared her sister-in-law's bloodthirstiness but he couldn't tell. Her expression was neutral. She was listening, but he had no idea what she felt—if anything.

"What's a scalp?" Sarah Ann's small voice punctured the sudden silence.

"It's what's on a man's head, Sugarplum," he replied.

"I thought that was hair."

"So it is," he said, "but under that is the scalp." He

watched her digesting that. It was always a miraculous procedure to him, that thinking process of hers.

The serving girl removed the soup and replaced it with the next course. Sarah Ann stared at her plate. "What's that?"

"Salmon," Lisbeth said. "Do you like fish?"

"I don't know," she said very carefully, "but Cully said I should eat everything on my plate. Good girls clean their plates," she said as if reciting an oft-spoken rule. "I'm not very hungry, though." Her voice drifted off.

"Who is Cully?" Lisbeth asked.

"Cully took care of me," she answered. "I miss her."

Ben's heart wrenched. He scooted his seat back and set her up on his lap, ignoring the others at the table. "You don't have to eat if you're tired. Or even if you don't want to." He didn't know how he'd missed the signs. She hadn't been good all this time because she was naturally so; she was simply scared. He should have guessed, but he knew so little about children, about their needs or feelings.

"I'm not tired," she insisted.

"I think it's time to retire," he said. "It's been a long day for Sarah Ann."

"The maid can take her to her room," Barbara said, disappointment flickering across her face.

"It's been a long day for me, too," he said. Then his gaze sweeping to Hugh, he added wryly, "But I thank you for your welcome."

He set Sarah Ann down and stood, favoring his left leg. Damn but it hurt.

Lisbeth too was getting to her feet. "I'll send up some warm milk and brandy."

"I'd prefer whisky, if you have it."

She hesitated a moment, then said almost reluctantly, "I would like to show you the stables tomorrow."

Sarah Ann suddenly perked up. He could feel her come wide awake.

"That would be fine." He leaned over and picked up the child. "You wouldn't have a pony, by chance?"

"There are some colts and a filly, but no pony to ride," Lisbeth said. "I'll ask Callum to check around the countryside for one."

"Callum?"

"Callum Trapp. He's our horse trainer."

"Thank you," he said, his eyes sweeping the room. Hugh had also gotten to his feet and looked none too pleased at the conversation.

"Are you planning to stay, then?"

Ben met his gaze steadily. "Did you think otherwise?"

"You don't belong here. You have no right—"

"Neither do you if Sarah Ann's claim is upheld," Ben said softly. "It's her birthright."

"Bloody hell," Hugh exploded. "Don't be so sanctimonious. You want the money. You'll take it and leave—"

"Think what you like." *Christ*, his leg was hurting. And the longer he stood the more it ached. He turned toward the ladies. "Good night."

Ben went through the door, carrying Sarah Ann, who clung tightly to him. A sip of that whisky Lisbeth Hamilton mentioned and bed. That was all he needed.

That and some relief from the turmoil in his mind. What had Barbara meant when she'd said that the Marquess's dream had killed Lisbeth's husband? Another accident? He remembered the crates in Glasgow. Accidents seemed to occur a little too regularly around here.

Thinking of Hugh's open hostility, Ben wondered whether the young man had the guile or stomach for violence. He certainly had one for bribery.

And Barbara? He suspected she was as shrewd as she was lovely. And she was protective of Hugh. Perhaps, together, they might have planned the attack at the wharf.

And Lisbeth Hamilton? He read her with more difficulty than the others. Her face gave little away, but she was obviously passionate about the horses she raised. Passionate enough to set villains on a stranger and child? But then, what would she gain by that? Hugh would inherit.

Hell, it was all a puzzle.

Ben pushed the troubling thoughts away as he entered the suite. Gratefully, he set Sarah Ann down and she made for Annabelle's basket, took the cat and cuddled it possessively. She murmured to Annabelle, then headed for the feather bed. Her mother's scarf was wound around her neck, and Ben knew she would sleep in it again. He had to think of a way to get it washed. Its sky-blue color had turned a smoky-gray.

Good girls clean their plates. Sarah Ann had tried so hard to be good. It was time for her to be a child again. And that meant the coveted pony.

The elderly butler paused at the open door of the room, then entered. Duncan carried a tray with two glasses, a pitcher of warm milk, and a bottle of golden whisky. Even a cigar was included. He blessed Lisbeth Hamilton, though he suspected ulterior motives behind such largess.

Ben sat next to Sarah Ann as she drank her milk, then helped her into a long nightgown. He fingered the scarf. "Maybe we could ask someone to launder this," he suggested.

She grabbed the end of the filthy cloth. "No," she said stubbornly.

"Someday, then?"

"Someday," she agreed in a sleepy voice.

It was obvious to him, though, that that someday might never come. He thought about slipping the scarf off after she went to sleep, but then considered the repercussions if she woke and found it missing.

Not yet. The time wasn't right to risk her trust only for the sake of washing a piece of cloth that represented security to her.

Annabelle eyed him suspiciously, as if she knew is every thought, then collapsed next to her mistress. The bed was meant to be his, but the young intruders would enjoy it much more than he.

With the slightest of sighs, Ben leaned down and covered Sarah Ann and Annabelle. The child's eyes flickered open for a moment. "I think I like it here. If I can have a pony."

"You will have your pony, I promise."

"Will you tell me a story?"

He thought of the glass of whisky . . . the cigar . . . and decided there was nothing he would rather do than tell her a story.

His supply of stories was limited, however. His father had never told him even one. But he'd found a book of fairy tales in Boston and had memorized a dozen. He'd tried to put a different twist on several, but Sarah Ann rejected that. She liked the same ones over and over again.

"Once upon a time," he said, "there was a beautiful princess who lived in a castle."

"Like this one?"

"Just like this one," he assured her.

"And she had a cat named Annabelle?" Sarah Ann asked.

"A *naughty* cat named Annabelle," he replied.

Annabelle took offense. She stood, raising her back and stalking about the feather bed several times before returning to the spot she deemed softest.

Sarah Ann giggled. "She understood you."

If he hadn't known better, he might have agreed. The damned beast was uncanny sometimes. The dangerous life in the Boston alleys seemed to have imbued Annabelle with extraordinary abilities.

"She doesn't think she's naughty at all," Sarah Ann said. "You don't either, do you?"

"Of course not," he lied, crossing his fingers in front of her. She had told him herself that it was all right to tell tiny lies if you crossed your fingers.

"And she's beautiful," Sarah Ann added.

Not for all the crossed fingers in the world could he tell that big a lie. The half-grown feline was too skinny despite a voracious appetite, her head was misshapen, her left ear half gone, and her eyes of different colors.

"Annabelle is . . . distinctive," he hedged.

Sarah Ann smiled happily. "What's 'tinctive'?"

"Different, Sugarplum."

"Pretty, too," she insisted.

She wasn't going to give up, so he nodded.

Satisfied, Sarah Ann returned to the story. "Go on," she demanded.

So he did for the next few minutes, until her thick lashes fluttered and her eyes closed. He leaned over and tucked the comforter around her, then just watched for several minutes, feeling contentment flowing through him. Both Sarah Ann and Annabelle looked lost in the big feather bed. Finally, he put out all but one kerosene lamp, which he lowered to a small glow, and left the room for his own smaller chamber.

He regarded the whisky and cigar with appreciation. He would have one glass, a smoke, and then retire.

He found the whisky excellent and the cigar superb. Yet he would have preferred being back in Colorado. He had come to love the mountains, and the freedom they inspired in him to be what he wanted to be. The idea of practicing law again had become increasingly attractive in the past few months.

He didn't belong here. He would try, for Sarah Ann's sake, but . . .

He recalled Hugh's bitter comment. *"You want the money."*

But Hugh was wrong. He didn't want the money. He didn't want Calholm. He didn't think he wanted anything to do with a family that traded barbs across the dinner table. He would give it two months for Sarah Ann's sake, but he wasn't going to leave her here alone, not the way things stood.

Ben finished his drink and cigar and, as was his habit,

took his gun from his valise and tucked it under his pillow. He doubted the presence of danger, and yet the accident in Glasgow nagged at him. It probably *was* an accident; still, years as a lawman made him wary.

Ben quenched the light, looking forward to tomorrow, particularly to visiting the stables. He'd always loved good horseflesh, and he longed to be in a saddle again.

With that thought, he closed his eyes and willed sleep to come, halfway wishing he had an outlaw to hunt. That was easy. Black and white.

Calholm was something else altogether.

❖❖❖

Lisbeth couldn't sleep. And the big man who had entered their household was responsible. She kept trying to remember Jamie, his sensitive face and kind hands. But the rough-hewn, plainspoken American pushed those memories aside.

She'd never met anyone like Ben Masters. He obviously didn't care what they thought of him; not even Barbara's opinion seemed to matter. And he had been so gentle with Sarah Ann. Her niece. Sugarplum, he'd called her.

She'd thought, like the others, that the American had latched onto the child because of the inheritance. Now she wondered. No one could feign the caring she'd heard in his voice.

At dinner, Lisbeth had felt Sarah Ann's bewilderment, though the little girl had tried hard to hide it. She'd felt it because she'd known the same kind of uncertainty at that age. But Ben Masters had a deft touch for comforting, a touch her own father hadn't possessed.

Rising from her bed, Lisbeth pulled on her dressing gown. The thought of Sarah Ann in a strange, frightening place made her ache inside. She would look in on her, see that she was comfortable.

Lisbeth lit a candle and left her room. The hall was dark, and the flickering flame cast dancing shadows against the walls. Calholm had never really been her home. Nonetheless, she had been safe here, and that had been enough.

Her slippers made no noise on the carpeted floor. She passed the door to the large room Ben Masters was occupying and went to the next one where Sarah Ann would be sleeping. Keeping the candle to the side, shading its light so it wouldn't wake the child, Lisbeth approached the single bed. The faint smell of cigar smoke drifted to her nose, and she stiffened. In the next instant, the bed seemed to explode.

Something grabbed her hand, and she went tumbling down to land on a hard object. The candle dropped from her hand, and something cold and round pressed against her side. Metal. Like a gun. An exclamation escaped her lips.

"What the hell?" a man's voice roared.

She couldn't answer. She'd been rendered speechless by the sudden awareness that she was lying atop Ben Masters, who held a gun to her side—and that he was stark naked.

Chapter Five

"What the hell?"

The words thundered from Ben's mouth before he realized that the soft body lying on top of his was female—a scantily clad, unarmed female of the grown-up variety.

She wriggled in his tight grasp, and the consequent stroking between them brought instant awareness to every nerve ending in his body, as if they'd been jolted awake from a long sleep. Ben cursed again, silently this time. He'd lived on the edge of danger so long that he didn't know how to react like an ordinary human being. When had he become an animal, like those he'd hunted?

The woman on top of him had gone very still. Ben tried to force himself to relax, but it was a losing battle. The feel of her, her warmth and softness, seeped through his skin and into his blood. His body responded, and he knew she felt the response. The smallest whimper escaped her.

Though he couldn't see her, he knew who she was. Perhaps it was the light scent she wore, or the slenderness of her form. Lisbeth Hamilton was lying full-length on top of him with damned little between them. And the blood pooling in his loins thickened at the thought.

He expected a scream, but all he heard was a sharp intake of breath. She wriggled again and, this time, he let her go. But when she slid across him, trying to rise, she increased the friction between their bodies. Ben had to stifle a groan. Fire ran through him like a wildfire racing through the Indian Territory prairie.

He rolled to his side and saw a flare of light on the floor. A flame. The candle that had fallen from her hand.

He shoved Lisbeth aside, reaching for the candle, grabbing it, clapping his other hand down onto the carpet to extinguish the fire. Then he sank back onto the bed with a sigh, and blew out the candle, plunging the room into total darkness.

❖❖❖

Lisbeth lay, stunned, against the wall where she'd been tossed like a rag doll. She didn't know whether to be outraged or grateful. Ben Masters had prevented a fire from spreading—but then, she wouldn't have dropped the candle if he hadn't attacked her.

Bloody hell. She had expected a sleeping child, and she'd encountered a volcano.

She pulled herself up to lean weakly against the wall, shoving the hair out of her eyes with a hand that trembled. In the next instant, she was attacked again—suddenly, inexplicably—by something flying out of the darkness. Something with claws. The claws dug through the light fabric of her nightdress and dressing gown, and she screamed.

"Dammit!" Masters erupted only inches away. "You want to wake the whole household?" he hissed.

A furry body walked over her, then disappeared in

the blackness. She uttered an epithet that would have made a stableboy proud, and she heard Masters chuckle.

That chuckle brought her anger to a boiling point. Bloody man. This was still her house. Until Sarah Ann was officially acknowledged, she was still mistress of Calholm.

Then Masters said quietly, "I don't think we want any visitors, do we?"

God's toothache! The implications chilled her. Though she'd never been one for convention, there were certainly some situations that were beyond the pale—and this was one of them. She was in a man's bedroom, wearing only a nightdress, and he was naked. Thoroughly naked. Not only that, but he was also in the throes of arousal, if what she felt just seconds ago was what she thought it was.

"I would suggest you put some clothes on," she said, trying frantically to imbue her voice with authority. It came out more prim than anything else, and she shuddered at the ridiculous sound of it.

"You would suggest?" he repeated.

She wanted to slap the amusement out of his voice. He should be as appalled as she at the circumstances. He was obviously no gentleman, for he was making no haste at all to remedy the situation. He even seemed to be enjoying it.

She reached out a hand and was even more dismayed when she encountered a muscular human leg. She jerked back, hitting the wall again.

Mortified, she sought a way to restore some dignity to the absurd situation. Impossible. It was black as pitch—now that the candle was out—but in her mind's eye she saw him. Naked. Close. Very close. Too close.

"The cat . . ." she managed weakly.

Another chuckle drifted across the space between them. But the chuckle turned suddenly to a curse, and she could only guess that he'd become the cat's next target.

"Annabelle," he warned in a deadly tone that Lisbeth knew she *never* wanted to hear directed toward her.

"Papa?" The terrified voice came from the next room.

"It's all right, Sarah Ann," he said. "It's just Annabelle."

Lisbeth sensed movement. Then a bulky form hovered over her.

"You stay here," he ordered.

As her eyes became accustomed to the darkness, she saw Ben Masters lean down and pull on something. There was the sound of a match being struck, then the flickering flame of a kerosene lamp.

The cat fled back to the other room, and when her eyes returned to the American, he was standing in front of her, partially covered by a pair of trousers. The rest of him, however, was quite bare . . . and impressive. For a moment, she wanted to flee, too, like the cat, but something held her back.

It wasn't his order that kept her there. She had never taken to orders very well. It was curiosity. The kind of curiosity that killed the cat, she reminded herself.

Still, she had to admit, the sight of the half-naked Ben Masters was *not* unpleasant. A tingle started in her spine and spread rapidly throughout the rest of her. Ben Masters's body was lean and very, very hard. His chest looked as if it had been sculpted from marble, the scar that ran along his side a mere slip of the sculptor's chisel. His hair was tousled, a lock falling onto his forehead, and his cheeks were covered with bristle. Never had she seen such stark masculinity. He dominated the small room like some giant, and his scowl would have frightened a host of angels. He muttered something she couldn't quite hear, turned around, and disappeared into the other room, taking the lamp with him.

Paralyzed by indecision, Lisbeth stayed exactly where she was, uncertain whether or not her legs would carry her from the spot. She looked around. By the lamplight coming from the other room, she saw Ben Masters's clothes neatly folded over the one chair in the room. There was no sense of the man other than the lingering power of his physical presence. But that was enough. More than enough.

Her gaze fell to the pistol on the bed. Another surprise. Far different from the antique dueling pistols she'd seen before, this one had a short barrel and plain handle. It looked businesslike. And well used.

She thought about the man who owned it—the speed of his reactions, the deceptive casualness of his manner, the strength and scarred condition of his bronze-toned body—and she came to one swift conclusion: Ben Masters was no mere solicitor. Not unless American solicitors were a great deal different from their Scottish counterparts.

So the question was, who and what was he?

Lisbeth took a deep breath and let it out slowly. Cautiously, she moved toward the door and unashamedly spied.

Masters was sitting on the big feather bed. His head was bent over, and he was whispering something she couldn't hear. Then he tucked a comforter around Sarah Ann, whose small form hardly made a ripple in the huge bed. He waited a moment, then rose with a kind of grace that belied his limp, which she'd noticed had grown more pronounced throughout the day.

He moved swiftly toward her, carrying the lamp with him, and very quietly closed the door.

"She's asleep," he said curtly. "Now perhaps you will explain your intrusion."

Lisbeth was very aware of his bare chest, his mussed hair, the expectant look in his eyes.

"I thought you would be . . . in the other room," she said, her voice shaking slightly.

His eyes turned very hard, as if her stumbling explanation was even worse than her invasion of his quarters.

"I thought Sarah Ann would be sleeping here," she

continued. "I only wanted to look in and make sure she was warm enough . . . and that she wasn't frightened."

His eyes held disbelief, and Lisbeth felt a chill. Suddenly, a horrifying idea flashed into her mind. "You *don't* think I intended to hurt her?"

"I don't think anything," Masters replied harshly. "I just don't like people sneaking around in the night."

Lisbeth was outraged.

"This is my house, and I don't *sneak*," she said through clenched teeth. "Neither do I have animals so ill-bred they bite their hostess—and their bloody owner to boot."

He was silent for a moment, then, amazingly, he began to laugh.

"You're right on one count," he said. "Annabelle *is* obviously ill-bred. We found her on the streets of Boston and she's so used to fending off villains, I guess her instinct is to attack first and ask questions later."

"Not unlike her owner," Lisbeth observed bitingly.

He unexpectedly winced. "Only with intruders in the night. Now, let me see that hand." He took hold of her arm, which was bleeding slightly from cat scratches, and, with one finger, pulled up the sleeve of her nightclothes.

Lisbeth's first reaction was surprise at his gentleness. How could such large hands be that sensitive? His thumb ran over the newest scratches, and the ones created earlier in the morning. "They're not bad, but I'll have to apologize for Annabelle," he said. "She won't do it for herself. She believes herself quite above the law. She pays attention only to Sarah Ann, and that rarely." His voice held a wry note of admiration, as if he thoroughly approved of the cat's unruliness.

Lisbeth frowned. Henry the Eighth was no paragon of virtue, but he didn't run around chasing cats or biting everyone in sight, not even Barbara, though, once or twice, Lisbeth had secretly wished he would. Sometimes Henry was too good-natured for his own good. The same certainly couldn't be said of Annabelle.

Her eyes had narrowed. "Annabelle. What an innocent-sounding name."

The corner of Masters's mouth turned upward in a crooked smile, and she had the impression he didn't smile often.

"It is, isn't it?" he agreed. "I've often thought her rather ill-named, but Sarah Ann was quite insistent."

He had finished inspecting her hand and arm, and his gaze rose to her face. The searching look in his sky-blue eyes seared through her bones.

"Your hand must have been burned," she said, trying to break the sudden intensity between them. "I'll get something for it."

He shook his head. "I'm not letting you get away that easily."

Lisbeth cocked her head.

"I still want to know why you came into the room."

"I told you," Lisbeth retorted, her anger returning. "I thought it was Sarah Ann's. This house gets very cold . . . and I know it must be a little frightening. I—" She stopped. She didn't want to tell him how many times she'd been terrified as a child.

His eyes were like a sword probing for a weak point in her armor.

"Why are you in this room?" Lisbeth went on the attack.

"Because Sarah Ann likes that bed, and I don't," he replied.

She looked dubiously at the single bed he'd chosen.

"I'm used to simple things," he said sarcastically. "Isn't that what you all believe? That I'm a fortune hunter who's latched onto a child heiress?"

It *was* what they all thought. *Had* thought. She wasn't so sure anymore what she thought. He was unlike any man she'd ever met.

"Maybe," she admitted. She could have lied, but it went against her grain. Nor would he have believed protestations of innocence.

"Believe it or not," he said, "I would return home in a minute if it weren't for Sarah Ann. But I won't take her heritage from her."

His gaze held hers, and it was so brutally direct, she believed him.

His hand went back to her scratched one. "You'd better see to this," he said.

"We both need mending," she agreed. "Would you go down to the kitchen with me? The medicines are there."

He looked toward Sarah Ann's room.

"She's safe here," Lisbeth said, reading his thoughts. Whatever else he was, whatever his motives, he cared for the child. She couldn't doubt that any longer. "No one will do her harm." She grinned suddenly. "I wish I could say as much for that cat."

He hesitated for a moment, then nodded. He reached for a shirt that lay on the chair and pulled it on, not bothering with the buttons. His careless masculinity was a powerful force, unlike anything in her experience. Jamie had always been careful about propriety. He'd undressed in the dark and had always worn a nightshirt, even while making love.

Ben Masters's assurance was daunting. He slept in the nude and, even now, was bowing only marginally to convention. The flame of the kerosene lamp seemed devilish, playing shadow games over his chest, making the blond hairs glow as if they were gold. She shivered with the unwanted feelings that assaulted her like waves against the Scottish coast.

He frowned. "Are you cold?"

"A little," she replied, but it was a lie. Her shivering had nothing to do with the chilly night. His gaze raked over her thin nightdress and dressing gown, and she felt as if he'd actually touched her. Awkwardly, she pushed a few strands of hair back behind her ear and started to braid them. She hated her hair; it was curly and unruly and never did what it should. And she'd seldom been as self-conscious about it as she was at that moment.

That thought stiffened her shoulders. This man held enormous power over her future, and she would be the worst kind of fool to let down her guard in front of him. She couldn't trust him—not even if she wanted to. Not yet. Perhaps never.

"Don't," he said suddenly.

She was bewildered. "Don't what?"

"Don't confine that hair. It's really very pretty." The words were appraising rather than complimentary, but their sincerity sent warmth flooding through her again.

She tried to move. But his gaze pinned her to the spot. She was so aware of his commanding size, of his self-assurance.

He touched her hair in a swift gesture that surprised her. Lisbeth reached up with one hand and took his fingers in hers, her thumb running over them. She felt the calluses. His hands were not those of a solicitor at all, adding another factor to the mystery.

She asked, "Are you quite sure you're a solicitor?"

"A lawyer," he corrected, smiling slightly at her disbelief. "I am."

"Do all American lawyers sleep with guns?"

"If they have unhappy clients," he said lazily.

"And how did you get all those calluses?"

His hand suddenly seized hers. It seemed tremendously large, like a bear's paw, but his fingers were gentle as they ran over her own calluses.

"A lady's hand?" he shot back.

"As you've probably noticed, I'm not always a lady."

"It depends on your definition of a lady," he said.

A flash of pleasure rushed through Lisbeth. But as soon as he'd made the comment, his eyes turned wary again. He still hadn't accepted her explanation of her presence in this room. And *she* still wasn't sure what he was doing there. His explanation was difficult to believe: that he would give up the large room for a child and a wayward cat. In her family, a child hadn't existed except as an object of anger.

Did he really think Sarah Ann was in danger? Was that why he'd put her in what should have been his room? The notion was ridiculous. No one here would hurt a child.

"Come," she said. "I'll get something for that burn."

He hesitated again for a moment, but then nodded. "My lady," he said almost mockingly as he went to the door and waited for her to lead the way.

When he closed the door behind them, she looked at him curiously.

"Annabelle," he explained. "There's no telling where she'd go if she got the chance. At least Henry's not around." The amusement was back in his voice again, and she thought how pleasant it was. No hint of nastiness colored it—as was often the case with Hugh's brand of humor.

She liked Ben Masters. An uncomfortable thought.

"Why is she always wearing the scarf?" Lisbeth asked as they walked side by side down the corridor.

"It was her mother's," he said. "She never wants it far away."

She wanted to ask about Sarah Ann's mother, but his voice had turned cold and hard. *He's hurting, too,* she thought.

He'd been so blunt, so direct . . . so American. It seemed odd, to run suddenly into a topic that caused him such obvious discomfort.

But then, maybe it wasn't so odd. Maybe he had very strong feelings about Sarah Ann's mother. Perhaps he'd been in love with her and mourned her still. That would certainly explain his tenderness toward Sarah Ann, a child who wasn't even his own.

Suddenly, it occurred to Lisbeth to wonder if Sarah Ann, in fact, was Ben Masters's daughter. Birth certificates could be faked. Perhaps Masters had entered into a conspiracy with the American solicitor Mr. Alistair had hired. Wouldn't Hugh love to prove that.

Lisbeth, however, found no joy in the prospect. She

didn't want Ben Masters to be a liar. For the sake of her own and Jamie's dream, she needed him and Sarah Ann to be exactly what they claimed to be. She refused to admit to herself that she might also have other, more personal reasons to want Masters to be honest and trustworthy.

They reached the bottom of the staircase, and walked through the lower floor to the kitchen. Lisbeth lit several lamps, then went to the storage room where herbs and the medicine box were kept. She also found a bottle of brandy kept for medicinal use. She didn't know whether the American needed it, but she bloody well did.

Loaded down with her supplies, she returned to the kitchen. He was lounging against one of the walls, looking like two tons of masculinity. He was barefooted. But he'd buttoned his shirt halfway, and she breathed a sigh of relief. Still, her gaze automatically focused on the part of his chest that remained exposed. God's toothache, she hadn't imagined its impressiveness, nor had the darkness exaggerated.

Lisbeth scolded herself for having such thoughts. He might well be a confidence man and thief. He might be anything.

And you need him. She had the fleeting thought that it might be like needing an asp.

Lisbeth felt a bit aspish herself and banged down the medicine box on the kitchen table. "Aren't you cold?" she inquired.

He took a long, lazy look over her nightdress. "Aren't you?"

"Do you always answer a question with a question?" She couldn't keep the exasperation out of her voice.

"Not always," he replied complacently.

Frustration boiled in her.

You need him on your side.

Even if he's a charlatan?

Hugh's the alternative.

She smiled through clenched teeth. "Where is your home?"

"In America?"

"Yes," she said, clenching her teeth even harder.

"The last place was Denver."

"The last?"

"I move around a lot."

"Where were you born, then?"

"Chicago."

It was like pulling teeth. He gave her nothing to fasten onto.

"Where was Sarah Ann born?"

"Denver," he replied shortly, then strode over to the table and started riffling through the medicine box. It had taken him four steps to cross the room. It would take anyone else seven. She wished she weren't so conscious of his size, or the way he loomed over her.

Her entire body tingled with awareness, especially as she recalled the way she had fallen on him a short while ago.

He pulled out some ointments and bandages. "Sit down," he demanded, and she wondered how and when he'd taken over. But then hadn't he taken over from the moment he'd walked onto Calholm?

Lisbeth sat, stunned by the authority in Ben Masters's voice.

He took her arm and studied the scratches, then washed them and soothed ointment over the area.

"I meant to doctor you," she said, thoroughly put out.

"I can doctor myself."

"So can I," she shot back irritably. She had been taking care of herself for a long time.

The side of his mouth turned up again in that crooked smile that was so uncommonly attractive.

"Tell me about Hugh and Barbara," he said.

She dropped her gaze and shrugged, trying to hide her dismay. She didn't want to talk about Hugh, and she particularly didn't want to talk about Barbara. She should have realized, though, that this was coming. *All* men wanted to know about Barbara.

"What do you want to hear?"

"You don't like each other." It was a statement.

"We disagree with each other," she insisted. "We admire different things."

"What do *you* admire?"

"People who work hard. Animals, who have a certain innocence. Honesty." *But I'm willing to use you even if you are dishonest.* She tried not to think about how much she might have to compromise her beliefs.

"And what does Barbara admire?"

"You'll have to ask her," Lisbeth replied, unwilling to appear the jealous shrew.

"And Hugh?"

"Ask *him*," she said with some satisfaction. She could be just as discreet as he was.

His eyes bored into her, and the smile disappeared. He seemed to be weighing her, judging her. She felt hideously wanting.

"Exactly how much power will I have if Sarah Ann is recognized as the heiress?"

"A great deal," she said. "She would inherit Calholm and all its land and much of its wealth and investments. Barbara and I have lifelong tenancies in the house, but you could make that untenable if you wished."

"You must resent that."

"I don't know," she said.

"Why?"

He was like a woodsman with a saw. Except he wasn't cutting into a piece of wood in this case. He was cutting into her.

"You might be the better choice," Lisbeth replied. She started to add "between two evils" but thought better of it. However, his eyes suddenly gleamed as if he understood too well.

"Better than Hugh George Alexander Hamilton?" Masters aped Hugh perfectly.

"He wants to sell off the horses."

"Are they worth that much?"

"Not as much as they will be in several years, when we have a champion."

"You're gambling on that?"

"Jamie's father gambled on that—and Jamie. It's what they wanted."

"And what you want?" he concluded.

"Yes," she said defiantly.

He paused, then asked, "How did your husband die?"

The question hit hard. It was impertinent and none of his business, and yet she heard herself answer. "The girth on his horse slipped when he was jumping. His neck was broken."

Masters finished tending her arm, and his hands dropped away from her, leaving her feeling vaguely bereft, empty. His fingers had felt good on her skin.

Hunting through the basket, Lisbeth found an herb mixture for burns. "Fair's fair," she said, grabbing his hand. She studied the burn again. Like her scratches, it wasn't bad, but a poultice would help the pain.

"Stay here," she ordered. She tried to sound as authoritative as he had.

Whether or not she had succeeded, he did as he was told. She added water from a pitcher to the herbs and brought the mixture back, then pressed a layer against the burn. His expression didn't change, and she couldn't tell whether the pain had eased or not.

His eyes were like ice and fire at the same time. They looked cool, but they seemed to burn right through her. She wished the herb poultice cured that sort of pain, too.

"Thank you," he said, somewhat stiffly.

"You're welcome," she said, thinking he didn't look grateful at all. He looked, instead, disconcerted. Had anyone ever taken care of him before? Had Sarah Ann's mother?

The questions nagged at her.

Masters stood. "Can I expect more midnight excursions?" he asked with that crooked smile.

"Not from me. Annabelle is too good a watch cat."

"What about Henry?"

"He's probably sound asleep on my bed."

"Smart dog."

Suddenly the air was alive with innuendo, the room crackling with electricity. Another minute of this and she'd be lost in the fog of intimacy surrounding them.

He touched her cheek. "It's been an . . . interesting evening."

Her legs were turning to water. "Yes."

"I think I might enjoy Scotland more than I thought."

"It's really . . . quite beautiful, particularly when the hills are covered with heather." She was babbling. She never babbled.

"You should see Texas in the spring, and Colorado in the fall."

God's toothache, she was being consumed by his eyes. She felt compelled to respond. "But it can't be grander than the loch nearby."

"The lake we can see from the window?" he asked, winning her nod of approval. "I've promised to take Sarah Ann there. Can you guide us?"

Pleasure suffused her, lazily and sensuously.

"I'll have cook prepare some Scottish delicacies. Scones and cream and jam."

"Sarah Ann will like that."

She wished he would say he'd like it, too, but he didn't. Despite the warm sensuality of his words, he kept his distance emotionally. For a moment, she wanted nothing more than to bridge the gap between them.

But she couldn't. She couldn't let wayward feelings get in the way of what she hoped would be a sound business relationship. Feelings were treacherous.

"Good night," Lisbeth said. "I'll quench the lamps."

Masters nodded, hesitated only a moment, then made

for the stairs. She stayed behind, eyeing the brandy bottle. She had never taken a drink alone.

The circumstances could be considered unusual, though, unusual enough to justify a drink for medicinal purposes. She poured herself a glass and gulped it, feeling the fiery liquid sear a path to her stomach. It didn't help at all.

Disgusted with herself, Lisbeth returned to her room. Henry was oblivious to the world, including the recent attack on her person—and her emotions. He was, instead, snoring quite happily on top of her bed. He barely lifted his head in acknowledgment as she lowered the lamp she'd taken from the kitchen and sat next to him.

"Useless dog," she complained affectionately.

He moaned. Henry moaned a lot, sometimes with pleasure, sometimes in response to her speaking to him. She liked to believe he understood a lot of what she said, though she knew he just plain adored being talked to.

She threw her arms around him, and he shivered with delight and moaned again.

"What do you think of him?" she asked.

He moaned.

"That's no answer."

He licked her hand sympathetically.

"That's more like it." She hugged him, happy for his uncomplicated presence—a great relief after the very complicated presence of Ben Masters. She wondered whether she would get any sleep at all this night.

Chapter Six

Ben was awakened yet again by a body bouncing on top of him. This time, however, the body was a tiny one.

What was happening to his instincts? Usually, the slightest sound woke him. It did last night; why not this morning? If people were going to continue to creep up on him while he slept, he would have to start wearing clothes to bed. So much for his old bachelor habits.

Sarah Ann gleefully bounced on him again, and an involuntary "oomph" exploded from his mouth. She was getting heavy.

"Can we get a pony today?"

Uncomfortably recalling several incidents from last night—or was it early this morning?—he looked around cautiously. Instead of answering, he asked, "Where's Annabelle?"

"Lady Lisbeth brought her some cream," she said.

Dear God, his instincts had gone straight to hell if

someone had entered Sarah Ann's room without his waking. "That was nice of her," he said noncommittally.

"It was . . . splen'id," Sarah Ann replied.

"Splendid?" he asked.

She nodded. "Yep, splen'id. That means *very* nice. Lady Lisbeth said Annabelle was a splen'id cat."

Lady Lisbeth was a liar. But bringing Annabelle her breakfast had been thoughtful, especially since the animal had twice scratched her.

"When did she bring it?" he asked.

"Just now. She was real quiet. She said she didn't want to wake you. She hushed me." Sarah Ann put a finger to her mouth and whispered, "Shhh."

"She did, did she?" Ben said, partly amused, partly even more concerned than before. What *had* happened to those damned instincts?

Of course the door had been closed between him and Sarah Ann. And he'd stayed awake a good piece of the night trying to figure out Lisbeth Hamilton. Apparently, *she'd* had no trouble sleeping if she had been visiting at this early hour. That was a disgruntling thought.

Annabelle joined them, cream dotting her ragged whiskers. She leaped next to Sarah Ann on his lap, kneading her paws on the trousers he'd decided to keep on when he'd returned to bed. The cat was perilously close to a part of him that he definitely didn't want clawed.

"Now that Annabelle has eaten," he suggested, "I think we might go in search of food."

"And then a pony?" she asked hopefully.

"Perhaps," he said. "I don't know how long it will take us to find one."

"I think we'll find a splen'id one today," she said confidently, quite pleased with herself.

He grimaced. He didn't want to dim her enthusiasm, but finding a pony might not be all that easy. Ben disengaged Annabelle and placed her on the floor, then sat upright. He set Sarah Ann on her feet.

"You wash," he said. "Do you know which dress you want to wear?"

She tipped her head in thought. "The blue one. A pony will like the blue one."

He sighed. He was not going to be able to divert her thoughts from that damned pony.

"All right," he said. "I'm going to shave, then I'll come in and help you with the buttons."

"I can button the blue dress myself," she said. Which was one of the reasons she liked it best, he knew. Managing the buttons, which were in front, made her feel more grown-up.

"Well, I'll help brush your hair, then."

"All right," she said happily, imitating the way he'd said it. "Come on, Annabelle. We're going to get a pony." She disappeared into the next room in a flurry of red curls and white nightgown.

He shook his head. A child's faith. And all her faith was placed in him. Somehow he had to find her a pony.

He also had to face Lisbeth Hamilton in the glare of daylight. The memory of her body pressed to his last night stirred an ache deep inside him. It had been months since he'd slept with a woman. The last one had been Sarah Ann's mother, a thought that sent a shard of pain into his heart.

He hadn't loved Mary May; he hadn't known her long enough. But he'd liked her more than any woman he'd ever met, and, given more time, he probably would have loved her. She'd had a zest for living that was rare. And a sense of humor to boot.

Lisbeth Hamilton had a sense of humor, too. Calling Annabelle "a splendid animal" certainly required a sense of humor; so did naming a furry behemoth Henry the Eighth. Ben stopped shaving long enough to grin.

But the grin faded quickly. *Instincts*, he warned himself. *Don't forget your instincts.* Lisbeth Hamilton, Lady Calholm, wanted something from him, and she probably stood to profit if there was one less heir.

Ben stared at his reflection in the mirror, at the lines in his face. Those around his eyes came from years of squinting into the sun. Others stemmed from less benevolent causes: war, pain, responsibility, too many split-second, life-or-death decisions. He was ready for a more peaceful life, and Sarah Ann deserved one, too—a peaceful life free from any more uncertainty and loss.

He wasn't sure Calholm was the place to find that life.

Ben finished shaving and pulled on a clean white shirt and changed to a pair of riding trousers. What did one wear in the morning in the Scottish countryside? He didn't know, and he really didn't care. He wasn't going to confine himself in a cravat and waistcoat.

He went into Sarah Ann's room. She had, as promised, dressed herself and was patiently lacing up her best pair of shoes. Her dress was a little askew, the buttons in the wrong holes. The dirty scarf was tucked in the collar of her dress.

She looked up at him. "You look very handsome," she said solemnly.

"And you look very pretty, Lady Sarah Ann."

"I'm not—"

"A lady, I know," he said, "but you soon will be."

"Ladies have ponies, don't they?"

"I believe so."

"Then I'll think about it."

"You do that, Sarah Ann," he said seriously. He brushed her hair and tied it back with a blue ribbon. She stood proudly before him, as if at inspection. As surreptitiously as he could, he fixed the buttons while looking at her admiringly. "You look very royal, Sugarplum."

"I like sugarplums better than ladies." She was very serious, and he had to stifle a chuckle. He had to hide his amusement often, for fear of offending her. Before he became her guardian, it was rare for him to even feel amusement.

"I can understand why you'd prefer sugarplums to ladies," he finally said, realizing she was waiting for approval.

"Do you like sugarplums better, too?"

He choked. "Depends."

"Depends on what?"

The infernal questions again. She looked at him expectantly as if waiting to hear a great truth.

"Depends on the sugarplum and the lady."

"Oh," she said, clearly stymied by the enigmatic answer.

He felt a moment of triumph, but it was quickly squashed.

"Do you like Lady Lisbeth?"

"Yes," he said cautiously.

"A lot?"

"I don't know her that well."

"What about Lady Barb'ra?"

"I don't know," he replied. "What do you think?"

She pondered the question. "She's very pretty."

"Yes."

Just then, Annabelle jumped into her lap, and Sarah Ann's thoughts were diverted. "Do you like it here?" she asked the cat.

Annabelle didn't deign to reply.

"I think she does," Sarah Ann proclaimed on Annabelle's behalf.

"Why?" Ben thought he would turn the tables on her.

"Because she'll have a pony to play with."

Turning the tables by asking questions seemed of no use. Sarah Ann couldn't get her mind off the blasted pony. "I don't know if Annabelle shares your enthusiasm for a pony."

"She will. She likes everything I like."

That was a dubious assumption, but Ben didn't really feel like a new round of questions. "Let's go, Sugarplum."

"We'll take Annabelle."

"I think we better leave her here and warn the maid. You don't want her to get lost."

"Henry goes everywhere," Sarah Ann argued.

"Henry doesn't scratch everyone."

"Annabelle doesn't, either. Just when she's scared."

Which was most of the time. "You can play with her after breakfast. I think she needs some sleep. She had a hard night."

"Did *you* have a hard night?"

"A very hard night," he said. "Now, come along." He picked up Annabelle and put her in the basket. Since the cat was quickly learning how to open it, the measure was temporary at best.

"What's a hard night?"

"It's one when a cat jumps up on you when you're sound asleep." Not an entirely accurate account of last night's activities, but true enough. Annabelle would ruin anyone's sleep—even without help.

"Oh," she said again, her face creasing with sudden worry. "Annabelle was a bad cat?"

"Annabelle was Annabelle," he soothed. "Now let's go eat."

Sarah Ann looked puzzled, but decided to leave well enough alone. She put her hand in his, and they left together for their first full day at Calholm.

❖❖❖

After bringing a bowl of cream to Annabelle and looking in on Sarah Ann, Lisbeth had taken Henry out for a run. Now she walked into the dining room, Henry at her heels.

Much to her shock, Barbara wandered in, looking splendid in a violet day dress, her dark hair caught in a chignon in back. The severe style, which would have looked terrible on Lisbeth, flattered Barbara's elegant face. Lisbeth felt a little like a crow in her black riding dress.

"You're up early," she observed pleasantly. "A special occasion?"

Barbara shot her a suspicious look. "I just wanted our . . . guests to feel at home."

"And Hugh?"

She shrugged. "He's a bear in the morning."

Lisbeth helped herself to the food on the sideboard. She had ordered more than usual, not knowing the eating habits of Ben Masters and Sarah Ann. She filled her plate with bacon and scones and eggs while noticing that Barbara took only a slice of toast.

Lisbeth liked to eat. And she worked hard enough during the day to wear it off.

"You have the appetite of a peasant," Barbara said distastefully as Lisbeth slathered cream over the scone.

"Aye," she replied contentedly. "You don't know what you miss."

"I don't see how you can eat anything in the morning."

"Sleeping well gives me an appetite," Lisbeth said. It was a lie, at least as far as last night was concerned, but it was as good a retort as any.

"How nice." The deep masculine voice came from behind her, startling Lisbeth and bringing color to her cheeks. Her skin prickled with awareness. She could literally feel the American's presence; she probably would have known he was there even if he hadn't spoken.

"Good morning."

He sounded so self-assured. The unbidden, unwanted memory of the feel and sight of his naked flesh made her face flame even brighter. Oh, why did her mind insist on thinking the exact thought she most wanted not to think at that moment?

Barbara smiled prettily. "Good morning, Mr. Masters, and to you, too, Sarah Ann. I thought we might go into the village. There's a little shop there and a dressmaker. We can order some new dresses for Sarah Ann. And a new scarf," she added with distaste.

"I don't want a new scarf," Sarah Ann said. She went over to Henry, kneeling and pressing her head against his, receiving a big swipe of a tongue in return. She giggled and stood, totally ignoring Barbara.

"Of course you do," Barbara said confidently, obviously certain she could turn Sarah Ann to her way of thinking.

Ben Masters simply leaned against the sideboard.

"No," Sarah Ann said flatly. "Papa said we could look for a pony, and I don't want a new scarf."

Barbara looked pleadingly at Masters. "I really would like to take her shopping."

He hesitated. Lisbeth thought that perhaps he wanted to accept Barbara's offer.

"I want my own scarf," Sarah Ann insisted stubbornly, "and I don't want a new dress. I want a pony."

"The scarf was her mother's," Ben explained kindly.

Lisbeth could see he felt sympathy for Barbara, and she wanted to kick him. Barbara was a superb actress; Lisbeth doubted she felt any real concern for Sarah Ann.

"Oh," Barbara said, giving Masters a grateful smile. "I understand." Turning to Sarah Ann, she said, "Then of course you must keep your scarf. And tell me something about your mother sometime."

Sarah Ann, having won her point, smiled.

Lisbeth watched Ben help the child select her food, bending down and asking what she wanted, and placing two scones and an egg on her plate. He filled his own plate with ham, salmon, eggs, and a scone, then carried both plates to the table. He set them down and held out a chair for Sarah Ann. The pillow was in place, and he shot Lisbeth a quick smile of thanks. She felt the impact of that smile all the way to her toes.

Sarah Ann was also looking at her. "You said we can go find a pony."

"It depends on your father," Lisbeth said. She gave him a challenging look, expecting him to take Barbara's offer instead.

Masters nodded. "I won't hear anything else until we do," he said. He turned to Barbara. "Perhaps we can take her shopping another time. Next week perhaps. I have to meet John Alistair in Edinburgh this week."

"I'll go to Edinburgh with you," Barbara said swiftly.

"I can introduce you to dear Mr. Alistair and to some other families. My family—the MacLeods—maintain a town house you can use."

Ben hesitated. He wasn't sure about the proprieties. "I think a hotel might be better."

"Oh, I'll stay with my sister," Barbara said. "She's married to a marquess who's in the Parliament."

Lisbeth noted that Barbara conveniently forgot the fact she and her sister disliked each other intensely.

"What about Hugh?" Lisbeth said and almost immediately regretted it. She attributed the question to the devil that sometimes ruled her tongue. She hated being snide, but Barbara seemed to bring out the worst in her.

Barbara cast an irritated glance her way. "Hugh can take care of himself."

"So can I," Masters said, "and I really would prefer a hotel. We'll just be there a day."

"We?"

"Sarah Ann and I."

Barbara's face fell. "I thought Fiona and Maisie could care for her here."

Fiona, Ben had learned, was the cook, and Maisie, Barbara's maid. Effie, Maisie's sister, was Lisbeth's maid. The sisters had helped prepare Ben's and Sarah Ann's rooms and tended to Sarah Ann's clothes.

"No," he said flatly.

Barbara shrugged again. "I would still like to travel with you. I need some new dresses."

This time, Lisbeth kept her tongue in place, merely lifting an eyebrow.

"And you, Lady Lisbeth," Ben Masters asked, "would you like to go with us?"

"Just Lisbeth," she insisted. "We are practically relatives, and I know Americans aren't comfortable with titles." She smiled. "Neither am I, actually. And thank you, but I have too much to do here. Shadow's training is critical now."

Ben Masters nodded and finished his breakfast. She enjoyed watching him eat, for he obviously relished it.

"You like scones?" she asked.

"I like anything except beef jerky and hardtack."

"What's that?" she asked.

"You don't want to know."

"Yes, I do."

She saw the doubt in his eyes, but then he answered. "Hardtack is a hard biscuit made of flour and water, and jerky is beef cooked so long you can hardly chew it. But they both keep a very long time if you're on a trail."

"On a trail?"

He hesitated, and she wondered why. Was he hiding something?

"A long ride," he said a moment later.

She puzzled over that. He'd said earlier that he rode "a little." Yet it sounded as if he'd eaten a lot of that hardtack and jerky that one only ate on the trail.

"Don't you have trains in America?" Barbara asked.

He looked amused. "Yes, but America is very, very large and there are great expanses of territory without roads, much less trains."

"I think I would like to go there someday," Barbara said dreamily.

"Despite the Indians?" he asked.

She shuddered. "Are there Indians in New York?"

"No. They're all pretty much west now."

"I'd like to go to New York, then."

"I would like to go west," Lisbeth said. "I've read about it. It's said the mountains are greater than our Highlands."

"Lisbeth is from the Highlands," Barbara said almost apologetically.

Lisbeth knew Barbara and Hugh considered being a Highlander akin to being a barbarian. She, on the other hand, considered most Lowlanders less Scottish, and knew them to be more favorably disposed toward their English neighbors. But she decided not to be affronted. She was too interested now that the American was beginning to talk.

"I would like to visit the Highlands someday," he said, turning the subject away from himself.

Lisbeth thought she would like to show them to him. She loved the craggy, majestic mountains. They had been her escape, a thing of beauty away from a home filled with ugliness.

"In the summer," she said, "they're covered with heather. That is the time to see the Highlands. They can be bitter cold in the winter."

"All Scotland seems cold," he said. "The wind bites through you."

"Is it not so in America?" Barbara broke in.

She looked decidedly irritated, Lisbeth thought, undoubtedly because it was the first time a man paid more attention to Lisbeth than to Barbara.

"In some places, it is," he replied. "Winters in Colorado and Chicago can be damnably cold, though there's not this constant damp."

Sarah Ann started squirming then, and Lisbeth rose. As much as she would like to learn more, she knew the child must be tired of sitting. She'd been very good to stay still this long.

"If you're ready," she told Masters, "we'll go down to the stables. Callum, our trainer, should be there, and he might tell us where we can find a pony. You can pick out a horse for yourself."

She noticed the quick flare of pleasure in Masters's eyes. Had he minimized how well he rode? She would soon find out.

"Sarah Ann will need her coat," he said.

"So will you," she replied. "I'll meet you at the front hall in five minutes."

Sarah Ann was wriggling with excitement, and it tugged at Lisbeth's heart. The child was already bringing something special into this cold house, a sense of wonder that had long gone.

She found her own long riding coat and made her way to the stables. Callum Trapp was brushing Shadow.

"Ye are late this morning," he observed. "Our lad is a wee bit impatient."

"Our new heiress has arrived."

He scowled. "Ain't right," he muttered. "Ye should 'ave Calholm. Ye are the only one who cares for it."

"I think it might be better in her guardian's hands than Hugh's," she said. She probably shouldn't use Hugh's name so informally. But Callum was a friend as much as a trainer. Since she'd come to Calholm, he had been the only one she'd been able to talk to. Even Jamie had considered the horses a business, and had often seemed indifferent to the wonderful sensitive creatures themselves.

"Neither Master Hugh nor the American should 'ave it," Callum said again, running his hand along the horse's neck. "Shadow's a proud one. He can make Calholm famous and show those bloody English."

"You should have seen him take the stone wall," she said proudly.

"Only ye could have done that. He only works for his mistress."

"Jamie was good with him."

He ignored that observation. "I'll ride wi' ye, and watch him jump."

She shook her head. "Mr. Masters and his . . . daughter are coming over to see the horses. Sarah Ann wants a pony, and I was hoping you might help us find a good one."

Callum muttered something, but she didn't take offense. He did a lot of muttering. She eyed him affectionately. He was small and wiry; though she knew he was in his forties, he looked ageless. He didn't like people much and made no bones about it, but he was unceasingly patient with the horses.

He had no family that she knew of and he never talked about himself, no matter how she coaxed him. As far as she could tell, he had only one love: horses. The objects of his hatred were wide and varied, ranging from all Englishmen to Scottish "nabobs" to "worthless" jockeys. She didn't know how he felt about Americans but suspected they would probably rank low as well.

"We need him, Callum," she pleaded now. "Be civil."

His gaze met hers. His eyes were a dark brown-black and impossible to read. "I willna tolerate a fool, not like that cousin of yours."

"I don't think this man is a fool," she said with a slight smile.

"Does he like horses?" Callum questioned fiercely, as if he would take a pitchfork to the man if he didn't.

"I think he likes animals," she said. "His little girl has a cat."

He wrinkled his nose in distaste. "A demmed cat's no lassie's companion. 'Tis good for one thing, and that's catching the rat."

"Sarah Ann thinks Annabelle is perfect," she said softly. "I think she's a lonesome little girl."

"He be a brute, then," Callum said with some satisfaction.

"I hope not."

The drawl came from the doorway, and Lisbeth whirled around to see Ben Masters. Sarah Ann was eyeing the interior of the stables with a look of great awe.

Lisbeth felt her face go red at being caught discussing him with an employee. Callum, however, merely stuck out his jaw pugnaciously.

"This is Callum Trapp," she told Ben Masters. Turning to Callum, she added, "Mr. Masters and Sarah Ann Hamilton."

"Sarah Ann Hamilton Masters," Masters corrected.

Lisbeth prayed for a moment that Callum would behave himself. Too much depended on this American.

"I hear she be wanting a pony."

He *was* behaving himself. Lisbeth breathed a sigh of relief. She didn't like the light in Callum's eyes, however, nor his suddenly subservient voice.

Sarah Ann was creeping up to Shadow, and Lisbeth placed a restraining hand on her. "Let him get used to you," she said gently, taking a piece of carrot from her pocket and putting it in Sarah Ann's hand.

Unafraid of the large animal, Sarah Ann held out the treat, and Shadow smelled it, then took it in his mouth. "He liked it," she said with a huge smile.

"So he did, and he doesn't do that for many. He's very selective about his friends." Lisbeth returned to the matter of finishing introductions. "Callum is our trainer, the best in all Scotland."

Masters held out his hand, but Callum turned toward the horses. Lisbeth winced inwardly as Masters gave her a wry look, then lowered his hand. Gentry didn't shake hands with servants in Scotland, but Lisbeth had read about American casualness and approved. She herself had always maintained a certain informality with servants and other employees. But it seemed Callum was determined to be difficult. He would protest later that he hadn't noticed the American's hand, waiting for a handshake.

"I'll show you the rest of the horses," she said quickly to cover Callum's rudeness. She led Masters down the two rows of stalls, introducing him to each of the twelve jumpers, three young colts, and one filly. She watched as, several times, he stopped to run a hand along the neck of a horse. He said little, but approval flickered in his eyes, and she took comfort in that.

Clinging to his hand, Sarah Ann cooed and ahhed over the horses, giggling when one reached his head down to nuzzle her.

When they were finished, Lisbeth waited for a reaction.

"They're fine animals," he said, and she had to settle for that. She had already discovered he seldom said much of anything, and never what he was really thinking.

"They are among the best in Scotland," she said. "We're getting offers to buy even from England."

"But you don't want to sell?"

"Not yet," she said. "If Shadow wins the Grand National next year, the horses will double in value."

"The Grand National?"

"It's the greatest steeplechase in the world," she said. "It's held at Aintree near Liverpool. We've duplicated the course as much as we can here with thirty fences spread over a distance of four and a half miles. Shadow's already won a number of hurdle races here in Scotland but the Grand National . . ."

Lisbeth heard the awe in her own voice. Grand National winners had made stables in Ireland and Britain both famous and prosperous. It was past time the Scots showed their mettle.

Masters was silent for a moment, his expression thoughtful. "You think Shadow can win?"

"I know it," she said. "And one of the two-year-olds shows signs of being a champion in another three years."

"Three years?" he said.

"It's rare for even a five-year-old horse to win the Grand National," she explained, "but Shadow's extraordinary."

"We race three-year-olds."

"But most American races are on flat tracks and aren't nearly as grueling as steeplechases," she said. "The Grand National requires strength and endurance that a young horse hasn't yet developed. It requires more training. *Years* of training. We've invested in those years." She looked up at him with a silent plea.

But instead of responding to the unspoken entreaty, he changed the subject. "About that pony . . ."

Callum, who had been tailing along behind, spoke in what Lisbeth recognized as forced civil tones. "Douglas might be knowing of one."

"Douglas?"

"The blacksmith in the village," Lisbeth explained.

Masters nodded, his gaze wandering with interest to the horses again.

"I'll take Shadow," Lisbeth told Callum.

"And which one for 'im?"

Lisbeth looked at Masters. "How well do you ride? We have horses ranging from gentle to . . . difficult."

"Gentle," he said. "Sarah Ann will be riding with me."

That told Lisbeth little. Was Sarah Ann an excuse? But there was an aura of competence about him that made her think he probably did everything well.

She nodded to Callum. "Samson," she said, then turned back to Masters to explain. "He's as big as his name, but has a much better disposition." He gave her that crooked grin, and she was utterly charmed by the way it changed the austere face.

"Sounds about right," he said.

She heard Callum mutter close to her ear something about Americans which she ignored.

"I can saddle my own horse," Masters said.

Callum shook his head. "Lady Lisbeth wouldna like any more accidents," the small Scotsman said and, with a disdainful sniff, retreated into the tack room. He returned shortly with a saddle, which he carried into a stall down the row.

Lisbeth ignored the American's questioning gaze as she quickly fitted a bridle and bit onto Shadow, then led him from the stall. She started to lift a small sidesaddle from a sawhorse, but it was taken firmly from her hands. She watched as the American competently tightened the cinch despite Shadow's nervous sidestepping. He touched the horse's neck, and Shadow instantly quieted.

"He's a fine animal," he said.

Lisbeth's legs trembled slightly as his hands roamed over the horse, quiet approval lighting his face. He knew more than a little about horses. Would he want Shadow for his own? Or would he try to sell him?

Masters's eyes were neutral as he helped her into the saddle. "I like the other way you rode better." He spoke as if they were sharing a secret.

"So do I," she said, "but Barbara and Hugh would never forgive me if I rode astride into the village."

"Do you care?"

The question caught her by surprise, and she didn't know exactly how to answer it. Part of her didn't care. But another part, the child in her, still wanted approval from those who never gave it. Defiance was the refuge of the lonely.

"No," she said finally.

His gaze searched her face with care and wariness. Was he a confidence man? She still wasn't sure.

A primitive roughness radiated from him despite his soft-spoken words and good manners. Perhaps the war had created that edge that proclaimed his familiarity with danger; surely the practice of law hadn't.

Regardless of the cause, Ben Masters intrigued and frightened her. He was dangerous in many ways. And she realized she wasn't going to be able to sway him as she'd so fervently hoped. He wasn't a man to be used.

She watched as he lifted Sarah Ann up onto the horse Callum had saddled for him, then effortlessly swung into the saddle behind her. Lisbeth recognized his easy seat, the grace found only in an experienced rider.

He'd said he rode a little. That was one lie he'd told. How many others were waiting to be uncovered?

Chapter Seven

Damn, but it felt good to be on a horse again.

Ben shifted in the saddle, relishing the feel of it. He liked its light weight. Cavalry saddles were light, too, though a little larger to accommodate a carbine sling, bedrolls, and saddlebags. The saddles he'd used for the last several years, however, were of the heavy western variety, designed for days of riding, outfitted to carry the paraphernalia necessary on a long trail.

The saddle beneath him was the closest thing to riding bareback and took him back to his young days in Chicago.

Sarah Ann had ridden with him in Texas, and she settled easily in his arms. He could feel her excitement; her little body was wriggling with anticipation.

The horse, Samson, presented little challenge. He had an easy rocking gait and a mild temperament that responded instantly to instructions. For a moment, Ben longed for the horse he'd left in Texas. Lucifer had been well named: sometimes angelic but more often stubborn and rebellious.

The penetrating mist of yesterday was gone; the air, though, was frigid, and the wind whipped his hair. His body protected Sarah Ann's from the cold, but he felt exhilarated. He didn't know if it came from being on horseback again, from the cold wind, or from the sight of Lisbeth Hamilton riding next to him.

He'd always considered sidesaddles clumsy and unsafe. But she looked truly lovely perched there in a gray riding coat and hat that highlighted her hazel eyes and made her auburn hair more striking. She was every inch an aristocrat this morning, with no trace of the ruffian hoyden he'd seen before, except perhaps in the stubborn tilt of her chin. In contrast, he felt like a stable hand in his sheepskin coat and cotton shirt and riding trousers, totally out of place.

The low hills were still green though spotted here and there with snow. Small stone cottages, from which smoke snaked up into a royal-blue sky, dotted the landscape, along with neat plots of tilled earth. Sheep and a few cattle grazed placidly, side by side. He smiled, imagining the reaction of Texas cattlemen to the sight of the animals coexisting so easily. Most Texans were violently opposed to sheep, convinced they ruined cattle feed.

"There's those funny cows with shaggy hair," Sarah Ann said. From the moment they'd first seen one, she had been fascinated by their unusual looks.

"You should see the cattle in the Highlands." Lisbeth cast her a quick grin. "They look like yaks."

"What's a yak?"

"It's a large hairy beast that lives in Asia," Lisbeth said.

"Where's Asia?"

Ben sighed. "With Sarah Ann, one question always leads to another."

"I've noticed," Lisbeth said with a smile. "It's rather nice to have some curiosity around Calholm."

"Lady Barbara?"

"Only about those items with lace and ribbons," Lisbeth replied ruefully.

"And Hugh?"

"All he cares about is sheep and—" She stopped suddenly, and shrugged.

"And you?"

Her grin widened, her face becoming vivacious and alive. "Horses and books."

He knew how she felt about the horses. The books rather surprised him. His surprise must have shown on his face because her chin tilted even more defiantly.

"Perhaps you can suggest some books for Sarah Ann," he said mildly. Her defiance faded quickly, and he could only guess she'd been reassured by his tone.

"Our library has some wonderful illustrated children's books," she said. "I always wished . . ."

She trailed off, and he wondered why. There was a mystery about her that puzzled him.

"Tell me more about America," Lisbeth asked, changing the subject. "You said it's cold, too. And I've read of blizzards and snowstorms."

"True," Ben replied. "But then there are parts that are warm year round."

"Truly?" she asked.

"Truly," he confirmed as solemnly as if he were responding to one of Sarah Ann's questions.

"Are you laughing at me, Mr. Masters?"

"Ben," he corrected her. "If I call you Lisbeth, you must call me Ben. And no, I'm not laughing at you."

She looked at him dubiously, then asked another question. "Which part of America are you from?"

"I was born in New York, but my father moved west to Illinois when I was a boy."

"But Mr. Alistair said you and Sarah Ann lived in Colorado?"

She wasn't feigning interest, he'd decided; she genuinely wanted to know—unlike her sister-in-law, who had seemed more interested in flirtation than his answers.

He shrugged. "I moved farther west after the war."

"And that ended three years ago?"

"Nearly four."

"And you've been a solicitor since then?"

"Among other things."

He saw the question in her eyes, but he still wasn't prepared to tell the truth, that he'd been a hunter of men rather than a seeker of justice. He'd asked Silas Martin, the solicitor who had found Sarah Ann, not to tell the family his full history. He was a lawyer; that was all they needed to know.

Ben still didn't know why he'd taken that precaution. Instinct, maybe, or distrust born of chasing criminals. He'd disguised himself plenty in the past, had fitted in with outlaws, had even established a sort of friendship with one named Diablo. But he'd learned to keep his own counsel, to give as little information as possible, to disarm and deceive. Not particularly attractive traits, but they were his now; he didn't know how to be otherwise. And Sarah Ann's future was at stake. He had to remember that.

But Lisbeth wasn't ready to give up.

"What other things have you done?" she persisted.

He shrugged. "How did you start raising horses?"

She was silent a moment, and out of the corner of his eye he caught her looking at him with a mixture of frustration and puzzlement. Then, with a sigh, she said simply, "I love horses. I always have, and when I came to Calholm, I thought I'd found heaven. Callum has taught me so much."

"And your husband approved of you riding astride?"

She bit her lip. "I didn't ride that way until after his . . . accident."

Her hesitation told Ben one thing: there was the possibility of murder in the death of Jamie Hamilton. Ben thought of the mishap with the crates. Were the two

events somehow connected? Or was the idea too far-
fetched?

"Look," Sarah Ann said, bringing him out of his mus-
ings. She pointed toward a horse and colt grazing in the
fenced paddock of a nearby house. "A pony!" she exclaimed.

"Not exactly," he said. "That's a young horse. It'll
grow as big as the horse we're riding. A pony is always
small."

"When I get big, can I have a big horse?"

"The finest I can find," he assured her.

Her questions ended abruptly upon their entering the
village. They had spent a few hours here, changing from
the Edinburgh coach to the hired coach, and she was just
as fascinated now as she had been then. All the small
villages along the journey entranced her. To her, the neat
stone exteriors and big glass windows were like pictures
from a fairy-tale book. They charmed him, too, Ben admitted. The air of solid permanence here was so different
from the air of flimsiness and newness of the boomtowns
in the west.

Lisbeth led the way along a cobbled street to a blacksmith's shop. She slipped down from her horse and
opened the wide barn door. A bell rang and a husky man
hurried over from a smoky forge.

He flashed a wide grin. "Lady Lisbeth," he acknowledged.

"Douglas," she said. "It's fine to see you again."

"And who be these strangers with ye?" The huge man
turned toward Ben and Sarah Ann, who flinched a little
at the booming voice.

"This is Ian's daughter," Lisbeth said. "And her
guardian—"

"Ben Masters," Ben interceded at her discomfort over
finding the right introduction.

"Ahhh, Ian Hamilton. He was a wild lad, he was. But
she's a fine-looking lass. And what can I do for ye?"

"A pony," Sarah Ann said bravely and determinedly.

Lisbeth gave the blacksmith a conspiratorial smile. "I told her Douglas MacEver just might know of one for sale."

Ben warned himself not to respond to her smile. There was too much he didn't know about her. He couldn't afford to lower his guard. *Remember another warm smile,* a voice in his head admonished. *And the betrayal that followed.*

He had held women at arm's length ever since, even Sarah Ann's mother, although Mary May had started to breach his defenses before she died. But, then, she had wanted nothing from him.

He wasn't so sure of Lisbeth Hamilton.

"I think I may know of exactly the one," the blacksmith said, turning to Lisbeth. "Mary Godwin has outgrown her pony. John brought in her new horse to be shod."

Ben looked at Lisbeth in question.

"They live on the edge of town. He's the doctor."

"Can we go now?" Sarah Ann asked.

"I see no reason why not," Ben said. He turned to the blacksmith. "Do you have a good riding horse for sale?"

It was Lisbeth who answered. "You can use any mount at Calholm."

"I would prefer my own," Ben replied. He knew he sounded stiff, but he didn't want anything from the Hamilton family. He was here because of Sarah Ann, and he wasn't going to take a thing he hadn't earned.

Surprise flittered across Lisbeth's face, and he realized instantly that she had believed, as Hugh Hamilton did, that he was using Sarah Ann to benefit himself.

Ben returned his attention to the blacksmith.

"Aye, I know of a few animals that might suit ye," MacEver said, eyeing him carefully. "Ye look like ye know horses."

"A little." He ignored the eyebrow that Lisbeth raised.

"Ye like a spirited beast?"

"Let's say a good one," he said.

"I 'ave two for sale, but neither compare to those at Calholm."

Ben said, steadily, "I don't need a jumper."

"Then ye be welcome to take a look."

Ben lowered Sarah Ann to the ground and dismounted, then followed the blacksmith into the stone barn. The two horses for sale were adequate. The blacksmith was correct—neither measured up to the horse he was riding or the others at Calholm. But then he didn't plan to be in Scotland long enough to need a truly fine animal. He chose a steady-eyed bay.

"His name is Bailey," the blacksmith said, "and he's a fair horse. Do ye be wanting to take him now?"

Ben shook his head. "I would be grateful if you could send him to Calholm."

The blacksmith looked at Lisbeth. She nodded, and Ben felt even more of an outsider. Calholm wasn't his home, would never be his home.

But could it be Sarah Ann's? And could he ever let her go, even for her own good?

❖❖❖

Any pony would have been acceptable. Lisbeth realized that long before Sarah Ann met Peppermint. But Peppermint was as perfect as a pony could be. He was a dandy fellow, white and dignified and well mannered, standing quite still as he was inspected. Love was instant and mutual.

Actually, Peppermint was not Peppermint before introductions. But Sarah Ann immediately renamed the snow-white pony from Prince to the name of her favorite candy. Peppermint apparently approved. The pony nuzzled his new mistress at first sight, and when Ben Masters lifted Sarah Ann onto the pony's back, Peppermint stepped carefully and proudly around the small fenced paddock.

"The young lass has a way with horses," Dr. John Godwin said happily.

"She has a way with all animals," Ben said.

Lisbeth heard the affection in his voice and couldn't help thinking of her own child. If only the bairn had lived . . . But she'd lost it before it could take even a first breath.

Lisbeth pushed those memories away and concentrated on Masters and Sarah Ann. While he studied the pony with knowing hands, the girl stood nearby, practically prancing with delight. "Can we take him now?" she pleaded.

"Do you mind?" he asked Lisbeth. "Will your jumpers welcome this little one?"

"They tolerate Henry," she replied. "I think Peppermint will make a fine stable mate."

"Then it's done," he told the doctor. "Do you have a saddle?"

"Aye," the doctor said. "My daughter's. She's outgrown it, just as she's outgrown Prince. She'll be well pleased to know he's found a good home."

"The pony will be feasting on carrots and apples all the day if this one has anything to do with it," Ben said with an affectionate glance at Sarah Ann.

The pony nuzzled his new mistress. "Annabelle will like him, too," Sarah Ann said.

A rueful look passed over Ben's face. "I wouldn't be so sure of that, Sugarplum."

"You'll see," Sarah Ann countered confidently.

"Aye," he said. "Perhaps we will."

The Scottish word sounded fine on his tongue, Lisbeth thought. She felt a pleasant tingle run down her spine, then a pang twist in her heart. She wished for a fleeting second that someone—anyone—had been as kind to her as Masters was to Sarah Ann. God's toothache but this American stranger affected her in strange and unwanted ways. Or were they unwanted?

Masters counted out some pound notes, then turned to her. "May I help you mount?"

She wished she didn't need his help, but the bloody sidesaddle almost required it. She didn't want him to touch her, not now, not when she was so confused by her reaction to him. Her worst fears were realized when his hand took her gloved one, and heat radiated between them. His fingers lingered on hers a moment and a flash of surprise crossed his face before he released her.

"Can I ride the pony?" Sarah Ann asked.

"Not yet," he said. "I think you need a few lessons first."

"But Pep'mint will be dis'pointed."

"He'll just have to suffer through it," he said.

"But—"

"But you have to get used to each other," Lisbeth interceded, noting Ben's suddenly helpless look. There was something vulnerable—and attractive—about such a big man being made to feel helpless by such a small child.

"I already love him," Sarah Ann protested.

One of Ben's eyebrows arched upward as if to challenge Lisbeth to answer *that* one.

"But what about Peppermint?" Lisbeth said carefully. "He's going to a new home, and he's probably a wee bit frightened."

"Like me?" Sarah Ann's face showed great concern for the pony.

"I know it must have been fearsome, coming to a new country," Lisbeth continued, "but it wasn't so bad when you got here, was it? But you didn't know that. And neither does Peppermint."

"Poor Pep'mint," Sarah Ann said, her eyes large with understanding. "I'll have to love him extra much."

Lisbeth wanted to clutch Sarah Ann to her breast, hold her tight. She knew the kind of uncertainty Sarah Ann must feel. She knew how hard and how frightening it was to hold it all inside.

Ben gave her a glance of approval, and Lisbeth felt as if someone had handed her a star plucked from the sky.

"And now, I think we best be on our way," he said.

Dr. Godwin disappeared and returned with a saddle and bridle, both of which he put on the pony. Ben prepared a lead, then lifted Sarah Ann to his own horse and mounted behind her. Sarah Ann leaned over to look adoringly at her new acquisition.

Lisbeth herself had yearned for a pony as a child, for a pet of any kind. For anything to love. She had Henry now. And Shadow and the other horses.

And a child? Perhaps, if Sarah Ann could learn to love her . . .

And Sarah Ann's father? What did she want from him? A partnership, certainly. But as for anything more . . . she simply didn't know.

Lisbeth did know she didn't want to be like Barbara, who jumped from bed to bed, allowing herself to be used over and over again. As a widow, Lisbeth had a degree of independence and she was loath to give it up for any man.

If only she weren't so intrigued by Ben Masters. If only she could stop thinking about their midnight encounter. If only her hand didn't still burn from his touch.

❖❖❖

Barbara watched the drive through the window. What could be taking the American and Lisbeth so long? Surely he wasn't attracted to Lisbeth. The possibility kept nibbling at her mind.

She felt Hugh's presence behind her, his anger, and she turned to face him. He didn't understand that what she was doing was for both of them.

"Still watching for that ruffian," he said bitterly.

"I simply don't want Lisbeth to poison him against us."

"Is that why you're going to Edinburgh with him?"

She put a hand on his fine linen shirt. "It's important to both of us that we know what he plans to do."

"Bloody savage," Hugh said. "Why couldn't Ian and his get have stayed lost?"

"Well, they didn't," Barbara said. "But if we can prove he's a charlatan, that she might not be Ian's child—"

"I checked his room," Hugh said. "I couldn't find anything about him." He was quiet a moment, then added softly, "I did find a gun."

"A gun?"

"It looks used," Hugh said. "*Well* used."

Barbara looked at him. "I sensed something . . . dangerous about him."

"He's no mere solicitor," Hugh said. "I would stake my life on it."

"You stake too much on too little," she retorted. "That's why you've lost so much."

"But not everything," he said suggestively, putting his hand to her breast.

She moaned slightly, instantly aroused. He always did that to her. She had loved him ever since he'd come to Calholm two years ago. He had stirred her blood as no man had before, not even Hamish, and their love had seemed so right, so fitting. But he had nothing if he didn't inherit Calholm, and she knew both of them couldn't live off her allowance—nor did she think his pride would allow it. Hugh knew sheep-raising and husbandry, but his reputation as a gambler and rake had made it difficult for him to find a position. His prospects had brightened only with Jamie Hamilton's death. No one had ever believed Ian could be located after ten years of silence.

Now he was back to where he'd been two years ago—with sizable debts and not a pound to his name, even though he'd managed Calholm's acres for the past two years, and had done well at it. He had taken pride in enlarging the flock of sheep and improving its quality. He could have done even more if Lisbeth and Alistair had not been so obstructive.

And now an American and a small child would take it away.

Barbara cursed the fates as Hugh held her. She would still try to help him inherit. And if that meant using her charms to seduce the American, then she would do it.

There was a clatter beneath the window, and Barbara moved away from Hugh's embrace toward the panes of glass. Looking down, she saw Lisbeth and the American, Sarah Ann seated with him on his horse, ride in toward the stables, a pony in tow. Bloody hell. She'd thought to woo the child with clothes; Lisbeth, who thought of nothing but horses, had apparently judged their small guest better than she.

But there was tomorrow, and there was Edinburgh, and she'd always been able to charm babes as well as men. The American and the girl would forget Lisbeth existed. She would make sure of it.

Barbara watched as Lisbeth waited for Masters to dismount and help her down. Lisbeth was smarter than she used to be, Barbara thought with no little malice.

With growing apprehension, she noted that the American held Lisbeth's hand a fraction of a second longer than necessary. Then, he lifted down the child, who immediately ran to the pony. Lisbeth said a few words to the American, then turned toward the manor.

Masters stayed at the barn with the child, stooping down next to her as Sarah Ann stroked the pony's neck.

Barbara gave Hugh a quick kiss before whirling toward the mirror to check her hair. She would stop by the kitchen for sugar, then go to welcome the pony.

Chapter Eight

Ben hadn't seen Sarah Ann so happy in a long while. Joy exuded from her as she proudly rode the pony for the first time. More days like this and she wouldn't need that scarf wrapped around her neck.

She finished her first riding lesson, and Ben was showing her how to brush the pony, when Barbara Hamilton appeared in a violet dress and matching coat that nearly took his breath away.

Barbara was perfect, too perfect for his taste, and he recognized the time spent in polishing that surface. Every hair was in place; the face paint was subtle but artfully designed to emphasize the violet eyes and ivory complexion. Her voice was moderated, as if she practiced every morning; she'd rid herself almost entirely of the Scottish burr that he enjoyed hearing so much in Lisbeth's speech.

Why did Barbara remind him so much of his fiancée, the woman who had urged him into battle, then deserted him the moment she thought he was crippled?

Barbara came bearing gifts—an apple and a rock of sugar for the new pony.

"That's a lovely pony," she told Sarah Ann.

"His name is Pep'mint," Sarah Ann proclaimed proudly, "and he's the most splen'id pony anyplace."

"I can see that," Barbara said. "I saw you riding him. You rode very well."

Sarah Ann eyed Lady Barbara carefully, and Ben knew she hadn't quite made up her mind about her. She had decided she liked Lisbeth, mainly, Ben suspected, because she'd helped find Peppermint.

"You can give that apple to him," Sarah Ann said, eyeing the treats enviously.

"I think it would be better if you did," Barbara said.

Had she said that out of generosity or reluctance to get her silk gloves dirty? Ben decided he didn't care when another smile spread over his daughter's face. She took the apple and held it out to Peppermint, who daintily took a bite, then another.

"Thank you," she said to Barbara in her most polite grown-up manner.

After consuming the apple, the pony nuzzled her again, evidently sensing the rock of sugar.

"Greedy little animal," Ben said affectionately, and Sarah Ann nodded sagely.

"All horses are greedy," Barbara said with just a shade of distaste in her voice. Obviously, she didn't share Lisbeth's love of anything with four legs and a tail.

Sarah Ann picked up on it, too. She turned all her attention back to the pony, the sugar held out in the flat of her hand. She giggled as the pony's teeth tickled her fingers in its eagerness.

"I want to ride him again," Sarah Ann said.

"I think that's enough for the day," Ben said. "You need some rest, and so does Peppermint. Remember, this is a new home for him."

"I think I should stay with him so he won't get lonesome."

"He'll have new horse friends," Ben said. "Don't you think they need to get acquainted? And you can see him first thing in the morning."

"Tonight," Sarah Ann bargained.

Barbara laughed. It was a pleasant sound, and he glanced up at her. Genuine amusement danced in her violet eyes.

"You might as well give up," she said. "I sense feminine stubbornness in that face."

"All right," he said, surrendering. "After supper for just a few moments. If you take a nap."

"I will," Sarah Ann promised solemnly. She hugged the pony. "You be a good pony," she admonished him. Peppermint nudged her shoulder playfully. "I think he likes me."

"I think so, too," Barbara said, taking the words from Ben's mouth. He wondered whether he'd misjudged her. He'd automatically assumed that because she was beautiful, she was also shallow, and even treacherous.

"Thank you for that," he said as he began to unsaddle the pony. He led the animal into a stall already assigned to him by the silent trainer who was nowhere to be seen. Ben made sure the pony had feed and water, then started back to the manor with Sarah Ann and Barbara, who had waited.

She glided rather than walked. Partway to the house, she put a hand on his arm, stopping him. "Do you miss your home?" she asked.

"Not particularly." He didn't mention that he hadn't really had a home in more than seven years. A bedroll, sometimes a bunk in a sheriff's office or a temporary bed in a hotel—those had been the extent of his home.

"No family?"

"Only Sarah Ann," he said. She was good, very good at coaxing out answers.

"Then . . . there's no one waiting for you?"

He shook his head, amused at the line of questioning.

She hesitated, then continued. "Mr. Alistair said Sarah Ann's mother died?"

"That's right." His tone was curt now. He didn't want to talk about Mary May, particularly with Sarah Ann just a few feet ahead.

"How did she die?" Barbara had lowered her voice but she wasn't giving up.

He gave her a look that had quelled outlaws, then started walking again, catching up with Sarah Ann and taking her hand in his.

Lady Barbara Hamilton hurried her steps to match his and was silent the remainder of the way to the manor. As they reached the steps, she stopped him again, a slight frown furrowing the lovely brow. "I didn't mean to pry."

"Yes you did," he said easily.

She looked startled. He wondered if any man had challenged her before.

She smiled suddenly. "So I did, and I apologize. Do you still want to go to Edinburgh with me?"

The apology was nicely said. He nodded.

"Day after tomorrow?"

He nodded again.

"I'll make the arrangements," she said. "Though I don't know if Sarah Ann will leave that pony."

Ben hadn't thought of that. He was still getting used to the needs and wants of a tiny person.

"We can leave her here," Barbara said. "She'll be well cared for."

Ben studied the beautiful woman before him, considering her motives. Why would she suggest leaving Sarah Ann behind? Thoughtfulness? Or something else? Sarah Ann was the heiress, not him, and any intended harm would be directed toward her.

"No," he said firmly. "Sarah Ann goes with us."

Barbara shrugged, though he saw disappointment in her eyes.

They separated inside the manor entrance.

"I'll see you at dinner," she said.

"My thanks for the apple and sugar," he replied, trying to ease the sting of his earlier brusqueness.

She hesitated, looking very, very pretty, and winked at Sarah Ann. "Have a good nap, Sarah Ann," she said, then hurried down the hall.

❖❖❖

Lady Barbara Hamilton could be as charming as Lady Lisbeth could be challenging. Ben thought about the striking differences in the two women as he watched Sarah Ann play with a disgruntled Annabelle. After tucking her and the cat into bed, he stayed a few minutes, listening to her chatter about the pony until the long dark lashes closed over her eyes.

Ben retreated into his own room to wash, and to think. He located one of his few remaining cigars and poured a small glass of the whisky. His bad leg ached, and he sat down, stretching it out into a more comfortable position.

He sipped the whisky, remembering how he and Mary May used to linger over a drink in the saloon where she had worked. He missed her, missed her warm humor and complete lack of subtlety. And he regretted holding himself back from loving her. He'd kept his feelings turned off for so long, he hadn't known how to deal with them when they started to emerge, simmering in some hidden part of him like lava about to erupt.

Ben had made plenty of mistakes. He'd spent his young life trying to please his father. His efforts, though, had not won the love he'd craved from the one person in his life he'd admired. So he'd looked for love elsewhere and thought he'd found it in a beautiful young woman. That had been another mistake—another regret.

War had drained him of boyhood illusions and had made him incapable of practicing law. He'd returned home to discover that he could no longer spend hours and days in a small office, representing clients who engaged in profiteering during the war. So he'd become a U.S. marshal, the opposite of what he'd been before the war. He'd taken a savage satisfaction in that, and in his solitude. He hadn't needed anyone, didn't want to need anyone ever again.

He'd clung to that belief even when he'd met Mary May. He'd clung to it when he'd promised her he'd take care of Sarah Ann. He'd clung to it the first few weeks he had the child. But then something happened. Sarah Ann's needs had become his. She'd squirmed into his heart and made him feel again. And he found he liked to have feelings. It scared the hell out of him, but he was ready to admit that he needed her as much as she needed him.

Ben rose and stalked around the room, then stopped abruptly when he realized something was not as it should be. His gaze searching the room, he recalled how the room had looked that morning.

It had been cleaned before he and Sarah left to see the pony; no one should have been inside since then. Yet he sensed intrusion. He checked the drawers of the bureau. His shirts were as he remembered. He opened the highest drawer, the one where he'd put his gun, a drawer too high for Sarah Ann to reach.

The gun was still there, but the barrel was staring straight at him. He'd left the barrel pointed toward the back of the drawer.

Someone had gone through his room.

Ben checked the valise he'd stowed in a corner, carefully studying the linings. They were intact. The papers were safe: Mary May and Ian Hamilton's marriage certificate, and copies of Sarah Ann's birth certificate and adoption papers.

Were they what someone had been looking for?

He went into Sarah Ann's room. She was still asleep. The room looked normal, just as they had left it earlier; but then Effie had put away her things, not him, and he had no way of telling whether they too had been searched.

Ben hated the feeling of being spied upon. He hated the invasion of his privacy. He cursed under his breath. Dammit, he would find out who had searched his rooms, and why.

❖❖❖

Dinner was as awkward as it had been the night before.

Lisbeth tried to lighten it, more for Sarah Ann's sake than her own. But Ben Masters wasn't helping. He was silent, his gaze studying the others at the table slowly and carefully, his eyes devoid of the warmth she'd glimpsed earlier in the day. He seemed too preoccupied to even pay the usual attention to Sarah Ann.

Hugh was late, and he arrived smelling of a distillery. He glared at each one of them, saving his most vicious glance for Ben. Hugh, like Barbara, could be irresistibly charming, but Lisbeth saw fear choking that charm now. Fear that he was about to lose everything he'd been counting on.

Sarah Ann most certainly felt the tension. She had eagerly talked about the pony for several minutes, then had fallen silent.

"Did you enjoy riding Peppermint?" Lisbeth asked to dispel the gloom.

"Oh, yes. He's a splen'id pony. Papa said I could visit him tonight. He's very lonesome."

"He won't be lonesome long," she said. "He'll have lots of friends."

"Lady Barb'ra brought him an apple."

"That was nice of her." Obviously, Barbara had no intention of giving up on the girl immediately, Lisbeth thought.

She glanced down at Henry the Eighth, who lay beside her chair being unusually quiet. She wondered whether Annabelle had cowed him or whether he too was affected by the American's dour attitude.

As if in answer to her thought, Henry mumbled. Lisbeth had never known a dog to mumble before, but Henry was very good at it. This one sounded like a complaint.

"Maybe he's lonesome, too," Sarah Ann offered.

"More like ate too much," Hugh muttered, "and is suffering from indigestion. Damn dog's a glutton. Eats better than we do."

Lisbeth looked over at Hugh's plate. It was brimming with lamb, potatoes, and steaming gravy. "At least he doesn't come to the table stinking of drink," she retorted icily.

Hugh's face went red, then he rose from the table, disregarding the chair that fell with a clatter. "Calholm should belong to me, by all rights, and you willna be telling me wha' to do." The Scot's accent had deepened in his anger. Lisbeth saw Sarah Ann huddle closer to Ben and his arm go around her. His face went rigid, and a muscle flexed in his cheek, a look far more deadly, more dangerous than Hugh's.

Ben stood slowly, and so did Sarah Ann. "If our claim is substantiated," he said slowly, "you will mind your tongue and your temper, or you can leave."

"And if it isn't?" Hugh taunted. "I don't think you have a valid claim. You probably forged everything."

"And did I bribe someone, too?" Ben replied in a low voice. "Or do you reserve that crime for yourself?"

Hugh's face went completely white, as did Barbara's. "I'll see you laughed out of court," he said, turning from the table and striding out the door.

A dreadful few seconds of silence followed. Lisbeth held her breath, waiting for Ben to make a move, to say something. Instead Henry barked and, in the next instant, Barbara spoke.

"I'm sorry," she said softly. "He didn't mean it."

"I don't like him," Sarah Ann sniffed.

"Do you ever say things you don't mean when you're upset?" Barbara asked. "Maybe if you hadn't gotten your pony today . . . ?"

Sarah Ann looked up, her insatiable curiosity aroused. "Didn't he get a pony?"

"Well, he didn't get something else he wanted very badly."

"What?"

Sarah Ann's fear was fading now, Lisbeth noted. She was amazed both by the child's resiliency and by Barbara's almost tender attempts to justify Hugh's behavior. Or was she simply trying to pursue Ben by showing interest in Sarah Ann?

"Can we go see the pony again?" Sarah Ann asked, breaking the awkward stillness.

"What about your dinner?" Ben asked, frowning.

Sarah Ann pushed her plate away. "I'm not hungry."

Lisbeth wished she'd held her tongue when Hugh had insulted Henry. Her eyes met Barbara's. Regret flickered in her sister-in-law's gaze, too.

"I'll have some food sent up later," Lisbeth said to Ben. "A meat pie, perhaps. How would you like that, Sarah Ann?"

"That would be nice," Sarah Ann said politely, but without enthusiasm.

Lisbeth's eyes met Ben's gaze. "I apologize for that scene," she said.

"I've always heard about English manners," he said, one corner of his lips curling.

"We're not English," she replied. "And we Scots are well known for our argumentative ways."

Barbara winced. "Especially the Highland Scots. I prefer peace."

Lisbeth arched an eyebrow. "Then why do you keep Hugh around?"

"He has as much right to be here as—" Barbara stopped suddenly.

"As who?" Lisbeth said, unable to help herself. It *was* true, what they said about the Highlanders. She'd never been able to back away from a challenge, not since she'd been old enough to defend herself.

Ben was watching both of them, watching and weighing. He seemed more guarded than ever.

"Papa?" Sarah Ann's question was more a wail.

Ben pushed back his chair. "If you ladies will forgive me, I believe Sarah Ann and I have an engagement with a pony."

Lisbeth nodded. "I'll go with you and see that everything is taken care of."

"That's not necessary," he said. "But I thank you for your concern." His tone was sharp, almost angry.

"All right," she said. "I'll have a meat pie and some sweets sent up in an hour." She hesitated a moment, then continued. "You might like to visit the library later. You mentioned wanting some children's books."

"That's very kind."

Did she actually hear a note of sarcasm in his words or had she only imagined it? She watched as the big man and small child left the room, hand in hand.

❖❖❖

Which one had searched his room?

Hugh was Ben's prime suspect, but they'd all had an opportunity, including Lisbeth.

She was quite frank about wanting something from him. Her passion for the horses was obviously very strong; he'd discovered long ago that people could justify almost anything for a cause they believed in. While passion had never frightened him, it made him wary.

He needed to talk to the solicitor. He needed to know who, other than Hugh, stood to lose by Sarah Ann's claim to the inheritance, and exactly what would happen if her claim wasn't upheld.

At the stables, he and Sarah Ann found the door open and Callum Trapp scolding one of the stable lads. Trapp turned as they approached, touching his cap in a sign of respect Ben hadn't expected. His tone civil, he said, "Yer horse came, Mr. Masters, and the lassie's pony has made himself at home."

Peppermint had indeed done so and was happily munching on fresh oats. He acknowledged his visitors with a swish of the tail.

"He seems a fine pony," Callum said with as close to a smile as Ben thought possible on the weathered, stern face.

"Oh, he is," Sarah Ann agreed, immediately warming to the praise of her prized possession.

"I hear you 'ave a fine cat, too, lassie," he said.

"I'll bring Annabelle to meet you," she promised.

Callum hesitated. "Perhaps you best not, lassie. There are some barn cats here who may not bless an intruder."

"She chased Henry," Sarah Ann said defensively.

"Ah, that one's a big coward," he said affectionately. "I keep telling Lady Lisbeth that, but she doesna care."

"We will take your advice," Ben said. He wanted no catastrophes.

Sarah Ann didn't agree. "But—"

"We'll discuss it later, Sarah Ann," he said, ending further protests. He wondered if the buts and whys would ever end. He doubted it. "I think you should say hello to your Peppermint," he said, "while I look in at my new horse." He looked toward Callum for direction.

"The last stall. He's fit enough," Callum said.

It wasn't exactly approval, but then Ben didn't care if the trainer gave it or not. Bailey didn't compare in bloodlines to the Calholm stable, but he looked fast and reliable—and he was his.

"I'll take him out in the morning."

"I'll be working with Shadow tomorrow," the trainer said, "and the grooms will be running other horses. Can you be saddling yer own horses?"

"I would prefer it," Ben answered.

"Good. If you don't be needing anything else, then . . . ?"

"I don't need anything at all," Ben said sharply. "Just stalls for the pony and my horse. I'll take care of the grooming and feeding."

Callum's eyes were cool. But then why shouldn't they be? Ben was the outsider, come to take something that never should have been his. He really couldn't even blame Hugh for his resentment, either. He probably would have fought too for something he truly believed should be his.

Ben ran his hands down Bailey's neck and murmured some words to him, allowing the horse to recognize and know him. The animal nickered with appreciation, and Ben left the stall, heading toward Peppermint and Sarah Ann.

Sarah Ann was feeding oats to the pony from her hand. Her absolute fearlessness with animals sometimes worried him, though he admired it. He watched for several minutes before he heard a scream outside the stable. He turned toward the door just as Maisie, Barbara's maid, came running in.

"The cat . . . the dog . . . the cat . . . your lordship . . . please!" she stammered, bouncing from leg to leg in anxiety.

"Annabelle," screamed Sarah Ann. She dropped the oats and scampered out of the stall, starting toward the manor house.

Ben scooped her up, then continued toward the manor. As he reached it, the door opened, and a stunned Barbara stood in the doorway. He stepped past her at the same time two animals streaked by him, followed by Lisbeth.

A table crashed and a porcelain bowl smashed to the floor, and they were apparently not the first casualties. An umbrella stand had tipped, and umbrellas lay scattered over the entrance floor. Suddenly the animals reversed course, the cat now chasing the dog as they pounded into the dining room. Another loud crash soon followed. Servants joined in the chase like swarming gnats, and Hugh appeared on the landing above, looking dazed.

Lisbeth shouted at Henry, but he was obviously having too good a time to pay attention. He chased Annabelle for several seconds, then Annabelle turned and chased him. It was next to impossible to tell who was chasing whom at any given moment.

Ben put Sarah Ann down, and, at the next pass of the two outlaw animals, he leaned over. He'd had a lot of practice in catching Annabelle, but, at the last second, she swerved, and he missed her. Instead, he caught Lisbeth. They smashed together; only his hands kept her from falling. Her head was inches away, and her hair had fallen from the tidy French twist she wore at dinner. She felt . . . soft. Even her stays couldn't disguise her softness.

"I'm sorry," she said breathlessly, and for a moment Ben was thoroughly distracted by those vibrant gold-flecked eyes, by the feel of her.

But then the animals came dashing through again, brushing by his legs. He heard another crash and wondered if there would be anything left of the manor by the time they were through. Slowly, he released Lisbeth. She too looked dazed.

All at once, Henry barked and the animals came streaming back into the hallway. Ben seized the moment—and the renegade cat. But Henry kept coming and hurtled into him. His bad leg collapsed under the impact and, the next instant, all three of them fell to the hallway floor. He was only partially aware of the wails and oaths surrounding him, mingled with Lisbeth's delighted laughter.

Ben maintained his hold on Annabelle as Henry set two feet on his chest and started licking the damned cat. Annabelle meowed coyly. Lisbeth's laughter grew louder; so did Sarah Ann's scolding of the cat. The servants huddled around, not quite ready to tackle Henry.

Ben tried to sit and soon gave up. A chuckle started deep inside him as he pictured himself sprawled in the middle of the grand manor's entrance, clutching a cat while a hundred-pound mongrel held him prisoner—with a bevy of servants looking on. Annabelle had most definitely taken a toll on his dignity.

Lisbeth knelt and plucked Annabelle from his chest, and Henry followed the cat adoringly. Sarah Ann, looking worried, approached. "Annabelle is a bad kitty," she said.

A gross understatement. Ben wanted to get up, but he couldn't. The chuckle moved up from his chest to his throat, and he couldn't keep it in. He started laughing. He laughed as he had never laughed before and the servants looked at him as if he were mad. But Sarah Ann giggled, and then threw herself on top of him, giving him a big hug. "I love you," she said.

Those words wrapped around his heart. Sarah Ann might seek comfort from him and hug him, but she was stingy with her words, as if to give voice to her deepest feelings made her too vulnerable. Ben held her close, not caring that his dignity, such as it was, lay in tatters along with other objects in the house.

"I think it's time," he finally said, "that your renegade cat goes to bed . . . and you, too."

"What's 'ren'gade'?"

"Someone who doesn't do what they're told."

"Is Henry a ren'gade?"

"Yes."

"I think I like ren'gades. Can I be a ren'gade?"

"Not if you want to be splendid," he teased.

She considered that. "I think I would rather be splen'id."

"I think that's a splendid idea," he replied with a big smile.

He ignored the host of grinning servants as he awkwardly rose, bowed with what dignity he had left to Lady Barbara, and took Annabelle from Lisbeth. He gave Lisbeth a rueful grin, then made for the bedchambers upstairs with his two little ren'gades.

Chapter Nine

After picking several children's books from the shelves, Lisbeth prowled the library in search of distraction. Any kind of distraction. Henry prowled behind her, unintimidated by his brief scolding. He knew he was easily forgiven; and she needed his company.

She had never known a man to laugh at himself before. It had nothing to do with pride—or perhaps everything. Ben Masters had pride: it was evident in the way he held himself, in his air of self-confidence. That was the difference. Only a man entirely comfortable with himself could find humor in being sprawled on the floor clutching a cat and being sat upon by a dog.

The image made her smile again. In that moment, he'd seemed so heroic to her.

Henry the Eighth moaned for attention, and she leaned down to give him a hug. "You're a renegade, too," she told him, "but an endearing one." He buried his large head in the crease between her breasts.

"Ah, the rewards of roguery."

She stood up abruptly at the sound of a wry masculine voice. Ben Masters had changed to a comfortable-looking, well-worn pair of denim trousers and a cotton shirt. The sleeves of the shirt were rolled up, showing muscled arms and a spattering of golden hair. She had never seen a man in denim trousers before, though she knew of the material and had even seen some in a dressmaker's shop. She couldn't help but notice the way it hugged his hard, lean body.

His eyes caught her gaze, and she blushed.

"I'll have to get more suitable clothes in Edinburgh," he said. "But these are comfortable."

"Wear those in Edinburgh," she said, "and every lady there will be . . ." she trailed off.

"Will what?" he asked with interest. He took several steps toward her, favoring his leg more than he had all day.

Guilt raced through her. His various misadventures at Calholm had evidently taken their toll.

She ignored his question, for she didn't want to speak the answer. "Henry and I seem disastrous for you," she said. "Is there anything I can get you for that leg? Some salve?"

He shrugged. "It's nothing. I'm used to its small rebellions. I thought, though, I might take you up on your offer of a book for Sarah Ann."

"What about a brandy?"

"That, too," he replied, "especially if you'll share one with me."

She hesitated. Ladies didn't drink with men, except wine at meals. But then he was American, and his customs were obviously different, freer. And perhaps drink would loosen his tongue; she hungered for more information about him. She hungered for other things, too, but she tried to ignore those needs. It was difficult when every nerve in her body was humming.

"All right," she said, walking stiffly over to the cabinet where they kept the brandy. She poured two glasses, giving him by far a larger portion.

She noticed he watched her carefully though he said nothing. He took the glass she offered and sat down in one of the chairs, stretching out his leg. Henry flopped contentedly next to him.

Lisbeth felt deserted. Henry usually stayed next to her and seldom hovered around a stranger for more than a moment's inspection.

"He likes you," she said.

"Probably because I make a great pillow," Ben said wryly. "He's just waiting for another chance."

She giggled. She couldn't help it. "I think Henry the Eighth's taken with Annabelle."

"God help us." He sighed. "Don't tell me he's as indiscriminate as his namesake."

Lisbeth giggled again, astounding herself. She never giggled. "Everyone is scared of him because he's so big, but all he wants is to be liked. I think he admires Annabelle because she isn't intimidated."

Ben raised a skeptical eyebrow. She imitated his shrug, and the corner of his mouth bent into what appeared an unwilling smile. Why would he be reluctant to smile at her?

He took a slow sip of the brandy. "It's good."

"Scotland is well known for the quality of its spirits."

"I thought it was known for consuming them."

She grinned. "That, too. What about Americans?"

"We hold our own."

She had noted, though, that he was cautious in his drinking. He usually took no more than a glass of wine during supper, and he was drinking very slowly now. Not like Hugh, or even Jamie, both of whom often drank to excess.

He was quiet, nursing his drink, looking around the library with an appreciation Lisbeth understood. She loved the room; it had become her private sanctuary since no one else ever used it. She hadn't even known so many wonderful books could exist in one home; the library—if it could be called that—at her childhood home had been small, its volumes concentrating on war and weapons.

"There's a great variety here," she said. "Jamie's father loved books. He bought everything he could."

"And Jamie?" he asked. "Did he also love books?"

"No," she said wistfully.

"What did he like besides horses?"

"Music, drink, tales of Scottish feats."

"Did you love him?"

It was an impertinent question, but then she had asked her share of the same. A week ago, she would have said yes, without reservation. Now, she hesitated.

She had been so grateful to Jamie. He had given her a home, and he'd always been kind. They'd shared pride over Shadow and the excitement of racing.

Besides, she'd never believed in the kind of love portrayed in books and song. Love had never existed in her home. Her mother and father had hated each other and her brothers considered their wives as slaves to be used.

Yet Ben Masters made her wonder if there wasn't something more to be had from love than what she'd had with Jamie. If Ben didn't make her blood run hot, he certainly warmed it considerably. The tight cloth of his trousers hid little, and every time her gaze dropped slightly, something deep and primitive—and new—inside her responded.

She sipped the brandy, though she was tempted to gulp it.

"You didn't answer," he reminded her.

"Why would you think I didn't love him?"

"No reason," he said. "I've heard of arranged marriages in Britain. Alliances. A system with some advantages, I suspect," he added with a shade of bitterness.

Lisbeth hesitated. Her marriage *had* been arranged. Jamie's father had been demanding that he marry, and since the Hamilton name was finer than her own, her father agreed readily enough. She had few illusions that

Jamie loved her. She had been in the right place at the right time when his father demanded marriage: she had a sufficient dowry and she was suitable, since her father was a clan chief, if not titled.

"I cared deeply for Jamie," she said simply. She didn't add that he had been the first person to show her any affection at all.

Ben's gaze left her face and went to the brandy in the glass. She watched him study its rich color for a moment, then she asked the question nagging her.

"Sarah Ann's mother? Did you love her?"

His mouth quirked upward in that enigmatic half-smile. "I cared deeply for her," he said, turning her own words back on her.

"You've never wed?"

"No."

"Why? You obviously like children."

"I didn't know that until Sarah Ann came along," he said. "And she is . . . unique."

"All children are unique."

"You and Jamie didn't have children?"

"I lost a bairn before it was born," she said, feeling tears well in her eyes.

"And Barbara?"

"She was married less than a year when her husband died."

"How did he die?"

She hesitated. It wasn't her tale to tell, and she'd never known the truth of the matter. "Her husband was shot," she said shortly.

"Another accident?"

Lisbeth shook her head. "A duel."

Ben's brow furrowed. "I thought they were illegal."

"They are," she replied, wondering whether he was avoiding her question by asking others. "Tell me about Sarah Ann's mother and Ian Hamilton."

Ben finished his brandy, then carefully set the glass down. "I don't know that much. She was married to Ian three years before he was killed during a poker game. Mary May was pregnant then. I know she had a difficult time of it, but she did a damn good job of making sure Sarah Ann was cared for." He remembered the first time he'd seen her, the way she'd boldly approached him in a saloon. "She was very courageous."

"It's almost as if the family is cursed," she said slowly.

"I don't believe in curses," he stated. "But why did Hamilton leave here?"

Lisbeth had heard whispers, though John Hamilton had forbidden anyone to use Ian's name in the house. "He'd been gone years when I met Jamie, and the family didn't talk about him. There was some scandal . . ."

"Cheating?"

She nodded reluctantly. "That's what I heard. How did you know?"

"That's what got him killed in Texas. Texans take it very seriously. A man caught cheating at the poker table doesn't simply get banished to another country."

He stood slowly, as if he were in pain. But once on his feet, he moved gracefully, even with the slight favoring of the one leg. He walked over to one of the bookshelves and read titles for a minute or two, then removed a book from the shelf. "If I may, I would like to borrow this."

Lisbeth nodded, and rose, too. She picked up the children's books she'd already gathered and handed them to him. "For Sarah Ann."

"I only have one children's book, and Sarah Ann has memorized all those tales. I'm afraid I'm not very good at storytelling."

She believed that. He had the look of a man who lived life, not of one who imagined it. And she doubted his real-life tales would be the kind fit for children.

"You're welcome," she said softly. "There's more if you need them."

He hesitated at the door for a moment, then turned to her. "You won't reconsider going to Edinburgh?"

Lisbeth was surprised. Why would he want her when he had Barbara? She was tempted, but she knew what would happen. She wouldn't be able to resist needling Barbara, nor Barbara her. And she wouldn't play second fiddle.

"I have too much to do here," she said. "We're trying to get Shadow ready for the Grand National."

His blue eyes suddenly turned piercing. There were unfathomable depths to him, and she was afraid she might drown in any attempt to reach the bottom.

"Would you like to go to the loch tomorrow?" she asked. "Sarah Ann can ride her new pony."

"She would like that."

"And would you?"

"I think any trip away from Annabelle would be pleasurable," he said lightly.

"I believe you really admire her."

"Perhaps I do," he said. "I've always liked independence."

Lisbeth swallowed hard. Was he referring to her?

"Will you stay here in Scotland if Mr. Alistair upholds Sarah Ann's claim?"

"I don't know."

"You could always designate a manager," she ventured.

"I could, couldn't I?" he said noncommittally. "But this conversation is premature. Thank you for the brandy, the books, and the conversation, Lady Calholm."

The room had suddenly turned cold. Lisbeth knew she shouldn't have made the last comment. It was far too soon, but guile was not one of her strong points.

"You're welcome, Mr. Masters," she said just as formally.

He looked disconcerted for a moment, then grinned. "Sounds sort of ridiculous, doesn't it?"

"About as ridiculous as 'Lady Calholm,' " she replied.

The ice in his eyes turned into heat. Yet she still

sensed a distance between them, one she desperately wanted to breach.

She stepped toward him, reluctant to let him go. Whether it was the brandy or the meeting of their gazes, awareness flashed and thundered between them, like a sudden Scottish storm.

His eyes burned through her, igniting waves of heat cascading along her body. Her fingers bunched into a fist as the impact of his gaze became overwhelming. A craving such as she'd never known gnawed inside her. She wanted to touch that hard face and watch it soften. She wanted to kiss that mouth and feel it move against hers. She wanted it more than anything.

He reached out and touched her hair, confined again in its French twist. Then his fingers moved to her face, tracing the line of her jaw with one finger. His hands were infinitely gentle. The gentleness contrasted with the heat those fingers left in their wake.

She fought her racing emotions. He knew she wanted something from him. She couldn't allow him to believe she was willing to trade her body for it. But she'd never felt like this before, barely in control of needs so intense they threatened to explode.

He moved toward her, and his mouth came down on hers. Hard and demanding and searching.

She wanted to respond. Needed to respond. But if she did, he would believe the worst. Her body ached with fierce wanting, but she managed to pull away. Lisbeth stood trembling, her gaze lowered, and slowly she backed away.

"Lisbeth?" When she looked up at him, she saw traces of suspicion and cynicism. She stepped back again from temptation. She couldn't afford the cost, the complete loss of her self-respect. The ache within her grew deeper, more unbearable.

"I won't trade," she said.

He was silent, and she knew he understood. She

turned her back to him, not wanting him to see the tear beginning to leak from one eye.

"I don't trade, either, Lisbeth," he finally said. "I think—"

"You wanted to see how far I would go?" she asked bitterly. "Well, now you know. Too stupidly far."

She was shaking now, and she felt cold, so cold. All the heat had drained from her body as if a pail of icy water had been thrown on her. "Please leave," she said, cringing at the break in her voice.

Silence, then a hand touched her shoulder and guided her around to face him. Fingers cupped her chin, forcing her gaze to meet his searching look. She wondered whether he ever took anyone at face value. She doubted it.

"I'm sorry," he said unexpectedly, and she suspected he seldom apologized.

"Don't be," she said, biting her lip. "I just thought . . . I suppose I didn't think."

"I'm not very experienced with emotions, but I *do* understand needs. I'm just not sure what yours are. Or at least which are the most important to you. Whether it's Calholm or—"

"Go to the devil," she said, then left the room. Her rage got her upstairs to her bedchamber before she started shaking again. She'd made a complete fool of herself.

But damn the man! She didn't understand him at all. For a few moments, he had seemed to feel the same attraction she felt for him. Or had he been testing her all the time?

Henry whined, asked for permission to join her on the bed, then climbed up slowly. Her usual amusement at his tentative approach—one leg at a time—was missing. She simply hugged him.

"Oh, Henry," she said. "What have I done?"

❖❖❖

Ben broke his own rule. He had a second drink, then a third.

Christ, he ached for her.

But he couldn't quiet his suspicions that Lisbeth wanted something from him that he wasn't willing to give. He sure as hell wouldn't trade Sarah Ann's heritage, and neither did he ever plan to give his heart away again.

But she'd looked so pretty in that library. The light from the oil lamp had glinted off her auburn hair, and her cheeks had been rosy, her lips inviting. She'd been the picture of a polished young woman at home in this elegant room full of books. She belonged here. He didn't.

Hell, he didn't even want to be here.

He thought back to what she'd said. A manager. That's what she wanted from him: a manager of her choosing. Perhaps she was even thinking that she should be the manager. He was a fool to think there was anything more to her feelings toward him. Not that he wanted more. She was pretty enough and she did stir a need inside him. But it was nothing more than lust.

Well, perhaps a need for companionship, too, he admitted reluctantly. But that was all. He refused even to consider anything more. He'd been a fool once in his life, and he had no intention of repeating that folly. Love between a man and a woman was a romantic fairy tale. In reality, there was lust, affection, companionship if one was lucky. He'd had all that with Mary May. But love?

Ben ignored the loneliness slicing through him. He had Sarah Ann, and he *did* believe in love between child and parent. It was, he thought, probably the only thing he truly believed in. Even his long-held belief in what was right and wrong had changed. An outlaw named Diablo had been responsible for that.

Hell, he wished he hadn't thought of Diablo. He didn't want to remember the looks that had passed between Diablo and the woman who had since become his wife, didn't want to think about the sacrifices each had been willing to make for the other.

Ben closed his eyes against the memory. With disgust, he placed his half-filled glass on a table, quenched the oil lamps and left the room. He'd had little sleep last night. Perhaps tonight . . . but he doubted it.

❖❖❖

"Where's Lady Lisbeth?"

Sarah Ann looked around anxiously as their luggage was loaded onto a handsome coach.

Ben wondered, too. He had seen only fleeting glimpses of Lisbeth since their meeting in the library two nights before. She hadn't joined them for dinner last night, nor had there been any further mention of a visit to the loch.

Ben didn't really blame her. He had been insufferably rude, and his only excuse was one that made him cringe. He had been protecting himself, striking out because she had hurt his pride, because, for a time, he thought she might be trying to use him. He had no intentions of ever being used again—by anyone.

God knows, he'd used people for his own purposes before. So he should be the last one to take offense.

Those days were over though. At least, he hoped they were.

Ben had wanted to apologize to Lisbeth yesterday, but he'd never found her. When he'd asked Callum Trapp where she was, the dour Scotsman had merely scowled at him. "Tending 'er business," he'd said, implying that Ben should tend his own.

"Papa." Sarah Ann tugged at his hand. "Where's Lisbeth? I want to say goodbye and ask her to take care of Pep'mint."

"She'll take very good care of Peppermint," he said. "You can be sure of that."

"I wish Pep'mint could go with us."

"I know, Sugarplum, but you'll be very busy and he would get lonesome in a strange place."

Barbara came down the steps, smiling. She was wear-

ing a violet traveling dress and a small hat that perched
fetchingly on one side of her head. Her dark hair glowed,
and her eyes danced with the prospect of going to Edinburgh.

She gave him her gloved hand so he could assist her
into the coach. Her hand was soft, not hardened by riding
calluses like Lisbeth's. Barbara gave him a grateful smile as
she settled down on the seat. Ben lifted Sarah Ann into
the coach, then placed Annabelle's basket next to her.
Sarah Ann refused to go anywhere without the cat. Ben
squeezed in between the basket and the door.

"You will like Edinburgh," Barbara said. "And I hope
you might reconsider using the town house."

He shook his head. "I think we should stay at a hotel."

"You need someone to take care of Sarah Ann while
you attend to your business. We have very reliable servants."

He considered that. He couldn't take care of Sarah
Ann every moment, nor did he wish to take her to see the
solicitor. Too much needed to be discussed, and she was
too smart not to comprehend at least some of it.

A loud meow rose from the basket and Sarah Ann
took Annabelle out and set her in her lap. The cat got up
and stretched before sitting down in regal silence. Her
eyes seemed to drill into Barbara.

Barbara ignored the cat and waited for Ben's response.

He really didn't want to be beholden to any of the
Hamilton family, but Barbara was right. He couldn't keep
dragging Sarah Ann to every place he went.

"Where is Hugh staying?" He knew that the man also
planned to visit his own solicitor in Edinburgh. He had
declined to travel in the carriage, though, saying he would
rather ride.

"With friends," she replied.

"Then perhaps I'll reconsider your offer of the town
house." He would reserve judgment until they arrived and

he could determine for himself how trustworthy the maid and butler were.

For the next several hours, he listened while Barbara chattered about people in Edinburgh and balls and parties, and how much he would enjoy them. Occasionally when the coach hit a rut, her hand went to his knee, and she blushed prettily. She did it all so naturally that he felt guilty for being skeptical about her motives.

She was trying to win over Sarah Ann, too, making a valiant effort to charm her. He listened to their exchange in fascination.

"You must like peppermint to name your pony after it."

Sarah Ann nodded. "Annabelle likes it, too."

"Of course she does," Barbara said as she eyed the sleeping cat with less vigilance than she had earlier. "Everyone likes peppermint."

"Even you?" Sarah Ann asked the question with such surprise that Barbara smiled. Ben conceded it was an honest-to-God smile.

"Even me." She leaned over and added confidentially, "I especially loved it when I was a little girl like you."

"I'm a *lady*," Sarah Ann said, astounding Ben. She'd always rejected the description before. Had she said it now to be obstinate? But her lips weren't pressed together tightly as they usually were when she was preparing for some kind of battle. Could Sarah Ann be testing Lady Barbara in some way? He shook that thought away. She wasn't that devious. Yet.

"Indeed you are a lady," Barbara said, darting a quick glance at him for an explanation.

He shrugged.

Barbara bit her lip, then struggled on. "Well, ladies like peppermint, too, and we'll buy loads of it for you and Annabelle in Edinburgh. And we'll take a carriage ride in the park. Would you like that?"

"Can Papa come, too?"

"Of course."

"All right," Sarah Ann agreed. "If Annabelle can come."

Barbara winced. Ben noted that Sarah Anne's eyes gleamed with mischief. No, he thought. She really *can't* be that devious.

"I wish Lady Lisbeth could come, too," Sarah Ann added after a moment of silence.

Barbara sighed, not with pleasure or agreement, Ben thought. He too wished Lisbeth was with them, but he was damned if he was going to show it.

In truth, he'd missed Lisbeth's challenging presence these past two days. He kept telling himself that she, like Barbara, merely wanted to win his favor. Only Lisbeth was not as practiced at seduction as her sister-in-law.

When he had agreed to travel with Lady Barbara Hamilton, he already knew he could have her in his bed on the trip. The invitation was bright in her eyes. And the thought did appeal to him. She was physically the most beautiful woman he'd ever met, and his masculinity responded to those artful touches and that soft smile.

But Ben had absolutely no intention of taking what she was offering with every look she gave him. Aside from his obligation to Sarah Ann, he didn't like being used by Lady Barbara any more than by Lisbeth. He had no intention of being trapped by Barbara's body or by Lisbeth's dreams.

So he merely gave Barbara a brief blank look, then closed his eyes and listened to the awkward conversation between a woman who obviously knew little about children and a child who was learning much too quickly about playing adult games.

❖❖❖

Ben liked the Scottish solicitor, John Alistair. He was seventy or older, thin and dour and straight as an arrow in his bearing. The kind of man who worshiped integrity.

Ben felt himself being judged as he took out the legal

documents he'd accumulated: Mary May's marriage certificate to Ian Hamilton, Sarah Ann's birth certificate, and her adoption papers.

After several moments of probing Ben with pale blue eyes under great shaggy eyebrows, the solicitor turned his attention to Ben's documents and studied them closely. He took papers from a pile on the desk, and matched them with the others, then looked back up at Ben.

"I took the precaution of asking our solicitor in America to check the official records in Colorado and Texas. Everything seems to be in order. I'll file the papers for official recognition of Sarah Ann Hamilton Masters as heiress to Calholm. Actually, she'll be heiress presumptive, and her son will inherit the title."

Alistair paused a moment, then continued. "We also have to petition Parliament to make you her official guardian. These adoption papers should ensure that. But I would like more information."

Ben had expected an inquisition. As an attorney, he would have demanded it. "What do you want to know?"

"I understand you're a solicitor yourself?" Alistair's voice ended on a questioning note.

"I studied law at Harvard and practiced in Chicago," Ben said.

"But not for the past few years. My American colleague said you've been a . . . marshal. A law officer."

He nodded.

"My American colleague said you wished to keep your . . . occupation private, and I see no obligation to divulge that information. As solicitor and trustee for the estate, my duty is to the heir, who now appears to be Sarah Ann Hamilton." The solicitor's gaze bored into him. "I am curious, though, as to why you wish to withhold information about the last few years."

Ben answered without hesitation. "Silas Martin told me there was an attempt to bribe him not to find Ian Hamilton. I know there's money involved—a lot of it— and I wasn't sure whether bribery would be the only, shall we say, *action* taken. I believe I can protect Sarah Ann more effectively if some of my other skills are unknown."

John Alistair continued to study him. "I was informed of Hugh's bribery attempt. I warned him I would press charges if it, or anything else untoward, occurred again. But surely you don't expect any violence." His tone became frosty as he added, "This isn't the wild west."

Ben permitted himself a slight smile. "You mean there's no murder or greed in Scotland?"

"I wish that were so, but I don't think the Hamiltons . . ." He shook his head. "They are a very respected family. The old Marquess, John Hamilton—"

"But there was an accident in Glasgow and—"

"What kind of an accident?" Alistair said, clearly alarmed.

"A stack of shipping boxes fell as Sarah Ann and I passed them. It could have been an accident. Then again . . ."

"I think you're wrong, Mr. Masters."

"And then there's Jamie Hamilton's accident . . ."

The frost in the solicitor's eyes became pure ice. "It *was* an accident."

"Perhaps," Ben said. "But I've learned that money— or lack of it—does strange things to people. And I aim to protect Sarah Ann."

The solicitor sat back in his chair. "What about yourself, Mr. Masters? You're gaining a great deal, too."

"I'm losing more," Ben replied. "My freedom, my career, possibly my country, if I stay."

Doubt crossed Alistair's face. "Then why—"

"Because it's Sarah Ann's heritage. She has a right to it, to reject or accept it. I can't take that away from her."

Alistair seemed to come to a conclusion. "I hope you do decide to stay. Calholm needs a strong, steady hand or it might well be destroyed. I'm not sure whether Hugh Hamilton can handle it yet."

"Yet?"

"He was a gambler in his youth. And a rake. I think

he has been trying to redeem himself these past two years, but if he obtains all rights, he might well fall back into his old ways."

"Is that why you looked so long for Ian Hamilton?"

Alistair nodded. "John Hamilton was my friend as well as a client. His own father was honored with Calholm for his service on the Continent. John wanted to preserve that honor. I knew Ian was . . . weak, but we'd both hoped that America would be the making of him."

"He was killed cheating at cards," Ben said flatly.

"Silas told me," Alistair said. "He also reported that Ian's wife worked in a . . . tavern."

"A saloon," Ben corrected. "But she had a special kind of honor, and she loved her daughter."

Alistair paused before saying, "You must have loved her to take her daughter."

"Before I knew she had a fortune?" Ben asked wryly.

"I made sure of that, too," Alistair said. "Mr. Martin informed me that you had started the adoption proceedings before he contacted you. You must have been close to the mother," he persisted.

Ben knew Alistair wanted his assurance that Sarah Ann was indeed Ian Hamilton's daughter, not his own.

But he couldn't explain the relationship he'd had with Mary May. She'd never wanted anything from him. Never asked anything. Not until she was dying and had no choice, and even then her request wasn't for herself.

"I met her this year," he said curtly. "If you check further back, I'm sure you will find we were in different parts of the country when Sarah Ann was conceived."

"Forgive me," the solicitor said, "but I must cover everything. Hugh Hamilton has already informed me he will contest our petition."

"Hugh Hamilton can go to hell."

John Alistair crooked a shaggy eyebrow at him. "You're willing to fight him, then?"

"Hell, yes."

"It could get uncomfortable."

Ben shrugged. "I've been uncomfortable before."

"You plan to stay, then?"

Ben hesitated. He had never gone quite that far in his mind. He had always wanted to see Sarah Ann happily settled in a family she could call her own. But after living at Calholm for several days he wondered whether that would ever be possible. It was a house divided.

"If I can find a good manager to run Calholm . . ."

"An ocean away?" Alistair questioned. "Scots don't care for absentee ownership. They've had too much of it from the English."

Ben winced. His options were being shredded by Alistair's calm arguments. And he had every right to argue. The solicitor's concern was for Calholm and the trust of his dead friend. Why should he fight for an American who planned to leave on the first ship back? John Alistair wanted a commitment that Ben wasn't sure he could give. He wasn't sure whether Calholm was the best thing for Sarah Ann.

On the other hand, he was sure it wasn't the best thing for himself.

"I can only promise you one thing," he finally said. "I'll do my best to preserve Calholm because it's Sarah Ann's. If it doesn't work out, if I don't believe Sarah Ann will be happy, we'll renounce the claim. I don't care about the money—either for Sarah Ann or myself. I can support us. I care only that she knows her legacy and has a chance to accept or deny it."

"Fair enough," Alistair said. "I'll start the proceedings immediately. I also would like to meet Sarah Ann."

"I'll bring her by this afternoon," Ben offered, "if that's convenient."

"It is."

The two men rose from their chairs, and the solicitor accompanied Ben to the door.

"One more thing," Ben said. "Would anyone other than Hugh Hamilton benefit if Sarah Ann didn't inherit?"

John Alistair looked discomfited. "The widows would," he said finally. "Unless a direct heir, such as one of the Marquess's grandchildren, inherited, the widows would receive a larger portion of the assets that are not entailed."

"Both of them?"

John Alistair nodded reluctantly. "Surely, you don't think—"

"Surely, I don't," Ben said, opening the door, but he knew the sardonic tone in his voice gave lie to his assurance.

Chapter Ten

Lady Barbara had been right about the town house. It was infinitely more comfortable than a hotel, and the housekeeper, Molly, was only too pleased to look after Sarah Ann. Ben felt comfortable with Molly, and Sarah Ann took to her immediately. She had the plump, jolly look of Mrs. Culworthy.

Still, Ben didn't want to leave Sarah Ann alone for too long, so he asked the driver of the hired coach to hurry back to the town house. Along the way he mulled over the conversation with the solicitor.

He felt trapped. He could take Sarah Ann back to America, resume the practice of law, and thus deprive Sarah Ann of her legacy. Or he could surrender any thought of returning home, along with hopes of a career and life of his own.

But then, how much would he be giving up? Until he'd met Mary May and Sarah Ann, he had been treading water, unable to make a commitment to any person or any place. Sarah Ann had put purpose back into his life, had given him a reason to care. A reason to feel. To live. It felt so good, caring about someone else, being the cause of a laugh or smile.

He went up the steps to the town house and opened the front door. The hall was quiet. Barbara had kept her promise to stay with her sister several blocks away. No one greeted him, and he felt a twinge of apprehension.

The house was much too quiet for Sarah Ann and Annabelle to be within. His footsteps sounded loud in the empty foyer as he crossed the smooth, polished floor, checking one room after another, including Sarah Ann's bedroom. No Sarah Ann. By the time Ben headed toward the kitchen, he was stiff with fear.

Then, he heard a giggle, and his pace quickened. To hell with his bad leg. He threw open the kitchen door and saw Sarah Ann perched on a tall stool. She was covered with flour from head to toe. Annabelle was on the floor beneath the stool; her calico fur was sparkling with sugar, and she was twisted in an impossible position trying her best to lick it off.

"Papa," Sarah Ann said, wriggling all over with delight, "we've made cookies for you."

He swallowed hard, wondering whether this was what being a parent meant: constant worry highlighted by moments of terror. He forced his voice to calmness. "You look like a cookie yourself with all that flour and sugar on you."

Molly looked worriedly from Sarah Ann to him. "I dinna think you would be home so soon," she said. "I hope I dinna do something wrong."

"Nothing that makes Sarah Ann smile like that is wrong. And Annabelle seems to be behaving."

"She's a dear, sweet cat, she is," Molly murmured.

He raised an eyebrow in disbelief. "I don't think that notion is shared by anyone other than Lady Sarah Ann."

Sarah Ann looked up quickly. "Is it true? Am I a *real* lady now?"

So she had understood his several laborious explanations. "Almost, Sugarplum."

"Will we stay at . . . Cal'om?"

"Would you like that?"

"If you stay and Pep'mint and Annabelle . . . and we can take Molly back with us."

Ben looked quickly at the housekeeper. Her face was red—and filled with pleasure. "Molly lives here," he said. "Don't you, Molly?"

"Yes, sir, but I wouldna mind a visit or two from the young lady." Her face grew serious. "There be a note for you from Lady Barbara on the front table."

Ben nodded and headed for the table, leaving Sarah Ann happily sprinkling more sugar onto her cookies and her cat. The note was on a silver tray with his name sprawled in large, bold handwriting: *I'll come by at two to take Sarah Ann shopping and for a ride in the park. I hope you can join us. Barbara.*

Ben's first impulse was to refuse. He hated shopping. Any effort beyond entering a mercantile and seizing a pair of trousers and shirt from a counter seemed a waste of time to him. But then he had to consider Sarah Ann. She needed more clothes, and he doubted whether she would go unless he did. And the truth was he could use some new clothes himself. If he were to stay, as he was contemplating, he needed to meet the people he would be dealing with, and he would have to fit the new role of country gentleman. That included dressing like one.

Ben looked at the note again. He had three hours before two o'clock. He would have liked a drink to help him face a shopping trip with Barbara. But it was much too easy to take that way out; he'd sworn never to do it again.

Instead, he selected a book from the library, a history of the Jacobin cause, and settled down to read.

❖❖❖

John Alistair's office was the first stop on the expedition. Barbara had reluctantly agreed to see the solicitor when Ben told her of his promise to introduce Sarah Ann.

Alistair's side whiskers wriggled as he greeted Sarah Ann, and he smiled when she curtsied as Mrs. Culworthy had taught her. But when he leaned over to shake her hand, Sarah Ann, who was fascinated by the whiskers, pulled on one.

"Sarah Ann," Ben exclaimed.

"My grandchildren do it all the time," Alistair said, his eyes roaming over the little girl. Was he looking for a likeness to Ian Hamilton and the rest of the Hamilton family? To Ben, Sarah Ann was a replica of her mother.

But John Alistair said nothing about resemblances, merely asked how she liked Scotland. She told him all about "Pep'mint," adding that "Lady Barb'ra is going to buy me pep'mint sticks."

"And what is this?" The solicitor said, his shrewd eyes resting on Sarah Ann's dirty scarf.

The smile left the girl's face. "It was Mama's. She's in heaven."

"I'm very sorry about that," he said, the burr thick on his tongue.

"I am, too. I miss her, and Cully, too."

"And who is Cully?"

"She took care of me before Papa."

"I think she did a very good job," Alistair said. There was a knock on the door, and he reluctantly rose from the chair. "She's charming," he said to Ben. "Thank you for bringing her by. I wish her grandfather had lived to see her." He shook his head slightly, then started to usher them toward the door.

"Lady Barbara," he said in parting. His tone was polite but not warm.

"Mr. Alistair," she replied stiffly.

The solicitor's gaze met hers directly, and Ben noticed Barbara's dropped first. These two had had battles, obviously, and Ben guessed they stemmed from the fact that Alistair controlled the estate and at least part of Barbara's income. If the solicitor had not persisted in the search for Ian or his heirs, her inheritance would have been greater—and her friend Hugh would have inherited the title and much of the estate.

Nevertheless, for the remainder of the afternoon, she showed no resentment toward Ben himself or Sarah Ann. Instead, she appeared happy as she suggested a tailor for him to visit while she took Sarah Ann to a dressmaker. He gave Barbara a sum of money for Sarah Ann's clothes and smiled at the excitement in his daughter's face. Apparently shopping had suddenly become fun. He wished he shared that enthusiasm.

❖❖❖

Ben made his purchases quickly and gave instructions to have everything delivered to Calholm.

"Some evening wear?" the tailor asked hopefully. Ben had already ordered a new dark gray frock coat and two pairs of trousers, after barely tolerating the measuring. "A cutaway coat, perhaps?"

"No," Ben said firmly. His purse was swiftly shrinking.

"Ben Masters, if the devil doesn't fool me."

Ben turned toward the voice in the doorway. Andrew Cameron stood there, a wide smile on his face. "Where's the little princess?" the Scot asked.

"Doing what females do best," Ben replied. "Shopping."

"You seem to be doing some yourself."

Ben winced. "So I am, but not happily."

"How is she doing?"

"She has her pony."

"Then that answers it," Andrew Cameron said. "I've never seen a child so intent on anything." His eyes suddenly narrowed. "And you? How are you enjoying our fair country?"

"Fair?" Ben retorted. "Does the sun ever shine in Scotland?"

"Occasionally. The rain and mist make us appreciate the sun more." Cameron lifted a quizzical brow. "How long will you be in Edinburgh?"

"Just until tomorrow," Ben replied.

Cameron's eyes went to the tailor, who nodded none too cordially toward him. "You will be pleased to know, Fitts, that I won at cards last night and can pay my bill."

Fitt's stern face eased only a little. "All of it, Lord Kinloch?"

"All of it," Cameron said without rancor. He turned to Ben. "Do these new clothes mean you plan to stay in Scotland?"

"They mean I need something to wear," Ben said shortly. He wearied of the same questions being asked over and over again, especially since he was also posing the same question to himself.

Cameron nodded. "Well, you picked the best tailor in Edinburgh."

Ben told himself the man was simply being friendly, but something about Cameron's appearance here, at this particular shop, rang alarms in his head.

He shrugged. "Lady Barbara's suggestion."

Cameron's eyes suddenly lit with interest. "Ah, one of the widows. And the other? Lady Lisbeth? I hear she's to have a horse in the Grand National in a few months."

"She's at Calholm," Ben said.

"And how are you and the widows faring?" Mischief fairly danced in Cameron's eyes. "I assume well, since you're squiring the fair Lady Barbara."

Ben scowled, but his displeasure seemed to have no effect on Cameron. "They've both been . . . cordial."

"I imagine," he said, almost too quietly to hear. "And which do you favor?"

There was a slight gasp from the doorway, then a rush of movement. "Mr. Cam!" Sarah Ann exclaimed, hurling herself at the Scot.

Cameron stooped, reached a hand behind Sarah

Ann's left ear and plucked out a coin. "Still not washing back there, heh?" he teased.

Sarah Ann giggled and took the proffered coin, then said excitedly to both Ben and Andrew Cameron, "Lady Barb'ra ordered me a riding dress. A green one."

Ben glanced at Barbara, who stood in the doorway. A riding dress to wear on her new pony. Very smart.

"We ordered two other dresses, too," Barbara said, her eyes on Cameron. "They'll be sent to Calholm when they're ready."

Cameron bowed. "I don't know if you remember me. We met—"

"Andrew Cameron, Lord Kinloch," she replied. "Of a certainty I remember you. Lisbeth introduced us several years ago at a steeplechase in Edinburgh."

He nodded. "You have a good memory."

Barbara glowed.

Ben looked from one to the other. *Lisbeth introduced us several years ago.* Cameron had said nothing about that on board the ship. How had Lisbeth come to know Andrew Cameron? Curiosity—and something that felt a lot like jealousy—started nagging at Ben.

"Would you and the ladies join me for an ice?" Cameron asked.

"Oh, can we?" Sarah Ann's eyes lit up like stars on a clear Texas night. He had yet to see a clear Scottish night. Ben looked at Barbara. "Lady Barbara?"

"That would be pleasant." She bestowed on Cameron a smile that belied her conservative answer. "We have a few moments before the carriage driver is to pick us up at the dressmaker's."

"I'll make my peace with Fitts," Cameron said, "and we can go to the tea shop around the corner."

Sarah Ann could hardly contain her excitement. She skipped ahead when they finally left the tailor. Ben was grateful to Cameron for his interest in her, but he remained cautious of the man himself. So at the tea shop he watched silently as Cameron and Barbara charmed each other, and Sarah Ann delighted in an ice and tart. Lady Barbara kept looking at him as if to gauge his reaction to her flirtation. Did she think—hope—he'd be jealous?

He again felt as if he were watching a play on stage, with everyone acting for his benefit. His biggest disadvantage was that he didn't know enough of the story for any of it to make sense.

Ben was jarred from his thoughts by a question Barbara asked Cameron. "You will come, won't you?" she asked.

"I would be delighted," Cameron answered.

Ben realized he must have looked startled because Barbara turned an innocent look on him. "I thought we would have a ceilidh so you can meet the other landholders in the area. Since Mr. Cameron is a friend of yours and Lisbeth's . . ." Her brows suddenly knitted together. "That is . . . all right, isn't it?"

"A ceilidh?" Ben had never heard the word.

"A party. Not quite as formal as a ball, or as grand, but a gathering with music and dancing."

"By tradition," Cameron broke in, "it's open to anyone who wants to come."

Ben was neatly trapped, and he knew it. He didn't have legal control over Calholm until Parliament upheld his petition on behalf of Sarah Ann. Barbara and Lisbeth had every right to hold a party. They also had a right to invite whomever they wished.

"I'm not much for parties," he said.

"Oh, I *love* parties," chimed in Sarah Ann, who had, as far as he knew, never attended one. "You can meet Pep'mint," she told Cameron.

"I will wait breathlessly for that moment," Cameron teased, rising from his chair. "Now, I'm afraid I have to leave this delightful company. I promised to meet some friends . . ."

Ben stood. "We have to get back, too. Sarah Ann's had a long day."

"My carriage should be at the dressmaker's," Barbara said.

Ben shook his head. "It's a short walk. We'll enjoy it." In truth, he felt suffocated. He had been alone too long; polite conversation no longer came easily.

Cameron bent down and tickled Sarah Ann under the chin. "I'll see you soon." Straightening back up, he turned to Barbara. "It's been a pleasure."

Ben nodded his own acknowledgment, and Cameron paid the bill and left the tea shop. Ben watched him disappear out the door, then he and Sarah Ann walked Barbara to her carriage.

"When do you wish to leave for Calholm tomorrow?" she asked.

"As early as possible," he replied, not particularly wanting to think about the reason he wanted to return so quickly.

Barbara winced at his answer but soon recovered. "Eight?"

He nodded, then turned to Sarah Ann. "What did you get besides the dresses?"

"A riding hat," she announced proudly. "It's the most beautiful hat in the world."

"I'll bet it is," he said, "especially on you." He turned to Barbara. "My thanks. I'm not very adept at choosing feminine apparel."

She gave him a saucy look of disbelief, as if she thought he was probably very experienced, indeed, but then the look softened. "I enjoyed it," she said, sounding surprised at herself.

Ben nodded. He understood. He had been surprised at how easily he had taken to Sarah Ann and fatherhood. It hadn't always gone smoothly, but it had proved rewarding. There was something about a small, trusting hand and an open smile that made him feel more heroic than anything else in his life.

After helping Barbara into the waiting carriage, he watched the carriage disappear down the cobblestone

street. The street was full of people. By instinct, he studied them before starting toward the town house a quarter
of a mile away. Nothing looked unusual, and, taking
Sarah Ann's hand, he began to walk, shrugging off a slight
unease, dismissing it as nothing more than his natural
caution.

They walked down two streets, stopping occasionally
to look through fairy-tale-like windows. Sarah Ann was
entranced by the toys and confections in some, and the
fashion dolls in others. They had started to cross a third
street when Ben felt a tingling sensation in his spine.

A horse neighed wildly, and Ben heard the pounding
of hoofs behind him along with several alarmed cries.
Without a pause for thought, he grabbed Sarah Ann and
hurtled them both against the brick wall of a shop, shield-
ing her body with his.

Pain ripped through him as the corner of a carriage
brushed against him. Sarah Ann started whimpering.

"Bloody fool!"

"Daftie."

Ben straightened, hearing the cries around him. The
carriage was gone; he'd caught only a glimpse of it as it
disappeared around the corner. Ignoring his own new
bruises, he looked at Sarah Ann. Her face was white, her
lips trembling. Her hand, where he'd pushed her against
the brick, was rubbed raw. Blood dripped from the wound,
and when she saw it her whimpering turned into a wail.

"Puir wee one," a bystander said.

"Did anyone see the carriage?" Ben asked of the
growing crowd.

One man shrugged. "It wa' going too fast."

Anger welled inside him. One accident might have
been just that, an accident.

Two? Never.

Someone had just tried to kill him. And Sarah Ann.
For the second time.

He brusquely thanked those who had stopped to help
them, quieted Sarah Ann's tears, and headed back to the

town house. Rage such as he'd never known burned in his gut. As a soldier, then as a marshal, he had been clubbed, shot at, ambushed, left for dead. But he'd never taken any of it personally. Such were the dangers of war, the risks of marshaling.

But *this* was personal. This time, someone was targeting Sarah Ann. *A child.* By all that was holy, he swore, someone would pay. Dearly.

❖❖❖

Lisbeth couldn't rid herself of the edginess that had plagued her since Ben had left for Edinburgh. Even Shadow felt it and had refused to jump.

Callum scolded her. "Attention, Lady Lisbeth. You must gi' 'im yer full attention."

But she couldn't seem to do that, and she didn't understand why. She had always managed to wipe everything from her mind when she worked with horses. They had always been her escape from both the past and present.

Yet she kept thinking of Ben Masters with Barbara, worrying whether she should have gone with them to Edinburgh, after all. She knew she could never play Barbara's games and win, could never match Barbara's beauty or witty conversation. But maybe she should have tried.

Lisbeth did try to convince herself that she cared only about the future of Calholm, of Shadow's future, of the families that called Calholm home. But she couldn't forget the feel of Ben Masters's body against hers, the touch of his hand, the somber steady gaze of those blue eyes. Nor could she erase the memory of his kiss.

"God's toothache," she swore as she curried Shadow. She always did that rather than allow the stable boys to do it.

Henry the Eighth whined behind her. After Ben, Sarah Ann, and the cat left for Edinburgh, the dog had spent a full day looking for Annabelle. Not finding her, he'd moped ever since. It was ridiculous, a dog pining for a cat, but then Henry was rather eccentric.

"They'll be back," she reassured him.

But when they returned, would Ben be under Barbara's spell? The idea was agonizing.

"Ye will have to work harder, Lady Lisbeth," Callum said, interrupting her reverie. "And keep yer mind on training or Shadow will no' be ready for the steeplechase."

Lisbeth continued stroking down Shadow's withers. "Do you really think he can win?" she asked.

"He's a fine, bonny horse, and he 'as heart. But he needs to know what's expected."

"I know," she said with a sigh. "But I'm just worried about what will happen to Calholm, and Shadow."

"Ye canna worry about anything but that horse," he admonished her again.

"I know." She ran her hand down Shadow's shoulder, feeling his shudder of pleasure. "What do you think of him, Callum?"

"I told ye. He 'as a strong heart, but needs a strong 'and."

"I mean . . . Ben Masters."

Callum was silent for a moment. "He be an American," he said.

"He likes horses," she said hopefully.

"He also went off wi' Lady Barbara."

"Because he had to see John Alistair."

Callum shot her a look of great disgust.

Lisbeth sighed and gave Shadow one last stroke of the brush. "You think she might convince him to sell the horses."

"She convinced Lord Jamie."

Lisbeth went still. "What do you mean? Jamie wouldn't . . ." She stopped at the grim expression on Callum's face.

He looked away. "I dinna mean anything, Lady Lisbeth. I just don't think ye should hope this American will share yer dream—not wi' Lady Barbara convincing him otherwise."

She convinced Lord Jamie.

Lisbeth suddenly felt sick. She was anxious to learn more, but Callum had disappeared.

He was lying. Or he was wrong. He had to be.

The sick feeling grew stronger as she headed toward the house that had never really been her home.

Chapter Eleven

Questions continued to whirl around in Ben's mind. Questions and suspicions.

He'd stayed mostly silent during the journey back to Calholm, blocking out Barbara's endless chatter, giving only the occasional polite reply.

She'd been properly horrified on hearing the news of their "accident." He would have preferred not to mention it, but he'd had to tell Barbara because Sarah Ann's hand was bandaged and she was chattering about it. The event had gone from being terrifying to adventurous in her four-year-old mind.

It was still terrifying to him.

Last night he'd thought briefly about returning to Denver with Sarah Ann. But dammit, that would be running from evil. He couldn't bring himself to do it. Pursuit of justice, he guessed, was ingrained too deeply within him. He couldn't allow the attack on Sarah Ann to bear fruit for the perpetrator. Besides, running might not be good enough. The murderer might follow them to Denver, unwilling to let them live in peace. Whoever the person was might believe the only way he—or she—ever would be safe from the threat he and Sarah Ann posed would be to kill them.

No, Ben concluded. Running was not the answer. He had to find the would-be murderer. Hugh had already tried to bribe the American solicitor. He also had the most to gain by Sarah Ann's death. But both widows had something to gain, too.

And opportunity? One person had had more opportunity than anyone: Andrew Cameron. In fact, he was the only person Ben knew who had been present on the Glasgow docks and in Edinburgh, who could have engineered and executed both attacks himself.

And Cameron was a friend of Lisbeth's.

Though he hated the direction of his thoughts, Ben wondered if Lisbeth had sent Cameron to trail Sarah Ann from America. There had been time. Ben had lingered in Denver, waiting for the final adoption papers. And what was the nature of Cameron and Lisbeth's relationship? Were they lovers or conspirators—or both? Cameron's motives could be love or money. And Lisbeth had made it clear what she wanted: the horses and a Grand National championship for Shadow—and Calholm.

Exactly how badly did she want to win the championship? Badly enough to commit murder?

The carriage rolled up to the manor house as dusk was falling. The wind was gaining strength, and the dark clouds blowing in only added to Ben's somber mood.

"I want to see Pep'mint," Sarah Ann said, barely able to contain herself. At that moment, Annabelle yowled piercingly from within her basket.

Sarah Ann pulled the cat out, hugging her. "I love you, too," she comforted, but the assurance apparently wasn't enough. Annabelle streaked out of Sarah Ann's arms, through the door that the coachman had just opened, and across the yard toward the house.

Barbara raised one eyebrow as if to say, "Not again."

Ben sighed. He had heavier thoughts on his mind than a temperamental wayward cat. "Let's go find Annabelle," he told Sarah Ann as he set her down on the ground, "and then see Peppermint."

Tears were welling in Sarah Ann's eyes. "I hurt her feelings, saying I wanted to see Pep'mint."

"I don't think so," Ben replied, getting down on one knee so he could look at her on her own level. "I think she was just tired of traveling and wanted to be home."

"Really?" she said hopefully. "Do you really think so?"

"I do, indeed. She's probably begging a bowl of milk right now, enraging the cook by walking over her table."

Sarah Ann giggled, and her tears stopped. There had been several angry outbursts from the cook concerning Annabelle and Henry. Also threats to leave, but each time Lisbeth had cajoled Fiona Ferguson out of her bad humor.

"Maybe she went to see Henry?" Sarah Ann said.

Most likely to bedevil the poor dog. "Maybe," he said.

"Maybe Lady Lisbeth can take me to see Pep'mint."

He hesitated. He didn't want to leave Sarah Ann alone with any member of this household, not even for a moment, but he didn't think anything would happen here. The other two incidents occurred well away from Calholm and were made to look like accidents. Still, he had to be cautious.

After all, Jamie Hamilton had died at Calholm and Ben had no way of knowing if the riding accident that had killed him had actually been carefully engineered.

Still, how was he supposed to keep Sarah Ann in sight every moment? Could he really protect her here? And from whom? And how could he find out the answers to all his questions?

The irony of his situation did not escape Ben. During his last assignment—the one that probably would have ended his career as a lawman even if he hadn't adopted

Sarah Ann—he had forced an outlaw to infiltrate and befriend a band of outlaws with the express goal of betraying them. Ben hadn't realized then how difficult it was to live among people you couldn't trust, to pretend a friendship that didn't exist.

He was now in the same situation into which he'd forced Diablo. He couldn't voice his doubts, couldn't ask questions, couldn't mention his suspicion that the carriage mishap had been planned. If he did, he would lose an advantage, make the guilty person wary and more difficult to detect. No, he would do far better to set a trap with himself as the tethered goat.

"Ben . . . Mr. Masters."

It was only then that Ben realized he'd left Barbara in the carriage. She was still awaiting his assistance.

"My apologies, Lady Barbara," he murmured as he took her hand and helped her down. She tripped on the step and fell directly into his arms.

She was all womanly curves, and he felt every one of them. And he knew he was meant to feel every one of them.

Ben was trying to set her on her feet when he saw Lisbeth. She was galloping in on Shadow, her body wrapped in those boyish clothes and her hair flying behind her. Horse and rider arrived with a burst of exuberance, but that exuberance seemed to fade as Lisbeth pulled up in front of the carriage and looked at Barbara, who was still clinging to him.

"Barbara, Mr. Masters," she said formally and with just the slightest note of disdain. "I didn't expect you back so soon. I'll inform cook."

"Lady Lisbeth . . ."

She had already turned the horse toward the stables, but Sarah Ann's plaintive cry stopped her. She turned back.

"May I go with you to see Pep'mint?"

"No," Ben said.

"Yes, of course," Lisbeth said at the same instant.

Their gazes met as Ben set Barbara away from him. Lisbeth's eyes were angry.

Unaware of the human drama unfolding, Henry bounded onto the scene, galloping to Sarah Ann, lifting one paw in greeting and giving her face a swipe of his tongue.

"I want to see Pep'mint," she begged.

"What about Annabelle?" Ben asked.

"You can find her. You're bestest at finding her. No one can find her as good as you."

Ben had no choice. There was no reasonable excuse he could give for not allowing Sarah Ann to go with Lisbeth.

"Just for a few minutes," he finally said, then looked at Lisbeth. "Sarah Ann needs her dinner and some rest."

Lisbeth nodded, her expression suddenly guarded. She leaned down and pulled Sarah Ann up in front of her in the saddle. Her strength didn't surprise Ben; she had to be strong to control a stallion like Shadow. He watched as they rode to the stable and Lisbeth dismounted, then allowed Sarah Ann to slide into her arms. They disappeared into the stable.

Barbara was still only inches away from Ben. "Horses will always be her only love," she said.

"What about Jamie?"

Barbara shrugged. "It was a marriage of convenience. At least for Jamie."

"What do you mean?"

"His father wanted another heir. Her family wanted a title."

"I thought—"

"That they were in love?" She smiled sadly. "There are few real love affairs among the peerage."

"What about you and Hugh?" he probed.

Her face suddenly changed, became shuttered. "Hugh needs . . . someone."

It was the last thing he'd expected to hear from her.

There was almost something painful, even wistful, about the way she'd spoken.

She looked up at him. "You have a freedom in America we don't have, we don't dare have. We all live in the past, with legends and history and myths. Love is secondary to family and custom and duty. And none of us are trained to do anything but look good." The last was said almost bitterly.

"Except for Lisbeth?"

"She's worse than any of us," Barbara said disdainfully. "She dreams impossible dreams and won't accept that they are impossible. She believes she can bring back the past and make Calholm what it once was."

"And you, Lady Barbara," he probed, "what would you make of Calholm?"

"Profitable." She hesitated. "We can double the income if we clear the training field and farmland and buy more sheep. We can't do that because we have no cash. It's all tied up in those bloody horses."

Ben's eyes narrowed. "Is that what Hugh would do? Clear the remaining tenants from the land and sell the horses?"

"That's what any sensible person would do," she said. "That's what every landowner in Scotland is doing, *has* been doing for the past century. With England's taxes, we have little choice. But Lisbeth will hear naught of it."

"I heard Hugh gambled away everything he once had."

"He did," Barbara said, "but he had very little, and he was desperate to make it into more. He and his mother lived on the sufferance of others for years. He craves to belong somewhere. He thought Calholm to be it. His bad manners are only a mask for his disappointment." Her voice had softened. "He can be . . . very pleasant."

Ben knew about disappointments. He knew about despair. He also knew about escape. He had turned away from everyone after being injured in the war, during those months when he thought he would lose his leg and his fiancée had broken their engagement to marry a banker.

Any further questions he might have asked Barbara were suddenly curtailed. A scream came from the open kitchen window on the side of the manor. However, it seemed a scream of outrage rather than terror, and Ben suspected Annabelle had been located. The cat was uncanny in finding its way to the kitchen.

He looked toward the stable. He loathed to be even farther away from Sarah Ann, but murder sounded in the offing inside the manor, so he hurried up the front steps and rushed to the kitchen.

The cook was chasing Annabelle around the room with a broom. The instant he appeared, the cat hurled herself into his arms, flinging custard everywhere—on his new clothes, the kitchen floor, her fur. Custard lay across the floor and over a table where a bowl had been overturned. Paw prints readily identified the culprit.

"Tha' cat goes, or I willna stay another day!" the cook said, her face trembling with indignation.

Annabelle swiped a rough tongue along Ben's hand. He didn't fool himself that it was a sign of affection. But the damn cat looked so pleased with herself as she curled up in his arms, a sound of satisfaction rumbling deep in her throat, that he had to brake a smile.

"Ah, Mrs. Ferguson, I am sorry," he soothed. "Especially if that custard is as good as everything else you cook."

Her face quivered again, but some of the anger faded from it. "Ye sure ye'd not be having some Irish blood in ye?"

He grinned at her. "Aye, I'm sure. And I promise I'll keep Annabelle in our rooms. You know how Sarah Ann loves her."

The face softened. "She's a dear wee lassie, but"—her voice rose again—"I'll no' be 'aving that cat in my kitchen!"

Ben nodded solemnly.

She turned back to the stove. "Almost as bad as that 'Enry," she mumbled. "A fine 'ouse is no place for such goings-on."

Containing a smile, Ben backed out of the kitchen, keeping a firm hold on Annabelle. But Annabelle had apparently had her adventure—and evidently a fine, rich meal—and was content to be carried. On reaching the rooms, she streaked into Sarah Ann's chamber, licked the last of the custard from her paws, and curled up contentedly on the bed.

Ben gave her one last warning look, then went to his connecting room. He relieved himself quickly of the frock coat, shrugging into his more comfortable sheepskin coat, and quickly made his way back down the stairs.

❖❖❖

Lisbeth wished the raw hurt would fade. Why had Ben hesitated before allowing Sarah Ann to come with her to the stables? The cool appraisal in his eyes had struck her as hard as any axe.

She rubbed down Shadow, keeping an ear open as Sarah Ann chatted happily with Peppermint several stalls away.

A rare delight had surged through her when she'd seen the approaching carriage but had faded quickly as she saw the look on Ben Masters's face. There had been no welcome, only hostility.

So Barbara had gotten to him during the trip.

No need to wonder exactly what means she'd employed. And now he was probably ready to sell all the horses, throw off the tenants, and buy sheep. As for his opinion of her . . . Lisbeth couldn't bear even to imagine it.

But his opinion of her didn't matter. She couldn't give up. Too much was at stake. People's homes, Jamie's dream, and, yes, *her* dream. In her entire life, she'd never been allowed to dream, so she had never imagined wanting anything that she had only a prayer of having. Jamie may not have given her passion or romantic love, but he had given her hope—hope that something she worked for and believed in could come true.

She wasn't giving it up. Not without a fight.

Lisbeth swallowed hard. She'd lived so long in a home without warmth or trust. Without love. And she supposed she could go on without those things for as long as she had to. If only Ben hadn't come along . . .

In the short time he and Sarah Ann had been here, they'd given her fleeting glimpses of what she had been missing. It made doing without so much harder.

Lisbeth finished rubbing down Shadow, and gave him the carrot she brought from the house, then went over to Peppermint's stall. He was nuzzling Sarah Ann as she chattered on.

"And we were almost trampled, but Papa saved us."

"Trampled?" Lisbeth echoed.

Sarah Ann turned to her. "That's what Papa said. He knocked me down? See." She took off the glove from her left hand and held the hand up for inspection.

Lisbeth noted the large bandage, and the redness of the skin around the bandage.

"Was your papa hurt, too?" she asked.

"I don't think so, but I don't always know. I'm supposed to take care of him, too, you know," she said quite seriously. "But he always says he's fine," she added with adult exasperation that Lisbeth found endearing.

"Grown-ups are like that," Lisbeth replied just as seriously.

"But that's silly. I *like* being taken care of."

Lisbeth found it difficult to argue with that logic. "He probably didn't want you to feel bad."

"I feel worse when he doesn't let me take care of him." Sarah Ann's eyes were sad and Lisbeth understood her frustration. She liked feeling needed, too. It had been a long time since she'd looked after someone in a personal, intimate way. Jamie had never been sick, and he had died instantly. He had disliked "fussing," so all of

Lisbeth's maternal instincts had gone to the horses, and to Henry.

"Men never want to admit they need anyone," she confided to Sarah Ann.

"Why?"

Lisbeth wished she knew. She had become independent, too, in self-defense. She hadn't realized she needed anyone . . . until Ben Masters had held her in his arms.

"Because then they feel . . . vulnerable."

"What's vun'ble?"

Lisbeth had seen Ben try to answer Sarah Ann's endless questions, and she had been amused. She wasn't amused now. Perhaps because she too was vulnerable.

"What's 'vun'ble'?" Sarah Ann persisted.

Lisbeth tried to come up with a good explanation. "That's when you feel you can be hurt easily."

"No one can hurt Papa. He's a lawman," Sarah Ann said proudly. "Cully said so."

"He's a solicitor," Lisbeth corrected gently.

"No," Sarah Ann insisted. "He got bad men."

Lisbeth began to say that that's what solicitors and barristers did—they sent criminals to jail. But she had hardly said a couple of words when a low, thunderous voice interrupted.

"Having an interesting conversation?"

Lisbeth whirled at the chilling sound of Ben Masters's voice and found him standing a mere hairsbreadth behind her.

❖❖❖

Ben had to stifle the urge to grin. Lisbeth's head was tilted almost straight back in order for her to look him in the eye. She appeared positively dumbfounded.

"Yes," she said a little defiantly as her surprise faded.

"And how did 'vun'ble' come up?"

She hesitated, then suddenly smiled. "She told me you never let her help you and asked why. I told her being helped made men feel vulnerable."

Her smile drove straight through his defenses to his heart. "It does, does it?" he finally managed to say after a moment.

"I have observed such."

Her Scottish lilt seemed more pronounced than usual. It was . . . enchanting. Ben tried to make himself remember his suspicions but they were disappearing quickly in the face of the attraction that radiated so strongly between them.

"What have you observed, Lady Lisbeth?"

"That men would rather die than admit a weakness."

"And women?"

"Are never as hardheaded," she replied serenely.

Her gaze was fixed on his now, searching, probing. He wanted to turn away, but he couldn't. He felt sucked in, like a man pulled into quicksand. Her eyes were so lively, so curious, so full of secrets. He wanted to know more of them, more of her. He wanted most to know how this lovely hoyden, who stirred him as no other woman ever had, could possibly be a murderess.

"Sarah Ann said you were nearly trampled in Edinburgh?"

The question was enough to jerk Ben out of his fascination with her eyes. Dangerous eyes. Were they also deceptive eyes?

Ben looked at Sarah Ann, who was standing next to Peppermint. "Why don't you talk to your pony for a minute?" he suggested. At her eager nod, Ben pulled Lisbeth out of the stall and down to Shadow's stall at the end of the stable.

"It was an accident," he said, answering her question, keeping his suspicions to himself at the moment. "A runaway carriage, apparently."

"Another accident?"

He remembered their first meeting. He shrugged. "I must be prone to them."

She didn't reply, but something new appeared in those lovely eyes. Fear? Disappointment over failed plans?

"I met a friend of yours in Edinburgh," he said.

He'd surprised her, he could tell.

"Andrew Cameron. He was on the ship from Boston."

"Lord Kinloch?" Lisbeth said with a smile. Ben felt a bite of jealousy. Her expression held no guile, no fear, no apprehension, only pleasure.

He wanted to say Cameron had been expelled from the ship after being accused of cheating at cards, but he held his tongue. He'd never been a talebearer, particularly when the tale concerned a man's reputation.

"Sarah Ann took to him," he said.

"Most women do. I haven't decided whether it's because of his reputation or in spite of it."

Ben raised an eyebrow, which he'd learned was an effective way to get information without revealing his own thoughts.

"Like Hugh, Andrew had little or no inheritance—other than his title. Unlike Hugh, he's usually successful at gaming and he's particularly fond of races. Jamie and I met him at the Edinburgh Steeplechase, and he was one of the few men who . . ."

"Who what?"

"Listened to me, I suppose." She was suddenly indignant. "No one thinks a woman knows anything about horses. Now that Jamie's dead, no one pays serious attention to our stable. That's why it's so important for Shadow to win."

"So you can show them all?"

"So *the Hamiltons* can show them all. There are naught that can compare with Calholm's stable." The Highland accent was strong again, growing stronger the more she talked of the horses.

Her face had flushed pink. Her curly auburn hair was wild, and her boyish clothes smelled of sweat and leather. Ben thought of the beautifully dressed and coiffed Lady Barbara and wondered why on earth it was Lisbeth who excited his senses, who created chaos in his usually logical mind.

Standing there in front of him, her eyes flashing golden fire and her lips still set stubbornly, she was more captivating than any woman he'd ever met. And challenging.

Ben told himself—commanded himself—not to touch. His fellow lawmen had often commented on his self-control, his absolute self-discipline, and the comments weren't always good-natured. The Iron Man, they'd called him.

But he wasn't iron now. He had thought himself impervious to the charms of women. For years, he had rejected anything more than a strictly physical coupling. But Mary May had unlocked the door, and now Lisbeth was opening it wide.

Don't! But he did.

He touched her cheek, and the fire in her eyes seemed to smolder. He leaned over, and his lips brushed hers, lightly at first. Exploring.

She stiffened, and yet her body seemed to inch into his.

The sounds of the stable, the neighing of horses and the clomping of hoofs, faded. The only reality was Lisbeth, the soft sighs of her breath, the pliant warmth of her lips.

The ache in his groin grew stronger. He felt the swelling and braced for the need he knew was coming. His kiss deepened, his tongue entering her mouth in a primitive mating game. She stilled for a moment, as if surprised, and then she responded with a passionate curiosity that kindled a recklessness he'd never known before.

Nothing mattered at that moment except the need they were creating as they fed on each other, tasting, exploring, reacting. He wanted her. By God, he wanted her. His hands wound themselves in her hair, and he was only aware of its silky texture, of the way the curls wrapped themselves around his fingers.

The slam of a stable door brought the kiss to an abrupt halt. She jerked away, staring at him in astonishment.

He tried to focus, to remind himself of where they were. Sarah Ann was several stalls down. Stable boys were moving up and down the passages. Damn, what in the hell had possessed him?

But as he looked down at her, at her dazed eyes just inches away, he knew. Her face had a softness he hadn't seen before, a sudden glow that fanned the fires deep within him. He had been seeking answers. But this was one answer he sure as hell hadn't expected.

"Papa?"

The call for attention demanded a response. But it didn't quench the flame still burning inside him. He was relieved his coat fell down past his thighs.

"We're both mad," Lisbeth murmured.

"Completely," he agreed. He more than she, he thought, since not twenty minutes ago, he'd been wondering if she were a murderer.

She shook her head, as if she could shake him off, shake the kiss off. But it had been more than a simple kiss, and he knew it. He knew she knew it.

Hell, how much more of a fool could he be?

"Papa!" Sarah Ann's voice was more insistent.

Lisbeth turned around—reluctantly, he thought— toward the sound of Sarah Ann's voice. He watched as her trembling hand moved along Shadow's withers, and the animal shuddered with pleasure. He knew exactly how the horse felt. Shudders were raking their way through him, too.

"Lisbeth . . ."

She stilled, but didn't turn back to him.

He'd lifted a hand, but it fell back to his side. "I'll see you at dinner?"

She nodded, still not looking at him.

It was just as well. He didn't know what he wanted to

say to her. He left the stall and walked toward his daughter.

❖❖❖

Lisbeth clutched her hairbrush desperately as she stared at herself in the mirror. She barely registered the disheveled state of her appearance—hair flying in ten different directions, clothes covered with horsehair. Her attention was focused entirely on the hot, liquid sensations coursing through her body.

What was happening to her? She could still taste him, feel him, feel his arousal crushed against her, the memory of which only intensified the throbbing in her belly.

No one ever had kissed her like that. Jamie's kisses had been almost chaste, respectful. He had never explored the inside of her mouth. She was astounded at how that intimate play had inflamed the rest of her body. Had she been too bold? Too wanton? She'd only wanted to prolong those new and mysterious urges. God help her, but she'd wanted more. She'd wanted to explore every one of those urges, follow them to . . . wherever they led.

Lisbeth swallowed hard. She made a bloody poor seductress. She'd planned to use Ben, to convert him to her way of thinking. Instead, she'd fallen victim to the sound of his voice, to the sight of his tall, lean body and his lined face and intense blue eyes. She was helpless against the feelings aroused by the feel of his lips on hers and his hands skimming her body.

One moment he'd been hostile and aloof, and she couldn't for the life of her think of anything she'd done to make him so. Then in the space of a heartbeat, he'd changed. When exactly had frigid reserve turned to searing heat? And when precisely had she lost control and become helpless in the face of his passion?

But she *couldn't* be helpless. She couldn't allow herself to fall prey to the sensations he aroused in her body. It mortified her to think that, twice now, she'd been on the verge of giving herself to a man who thought she was willing to trade her body for a few acres of land and a stable of horses. For that was what Ben thought. And why shouldn't he? He had every reason to—because she'd given him every reason.

Angrily, Lisbeth ran the brush through her hair. She wasn't angry at Ben, but at herself. She'd worked for years toward a goal that was now in sight. She wasn't going to lose her way along the path in a fog of lust. For that was all it was—lust. And what she needed was cool logic to convince Masters to support racing Shadow.

With that plan in place, Lisbeth chose a plain, almost prim, gray dress for dinner, and tamed her hair into an equally prim knot. She only wished her wayward emotions could be tamed as easily.

Chapter Twelve

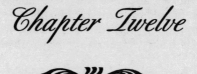

The loch glimmered in the morning mist, the ruins of a Scottish castle providing a haunting backdrop.

Ben reined in Bailey and caught his breath as he neared the gray-blue waters of the loch. But it wasn't the lake that drew his attention. It was Lisbeth.

She had ridden ahead on a fine gray horse and now waited at the lake's edge. She was wearing a green riding dress, a matching hat perched rakishly on her auburn hair that was subdued into a twist. He had never seen a woman who rode with as much confidence as she did, or who sat a horse as gracefully. Even the light rain appeared to cause her little bother. Indeed, her face looked heavenward, as if in welcome.

She turned toward them and watched as they approached. Sarah Ann was mounted proudly on her mild-mannered pony. She had been practicing diligently during the past several days, and Ben had finally decided she rode well enough to make the short trip to the loch.

Still, he kept a lead on the pony, though he allowed Sarah Ann to hold the reins. He himself had saddled Peppermint, inspecting every part of the saddle first, as he had his own. He hadn't forgotten the way Lisbeth's husband had died.

Sarah Ann, wearing her own new riding dress with a matching coat and hat, chattered excitedly to Peppermint. Her face was flushed with excitement, and Ben had to smile at the picture she made. He dearly coveted a painting of Sarah Ann as she was at this moment.

His thoughts of Sarah Ann were more welcome than usual—anything to distract him from thoughts of Lisbeth. He'd been trying his damnedest to stay mentally removed from her. Meals were tolerable enough. Hugh had returned, and he and Barbara usually kept a conversation— or argument—flowing. Barbara couldn't seem to keep from flirting with both Hugh and himself, and Hugh invariably took offense. Ben equated living in the manor with living in a building full of dynamite. He never knew when someone was going to light the fuse.

He'd come close to refusing Lisbeth's suggestion that they take Sarah Ann to the lake this morning. Both he and Lisbeth were as much a part of the dynamite as Hugh and Barbara, and the electricity they generated was dangerous. But Sarah Ann had begged so. And he *had* promised her days ago that they would explore the lake.

But he didn't need to be this close to Lisbeth, nor did he want to be enchanted by her plans. Yet the boy in him warmed to the idea of a lake, Scottish castle ruins, and a picnic in the rain.

A picnic in the rain, and a formal party. That seemed to characterize the personalities of the two mismatched sisters-in-law.

Lisbeth galloped back to where he had stopped. "It's very bonny, do you no' think?"

He pushed up the collar of his sheepskin coat, and she laughed, a clear happy sound. She always seemed happier, more relaxed, away from the manor.

"Aye," he said, but he was looking at her, at the dancing pleasure in her eyes.

She appeared not to notice. "The castle across there belonged to one of the Hamiltons centuries ago. It was taken and destroyed by the king after the Forty-five— when Bonnie Prince Charlie was defeated and so many Scots slaughtered at Culloden. They say it's haunted."

"And what do you say, Lady Lisbeth?"

"Every castle an' every ruin in Scotland is haunted," she said, her smile disappearing, "but mostly, I ken, by memories. Scottish history is full of tragedy and feuds and revenge. I think it must be hard for Americans to understand."

"We've had our share of tragedy and feuds. But our wounds are mostly fresh ones."

"But there are no old wounds to the Scots. They relive each one of them every day of their lives and take perverse pleasure in doing so. The hurt of forty-five is as fresh today as it was more than a hundred years ago."

Ben had learned enough of Scottish history to know that Culloden, the site of the bloody climax to the uprising of 1745, was sacred to the Scots. The war had divided Scotland into two factions, the Jacobites who supported independence and those Scots who allied themselves with England, and had destroyed the clan system.

"And what of your family, Lady Lisbeth?" he asked. "Barbara said you came from the Highlands."

"Aye," she said. "I was a Mackay, a clan well known for its fighting. Within the family as well as without."

There was something sad and wistful about her words. She had said very little about her family, or background. She seemed very alone except for her horses and dog.

"You have no brothers or sisters?" he asked.

"No sisters," she said. "Four brothers."

"Is that why you ride so well?"

She looked at him, puzzled.

"Did your brothers teach you?"

"No." Something about the way she said it made him

hesitate to pursue the subject. It was really none of his business.

Sarah Ann had been sitting patiently on her pony, but she'd apparently had enough of conversation. "Can we go to the castle?" she asked.

Lisbeth looked to him for an answer.

He gave her a non-committal shrug. "Is it safe?"

"There really aren't any ghosts or goblins," Lisbeth said with a bit of a smile. "Jamie used to love the place when he was a boy. He told me he used to prowl and pretend he was an outlawed Jacobite. He took me there several times and showed me some passageways that still exist, and once I nearly fell into an old well. There are a lot of those—old holes and loose stones." She turned to Sarah Ann. "You will have to hold tight to your fa's hand."

"What's 'fa'?"

"Papa," she said. "Father. We Scots just shorten it a little bit."

"Fa?" Sarah Ann rolled the sound around in her mouth.

Ben grimaced. He was just getting used to "Papa," for goodness' sake.

"There's one place that's partly covered where we can eat," Lisbeth suggested.

"I wondered about the . . . picnic," he said.

The rain was still falling, shrouding the hills and giving them a magical quality. Occasionally a ray of sun, like a rapier blade, struck through the grayness for a fraction of a second, then disappeared. The castle ruins looked mystical—grand and tragic at the same time.

A pounding started in his heart. He had never been fanciful, nor had he ever felt this sense of fate, not even before a battle during the war. But suddenly his mind was clouded with images and emotions and even a premonition. It made no sense, none at all.

He tried to shove it all aside. Lisbeth was the cause, he knew. Lisbeth, with her eyes, and the lyrical lilt of her voice and speech that drew him to this land and all its violent emotions. He had wanted to get away from violence. He'd wanted peace. But he felt swept into centuries of furious passions.

He wasn't sure at all that he wanted to go near that castle.

"Mr. Masters . . . Ben?"

He liked the sound of his name on her lips.

Liked? Hell. Already tendrils of desire were curling in his groin. Her eyes were wide as they watched him, and he suspected she was seeing straight inside him, seeing the confusion that plagued him. He was a man who viewed the world with cynical practicality. He'd never considered that he could be seduced by swirling mists, echoes of dead armies—or by the wistfulness in a lovely woman who might be a murderer.

"Papa?"

He looked down. At least Sarah Ann was real. She was everything she appeared to be.

"Please can we go to the castle?" she asked impatiently.

He didn't want to go. Frankly, he was afraid to share the magic of the place with Lisbeth. But to refuse was to surrender to unnamed and irrational fears.

The rain dwindled to a mist, which was already lifting, and more shafts of light sprinkled the loch, like thousands of small diamonds thrown onto its surface. Ben looked toward Lisbeth, who returned his gaze with a puzzled one of her own. He wondered whether she had felt the strange pull from the past that he had.

Thrusting his misgivings aside, refusing to let them guide him, he made a decision. "I think a princess needs a castle," he said, looking down at Sarah Ann, who rewarded him with a bright, open smile. It had been days since her last nightmare, since her face had clouded with poignant sadness. She still wouldn't relinquish her scarf, though today she had allowed him to tuck it underneath her fine, new riding dress.

Lisbeth grimaced. "It's rather a sad castle now."

"We'll make it feel better," Sarah Ann said.

"Aye, I ken you will." Lisbeth smiled. She turned and this time she kept a companionable pace with Ben. He was reminded of a similar ride months ago with Mary May. Like Mary May, Lisbeth was comfortable with silence.

Even Sarah Ann fell quiet, full of awe apparently for the ruins, which loomed ever larger as they approached. Watching her, Ben knew that it would only be a few more days before she would be begging to ride without a lead. He wished he knew what boundaries to set, but parenting was too new. He wanted to give her the sun and moon and every star in the sky. The word "no" had become difficult, if not impossible to say.

Christ, his life—and he himself with it—had become unrecognizable.

Ben was conscious of Lisbeth's occasional gaze turning his way, the questions in her eyes. Every time their gazes met, heat flashed through his body, like lightning on a hot, dry Texas night. He felt every intense strike to the core of his being. She felt it, too. He sensed it, saw her flinch several times and move her gaze away quickly from his; but it always returned, just as his did to hers.

God, how he wanted to hold her. He wanted to fling away that jaunty little hat from her hair, take out the pins and run his hand through the long auburn strands. He'd thought Sarah Ann would be protection against feelings he didn't want or understand, but she obviously wasn't. The need for Lisbeth was still hot within him. Burning, in truth, and not even the cold mist of morning cooled it.

They reached the outer ruins of the castle, and Ben dismounted, then helped Sarah Ann down. Lisbeth waited for him to help her, too, though she never had required help before. He gave her his hand and caught her as she slipped down, feeling her body move against his. A new rush of heat coursed through him, even more painful than the last.

He hesitated a moment before stepping back, unwilling, unable, to move. She looked up at him through thick dark lashes that framed her hazel eyes. A shudder ran through him, a shudder of pure desire, and he felt her tremble in response.

"Papa?" Sarah Ann's voice was insistent. "I want to see the castle."

He closed his eyes a moment, trying to jerk himself back to reality. Lisbeth didn't try to move away, and he felt her tremble again.

"Damn," he whispered, finally forcing his hand to relinquish its hold.

"I know," she whispered back, surprising him.

She brushed a damp curl off her face, and slowly he stepped back.

"You're very pretty," he said softly.

She wrinkled her nose. "I'm wet."

"You're particularly lovely when you're wet." His hand reached for the damp, wayward curl.

"And the mist ha' blinded you," she said, but a smile played around her lips. "My sister-in-law is much prettier."

"Depends on the beholder," he said.

"I dinna think you were a man for compliments." Her brogue was deepening again.

"I'm not," he said. "I don't say them very well."

Her eyes sparkled. "I think you say them very well."

Their eyes held, and he felt suddenly lost. He was like a schoolboy with his first love. And she was a woman he didn't entirely trust. He wanted to, but the lawman in him knew about human greed. He'd seen plenty of disarming murderers, charming thieves, and smooth swindlers.

He didn't really believe Lisbeth was involved in the recent accidents, but he simply couldn't take chances where Sarah Ann was involved.

His smile faded and he saw a frown flicker across Lisbeth's brow. There was nothing he could say to her so he busied himself with tethering the horses to a tree.

"Did children live here?" Sarah Ann asked Lisbeth as she stared at the ruins with fascination.

"Many, I ken." Lisbeth untied the picnic basket. She carried it in one hand and took Sarah Ann's hand in the other, while Ben took the little girl's free hand.

Ben considered the picture they made. Anyone would think the three of them had always been together. An unfamiliar ache settled in his chest. He was thirty-five years old. He'd never thought he'd have a family, not after the war. He hadn't missed it, because he hadn't allowed himself to think about it. He'd taken satisfaction in his freedom, in his independence. Only now was he realizing what he'd missed. What Sarah Ann was missing without a mother.

He didn't want her to lack for anything, especially not a mother's love. The fact that Sarah Ann had so taken to Lisbeth proved she needed it.

He wasn't sure, however, whether he could ever trust a woman again . . . and especially one who wanted something from him.

Claire. His fiancée who had eloped with another man when she learned he might lose a leg. Claire had vowed eternal love when he'd ridden off in a tailored captain's uniform. But her face had paled when she'd seen him in the hospital, consumed with fever, his face rough with beard, and his forehead wet with the sweat of pain. She couldn't leave fast enough. Then he'd received the note . . .

He hadn't lost the leg—mainly through sheer force of will and his refusal to allow the surgeon to amputate—but he left the hospital with a bad limp and an abiding suspicion of all women. Until Mary May had sneaked her laughing way through his defenses. But then she too was gone, knifed to death.

And now there was Lisbeth, who made no secret of the fact that she had dreams for Calholm. He would be a fool to subject himself to another betrayal. And he would be a poor father, indeed, to subject Sarah Ann to another loss.

They reached the partially standing wall, and Lisbeth released Sarah Ann's hand to lead the way through a break in the pile of stones.

"This was the gatehouse and outer wall," she said. "The cannon balls that were used in razing it are still here. Over yon is what's left of the castle and its towers. Farmers have carried off many of the stones for their houses and walls. Little is still standing."

Sarah Ann disengaged her hand from Ben's and stared at the ruins in wonder. He wasn't surprised. As a boy, he would have loved these piles of stone and their legacy of battles.

Sarah Ann started walking toward the stone wall, and he trailed behind her. Lisbeth stopped them.

"There are several wells. Be careful," she said, pointing out depressions in the ground. "Part of the chapel is still standing," she said. "The chapel and one of the towers are all the original buildings that remain."

Sarah Ann took Ben's hand again and pulled him toward the ruins. Lisbeth stayed close. Too close. He was aware of the scent of flowers, of femininity, of the temptation to draw her into his arms. He kept his eyes on Sarah Ann, as much to keep them off Lisbeth as to watch his daughter, who was obviously being careful.

His leg was beginning to ache, as it did when he walked too long, or when the weather was about to change. Sarah Ann stumbled ahead, letting go of his hand. As he reached for her, a sharp, almost blinding pain shot through his leg and suddenly it failed him. He started to fall. His hand swung out and caught Lisbeth.

They went tumbling down together. He twisted so he would hit the ground, and she landed on top of him with a gasp of surprise.

His first thought was, *Not again!* He was only too aware of the number of times he'd ended up on his back in Lisbeth's presence. First in the carriage, then in his bedroom, in the manor entrance, and now here.

"Damn, but this is becoming a bad habit," he muttered.

She chuckled, and the sound reverberated against him.

Her face was inches from his, and her laughter faded as she took note of the look in his eyes. She moved slightly, but that only made things worse. He groaned.

She stilled. "Are you hurt?"

"Only my pride," he said.

"That should be easily remedied," she said. "Men seem to have a great deal of it."

"That was cynical."

"Was it?" she asked innocently as she moved—carefully—from atop him.

"Are women immune, then?"

"From pride?" She righted herself into a sitting position, her hand straightening the hat that had shifted so the feather hung down in her face.

"Aye."

"Ye be learning the Scots speech."

"And ye dinna answer my question," he mocked.

"And I don't think I will." A grin spread across her face as she regarded him mischievously.

Ben was suddenly aware that Sarah Ann was peering at them, with something close to jealousy in her eyes.

"Why are you doing that?" she asked.

"What?" they both said in unison.

"Lying there."

He traded glances with Lisbeth, then wished he hadn't. Shared amusement turned into heat, raw, hungry heat. She was the first to drop her gaze. She rose gracefully, then held out a hand to him.

Ben hesitated. He could get to his feet by himself, but only very clumsily. But if he took her offer of help, he might well bring them both down again.

"I'm strong," she said, "unless, of course, I'm taken by surprise."

He took her hand then and stood.

"I'm hungry," Sarah Ann wailed suddenly.

It was only then that both Ben and Lisbeth became aware of the basket lying on the ground, its contents spilled over the rocks. She'd dropped it when they fell.

They scrambled to save what they could. A container of tea was intact, as was a pot of jam. The fresh bread was salvageable as were several scones. The meat pies were a total loss.

"We'll make do," Lisbeth said, taking quick steps toward the remnants of the stone chapel.

Ben followed, his leg complaining all the way. His pride *had* been hurt. He'd been able to ignore the leg for the past five years, mainly because he'd ridden most of the time and had been able to limit his walking. But the past several weeks had proved he couldn't ignore the weakness. If he did, he might endanger Sarah Ann. Now Lisbeth knew how weak it was, that he really was a cripple.

Cripple. Claire had called him that in the note she'd left. *I'm sorry. I can't marry a cripple.*

He'd fought that image. Perhaps that was why he'd started marshaling. The job had given him back his self-esteem as well as allowed him to pursue a personal quest, one that had ended only months ago.

"Ben?" Lisbeth's voice was soft, questioning. They had reached the entrance to the chapel, an opening without a door. He entered. There was only a partial roof. A stone altar stood at the far end; no other sign remained that this had once been a place of worship.

But the walls cut the wind as well as the dampness.

The stone floor was broken, and he walked cautiously. He was damned if he was going to take another spill. They had reached the middle of the room when the sun suddenly hit the opening in the roof and sent a splinter of light down to illuminate the altar.

"The light always shines on ʰat spot," Lisbeth explained. "It's as if the builder planned it, even to the hole in the ceiling." Her voice was soft, reverent.

"Have you ever tried to find out anything about the families who lived here?"

"Yes," she said. "I asked Jamie, and he told me a little. It's a very sad history. There was a shortage of sons, and many stillbirths. There are legends of course, but none associated with the chapel. And no deathless loves," she added drolly.

She abruptly turned away from him. Locating two large stones that had fallen on the floor, she sat on one, gesturing for Sarah Ann to join her. Ben sat down on the stone floor, stretching out his leg and taking pleasure in watching Lisbeth.

Sarah Ann's eyes also followed every movement Lisbeth made as she served their repast. Ben would have sold his soul at the moment for a cup of strong American coffee, but at least the tea tasted good and warmed him.

Sarah Ann's momentary flash of jealousy having disappeared, she proceeded to ply Lisbeth with questions about the castle and people who lived in it. What happened to the roof of the chapel? Why would anyone hurt a church? Why was there a battle? Why did men kill each other?

The last question was one Ben himself couldn't answer though he'd participated in a war. He'd known why he fought. He'd believed in the Union. He'd thought he believed in the right cause, until he'd discovered his enemies thought the same and every bit as deeply. And one of those enemies had risked his life and surrendered his freedom to save him. He'd never been so arrogant again as to believe he was the only one to know right and wrong.

He listened as Lisbeth haltingly tried to answer the questions, inviting new ones as a reward.

"I ken it's all very confusing, and I don't understand it myself," Lisbeth said slowly. "Sometimes people believe in something so strongly that they feel they must fight for it, or they need to protect something or someone they love."

"Like Calholm?" he asked softly.

Lisbeth looked startled. "Like Calholm," she said. "And like Sarah Ann."

"The man who killed my mother," Sarah Ann said. "Was he protecting someone?"

Lisbeth turned helplessly toward Ben. She hadn't realized Sarah Ann had been listening carefully, and understanding so much.

He scooped up Sarah Ann and held her in his lap. "Sometimes, Sugarplum, people are also greedy. And they don't care who they hurt as long as they get what they want."

Sarah Ann huddled against him. Her small body seemed so slight that his heart ached for her. "I'll never let anyone hurt you," he said. "I promise you that."

She pressed closer to him. He wished they hadn't come here. He wished she hadn't been reminded of what she'd suffered. He looked over toward Lisbeth. He couldn't read her eyes. It was as if she'd thrown a silky veil over them.

Lisbeth turned away to face the altar. Then she stood and walked over to it.

Sarah Ann wriggled, apparently having been comforted sufficiently. She gave him a hug, smearing jam on his face, and he silently blessed the resiliency of children. He stood awkwardly and walked over to Lisbeth. One of her hands was clutched in a tight ball at her waist. He reached out and touched her, but she shied away.

"Lisbeth?"

"I used to be afraid," she said softly. "It can be a terrible thing." She was trembling, and he reached for her a second time, but again she flinched.

"I think it's time to go," she said finally, still not looking at him. "I have to work with Shadow."

She had shut him out, closed the door to that sweet

intimacy they'd shared earlier. But had they really shared it? Had she detected his suspicion? Interpreted a warning?

Lisbeth walked back to where they had been sitting and quickly gathered what was left of their small picnic.

Why did he feel as if he'd lost something? When it was something he'd never actually had.

Chapter Thirteen

From his second-story window Hugh Hamilton had watched Ben Masters, Lisbeth, and Sarah Ann ride out from Calholm. The sight didn't help his hangover one bloody bit.

His solicitor in Edinburgh hadn't been encouraging. John Alistair had a fine reputation, according to his solicitor, and his recommendation almost certainly meant the naming of Sarah Ann Hamilton Masters as heiress to Calholm.

Hugh felt sick inside. He had depended on this inheritance for the last two years, depended on it so much that he had accumulated a mountain of debts based on his prospects. He had absolutely no way of paying those debts now; what small reputation and pride he had left would disappear.

The simple truth was he didn't have the funds to fight Ben Masters, and no solicitor would take such a risky case without some assurance of being paid.

His luck was just rotten, had been since he was a boy, the only son in a family already depleted of everything but title. His father had shot himself when he'd lost everything in an ill-advised investment, lending even more indignity to the family name. He and his mother had been passed around from relative to relative, and he was sent to inferior schools by long-suffering relatives.

But he had learned charm—beggars often did—and his good looks made him a sought-after guest if not quality husband material. He always enlivened a party with sophisticated chatter. God, how he hated what he had become during those years. And then two years ago, the eldest Hamilton son—Barbara's husband—died. With the younger son long missing and the current heir—Jamie—without children, he became next in line to inherit. He had been invited to Calholm for a hunt when Jamie had died, and suddenly his prospects were bright.

As the heir presumptive, he'd moved into Calholm, and he and Barbara, whom he'd met on several previous occasions, had fallen in love. Bloody hell, how he had fallen in love! And for the first time in his life, he seemed to have a future.

But he also knew that Barbara enjoyed wealth and the things it could buy. She might love him as she claimed, but he had become a realist: love existed only as long as the purse stayed full. When Alistair persisted in his search for Ian Hamilton or his get, he'd died a thousand deaths. In desperation, he had even attempted to bribe the American solicitor to end the search. Unfortunately, the man had reported the attempt, and Alistair became determined that Hugh would never gain control of Calholm.

He knew his attempt at bribery had been stupid, but he had been so obsessed with Barbara and Calholm. It just wasn't right that a piece of Scotland should fall into the hands of an American who cared not a farthing for it. If anyone was a fraud, it was the arrogant American.

Hugh's only satisfaction was that Barbara's flirtations

didn't seem to affect the American at all. Hugh couldn't understand why anyone would prefer a bluestocking who dressed like a man to Barbara, but he was grateful for that small blessing.

But what would he do now? Where would he go?

He could manage Calholm. He *knew* it. He also knew no one else believed it. But he had studied husbandry at Edinburgh University and had taken an interest in the estates where he'd stayed for brief periods with his mother. He'd always had hopes, if little else.

Hugh realized now his mistake had been waiting, expecting that life would hand him what his mother had sworn would be his. He'd never prepared himself for making a living by other means than owning and managing land. And now no one would trust him.

As he watched the three figures disappear toward the loch and the old castle ruins, he fought back bitterness, hopelessness. Dammit, the American didn't deserve Calholm. Nor did the child.

He felt a hand against his back, then smelled Barbara's scent.

"It appears he favors your sister-in-law," he said bitingly, unable to stop the cruel words. He had been barely able to suppress his temper—and anguish—as she'd teased and tempted the American these last few weeks.

She leaned against him, and he fought his need for her. "I favor *you*," she said.

"Only because you've had wee luck with him." He wanted to take her in his arms. He wanted to sink himself in her body and forget everything else—his poverty, his debts, his lack of a future.

She sighed. "You know me, Hugh. And I was just trying to find out something about him, whether he's the fraud you think he is."

"And did you?" he asked dryly.

"No," she admitted. "He loves the child, but he doesn't say much about himself."

"Does he kiss well?"

"He didn't try."

"You're losing your touch, my love. I'll wager he's kissed your dear sister-in-law."

"That's why you don't have a farthing," she retorted, and he knew his words had stung her pride. "He couldn't like that . . . hoyden."

"You didn't see them ride away a few moments ago . . . toward the ruins. A romantic trysting place."

"The child was with them," she said, and he knew then she'd been watching, too.

His jaw set. Every reminder that a four-year-old girl was taking what should be his made his blood boil—and his heart freeze. Why hadn't his bribe worked? Why had Alistair persisted? A true Scot should have protected his own. "Damn them!" he said.

"The child is rather sweet."

He raised an eyebrow. "Maternal feelings at this late date, Barbara? You know what she's costing us?"

"I know, but she's a precocious child, and she gets that sad look—"

"Bloody hell, not you, too," he said, exasperated.

She looked him in the face. "She has the Hamilton look about her despite that red hair. John Alistair says all the papers are in order. There's little we can do but accept it."

"*You* can accept it," he said bitterly. "You have your rights in this house and the trust. I have nothing."

"You have me."

"For how long?" he said. "I know you too well, love. As soon as Alistair's petition is approved, I plan to leave Scotland—just a step ahead of my creditors."

Barbara stood there stunned. "Where . . . ?"

If he hadn't been in such a terrible mood, Hugh might have felt some satisfaction at the strong emotion in her voice. He shrugged. "Maybe Australia or America. There's gold to be found, I'm told. It's better than poverty here."

"I have some money . . ."

"It's not enough, my love, and I'll not live off you in any event. You'd end up despising me."

"There has to be something . . ."

"With the exception of another accident, I don't see anything."

"An accident?"

"Jamie . . . your husband. Accidents seem to occur frequently in this family."

She shivered, and he pulled her into his arms. She turned her head to him, and his lips came down on hers. Desperation fueled his passion. How could he lose her?

Her arms went around his neck and seconds later they were on his bed, consuming one another.

❖❖❖

Ben watched Sarah Ann's eyes close. Annabelle, who'd complained long and loud about being left in the room, was now nestling in the crook of one of her arms, reeking of the fish she'd just consumed.

Tenderness threatened to drown him. He hadn't known it could be so strong, so powerful. He hadn't known he could turn to mush just by looking at a tiny person. He pulled up the soft down comforter to cover her and found his hand lingering on her shoulder. Dear God, he wanted to keep her safe and happy forever. He didn't know how he would ever be able to let her go.

Ben straightened and forced himself to leave the room, going into his own room and closing the door. He changed to a more comfortable pair of denim trousers and cotton shirt, and pulled on his sheepskin coat. He needed some time alone—on horseback, where he could think. The inactivity, the lack of anything worthwhile to do, was eating into him.

It was time to start learning about Scottish estates and Scottish farming. Because no matter what he decided—whether to stay or to find a manager to run Calholm—he wanted to make sure it was the best choice.

The first step was to explore the estate. He already

knew its boundaries from descriptions given to him by Alistair and Lisbeth. He'd not seen the outlying farms, though, the ones under dispute between Lisbeth and Hugh. The south fields, he'd been told, were used as the training field for Calholm's jumpers. The north and west were mainly occupied by sheep, and the east by some twenty families trying to hold a few acres each in tenancy. Barbara and Hugh wanted to put sheep on those acres, too. The few shares of crops Calholm received from tenants were only a fraction of the income additional sheep would bring.

He knew the argument. He'd been through it with Alistair, who had expressed the hope that Ben would preserve the farms.

Although he'd made no commitments to anyone, Ben's inclination was to preserve the farms. He'd seen land wars in his years of marshaling, and his sympathies had always gone to the homesteaders, who often worked from dawn until past nightfall to build something for their families. At times, he had been charged with the duty of ejecting homesteaders because they had settled on land that belonged to the government or to others. He'd hated that duty.

But neither did he believe he could be a farmer. Or a sheepman.

Ben made his way to the stable, greeted Geordie, the stable boy, and declined his offer to saddle Bailey. Ben found a saddle, and while he was checking the buckles, he heard barking from a back room. He looked curiously at Geordie.

" 'Enry," the boy said. "He dinna like being left behind."

"Do you think it would be all right if he came with me?" Ben asked.

The boy shrugged. "I dinna know why not. Lady Lisbeth dinna want him to ruin Shadow's practice, but if he be wi' you . . ."

Ben saddled his horse, then liberated Henry from his

prison. The dog exuberantly planted his paws on Ben's chest.

Ben rubbed the animal's head. He'd never had a dog; his father had forbade it during his childhood, and then it had never seemed possible—or fair—given his long days as an attorney, then the war and the demands of being a marshal. So he'd been an easy victim when Sarah Ann had pleaded to save a half-starved cat.

Henry barked enthusiastically and raced about as Ben swung into the saddle and trotted out of the stable heading eastward toward the tenant farms.

The sun had made its way out of the ever-present Scottish clouds, warming the air and shining down on the gorse and the dark green hills. He thought he saw a rainbow, then decided it had been an illusion. So many things about this country seemed to be an illusion: the peaceful hills belying years of warfare and treachery and yet uncommon valor.

As he crossed a hill, Ben saw smoke floating lazily into the sky from the chimney of a stone cottage below. Neatly kept fields, now lying fallow, carved patterns around the structure. He knew that the Calholm manor was staffed almost entirely by offspring of the tenant farmers; the small plots provided insufficient income for the tenants to live on.

A dog barked, and Henry ran ahead, his own thunderous barks drowning out the others.

As Ben approached, the door of the cottage opened and a woman peered out. A dog dodged past her body and ran toward Henry. The dogs greeted each other enthusiastically as Ben swung down from the saddle.

"I'm—" he began.

"I know who you be," the woman said. "The new master." Hostility flickered in her eyes.

Master. The word startled him. He had fought a war so no one would have to use that word again.

"Are ye going to run us from our land?"

Ben couldn't stop the slight smile that curved his lips.

Being a master apparently did not make him the automatic recipient of servility. "I have no authority to run anyone from the land," he said.

"But ye will. My nephew Geordie said so."

"Then Fiona is your sister?"

"Aye," she said carefully.

"She's a fine cook."

"Na as fine as me," the woman said belligerently. "I make the finest meat pie in the district."

His eyes narrowed. "Better than Fiona's?"

She straightened her shoulders, age seeming to melt away from her, pride erasing tired lines. "I wouldna work for the grand house, na for any of the Marquess's sons."

"Not even Jamie Hamilton?"

She sniffed contemptuously. "He wa' the worse of the lot. A wolf in lamb's clothing he wa'."

They were the first unfavorable words Ben had heard about the sainted Jamie Hamilton, and they surprised him. "You are . . . ?"

"Eliza Crawford, and ye can go tattle to Lady Lisbeth. She never saw 'im for wha' he was."

"I won't go tattle to anyone," he said. "And I have no intention of running anyone from their land."

A smile spread across her face. "Then ye be welcome to my home to 'ave a wee taste of my cooking."

Ben entered the cottage, noting the thatch roofing and the stone fireplace that also served as the stove. The one room was primitive, even compared to some of the sod shelters in the prairie. The smell of peat permeated every nook; it even dominated the smells coming from small crannies in the fireplace where pastries and bread were being baked.

" 'Tis not verra grand," the woman said, "but it's far better than the slums of Edinburgh or London."

"I've lived in much worse," he said, and he had. Violent storms and winter blizzards with only a cave for protection.

"In America?" she asked doubtfully. "I hear there be gold for the picking."

"Many believe so," he said, "and many are disappointed. There's gold, but it's hard—and often dangerous—to find."

"Young Ian went to find gold."

"I know." Ben took a seat at a table, and the woman placed in front of him a plate with a warm sweet bun and a crock containing freshly churned butter. The pastry practically melted in his mouth. "You have the right of it, Mrs. Crawford," he said. "You are a magnificent cook."

"Better than Fiona?"

He grinned. "Ah, you're not going to put me on that hot rock, are you?"

"Ye do no' look like a coward." Her eyes lit with life, and he thought she must have been a very pretty girl. Now, she looked weighed down by life and sorrow.

"When it comes to judging cooking, I am," he said. "And I'll not stand in the middle of a fight."

"I think ye be doing that right now," she said, sobering instantly.

"Between the sisters-in-law?"

"Aye."

"It's not a position of my choosing."

She looked at him with shrewd eyes. "But ye have chosen, haven't ye?"

"I don't have the law on my side yet," he said, "so I can choose nothing."

"Ye said ye have no intention of making us leave. Hugh Hamilton and Lady Barbara believe this land should be cleared for the sheep."

"Should it?"

"The first marquess swore that our grandfathers—an' their families—could live here forever."

"But he didn't put it in writing?"

She shook her head. "He saw no need. He told his son, and his son told his."

"And now there are no more sons."

"Nay," she said sadly. "We know other tenants have been put from the land they tilled for years."

"Your husband?"

"Dead these past ten years. My son, Alex, tends sheep for Calholm, but he loves the soil. His heart be in those fields outside."

Ben nodded. He'd known many westerners who had the same passion, and though he did not share it, he understood and had envied their love of land.

"Did ye know young Ian?" she asked, changing the subject.

He shook his head. "No, but there had to be good in him for him to have produced a fine daughter."

"He was a bonny lad, but wild," she said sadly. "Nothing like the Marquess. None of the sons were. John Hamilton had honor."

"I think he would be proud of his granddaughter. She has a huge heart."

"So do ye, I think," she said, "though ye try to hide it."

No one had accused him of that in years. Before Ben could think of a response, Eliza Crawford announced, "I would like to see the child. Geordie said she's very bonny."

"Then you shall," he said. "I'll bring her by tomorrow."

She grinned toothlessly. "I'll 'ave a meat pie ready."

"That's an offer I can't refuse," he said. "Tomorrow afternoon, then."

"I be waiting."

"It's been a pleasure," he said, taking his leave. He noticed the sparkle was back in her eyes, and he felt his spirits lift as he strode out the door and to his horse.

❖❖❖

Despite the cool air, Lisbeth was bathed in sweat when she returned from an afternoon of jumping Shadow. She had ridden him ruthlessly, trying in vain to escape her tortured thoughts and the feelings that this morning's expedition with Ben and Sarah Ann had aroused.

She kept the stallion to a canter as she approached the stable yard, but slowed when she saw another horseman riding in from the east.

Ben. Delightful. She'd spent most of the afternoon cursing his name.

He pulled up, waiting for her. Henry the Eighth, who had apparently persuaded Ben to free him, came barreling on, barking rapturously when he saw her. She thought she also detected the slightest note of triumph in his greeting.

Lisbeth's hand instinctively pushed back the hair that had escaped its ribbon.

Pulling his horse level with hers, Ben gave her that bloody crooked smile that made him look so infernally intriguing.

"Lady Lisbeth," he acknowledged.

She hated it when he used that title. She knew most Americans disliked titles. For heaven's sake, the colonials fought two wars with England to separate themselves from a title-plagued society.

Lisbeth dearly wished she had a retort, but none came to mind, so she simply turned Shadow toward the stable. But a moment later, her curiosity got the best of her. "Deigning to view your new domain?"

He raised an eyebrow at the asperity in her tone. "I thought it might be wise," he said mildly. "I met Fiona's sister. She's an interesting woman."

Lisbeth was afraid to ask why. She liked Eliza Crawford, but the woman was opinionated and didn't hesitate to express her views about the current members of the Hamilton family.

"She didn't care for your Jamie."

Lisbeth immediately stiffened. However, she ignored his comment, dismounting her horse and leading him to the door of the stable.

Ben dismounted too and opened the stable door for her. Hugh had called Ben a ruffian, but, in truth, his manners, except for the occasional brusqueness, were impeccable.

Timothy, one of the boys who worked in the stable with Geordie, approached her. "I'll take yer horse and cool him down, my lady. And yers, sir."

Ben shook his head. "I'll do it myself. Bailey and I are still getting acquainted."

Relinquishing Shadow to Geordie, Lisbeth hesitated a moment, reluctant to leave. "I'll help you rub him down," she heard herself saying to Ben. Now, why had she done that? Lisbeth could have kicked herself.

He smiled. "I accept the offer. Sarah Ann will be up from her nap before long."

Lisbeth watched Ben as he deftly unsaddled the horse and undid the bit, then led the horse around the interior of the stable several times before leading him into the stall. She fetched two currying brushes from the tack room, giving one to him and keeping the other. Wordlessly, she started brushing the horse, trying desperately not to notice Ben's strong hands moving along the animal's withers.

He started whistling a tune she'd never heard before, a lovely but rather mournful melody.

"What is that song?" she asked when he finished.

" 'Lorena,' " he said. "We used to sing it during the war, though it started out as a Reb song."

"What are the words?"

He started singing softly, his voice a true tenor, and she was transfixed by the pure longing of the words.

Years creep slowly by, Lorena.
The snow is on the ground again.
The sun slips down the sky, Lorena.
The frost gleams where the flowers have been."

"It's lovely," she said.
"It's ingrained in my mind," he replied. "You can't

imagine how many times I heard it. Someone said war was ninety-nine percent boredom and one percent pure terror. Songs were all that relieved the waiting. Nothing relieved the terror."

She couldn't imagine Ben Masters being terrified of anything or anyone.

"Were you ever in love?" she asked. The way he'd sung pricked her curiosity.

"Once upon a time," he said. "At least I thought I was. I thought *she* was."

Noting the cynicism in his tone, Lisbeth ventured to ask, "What happened?"

"She didn't want to marry a cripple," Ben said flatly.

Lisbeth's eyes widened in shock. "She was a fool."

His hands were moving along the horse's neck now. "Oh, I don't know," he said. "The doctors all said I would lose my leg. I couldn't blame her."

Lisbeth could. No wonder he eyed her with such suspicion. His opinion of women had to be dismal.

"What happened to her?"

"She married a banker."

"And you went back to war?"

"To staff headquarters. A weak leg didn't matter so much there."

"You could have stayed home."

"I could have," he said, "but there was something I had to do."

"What?"

"I had to find someone." He finished his side of the horse, noticed she had completed hers, and placed a blanket on Bailey.

"It's time to look in on Sarah Ann," he said.

Question-and-answer session was over. He wasn't going to say any more. He was probably sorry he'd said as much as he had.

"Are you going back to the manor?" he asked.

Lisbeth shook her head. "I have to talk to Callum."

"I'll see you at dinner, then."

She didn't want to sit at the same table with him. She didn't want to subject herself to another rebuff. She didn't want to *need*.

"I don't know," she replied.

"Sarah Ann will miss you."

And will you miss me? She couldn't ask.

"Good evening, then," he said. "Sarah Ann enjoyed our morning ride. Thank you for it." He left without another word, leaving her feeling bereft and more confused than ever.

❖❖❖

Ben cursed himself for being every kind of a fool. Why the hell had he told Lisbeth about Claire? Why had he sung that damn song? Why had he even thought of it?

Pure instinct. He had been seeking a way to put distance between himself and Lisbeth. Instead, he'd succeeded in narrowing the gap. In those few minutes he'd spent with her currying the horse, he'd felt a closeness he'd never felt with another adult human being. Not Claire. Not his father. Not Mary May.

The intimacy had been almost painful, yet, paradoxically, he'd felt an intuitive yearning to seek out that intimacy. As if blinders had been removed from his eyes, he suddenly realized that the closeness he'd shared with Lisbeth was the experience he'd been searching for all his life.

And it scared him to death. Scared him as he'd never been scared before. He wanted more of it, wanted it so badly he could taste and feel and smell it. But if he allowed Lisbeth to get any closer to him, would she betray his trust? Or would he find out he'd been taken in by a woman who didn't care for him but only wanted to use him to further her own ends?

He couldn't afford another betrayal. He doubted he would survive another. Hell, after the last one, he'd headed straight for the bottle, and it had taken months to regain control of his life.

But as Ben thought about her kind and lovely eyes and felt yet again their pull, he wondered how long he could go on denying himself the chance to have what his heart so clearly wanted.

Chapter Fourteen

Ben warily eyed the formal wear of the past Marquesses of Calholm.

Barbara's ceilidh was in four days, and he had no appropriate clothes to wear, nor any desire to spend a fortune for clothes he might wear once or twice. Lisbeth had suggested that he investigate the wardrobes still containing clothes from the past masters of Calholm.

There were linen shirts and formal jackets, wide belts, and kilts made of Hamilton plaid. There were no trousers.

He took a kilt out of the wardrobe and studied the infernal thing. The butler stood by watching him. Worry that nothing would please tugged at the old man's lips. Ben knew Duncan remained puzzled by his habits, especially his refusal of a personal servant.

"How do you wear one of these?" he asked, not sure at all he wanted to know. What he did know was that kilts were honored possessions. Barred after the '45 by the English but revived in the early 1800's, in part because of

Walter Scott's romantic novels, they were now part of Scottish national heritage. To wear American clothes would only make him more of an outsider. He didn't want that for Sarah Ann.

So he eyed what seemed to be rolls of worsted like a Texan eyed a rattlesnake: with extreme and respectful caution.

"Lord Jamie wa' not quite as tall as ye," Duncan said, "but closer than the others." He reached in and brought out another roll of red and blue plaid, handling it almost reverently as he unrolled all six yards of it.

"Ye must undress before I can fit it, sir."

Ben was not a modest man. Modesty didn't survive long in a war, nor on long days on the trail with other lawmen. Yet, something about trying on a damned skirt in sight of a stiff, formally dressed butler was uniquely humiliating.

But hell, if he was staying in Scotland, he'd damned well better get used to it.

The thought stopped him. He hadn't realized it, but he really was considering staying.

Stunned, Ben dropped his trousers and underdrawers and submitted to the fitting. The butler showed him how the straps were fastened. The pleats went in the back, the "apron" in the front. Duncan eyed him from every possible angle and nodded. "It will suffice."

Ben wasn't at all sure. He felt naked. "What do you wear under it?" Clearly his longjohns would not do.

The man looked at him as if he'd just committed sacrilege. "Why, naught," he said.

"Naught?" Ben hoped he hadn't heard correctly.

"Naught," the man insisted.

"Doesn't it get cold?"

Duncan cracked a thin smile. "Scots do no' get cold. They used to go into battle stark naked."

"Must have disconcerted the hell out of their enemies," Ben muttered.

Duncan's smile grew a little wider. "Aye."

Ben grinned. "I'll remember that." Then, moving to the nearby mirror, he looked at his reflection. He wondered whether he looked as ridiculous as he felt, whether he could ever parade in front of a hundred guests in this . . . skirt. But he had little choice.

He walked around the room several times, trying to gain some measure of comfort. A damned skirt. Worse, it was a dead man's skirt. What in the hell was he doing?

What would Lisbeth think?

Why did he even care?

By his third turn, he was beginning to wonder why men ever wore trousers.

"Ye look like a Scot." Duncan said in a reverent tone.

"Thank you," Ben said solemnly. "Can you help me get out of . . . this?"

Duncan's face wreathed into a smile. " 'Tis fine to be of service, sir."

The man was so clearly pleased to be of assistance, Ben felt regret, even guilt, at having rejected it so many times. He wondered whether he had hurt the other servants, as well. Still, Ben couldn't imagine anything worse than to have a servant hovering over him day and night. "I thank you," he said. "Not only for helping me with this but for tolerating an American."

Duncan straightened. " 'Tis an honor, an' the young lass be a joy to this house. Maisie, Effie's sister, is making her a fine gown for the ceilidh."

Ben nodded. "What else do I wear with the kilt?"

"I'll have everything ready for ye," Duncan said.

Ben thought it might take more courage to wear those clothes at a ceilidh than it did to go against the Rebs at Vicksburg.

"My thanks again, Duncan." He put on his trousers, feeling a great deal more like himself, wondering whether he would ever be comfortable as a Scottish gentleman.

Ben left the chamber, heading toward the kitchen, and Sarah Ann, whom he suspected was waiting impatiently for her afternoon ride. Annabelle, he hoped, was safely in the bedroom.

In the past few days, he'd made two important discoveries. First, Sarah Ann, like Lisbeth, was a born rider. Second, Annabelle was pregnant; her widening girth wasn't entirely due to the cream she was eating, after all. He decided she'd probably gotten pregnant by one of the mousers on the ship during the voyage over.

Annabelle was enough of a trial. How would he cope with a host of little Annabelles? Ben could see it all now. A half-dozen kittens or more waging war on poor Henry.

Kilts. Swirling mists. A woman who constantly mystified him. Now, a pregnant cat. And not just any pregnant cat but Annabelle! He wondered whether life would ever return to that state he used to think of as normal. Probably not with a little girl around, especially one with unbounded love for all creatures.

Or with Lisbeth around. He'd seen little of her these past days. She was out most of the time with Shadow and Callum, and he made no attempt to join them. She was too dangerous to his peace of mind.

Hugh was also avoiding him, he'd noticed, often disappearing for days at a time. The Scot, though, had held his tongue during the few meals they had shared. Once, Ben even thought he'd seen Hugh smile at something Sarah Ann said. It was a fleeting smile, though, quickly absorbed in the cynical mask the man usually wore.

Ben had grown curious about Hugh, having come to feel more than a little sympathy for him. It had to be difficult to expect so much and get so little. Once the Parliament officially declared Sarah Ann the heir presumptive to Calholm, he planned to have a long talk with Hugh.

Meanwhile, he had spent long hours riding the land and meeting the other tenants. He was reading a history of Scotland and books on husbandry. He'd gone over the estate books kept by Hugh, as well as the stable's records provided by Callum.

Ben had to admit he was coming to understand Barbara and Hugh's position. Calholm was barely making enough to pay the taxes; a killing storm during lambing season could bankrupt the estate, and the horses simply weren't paying their way.

But there had to be a middle ground.

Ben found Sarah Ann, as he had thought, still in the kitchen with Fiona. Annabelle was snaking in between chair and table legs in search of any tidbit. Sarah Ann, already looking the proper horsewoman in her new riding dress, bounced off her chair when she saw him.

"I tried on Maisie's dress, and it's very bonny."

"Bonny?" So she was beginning to use Scottish words.

"Oh, very bonny, Papa. I can't wait for the party. Lady Barbara says everyone wants to meet me." She frowned for a moment. "Except I don't think Cousin Hugh likes me."

"I think you're wrong, Sugarplum. He just has other things on his mind."

"I don't think he's very happy."

The child never ceased to amaze him. She had a little fountain of insight within her.

"I don't think so, either," he replied.

"Maybe we can make him feel better."

"Maybe."

"Can we go riding now?"

"I think that's a fine idea."

"Can we see Mrs. Crawford again?"

The visit to Mrs. Crawford's home had been a great success, but then Sarah Ann took to almost anyone who showed her the slightest interest. She was blossoming under the attention of everyone at Calholm, and she'd not had a nightmare for the past two weeks. Maybe soon she would even give up Mary May's scarf.

"We will wear Mrs. Crawford out," he said.

"Then can we go see Lady Lisbeth ride Shadow?"

Sarah Ann had been asking that question daily, and Ben had purposely ignored it. Lisbeth was like lightning to his thunder. They went together, but the mixture created an explosive storm. He wasn't sure how many more storms he could survive.

But surely watching couldn't hurt. "All right," he said. "We best put Annabelle upstairs first."

Fiona shook her head. "Annabelle and me, we be getting used to each other."

"Are you sure?" he asked dubiously.

"As long as tha' big lout of Henry is outside."

Ben was afraid the cook was remembering that scene in the foyer several weeks ago. A twinkle in her eye affirmed it.

Sarah Ann was grinning, too. She was beginning to love this place, he sensed, and people were beginning to love her. His goal, when he'd decided to come to Scotland, had been to give Sarah Ann up if she found her true family—and a happy home. He was no longer sure he could do that. But neither was he sure he could stay forever in a country that wasn't his.

But the decision didn't have to be made yet. There were still mysteries to solve.

The quiet and peace of the past weeks, since he'd returned from Edinburgh, had almost made him believe the accidents had been just that: accidents. *Almost,* however, was not *certain.*

"Papa!"

His attention was being demanded.

"All right, Sugarplum. Annabelle can stay here with Fiona, and may the saints preserve them both." He gave Fiona a wink. "We'll go watch Lady Lisbeth."

❖❖❖

Lisbeth put Shadow through the usual routine. The horse no longer balked at any of the hazards, and she was delighted by the smoothness of his jumps. She felt she could fly over the moon with him.

Geordie was watching today. Callum meant to start him riding Shadow soon. He would be Shadow's jockey for the Grand National if the training went well. She hated turning Shadow over to another rider. But a woman couldn't ride in the steeplechase, and it was time Geordie got some experience.

Still, it would be like giving up a part of herself. Shadow's training for the Grand National had been like a beacon in a storm of grief and loneliness and isolation. She'd taken a headstrong yearling and turned him into something magnificent. From now on, she would only be an onlooker.

Unless Ben Masters came to share her vision.

It always came back to him. She might train dozens of horses like Shadow in her lifetime, if Ben kept the stables at Calholm. She might have a purpose and a home then. She might get to help raise Sarah Ann, to delight in her childhood and watch her grow into a woman Calholm would be proud to call its Lady. She might even live long enough to come to know Ben Masters.

Although how she would ever live peacefully under the same roof with him, she didn't know. As things were now, she could barely eat or sleep. A single thought or glimpse of him could make her furious or bewildered—or ready to fall into his arms.

Disgusted with herself, angry at having no control over her life or her emotions, Lisbeth gathered Shadow's reins and prepared for the next jump. She had started her approach when, out of the corner of her eye, she caught sight of Ben and Sarah Ann riding into the meadow. It shouldn't have mattered; she was used to people coming and going. But her attention shattered the instant she knew Ben was there, watching her.

Shadow sensed her mental lapse and lost stride, swerving at the last moment and stumbling, going down. Lisbeth threw her feet from the stirrups to clear the horse's body and crashed into the heavy bush. Even as her body registered pain, she frantically looked for Shadow.

He had regained his footing and stood trembling on all four legs. *Thank God and all His angels.* She tried to stand, but pain shot up her left leg, and she fell back down. She saw Ben leaping from his horse and running toward her with no hint of a limp in his stride.

Callum reached her first.

She gave the trainer a reassuring smile. "I'm all right. See to Shadow."

He turned and glowered at the approaching Ben Masters. "Daft man."

"It's not his fault," she said. "You yourself often ride in when I'm jumping Shadow. I just . . . lost my concentration."

"Better he go back where he came from," Callum muttered.

"Callum, please see to Shadow. He's nervous."

Callum did as she asked, but he glared at Ben, who had reached her and knelt by her side. "Are you hurt?"

She grinned at him despite the pain. "As you said the other day, only my pride."

He didn't smile. Instead, his hands moved over her leg carefully and very gently. When he reached her ankle, she couldn't help but cry out.

"It was my fault," he muttered. "I should have known better."

How could he? How could he know that he disrupted her every thought and shattered her peace of mind?

"It wasn't anyone's fault but my own." Her words faded to a choked whisper when he started to pull off her boot. The ankle was already swelling, and she held her breath until he finally tugged it off. The pain rolled through her and, for an instant, she thought she might faint.

Ben's hands touched her stockinged ankle, as light and sensitive as any surgeon's. "I don't think it's broken," he said. "Probably just a bad twist. Some cold water and tight bandages will probably fix it." He then checked the bloody scratches on her arms and hands.

She thought about his easy dismissal of his own war

injuries and felt like a total fraud. "It's nothing. If you can help me up?"

"Aye," he said but then he leaned down and scooped her into his arms.

"I can—"

"Nay, you canna," he said, gently mocking her. "It is just starting to hurt."

"How do you know?"

"Every soldier becomes a doctor of sorts," he said.

Lisbeth surrendered. He wasn't going to put her down, and, anyway, she liked being carried. She'd never been held this way before, not even when she was a child. Jamie had never carried her, nor showed her the tenderness Ben was showing her now.

She heard the beat of his heart, felt the whisper of his breath against her cheeks, felt the strength in his arms and chest as he cradled her against him. Her arms went up and around his neck—to help him, she told herself. But she knew the truth was she wanted to touch him.

He released her when he reached his horse, helped her stand on one leg, then assisted her into his saddle and mounted behind her. The feel of him pressed tightly against her was enough to make the pain in her leg fade. She found herself leaning back, burrowing against his chest.

Lisbeth had barely been aware of Sarah Ann riding silently beside them. But when she turned her head and saw Sarah Ann's pinched face and her hands clasped tightly around the reins of her pony, her heart broke. The child had seen more than her share of accidents. And every one of them must remind her of her mother's death.

Lisbeth suddenly felt cold, and snuggling against Ben Masters didn't help.

When they reached the manor, Ben dismounted first and tied Bailey to one of the posts. He helped Sarah Ann down and tied her pony to another post, then returned to Lisbeth. He reached for her and lifted her again into his arms. Her arms went around him without thought this time. "I'll take you inside and we'll do something about that ankle."

He carried her into the library and lowered her onto a sofa.

Duncan appeared immediately. "Lady Lisbeth? What happened?"

"I fell from Shadow. I only hurt my ankle a wee bit. It will be fine tomorrow."

He looked stricken. "Lord Jamie . . ."

"It was nothing like that," she said. "But we could use some chocolate for the lassie."

Duncan turned around. Sarah Ann was hugging the door, her scarf clutched in her hand.

Ben swore softly, then quickly crossed over to the child. "We can use your help, Sugarplum," he said. "Go ask Fiona for some bandages, some soap and water."

Sarah Ann hung back. "Will she be all right?"

Lisbeth bit her lip at the fear in the child's tone. "Of course I will," she said. " 'Tis just a small bit of inconvenience."

Sarah Ann crept toward her. "You're not going away?"

"Of course not, love."

Sarah Ann's eyes reflected disbelief.

"Come over here," Lisbeth said, and Sarah Ann moved to her side. "Surely you've had a wee fall and were just fine."

Sarah Ann nodded.

"And I imagine your papa was a bit of a fussabout then, wasn't he?"

Sarah Ann smiled and took her hand. "He scolded me, too."

"That was because he cared about you."

"Why doesn't he scold you?"

Ben stooped next to her. "I was just about to do that, Sugarplum. But no one likes being scolded in public, so you'd better run and get some linen for Lady Lisbeth."

Sarah Ann hesitated, leaned down and kissed Lisbeth. "I'm glad you're fine." Then she whispered loudly, "He really doesn't mean it when he scolds, you know," before skipping from the room.

"So much for my authority," Ben grumbled.

"She loves you."

He looked uncomfortable.

"What happened to her mother?"

Pain crossed his face, and she wished she hadn't asked. She couldn't take the words back, though.

"A man killed her."

"Why?"

"He wanted information."

Something about the way he said it made her think he had been involved in some way.

"Sarah Ann wasn't there?"

"No, thank God, but the woman who had been caring for her had to leave at the same time Mary May died. Everything and everyone she knew disappeared within a few weeks. That's why she holds onto the scarf for dear life. It's one of the few things remaining, that and her doll."

"But she had you."

A moment passed, then he said, "She'd just met me."

"So you took on a child you barely knew?" Lisbeth couldn't help the skepticism in her tone.

A sad smile crossed Ben's face. "I made a promise," he said, his hands gently massaging her ankle.

A promise. Other people made promises, too, but she'd found they seldom kept them. Unless Ben had made his promise to take care of Sarah Ann because he'd known about the inheritance.

"And," he added with a bit of embarrassment, "the arrangement has turned all to my benefit."

Because of the inheritance?

"I can't imagine being without Sarah Ann now," he added.

"But it must have been difficult. It must have completely changed your life."

"It has done that," he said dryly. "I hadn't realized—"
He stopped in mid-sentence.

"Realized . . . ?" she prompted, but then a parade of
servants led by Duncan entered the room, carrying water,
bandages, soap, salve. Ben Masters stepped back as Fiona
assumed command. Sarah Ann sidled in, going directly to
his side, and he placed a hand on her shoulder.

As Fiona mumbled and scolded, Lisbeth's attention
was riveted completely on the man and child. There was
something exquisitely tender about their relationship. It
hurt to watch them together, though she didn't know
why.

Perhaps because she had never felt a hand rest affectionately on her as a child, nor had she ever experienced
the smiles Sarah won so easily from the man she called
Papa. To see them, to experience them, was both glorious
and heartbreaking; heartbreaking because it opened the
wounds from her young life, making her feel again the
emptiness and pain she'd thought she'd banished. But
wishing for a different past was selfish and self-indulgent,
so she swallowed hard against the senselessness of it.

Still, if only my own child had lived . . .

Fiona finished cleaning the cuts and applying salve.
She was looking at the swelling ankle when Ben Masters
stepped up. "I'll carry her to her room and put some cold
compresses on it."

Fiona looked at Lisbeth for approval, and she nodded.

At that moment, Barbara came into the room, her
gaze moving from Lisbeth to Ben and back again. "I heard
there was an accident."

Lisbeth sighed. Hugh would probably show up next.
"Just a small fall. I wasn't paying attention."

"Hugh and I warned you about riding," Barbara said.
"Perhaps now you'll—"

"I have no intention of not riding," Lisbeth said.

"But . . . ?" Barbara looked up at Ben appealingly.
"Maybe you can convince her to give up those horses.

They're dangerous. They've already killed one member of this family."

Lisbeth clenched her teeth together. It was just like Barbara to use this mishap to pursue her own cause.

Ben misinterpreted her expression of irritation as pain. "I think this discussion can wait," he said. "I'm taking Lisbeth upstairs."

Barbara bit her lip. "I'll come with you."

"I want to come, too," Sarah Ann echoed.

"I think Lady Lisbeth needs a little rest," he said. "Maybe Barbara can read you a book."

He had neatly trapped Barbara. She could only nod her assent. Ben looked at Sarah Ann until she too agreed, though not too happily.

"There are several books in her room," Ben said, then he leaned down and lifted Lisbeth.

Lisbeth saw Barbara's frustration, Sarah Ann's pout, the servants' amazement—and then she closed her eyes and allowed herself to melt into Ben's arms.

Chapter Fifteen

Ben didn't know whether he was really being protective of Lisbeth or he simply wanted his arms around her again.

When he'd seen her fall, his heart had stopped. Until that moment when he'd faced the possibility of losing her, he hadn't realized how much he cared for her. He *did* realize how unwise it was, even putting aside the suspicions that still lingered in his mind. As much as he was beginning to like Scotland, it would never be home, and he doubted whether he would ever be comfortable at Calholm with its grand house and host of servants.

Lisbeth, a Scot used to every luxury, would not adapt easily to the kind of life he now knew he wanted. The ideas had been dancing around in his head, and though they hadn't yet come together, a few things were clear. He wanted to return home. He wanted to practice law again. Not the kind of law he once practiced with his father— the dry, passionless pleadings for railroad companies and businesses—but the kind that had to do with justice.

He probably should have ignored the summons to Edinburgh. But he'd been compelled to discover the truth about his daughter's inheritance. Now he wondered whether the journey had been a mistake, whether it was wrong to take from others because of an accident of birth. And whether Sarah Ann would truly be happier here than in Denver.

He didn't know. He didn't think he would ever know what was best. And he was driving himself crazy thinking about it.

Ben reached Lisbeth's room with Duncan and Fiona trailing behind, carrying linens and water. Henry had appeared from somewhere and anxiously padded along at his side, his tail drooping close to the ground.

Ben gently placed Lisbeth in a sitting position on her bed, and he was immediately nudged aside by Henry, who desperately licked his mistress, first a hand and then the injured foot, trying to make whatever was hurt well again.

"I don't need a compress," Lisbeth said with a small giggle that made Ben smile.

Duncan tried to push Henry away but the dog had no intention of moving or quitting his ministrations, and frail Duncan was no match for him. Lisbeth didn't intercede. Mischief sparkled in her eyes as she regarded the affronted servants.

"Thank you for your concern," she said, trying to keep a straight face, "but there's been too much fuss already. I promise I'll survive." She scratched Henry's ears as if to convince him of the same thing.

"Are ye sure we canna do something more for you, Lady Lisbeth?" Fiona said worriedly.

"I'm sure," she said, and it was clearly a dismissal.

Duncan and Fiona backed out, obviously not convinced any more than Henry was that their help was no longer needed. When they were gone, Lisbeth looked at Ben. "Thank you," she said huskily.

He raised an eyebrow. "For startling you? It was a stupid thing to do."

" 'Twas my own fault for not concentrating," she said. "Not yours. And I've taken falls before."

That didn't ease his guilt.

"I am sorry about one thing—I made Sarah Ann worry so," she added softly.

"She's all right now," he said, "but I think you're going to miss dancing at the ceilidh."

She shrugged. "The ceilidh is Barbara's affair, and so is the hunt. I will not miss it at all." She grinned suddenly. "I ha' the perfect excuse now."

"I was looking forward to a dance." He hadn't meant to say it, but he realized he'd looked forward to holding her in his arms. "It was to be the one consolation of attending this ceilidh of Barbara's."

She glanced down at his injured leg.

Reading her mind, he said, "I can manage a waltz."

She flushed.

"Don't," he said gently. "I learned to live with it long ago."

"I hate ceilidhs," she blurted out. "I did not even know how to dance until I came here."

That took Ben by surprise. He'd supposed all young ladies of her rank would have had dancing lessons, just as he'd assumed her brothers had taught her to ride. He was wrong on both counts.

He tried to remember other things she'd said, things that hadn't seemed right to him. But he wouldn't pry. That would give her the right to delve into his life, and he wasn't ready for that.

"Will you be riding Shadow in the next few days?" he asked, hoping her answer was no.

A cloud passed over her face. "Geordie will ride him. He was going to start in any event. He'll be jockey at the Grand National."

"You want to ride him yourself?" he said quietly.

"I would give anything," she said fervently. She chewed on her lip. "Do women have more freedom in America?"

Henry had stopped licking her ankle, so Ben started to wet some of the linen and wrap it around the swelling ankle.

"Perhaps a little," he said. "Particularly in the west. But they pay a high price for their freedom."

"Tell me about it."

"It's a hard land. Often harsh. It takes strength to survive. The women usually work as hard or harder than the men. They grow old long before they should." He looked around the room, at the richness of it. "There are few servants."

"You miss it?"

"Yes."

"Is it beautiful?"

He hesitated. "Yes. It's nothing like your hills, though. There are plains that stretch as far as the eye can see, then dry and bare deserts that kill. But even they have a certain beauty, particularly when the cactus bloom. And the mountains . . . they're pure glory."

He stopped talking, and Lisbeth remained silent. Henry had flopped down on the floor, watching Ben's every move with suspicion.

When he finished wrapping her ankle, he started for the door, thinking it the wise thing to do.

"Don't go," she said softly.

He hesitated.

Henry whined.

Ben smiled. "Does he want me to go or to stay?"

"I don't think he knows himself," she said. "He's very possessive, but he likes you."

"How can you tell?" Ben said, amused.

She shrugged. "Have you ever had a dog?"

"No."

"But you like them," she said with assurance. "Henry knows you like him."

"Oh, he does, does he?"

Her face was so serious as she tried to explain dog behavior that he wanted to lean down and kiss her.

"He greets you," she said.

"Doesn't he greet everyone?"

"No. You're really the first," she said, blushing a little at the admission. "You have a way with dogs and children."

"But not with people?"

"Ah, isn't Sarah Ann a wee person?"

He agreed. "Much wiser than she should be."

"She's lucky to have you," Lisbeth said, an invitation in her eyes.

A kind of magic wrapped around them as their eyes met and held, as they spoke a language that needed no words.

Ben hesitated in the doorway a moment longer, then slowly moved back into the room, closing the door gently behind him. It was a damn-fool thing to do, he told himself, but . . .

He returned to her bedside, stood there awkwardly, then sighed as he sat next to her.

Lisbeth's hand stole into his.

"I'm glad you came to Scotland, Ben Masters. But I'm frightened, too."

Astounded, he lifted his other hand to her face and pushed back a curl. "I can't imagine you being frightened of anything." He thought of her racing Shadow over stone walls, something he wouldn't be eager to do, not even with his years of riding over rough country.

But those hazel eyes, golden now with some beseeching quality, were afraid of something. And her fear melted whatever reserve he'd sought to maintain. She turned away but his hand caught her chin, forcing her to face him.

He felt her tremble. He felt himself react in a dozen ways. He felt compelled to kiss her.

He did. Lazily at first, lips touching lips with featherlike gentleness. Then a searching kiss as he sought to explore the essence of her and of his own feelings as well.

Need quickened inside him, and something new, something even more powerful.

The kiss slowly deepened. They relished each step before proceeding to the next, savoring every touch, every new sensation. His hands touched her hair and unraveled the braid, even as his lips and tongue seduced and enticed. Tendrils of curls wove around his fingers as if they longed to be there.

Her fingers touched and explored the back of his neck, drawing patterns that created an exquisite tingling that seemed to reach to every part of his being.

Her lips were alternately gentle and hungry, and her tongue both curious and passionate, shy and bold. When he looked into her eyes, they were startled, like those of a surprised deer. Yet the gold in them seemed to glow with the same desire that was filling him.

He felt sensations new and poignant and aching and glorious. As his hands and mouth sought to give and teach pleasure, he knew he had never really made or given love before. Her body was soft and yielding against his, and his own desire was flaming.

The moments stretched into infinity as he savored the sound of her heartbeat, the sweetness of her mouth, the tender touch of her fingers against his skin. The exquisite sensations built and built until the world was a swirling top of uncontrolled emotion and needs. His hands drifted lower, untying laces at the front of the shirt she wore and moving under her chemise. His fingers caressed her breasts and she moaned slightly, her body going so tense he thought it might break.

His fingers stilled.

"Don't stop," she whispered.

"I was afraid—"

But her mouth closed on his, her lips as greedy as his had been. She undid the buttons of his shirt, and her fingers roamed his chest, sending hot rushes of heat roaring through his body. Her body stretched toward his, and the sudden, sure knowledge that she felt the same need that filled him humbled and excited him. Every part of him was alive and tingling and wanting.

"The servants?"

"They won't come in without knocking."

He still hesitated, want warring with years of discipline, of reluctance to involve himself in anything but the briefest liaison. Only once had he allowed himself anything more—and Mary May had died because of it.

"Ben?"

Even his name sounded lyrical on her lips. Her uncertainty was his undoing. She was so independent, yet so vulnerable—and the combination was irresistible. He swallowed, then with a smothered curse he leaned down and his mouth found the nipple of her right breast.

Soft. So soft. He felt her hand tense in reaction to his touch.

"Dear Heaven," she whispered with a sigh that floated in the air around them. He moved away and lifted her shirt over her head. She raised her arms to help him. There was so much trust in that small gesture that any caution left within him fled.

He'd never wanted anyone so badly.

Their lips met again, their breaths intermingled. She touched his face with a searching tenderness that made him weak. He needed that tenderness, needed it to the depths of his soul. He hadn't known how lonely he had been.

He felt the tremors in her body, as well as in his own. His mouth suckled her breast, his tongue teasing and circling and seducing. Her body arched, and then her hands were doing to him what his were doing to her. The nerves in his body became raw and burning, his manhood hot and throbbing.

He unbuttoned his trousers, did the same with hers, and then both pairs of trousers lay tangled together at the edge of the bed. Only their undergarments lay between them, pieces of cloth that tempted rather than protected.

She arched again, seeking contact.

He hesitated, aware of her injuries. "Lisbeth . . ."

She raised a finger to his lips, quieting him. "You have a handsome mouth, but it doesna smile enough," she said.

"You must hurt—" he began.

"I do," Lisbeth said. "Too much and in ways I shouldn't, but not from the fall. I did not know I could feel like this." He looked as baffled—and as enchanted—as she was, she thought.

He touched her mouth. "You have a lovely mouth but you do not smile enough," he mocked tenderly.

She sighed. The aches and soreness from her fall had disappeared, replaced by need. The need frightened her, the sheer strength of it. The raw hunger was one she had never known before. But for the first time in her life, she felt wanted and needed, and she couldn't keep her hands from wandering all over his body, exploring every inch of him, even as he explored her.

She felt his arousal pressed to her thigh, and her fingers caressed. He groaned deep in his chest, which only encouraged her. She, who had always been so contemptuous of Barbara's affairs, was now beginning to understand.

Jamie used to take her quickly in the dark of their bedroom and then leave for his own room. It was his duty, he'd said, to provide a child, and he'd performed it as such. The love act had not been unpleasant after the first time, but neither had she ever felt much pleasure. But then Jamie had never touched her as Ben was touching her. She'd never known that her body could sing, or that she would want to touch and feel and taste a man. It seemed right and natural. And wonderful.

She had to say so. "I didn't know lovemaking could be like this."

His hands paused in their exploration. "Jamie . . . ?"

She didn't want to criticize Jamie, not now. She didn't want to think of him, didn't want to think that perhaps everything hadn't been perfect at all, that he'd merely needed a son and she'd merely been grateful. She'd made the marriage into something it wasn't, simply because she'd wanted it so badly.

She let her gaze speak the words her lips could not and he pulled her tight against him, his arms offering a safe haven she'd never known. Feelings welled inside, almost overwhelming her. She had always thought love was something you planted and nurtured and harvested. She'd tried so hard to do that with Jamie. But here it was, in full blossom without seeding or tending.

She loved Ben Masters. She'd realized it when he'd leaned over her and picked her up after the fall.

Shyly, she reached for his underdrawers, her hands resting there for a moment. He didn't help. His own hands had stilled, and he watched her with an expression she couldn't decipher.

He took her chin in his hand and forced her eyes to his. "Are you sure?"

"Yes."

"You're hurt." His concern for her filled Lisbeth with a warming tenderness.

"It's nothing," she said, then added with a quick grin, "Perhaps tomorrow . . . I'll be a wee stiff."

He still hesitated, and she wondered whether there was another reason for his reluctance.

"My leg . . . it's not very . . ." he began.

She remembered his fiancée then, remembered the bitterness in his voice as he'd told her about the woman who didn't want a cripple. Ben Masters was anything but a cripple. He possessed a strength that defied the weakness in his leg.

"It does not matter," she said.

After a moment's hesitation, he pulled off his longjohns. It was immediately clear to her that his leg had been nearly ripped apart. Ugly scars covered nearly every inch of it from just above the knee to the ankle. Her fingers gently ran over the scars, wishing that she could go back in time and take away some of the pain he must have felt. She was awed by the stubbornness and will that must have been required to regain the use of the leg.

Ben was tense, as if waiting for her disgust.

She leaned down and put her cheek against the scars. "How did it happen?"

"A place called Vicksburg," he said. "Shrapnel from a cannonball." He paused. "I would have died on the battlefield if a Reb hadn't stopped to give me water and stop the bleeding."

"A Reb?"

"A Confederate soldier. My enemy."

Something in his voice made her ask, "You knew him?"

"Not then. He was captured because he'd stopped to help me, and I couldn't do a damn thing about it. I looked for him for years."

"Why?"

"I owed him," Ben said simply. His hand holding hers tightened.

"Did you find him?"

"A few months ago."

She couldn't imagine a man searching for years to thank someone. Now she understood why he'd come to Scotland with Sarah Ann. Not for himself but for Sarah Ann, for his sense of duty. She had never met anyone like him, hadn't known anybody like him existed.

Lisbeth moved against him, and she felt his immediate response. "You are a very unusual man."

He chuckled, and she felt every rumble through the only scrap of cloth remaining between them: her chemise.

"Unusual? Usually I'm called hardheaded by the kindest of people."

"I think I like hardheaded," she said.

"And I think you have some of that quality yourself."

"I do," she said proudly.

He leaned down and kissed her, and without further hesitation, he lifted her chemise over her head. Then there was nothing between them to prevent their bodies from touching. She felt his arousal, and the yearning inside her turned exquisitely painful.

He pressed her down gently against the mattress, and slid his hand to the triangle of auburn hair between her legs, his fingers soothing and searching, creating shock waves of sensation. His mouth came down on hers. There was little gentleness now, just hard, driving need that fired her own. Her body arched toward his in instinctive demand.

He raised himself, just enough so that his manhood touched the triangle he'd stroked. He moved slightly, probing, exciting, teasing until she was almost crazy with need for him.

Her arms went around him, drawing him to her, into her, and she felt billows of delicious sensation surge through her as he probed deeper and deeper. Slowly, sensuously, until she was crying with a need she'd never experienced before. His movements quickened. Feelings, exquisitely intense, built one upon the other. Her own body was reacting in new, instinctive ways, dancing to the beat of his. Giving, taking, wrapping around him.

"Lisbeth."

It was more a moan than a word as suddenly the world exploded in a kaleidoscope of brilliant colors and cascading sensations. She felt a warm fullness, then quivers of reaction. The urgency faded, but a honeyed sweetness remained as Ben lowered himself and turned slightly so he lay next to her, their bodies still touching, still intimate, still trembling from the splendid journey.

She felt his heart beating. His breath still came in small pants. His arms surrounded her, cradled her, protected her. She loved his nearness, the way her body curved so easily into his.

His hand moved down to hers and clasped it. "Are you all right?"

"Yes," she said softly.

"Your leg?"

"What leg?" she replied, still lost in the magic.

His grip on her hand tightened.

"You're beautiful, Lisbeth."

"No—"

"Dammit, you are. Who made you think otherwise?"

She was silent. No one had ever called her beautiful before. Not even pretty. Her brothers and father had always told her she was homely, too homely to bring about a good alliance, which was the only thing girls were good for. She had been made to feel worthless from the day she was born.

Jamie had wanted her, though. A lord. A future marquess. Even her father had been impressed enough to give her a good dowry. Yet even Jamie had not called her beautiful. Only Ben. How little she still knew about him. How much she wanted to know.

"What happened when you found the man you were seeking?" Somehow, she sensed that man was the key to one of the mysteries surrounding Ben.

He suddenly tensed, remaining silent.

"Is he alive?"

"Yes."

"And well?"

"I imagine so."

"Do Americans always say so little?"

"Yep."

She tried another subject. "Your skin is so dark. Are all Americans bronzed like you?"

"You're asking as many questions as Sarah Ann," he protested, but his tone said he didn't really mind.

"Because I want to know everything about you."

"There's very little to tell."

She twisted her head to meet his gaze. "You are a very complicated man."

"Am I?"

"Yes. I don't know anyone else who would search for years to find someone who had done them a favor, or would take responsibility for a child who wasn't his own." With a smile, she added, "Or for Annabelle."

"You have Henry," he countered. "I don't know anyone who would adopt a hunting dog that doesn't hunt."

"Henry needed me."

A gentle silence ensued. She dropped her gaze and rested her head against his chest. He cradled her, and she was stunned at the contentment—and joy—she felt simply from being held. How could such a thing happen? She'd been so determined to make her own way after Jamie's death. She'd ignored raised eyebrows and Barbara's horror when she'd decided to continue raising jumpers, and especially when she started wearing trousers. She'd resolved to build something of her own. She'd defied convention and scoffed at Barbara's obvious need for a man.

Lisbeth had sworn she would never be like that, that she would never be dependent again.

But, now, for the first time she knew how it felt to be a woman, a desirable woman. She knew how it felt to be touched as if she were a jewel.

"Ben?"

"Ummm?"

"Is your name really just Ben?" she asked.

He raised his head and looked at her, his blue eyes warm and sensuous and amused. The suspicion was gone.

"Does it matter?"

"No. But I told you, I want to know everything about you."

"Everything?"

"Well, your name will do for the moment," she amended hastily, fearing he might retreat from her again, that the suspicion might return.

"It's Bennett Sebastian Masters," he said, kissing her lightly.

"Bennett Sebastian Masters," she mused. "It's very impressive, but I think I like Ben."

"So do I." His mouth curved up in that crooked smile of his.

She wriggled against him, and she felt his arousal.

"God help me," he whispered.

"In for a pence, in for a pound," she said.

He didn't chuckle this time. He laughed. The sound rumbled over her like benevolent thunder. God's laughter. She'd always felt that way about storms.

But she didn't have time to explore that particular thought because he had moved back on top of her, and the sensations she'd felt a while ago paled in comparison to the conflagration that swept through them both.

Chapter Sixteen

What in the hell had he done? Ben asked himself as he changed clothes for dinner.

He had felt like a boy earlier, had even found himself whistling. But then reality had played havoc with the euphoria he'd felt.

He grew hard just thinking about the past couple of hours. And his heart constricted every time he recalled the warm, lazy passion in Lisbeth's hazel eyes or the way she so trustingly wrapped herself around him.

She was so honest with her responses that his suspicions had melted away. If someone intended harm to Sarah Ann or himself, it wasn't Lisbeth. He would bet his soul on it. He *had* bet his soul on it. But problems remained, problems that might well make her hate him.

Ben buttoned his linen shirt, shoved arms into a gray vest and a frock coat, and took a moment to straighten the cravat at his neck. A hell of a lot of clothes to wear just to eat. He hadn't questioned that gentility as a child or young man, but after years of freedom on the plains he resented every last stiff, confining garment.

He kept trying to think of everything but Lisbeth, of the realities he had to face. He still had difficult decisions to make. And he had to focus on the fact that someone still might try to permanently rid themselves of the Masters—father and daughter both. Indeed, he might have succeeded in putting Lisbeth in danger, too.

Ben didn't doubt he was only the second man to bed her. He hadn't intended it to happen, and he'd taken no precautions to prevent creating a child. He was determined that it wouldn't happen again, not as matters stood, not when he might well return to America.

The door opened between his room and Sarah Ann's, and she stood there in her favorite dress. Maisie had helped her with her bath and with dressing. "You look very handsome, Papa," she said.

"And you look ravishing," he told her.

Annabelle haughtily entered the room behind her, tail up in a fit of pique. "Annabelle doesn't look happy," he observed.

"I think she knows we're goin' to leave her again." A bit of wistfulness passed over her face. "Can't we take her to dinner with us?"

"You know she and Henry don't—"

"They really like each other," Sarah Ann assured him. "Really. Lady Lisbeth said so."

"She did?"

Sarah Ann nodded enthusiastically. "Annabelle needs a friend."

"She has you."

"An *animal* friend," Sarah Ann insisted.

Ben sighed. Annabelle didn't look as if she needed anyone at the moment. Despite her natural scruffiness, she obviously thought herself a queen.

"She's lonesome." Sarah Ann pressed her advantage at his silence.

He raised an eyebrow.

"Please. Lady Lisbeth—"

"What about Lady Barbara? And Cousin Hugh?" He didn't really give a flip what either thought, but neither did he wish to end up on the floor again.

"Lady Barbara likes Annabelle. She said so."

Sarah Ann waited patiently, moving from one foot to another as she did.

Annabelle *had* been on her best behavior. And she couldn't stay in the room the rest of her life. Ben closed his eyes, remembering the horrific scene in the foyer: porcelain shattering, armor clanging over the floor, furniture tumbling about.

But he couldn't dash the hopeful expression on Sarah Ann's face. "We'll try it, but—"

"She'll be good. I know it." She hesitated. "She feels like she's been . . . in jail."

Jail. What did Sarah Ann know about jail? He narrowed his eyes. Had she heard him talk about Diablo? Or had she heard her mother say something?

He decided it was best to ignore the comment. To ask was to invite questions he really didn't want to answer. And she was just waiting to ask those questions. He knew it. She may not know what she was asking, but she sensed a new subject, a new adventure. Four years old, and she was as tricky as a forty-year-old.

Well, he'd been clay in her hands long enough for one day. He wasn't going to spend the evening answering questions.

Ben bowed and offered Sarah Ann his hand. She curtsied, grinning, and took his hand. They left the room together, Annabelle prancing royally behind them.

❖❖❖

After Ben left her room, Henry demanded his share of Lisbeth's attention. It was quite obvious to her that his displacement from her bed had wounded him deeply. He'd whined and mumbled, rolled onto his back with his legs awkwardly waving in the air and wriggled until she scratched his stomach.

"You are an impossibly ridiculous dog," Lisbeth told him. Henry growled in happiness. He loved praise. His legs waggled harder.

"But then I'm ridiculous," she continued. "I have you. I don't need Ben Masters." She kept telling herself that. She *couldn't* need him. She *couldn't* want him this badly.

But she did. Her blood turned to molten lava as she thought about touching him again.

Henry whined. She scratched his stomach absently. When had everything changed? When had Henry and the horses faded into the background of her mind, supplanted by Ben Masters?

Ben and Sarah Ann. A man who made her senses sing and a child who made her yearn for one of her own. She wanted to tease a laugh from them, prompt a smile, drive away the ghosts still haunting both father and daughter. She grinned at such fanciful notions. But it was true. She'd rather receive a smile from the four-year-old cherub than ride Shadow to victory. And, God help her, she'd rather make love with Ben than do anything else on earth.

"Darling Henry," she said wistfully. "Why do you suppose your namesake took so many wives? Is love fleeting? Or is it merely lust?"

Henry barked as if he approved of lust, or might like some himself.

"You're such a handsome lad," she said. "We'll have to find you someone." For the first time, she truly understood the joy of mating. The joy and ecstasy and bewilderment. The longing and ache. The uncertainty and fear.

The glory.

It swelled in her as she recalled Ben's every touch, every feeling he evoked in her, every emotion. She thought of those cautious blue eyes that had turned so warm.

What would he be like at dinner? Cool and watchful as he usually was? Warm and teasing as he had been in her bed? Would she be able to keep from reaching out to touch him? Would Barbara realize what had happened?

Full of hesitancy, Lisbeth finally rose from the bed and chose a gown for dinner, one she hadn't worn since Jamie's death. It was subtle and modest, nothing like Barbara's gaily colored finery, but she knew the gray-green silk made the most of her eyes and hair. Barbara and Hugh would raise their eyebrows at it and wonder, but she didn't care. She wanted to look her best, to pale as little as possible next to Barbara.

She was still amazed that Ben preferred her. It was a miracle.

Bennett Sebastian Masters. She allowed the name to roll off her tongue.

Henry started pacing the floor, signaling that he had to go outside. She opened her bedroom door, knowing that Duncan would open the one downstairs. Effie should be up any moment to help her dress. God's toothache, but she disliked dresses with buttons in back, which meant she hated nearly all of her dresses.

Henry bounded out, down the stairs, barking as he went. He was in more of a hurry than usual. She started to close the door, and then she heard a crash. And another one.

She winced.

Then something else crashed, and she heard a screech that sounded as if it came straight from hell.

Annabelle!

A yowl. A child's scream.

Lisbeth opened the door and heard Ben's firm "*Annabelle*," then a string of curses that would have startled the devil himself.

Oblivious that her hair was down, still mussed from lovemaking, and that she wore only a flimsy dressing gown, she limped toward the stairs. At the bottom step, her ankle gave way and she stumbled straight into Ben.

The shock—and immediate physical reaction—kept her from moving for a moment. Then she was aware of silence. Complete, absolute silence.

She lifted her head from his shoulder and looked around. The entire household had gathered in the foyer. Duncan had horror written all over his face. Effie stood, her mouth open in astonishment. Hugh and Barbara were looking on with dismay. Sarah Ann, eyes wide, watched everyone with great interest.

Henry and Annabelle, oblivious to everyone, occupied the center of the foyer. Henry, stretched out, panted heavily. And Annabelle stood directly in front of him, either challenging him or claiming victory, Lisbeth wasn't sure which.

Annabelle's back wasn't arched though—a hopeful sign—and she wasn't hissing at Henry. The armor had fallen again, and so had the fragile table that held the silver bowl designed for visitors' cards.

That was all she noticed before she felt every angle of Ben's body and his heat singed her. She looked up at Ben, and saw amusement dancing in his eyes. God's toothache, but she loved him when he looked like that.

"Lisbeth!"

There was something ironic about Barbara's horrified cry; after all, Barbara had never been subtle about her own affairs.

Lisbeth knew she should move. She was being held by a man in full sight of the entire household. But Ben made no attempt to let her go, and her own legs were none too steady for her to stand on her own.

"Lady Lisbeth." Hugh spoke in a righteous voice that Lisbeth just couldn't take seriously.

"I heard . . . noises," she tried to explain, but it sounded weak even to her. What was she doing in the late afternoon dressed only in a dressing gown, with her hair tumbling down her back, and her face flushing brightly? "I was resting," she added.

Hugh narrowed his eyes and darted an accusing look

at Ben. Barbara looked hurt. Sarah Ann looked interested.

"I'll carry you back up," Ben said. "I think there's been a truce of sorts down here," he added, eyeing Annabelle and Henry. Annabelle had perched herself on Henry's stomach and seemed to be grooming the big dog, who growled contentedly.

"I told you she needed a friend," Sarah Ann said, and everyone turned to stare at her. Barbara and Hugh obviously hadn't noticed her until just then.

Duncan stiffened even more. "I shall see to dinner," he said.

Effie giggled. "I'll be there to help ye dress, Lady Lisbeth."

"This is really quite . . . scandalous," Barbara said, but her lips twitched. Lisbeth thought that perhaps Barbara had a sense of humor after all.

Only Hugh's expression remained black and grew even darker when Ben picked her up. His arms were becoming quite familiar to Lisbeth. His hands seemed to burn right through the dressing gown. She studied his bronze face above the snowy-white shirt and tie. He really was handsome, even with a clenched jaw and a muscle twitching in his cheek.

They were silent until they reached her room and he lowered her to the bed, then sat next to her.

"I think we've just created a scandal," she said.

"I think we did," he said, his lips twitching. "Your sister-in-law was genuinely appalled."

"Only because it wasn't her," she said.

His hand rested on her bare arm. It burned her. He must have felt the heat, too, for he suddenly let go. His eyes devoured her, though.

"At least Henry and Annabelle seem to have made peace." She tried desperately to hold on to some control.

"Annabelle is mellowing with the coming of motherhood. Still, I wouldn't be surprised to see her chasing Henry tomorrow. She can be rather fickle."

Lisbeth had heard only one word he spoke: mother-hood.

"I'm pretty sure she isn't getting that fat with cream," Ben continued.

"Sarah Ann must be delighted."

"She's not the one who has to find homes for Anna-belle's litter. It isn't going to be easy. Annabelle isn't ex-actly the most beautiful cat alive. And God knows her temperament would test His fondness toward all living things."

"Sarah Ann thinks she's beautiful."

"Hmm," he murmured.

Intimacy was cocooning them again. She was aware only of him, of the warmth that flooded her body, of the headiness of being with him. She closed her eyes, en-joying the sensations, relishing the closeness. Then, she felt a sudden chill, and she opened her eyes.

He looked at her strangely, his head tilted as if in question. He was no longer smiling. The muscle contin-ued to twitch in his cheek, though. "I'd better leave be-fore more damage is done to your reputation," he said stiffly.

Hurt and bewildered by his change in mood, she tried to shrug indifferently. She wanted to ask why, but she couldn't. Everything was too new, too fragile.

"Barbara will always think the worst, and so will Hugh," she stated.

"And the servants?"

"I'm not sure."

He hesitated a moment, as if he wanted to say some-thing, but then he rose. "I'll see you at dinner." He turned and disappeared out the door, leaving her feeling more than a little bruised, but not from the physical injuries.

❖❖❖

Dinner was a stiff, formal affair. Hugh was barely polite. Barbara chattered but her gaze kept moving from Ben to Lisbeth and back again. Sarah Ann said little and was watchful. Lisbeth was silent, looking more than a little mystified. Ben couldn't blame her.

What the hell he was doing? He had compromised Lisbeth in more ways than one. A gentleman would propose marriage. But he had no intention of marrying. His luck with women was dismal; his judgment lacking. And he couldn't escape the fact that Lisbeth wanted something from him, something he wasn't sure he could give.

The more he studied Calholm's books, the more he realized that Hugh and Barbara were right. Continuing with the horse-breeding could mean the bankruptcy or loss of Calholm, Sarah Ann's legacy. Even if Shadow won the Grand National, he doubted the horses would ever pay their own way. But doubling the number of sheep would double the income. Ben could never evict the tenants, even if he had the right, but the training and hunting fields could be turned into pasture for sheep.

How would Lisbeth feel about him then?

He already knew, dammit.

He'd been a fool to make love to her. He'd been a bigger fool to make it public, even inadvertently.

"Ben?"

Barbara's decidedly cool voice brought him back to the dinner table.

"I just thought you should know I've employed extra servants for the next few days for the ceilidh. Some of the guests will be staying two nights."

He nodded, but his gaze lingered on Lisbeth, on the way she looked in a silk dress that emphasized every slender curve and made her eyes deep and mysterious.

"I'll give you a guest list tomorrow and go over them with you," Barbara persisted.

Ben had no choice but to turn his attention to her. Hugh was frowning, jealousy apparent in his stare. He abruptly got up from the table and left without an explanation.

Barbara looked flustered for a moment. "I don't think . . . he feels well," she said, trying to excuse him.

Lisbeth sighed. "Hugh told me this morning he plans to leave Calholm after the ceilidh."

Barbara visibly paled. She bit her lower lip before covering her dismay with a slight smile. Her hands trembled, though.

"He told *you?*"

"He was saddling his horse when I went out to ride Shadow," Lisbeth said. "He told me he would be sorry not to see Shadow at the steeplechase, and I asked why. He said something about Australia or America."

Ben watched Barbara's fingers tighten around her wine glass, and saw the fear in her eyes. Did she really care about Hugh that much? Even if she did, it hadn't stopped her from trying to seduce Ben and secure control of Calholm. That her heart might belong to Hugh had to be little comfort to the man who obviously loved her . . . and coveted Calholm.

Ben's gaze met Lisbeth's. She was obviously searching for an explanation for his bewildering change of mood. He couldn't explain. Not now. Maybe not ever.

Ben was the first to lower his gaze, but not before he saw the hurt in Lisbeth's face. He wanted to erase it. He wanted to kiss it away. But it would be a lie.

He would hurt her again and again. He simply couldn't trust totally. He had used too many people in his days as a lawman to believe others didn't do the same.

He'd never realized until now how bitter that legacy was.

Chapter Seventeen

Calholm filled rapidly with guests. Standing in the foyer with Sarah Ann beside him, Ben greeted them as they arrived. He tried to keep all their names straight. There were countless Hamiltons, many with the same first names. Then there were Lockharts, Flemings, Douglases, Montgomeries, Carmichaels, Boyds, and Cunninghams. And amidst the chaos, an army of servants, most hired from the village, scurried around like ants.

After an hour of shaking hands and introducing himself and Sarah Ann, Ben was beginning to feel like an exotic insect on display, a "colonial" to the Scots, who wanted tales of gold and Indians. Moreover, his ears tired from deciphering the often heavy Scots accent. Added to that, he knew he would never get used to appearing in public wearing a skirt with nothing under it—and it didn't make him feel one bit better that every other man in attendance was wearing one, too. He felt naked and embarrassed.

To top it all off, he was wondering who was paying for all this. Calholm could ill afford the extravagance.

Ben sighed. It was too late to do anything about any of it. All he could do was continue to shake hands and remind himself that it was for Sarah Ann, which made it worth the discomfort.

So, he endured the newcomers' questions, their inspection and their obvious skepticism. All knew about the missing heir, the adoption, the guardian. All had a fair amount of suspicion in their eyes. He was incredibly proud of Sarah Ann, who smiled and chatted courteously and curtsied again and again, charming everyone who met her.

While Ben was patiently trying to answer two elderly Scotsmen's questions about Indians, he saw Duncan admit the one guest he had hoped wouldn't come: Andrew Cameron. The damned Scot swept in as if he were Bonnie Prince Charlie.

Sarah Ann saw him, too, and before Ben could stop her, she ran to Cameron. He swung her up into the air, earning gales of laughter and demands for a repeat. Cameron complied, then headed straight toward Lisbeth, who was sitting on a sofa in deference to her ankle and looking lovely in a gray silk gown. Cameron took her hand and held it much too long for Ben's taste. The two exchanged greetings, then Sarah Ann whispered something in Lisbeth's ear and Lisbeth whispered back, and Sarah Ann giggled. Then Cameron said something that made both females giggle.

Ben felt left out, and thoroughly irritated. He didn't want to believe his reaction had anything to do with jealousy.

"Ben said you two had met."

Ben barely heard Lisbeth's words to Cameron. His ear was being bent by Alex Douglas, who was rambling on with some nonsense about Indians he'd read in a book written by an author who obviously had never set foot in America.

When the man paused for breath, Ben heard Cameron say to Lisbeth, "And how do you like the new . . . master of Calholm?"

And then Alex Douglas began talking again, and Ben couldn't hear anything else. But he saw Lisbeth laugh, and the beat of his heart slowed. His throat felt constricted, and he wanted to march the few feet toward Cameron and land a fist in his face.

"Don't Indians scalp their enemy?" Douglas said. "And run around naked?"

Ben wanted to retort that compared to the Scots and their kilts, Indians were overdressed.

"I heard your Scots army fought naked," he said instead.

"But that was hundreds of years ago," Douglas pointed out.

"Have you ever been in an Arizona desert?"

"I have not." The Scot drew himself up indignantly.

"I suspect if you had, you might think nakedness rather desirable," Ben said. "And now if you will excuse me . . ."

He made his way over to Andrew Cameron and Lisbeth. "Cameron," he acknowledged shortly.

"Drew," Cameron said. "Friends call me Drew."

Ben nodded, his gaze dropping to Lisbeth's, noting the slight flush on her cheeks. Even Sarah Ann looked at Cameron with uninhibited adoration.

The jealousy he'd tried to deny sliced through Ben like a sword. He'd never known anything like it before, had never tasted its bitterness.

He hated it. And he didn't understand it. Drew Cameron didn't threaten anything he had, or wanted.

Liar! an inner voice mocked him. *You want Lisbeth, and you know it.* The voice was so strong, so honest. He did want her. Not just for an afternoon or a night. He wanted her forever. He wanted her laughter and her determination, and her gentleness with Sarah Ann, and her love for Henry, whom no one else had wanted.

"Drew is going to ride Shadow for me tomorrow," she said, and Ben realized only an instant had passed, not the lifetime that such a soul-shattering discovery should take.

The jealousy cut even deeper. The hunt would be for grouse in the morning, followed by races over the steeplechase course in the afternoon. They would take the place of a fox hunt, which Lisbeth refused to sanction. The race would give her a chance to show off Shadow, and she had planned to ride herself until her fall.

Ben raised an eyebrow. "I thought Geordie—"

"He's not experienced enough," Lisbeth said. "Drew's raced in steeplechases before. That's how Jamie and I met him. He's a superb rider."

Ben realized his resentment was unreasonable. He had consciously played down his riding and shooting abilities. He was also intelligent enough to know that riding through mountains and deserts and valleys was not comparable to navigating a steeplechase course, with its closely placed hazards, some six feet high. He had few doubts he could keep his seat, but he would hold the horse back.

"I wish you luck," he finally told Drew. "I know how much this means to Lisbeth . . . and to Calholm."

"It will be good to have a Calholm mount again," Drew said. "They're the best in Scotland."

"In Britain," she corrected him.

"In Britain," he agreed with a smile.

And I might be the one who has to take them from her. Ben's lips pressed together into a thin line. There had to be another way.

Drew turned to him. "You've decided to stay in Scotland?"

"I'm still waiting for word from your Parliament," he replied.

"I'm thinking about going to your American West," Drew said.

Ben hid his surprise.

"Where would you suggest?"

"Depends on what you're after."

"Money." Drew shrugged. "Gold. Excitement."

"Like Ian Hamilton?" Ben knew it must be common gossip now how Ian had died, shot down during a poker game.

"I don't intend to end up like Hamilton." There was something suddenly hard in Drew Cameron's voice, and Ben wondered whether he had underestimated the Scot, dismissing him as an aimless young lord who made a precarious living at gambling.

"There's gold fields in Colorado, silver mines in Montana. Mining camps are good places for gamblers . . . if you're honest. If you aren't, you'll likely end up at the end of a rope. There are few formalities in the west."

Drew nodded. "I'll take your advice. As you've probably discovered, there's many an impoverished gentleman in Scotland. Ships headed for America are loaded these days."

Ben thought of two other impoverished Scotsmen: Ian and Hugh. It had to be difficult to be born in wealth, grow accustomed to it, and then be left with little or nothing because of archaic inheritance and tax laws.

Regardless, he would be glad as hell to see Drew Cameron leave Scotland.

Barbara came over then, drawing Ben away to meet two new arrivals. Sighing inwardly, he followed her. He would have sold his soul at that moment to be able to toss Lisbeth and Sarah Ann, even Henry and Annabelle, onto the nearest ship and take them to Colorado. He wished for his own horse, and he longed for the mountains and rich valleys. He longed for the home he hadn't really considered a home until he thought he might lose it. He longed most of all for Lisbeth to share it with him.

He longed for much more than he'd ever had.

But at the moment, a kilted Scot and his wife stood waiting for introductions, and Ben could see the questions about barbarous Indians and ruthless gunslingers on the tip of their tongues, waiting to be asked.

❖❖❖

Lisbeth couldn't dance with her twisted ankle, but she watched and tapped her foot to the tunes provided by the small band of musicians Barbara had hired. She loved the fiddles and flutes, the infectious gaiety of Scottish music.

Barbara, as usual, was in great demand, but she was saving most of her dances for Hugh, which was odd. Usually, she flirted with everyone, giving no man more than a dance or two. She had been unusually attentive to their distant cousin lately.

And Ben. Dear God, he looked magnificent in the plaid and jacket. His primal strength was emphasized by the heavy belt and jeweled dirk. He towered over everyone present, and his hard bronzed visage was striking among the paleness of many of the other faces. He looked, in fact, like a chief of old, dominating the room with his very presence.

Lisbeth noted that despite Ben's bad leg, he danced well. She'd already known by his speech and manners that he'd been raised as a gentleman, and this evening she'd seen further proof of it. In selecting partners who had few offers, he showed an innate kindness and compassion.

Ben Masters was truly an extraordinary man. She only wished he wasn't such a puzzle, a living, breathing contradiction. She was quite convinced he was a man who had lived on the edge of danger and had never stopped looking for it, even though he claimed to be a lawyer. He was also a man used to being alone. What else could explain the distance he tried to maintain between himself and anyone else, including her?

"Lisbeth?"

Lisbeth tore her gaze from Ben and looked up to see Drew Cameron standing beside her. "You look lost in thought."

"What do you think of Ben?" She shouldn't ask such a question, but she trusted Drew's judgment. There was much more to him than the profligate gambler he appeared to be. She often wondered why he flitted around like a gadfly when he had a mind like a steel trap.

His face screwed up thoughtfully. Then, sitting beside her, he said, "He's what he seems, and he's not."

"That's cryptic enough."

Drew grinned. " 'Tis the best I can do. I have few doubts he's a solicitor. He thinks like one. But he's more than that. I can't put my fingers on it, but . . . there's a sharp edge to him. He doesn't trust me, but I can't fault that."

"I think you're one of the most trustworthy people I know," she protested.

"Few would agree with your discerning generosity concerning my character," he returned lightly.

"I don't think he trusts me, either," Lisbeth confided. She needed to talk to someone, and Drew was the one person, other than Callum, she really considered a friend. He always made her feel comfortable and worthy of respect, perhaps because he too came from the Highlands.

"I've seen the way Masters looks at you," Drew said. "He practically devours you. And your eyes shine when you look at him."

"Is it that obvious?"

"I'm afraid it is, my dear."

She sighed. "Barbara wants him."

"I think Barbara is occupied with Hugh. And in Edinburgh your Ben Masters didn't look at her the way he looks at you."

"He isn't mine. I'm not sure I even want anyone to be mine."

"Why?"

"I like being independent," she said, biting her lip. "I didn't know how much until . . ." She stopped, realizing she'd almost said "until Jamie died." She said a quick prayer for forgiveness.

"It's all right," Drew said gently. "You didn't cause his

death. Don't blame yourself for finding a measure of freedom."

She reached out and touched his hands. "Thank you," she said. "And now you'd better go and dance with Miss Carmichael. She's been looking at you expectantly."

"And Masters is looking at me as if he'd like to cut my throat," Drew said with amusement. "Always a good sign." He rose and went in the direction of Flora Carmichael.

Flora's father took the seat next to Lisbeth. "Tha' Masters looks like a sensible lad, not a wastrel like some." His eyes went to Drew Cameron and his daughter.

Lisbeth held her tongue. She knew Drew was not considered good husband material, but she also knew Drew *would* make a good husband. Like Ben, there was a kindness in him that some mistook for weakness or even deception.

Alex Carmichael grumbled a few more sentences about ne'er-do-wells, then switched to the subject of horses. "I've been hearing about that jumper of yours. Lookin' forward to seeing him. Too bad there's no fox hunt. Can really test a horse that way."

"He's a fine, spunkie lad," she said. And Carmichael had a stallion she would dearly love to mate with Shadow's dam.

"We'll see," Carmichael muttered. He'd brought two of his own horses to race Shadow, one for each of his sons.

"Mourning's 'bout over," he said, abruptly changing the subject as he eyed her gray silk gown. "Been two years since young Jamie fell."

She nodded, afraid of what was coming next.

"My two lads are anxious to marry," he said hopefully.

She doubted that. His sons had populated the midlands with bastards.

Lisbeth was saved from an answer by the arrival of Ben, who had completed a dance with one of the Fleming daughters. Something dangerous sparked in his eyes, and that menace she sometimes sensed in him vibrated like a scream in a Highland valley.

Alex Carmichael must have sensed it, too, because he quickly excused himself, heading toward Drew Cameron and his daughter, who were whispering in a corner.

Lisbeth could almost taste Ben's fury, so strong was it, and she couldn't imagine what it was all about. Surely not because Drew had been sitting with her.

Ben stared at her as if he'd never seen her before, and she felt a sense of foreboding. His mouth twisted as if he'd discovered a very unpleasant truth.

Was it something Barbara had said? Or someone else?

"Are you enjoying . . . this?" she asked inanely, desperate to break Ben's menacing silence.

"Your Scottish dances are confounding," he said. His jaw was clenched and his eyes wintry.

"I'll teach you when this ankle works again."

"Will you, now?" he asked.

A shiver passed through her body. He was a stranger, as much a stranger as when she found him in the wrecked coach.

"Aye," she said, puzzled.

She would have given anything to know what he was thinking. She felt small, as if he'd suddenly found something lacking in her. How many times had that happened before? She bloody well wasn't going to endure it again.

She looked directly into his eyes and went on the offensive. "You seem to be doing well enough. You don't need anyone, do you, Ben Masters?"

"No," he said, and turned away. He headed toward Flora Carmichael, who, with the exception of Barbara, was probably the prettiest woman at the manor that evening. Pain tugged at Lisbeth, and she struggled against tears that formed rebelliously in her eyes.

She stood unsteadily for a moment, trying to regain her composure. It was too early to leave without being noticed, but she couldn't stay in the same room with Ben Masters.

"Lady Lisbeth?" Duncan was at her side. "The little lass. Effie took her up to her room, but she . . . willna go to bed. She wants her fa."

Lisbeth looked at Ben, who was dancing with Flora Carmichael as Flora's father watched and beamed. If that was what Ben wanted, he was bloody well welcome to it. Flora Carmichael didn't have a brain in her head.

"I'll go up," she said, relieved to have an excuse to leave. The room was suffocating, unbearable.

Lisbeth limped up the stairs. The pain in her ankle was nothing compared to the pain in her heart. Was Ben rejecting her because she had lain with him? Had she not lived up to his expectations? Had she been so inadequate? But then she remembered the fury she saw in his eyes.

Blindly, she stumbled to her own room. Henry wagged his tail so frantically and moaned so pitifully, she decided to take him to Sarah Ann's room with her.

"You be good," she warned him, though her heart wasn't in the warning.

When she reached Sarah Ann's room, the little girl was standing on the bed in her nightgown, her red hair flowing down in tight ringlets. Tears ran down her cheeks. "I don't want to go to bed," she said the moment she saw Lisbeth.

Lisbeth went over to her. "Why?"

"I just don't," Sarah Ann said stubbornly. Annabelle, who had taken one of the huge pillows as her bed, eyed the dog warily but stayed put.

"All right," Lisbeth soothed. "I'll stay here with you."

Sarah Ann looked at her suspiciously. "You'll leave me, too."

Lisbeth now understood—and sympathized. "Is that why you don't want to go to sleep? You're afraid no one will be here when you wake up?"

Now that she thought about it, Ben had put the child to bed each night. Had he stayed by her side until she went to sleep? It was a new side to the American. Lisbeth couldn't imagine another man being as devoted to his child as Ben was.

Lisbeth's fear when she was growing up was different from Sarah Ann's. Lisbeth had been afraid of her father, had not wanted him around. His anger would explode without warning, his fist would strike her for some infraction she didn't understand.

"I'll stay with you," Lisbeth assured the child.

Sarah Ann brightened. "Will you?"

Lisbeth smiled. Sarah Ann's trust was like a balm to recent wounds. "Aye. I'm a bit lonesome, too."

Sarah Ann sat down on the bed. The doll, Suzanna, was with her. Annabelle made a slight hiss of annoyance at being disturbed. Lisbeth sat down, too, and Sarah Ann cuddled into her arms. "I love you, Lady Lisbeth," she said.

Lisbeth's heart turned to jelly. No one had ever said that to her before. Not even Jamie.

"I love you, too, Sarah Ann," she said.

"I want you to be my mama."

Lisbeth went absolutely still. She had no idea what to say. So she hummed a lullaby instead, a song one of her nannies had sung to her, until she felt Sarah Ann relax against her. In minutes, the child's breathing was soft and regular.

Lisbeth lowered her to the bed, then she lay down next to her, keeping an arm protectively around the child.

I love you. Such incredibly sweet words. No pretense. No reservations. No doubts.

Not like Sarah Ann's father.

❖❖❖

Ben suffered through the rest of the night until early morning, when the guests either retired to the rooms they'd been given in the manor or went home. He was left with Barbara, whose face was flushed with success, and

Hugh, who stood in the library doorway with a glass in his hand.

He lifted it in salute. "Congratulations," he said with a trace of bitterness. "The King is dead. Long live the new King."

Barbara's flush deepened. "Hugh . . ."

Hugh silenced her with a look, then turned back to Ben. "I heard from one of our guests that Parliament is about to approve your petition. They couldn't wait to reveal the news."

"Sarah Ann's petition," Ben corrected.

"Don't be a hypocrite," Hugh said. "You're going to benefit from this in no small way. Would you have come all this way otherwise?" His face was red with drink and anger.

Ben looked at Barbara. "Would you excuse us?"

She hesitated.

Hugh's angry expression faded. "It's all right, Barbara. I'm not drunk enough to hit him, and dueling went out years ago."

Barbara went white, and she rushed from the room.

"Don't worry, Masters," Hugh said harshly. "I'm not contesting your bloody petition. I don't have the money, and no solicitor would touch the case without it. I'll be leaving Calholm in a few weeks."

Ben ignored the other man's hostility. "You told me Calholm could be run profitably. Did you mean it?"

Hugh narrowed his eyes. "Not without selling those horses off."

"And the tenants?"

Hugh shrugged. "If sheep grazed the acres now being used for the horses, we could use more shepherds. It would make some sense to keep the tenants."

"Where do you plan to go?"

"Where do all the impoverished go? To America. God knows I hate running away from debts, but now I have no way to pay them. Perhaps someday—"

"How much?"

Hugh hesitated. Ben could almost read his thoughts. Why did he want to know?

Hugh finally shrugged and said, "I suppose you might as well know, too. It's common knowledge and my creditors will probably try to collect from you." He hesitated, then added, "Nearly five thousand pounds."

"I'll pay them when the inheritance is settled," Ben said.

Hugh stared at him. "Why in the bloody hell would you do that?"

"The Hamilton name is involved," Ben said coldly. "I don't want Sarah Ann's inheritance tarnished." That wasn't why at all, but he suspected it was an explanation Hugh would accept. He didn't want to explain his other reasons. Not yet.

Some of the petulance left Hugh's handsome face. His mouth worked slightly and he turned away, toward the window that looked out over the wide expanse of gardens.

Ben left without another word. He climbed the steps up to his room. Though the house was full, there was an eerie emptiness about it at this early hour of the morning. He wondered whether that was true of every large house, and whether one ever got used to it.

The door to Sarah Ann's room was closed. Ben opened it. A small flame flickered from an oil lamp in a corner, and he saw several forms in the feather bed. He finally made out Henry on the end, Annabelle curled between his two mammoth paws, and Lisbeth's arms around Sarah Ann.

Lisbeth was still dressed in her gown, and her curls had fallen from the twist laced with flowers. Petals lay spilled on the pillow. She looked fragile in the huge bed. Fragile, innocent, and so desirable.

He felt his loins ache again as he remembered their lovemaking, the incredible sweetness of it. Something he couldn't allow to happen again. But God, how he wanted it. Needed it.

Quietly he entered his own room. He undressed hurriedly, leaving only a shirt on his back, and poured himself a drink before sitting down on the bed and stretching out his leg, now aching from the night's activities.

Tonight, he hoped he had eliminated at least one of the potential dangers to Sarah Ann. He had thrown Hugh Hamilton a rather large, tasty bone, which should reduce at least some of Hugh's desperation.

And Lisbeth? Christ, he couldn't think logically about her. Especially when she slept in the next room.

He'd heard some of the words that had passed between her and Drew Cameron. He'd also seen the affection and intimacy between the two. Everything in him had fought against the idea of their being conspirators. But Cameron had been present both times Ben and Sarah Ann had been in "accidents." Cameron and Lisbeth appeared more than friends. And Lisbeth stood to inherit more money if Sarah Ann died, perhaps even enough to support a stable or at least Shadow.

And maybe the accidents had been just that: accidents. Maybe pigs danced the waltz.

He finished the glass of whisky and placed his pistol under his pillow.

God, how it would kill him if he found out Lisbeth had plotted murder—and that his trust had been misplaced. Again.

Chapter Eighteen

Ben did not look forward to the grouse hunt. He'd hunted for food, but he'd never understood the allure of killing for sport.

Nevertheless, he took the shotgun provided by Duncan, mounted Bailey, and rode with the other men to a wooded area beyond the loch.

His eyes kept going to the ruins. Like the day he visited it with Lisbeth, mist rose from the green hills, enveloping part of the castle ruins and leaving the remainder to rise like a magical kingdom from the clouds.

Some of the guests had brought their dogs. Once the men were in position, the dogs would flush out the grouse.

Ben tried to be polite to the other hunters but he had little in common with them. They lived for sport, for social occasions, for the politics of their country. Several, he'd discovered, were in Parliament. He felt different, an outsider tethered to events he despised for the sole reason of securing a future for his daughter. He was beginning to feel more and more it wasn't worth it, neither for himself nor for Sarah Ann. He didn't fancy her having a life like Barbara's: empty, aimless. Lisbeth had done something with hers, but at the expense of convention, and he'd discovered few other women in Scotland took life by the tail as she did.

Damn, he wished he knew what was best. For everyone.

He had looked in on Sarah Ann before joining the hunters. Lisbeth and Henry had already left, but Lisbeth's flowery scent remained, filling him with a longing that was becoming entirely too familiar. A sleepy Sarah Ann gave him a lazy hug when he sat down on the bed and woke her. He hadn't wanted her to wake up and find she was alone. She still became frightened, still clung to her doll and the green scarf.

"Where's Lady Lisbeth?" Sarah Ann had asked sleepily.

"I think she had to go look after guests," he'd replied, thinking it more likely that she'd wanted to avoid him. Well, he had done a good job of making sure she felt that way.

He'd thought about her all night, kept seeing the image of Lisbeth lying on the bed holding Sarah Ann. It just wasn't possible that she would be involved in the recent accidents.

He'd gone looking for her. He knew he'd hurt her last night and wanted to say something to her to make things right. But though he had searched for an hour, he couldn't find Lisbeth and finally gave up.

Now, he and the hunters arrived at the woods where a groom took the horses and the men divided into small parties. Ben was recruited into one with the Carmichaels.

"Are ye any good with that shotgun?" the elder Carmichael asked.

Better than good, but he didn't plan to show it today. He had no intention of killing birds on this cold Scottish morning. "I don't have much time for sport."

"My lads are fine marksmen," Carmichael said as he released his dog. The animal went straight into the bush, and in several seconds, the bush seemed to come alive as a flock of birds rose into the sky. The Carmichaels started shooting, while Ben watched. He heard shooting from other parts of the woods and saw birds flutter into the air and go down.

"Mr. Masters?" Carmichael said. "Ye have no taste for hunting?"

If only Carmichael knew how little taste he did have, and why. He'd been a hunter of much bigger game for much too long. At the same time, he knew he would be considered both odd and cowardly if he didn't participate. For Sarah Ann's sake?

But he couldn't.

"No," he said abruptly. He was tired of trying to be something he wasn't. The decision that had been forming in his mind solidified. "I'm going back to the manor."

Carmichael frowned, but then a new flock rose from the bush, and he muttered something about foreigners and went back to shooting.

Ben felt a sudden freedom. He started back toward the horses, cutting through the quarter mile of dense woods. Behind him, he heard the pounding of gunfire. For a moment, he was back in battle, back at Vicksburg, the thunder of cannon and rifle echoing in his ears, in his soul. Men were falling, crying out in surprise and agony.

He stopped, leaned against a tree, willing the memories to go away, but they were so real, so alive. Smoke. So much smoke. His troop was retreating. And then the pain, the overwhelming pain—and the thirst. He heard himself calling for water. He would die without water. He wanted to die. . . .

The images wouldn't go away. Neither would the noise. And then he heard a different sound and saw a movement not far from him. He started to lift his gun when a bullet hit the trunk a fraction of an inch from him.

While his gaze searched the woods, another shot kicked up dirt in front of him. He tried to blend into the brush. He couldn't expect help. No one would think anything of another shot. A yell for assistance might put other hunters in jeopardy.

He saw a movement, and his finger started to tighten around the trigger, but he hesitated. The figure was between him and the other hunters, and he might hit one of the innocent guests. He caught a glimpse of brown, but the shooter blended well into the woods. So did most of the hunters in their dark tweeds.

A dog barked, then something moved behind him, and the crack of another shot split the air, spitting up earth several feet away. The shooter could no longer see him, at least.

Dropping down onto the ground, Ben crawled to the left. Inch by inch he moved, keeping his gaze on the place where he thought the last shot had come from. If he could get between the shooter and the hunters, he might have a chance at his attacker.

He moved a dozen yards or more in a kind of circle. He saw nothing. He heard nothing. Whoever was out there was an experienced woodsman.

Sweat broke out on his forehead and his hands, despite the coolness of the air. Then he heard the crackle of a dry leaf. To his left. He moved the shotgun to fit into both hands and rolled to another position.

Another crackle. Then voices. Laughing, victorious voices. He looked back toward where he'd heard the first crackle. Nothing. The shooter was gone. Every instinct told him that. How long had it been? Ten minutes, thirty? He rolled into a sitting position, then stood upright, just as Carmichael and his sons appeared.

Alex Carmichael stared at him, at the dirt staining his sheepskin coat.

"Did ye fall now?" he asked in a somewhat pitying voice.

He shrugged. "An old injury. Sometimes, my leg collapses on me."

"Lady Barbara said ye ha' been in the American war. Can we gi' ye a bit of help?"

Ben shook his head and looked at the grouse the two strapping Carmichael boys carried. "I see you did well. Are all Scots such good shots?"

"All worth their salt," Carmichael said as his two sons beamed with pride. "It's part of bein' a man."

Ben hesitated, then asked, "I thought I saw someone go in your direction."

Carmichael shrugged. "We dinna see anyone."

Ben cursed silently, but fell in with the three men. Whoever had tried to kill him could have joined anyone by now. Or disappeared.

At least he knew this hadn't been an accident, just as the other incidents had not been accidents, either. Someone had killed Jamie. Someone had twice before tried to kill him and Sarah Ann.

If he'd been killed, what would happen to Sarah Ann? Who would protect her? Her nearest kin would be the Hamilton widows. He tried to reason. Lisbeth couldn't have moved that swiftly with her injured ankle. Barbara probably had never held a gun in her hand. That left Hugh. And the one man who had been present each time danger had threatened: Drew Cameron.

Lisbeth's friend. Maybe her lover.

His heart denied it. He'd been so certain this morning that she couldn't be involved. But his brain couldn't discount the possibility.

Lisbeth's arms around Sarah Ann. She'd said she'd wanted a child. Suspicion ate at him like vultures picking from a corpse.

Ben and the three Carmichaels reached the horses, and Ben reluctantly handed one of the grooms his shotgun. He kept his voice light when he asked if any others had recently left for the manor.

"Lord Kinloch, sir, and the Earl of Gaibreaith an' his party," the groom said.

"Together?"

" 'Peared to be." He turned when several other hunters came into view.

Ben went to his horse, inspected the saddle belt cinch, then mounted. Lisbeth would be at the stable, no doubt, soothing Shadow in preparation for this afternoon's race. Would there be anyone with her?

Without waiting for the Carmichaels, Ben dug his heels into Bailey's side, and the horse jumped forward and raced toward Calholm.

❖❖❖

Lisbeth spoke softly to Shadow as she brushed his gray coat to perfection, telling him how much she wished she were riding him. Sarah Ann was in the stable with her, grooming her pony, or at least trying to. Lisbeth had found her a step stool, and when last seen, Sarah Ann had been as covered with soap suds and water as Peppermint.

The two of them—and Henry who lay contentedly outside the stall—were blessedly alone. Callum had left an hour earlier to check the course for the upcoming race, and the grooms were with the hunters. This hour provided the peace she needed.

Lisbeth had not seen Ben that morning. She had woken when the first shards of light had hit the window. At first, she'd wondered where she was. A small bundle of child lay in her arms, and she felt good. Too good. It had made Lisbeth ache with regret.

And then she'd realized she was still fully dressed, and Ben was only several steps away. His eyes, so damning last night, remained fierce in her memory. She hadn't wanted him to find her there, and she'd carefully unwrapped herself from Sarah Ann and tiptoed from the room.

She wondered whether he still slept naked, and still kept a gun under his pillow.

She wouldn't think about it. She couldn't. She'd

gone to her room and sat watching the sun rise and listening to the sounds of an awakening house . . .

Lisbeth gave Shadow one last stroke with the brush. Why had Ben glared at her as he had last night? Almost as if he hated her. What had caused that warm, almost possessive look from his eyes to turn into anger?

This time, she determined, she would ask.

"Oops!"

She heard the exclamation from several stalls down, and hurried to Peppermint's stall.

The sight that greeted her made her giggle. Sarah Ann had fallen from the stool onto the soft hay. Her lap was full of suds from the pail of water, and she had such a look of astonishment that Lisbeth couldn't help but laugh.

Sarah Ann narrowed her eyes, then looked down at her ruined gown, thought about it for a moment, then grinned. "I fell, too," she said proudly, as though it were a great accomplishment.

"I see," Lisbeth said seriously. "Did you hurt yourself?"

Sarah Ann considered, then looked at Lisbeth's twisted ankle. "I might have hurt my a'kle. I might need a ban'age."

"I think that's entirely possible," Lisbeth said, now trying to hide her smile. The stool was only a foot tall, and Sarah Ann had obviously been surprised more than injured. A bandage, though, wouldn't hurt a thing.

"Will you carry me, like Papa carried you?"

She started to reach for Lisbeth when she heard the clatter of horses at the front of the barn, and then seconds later, Ben Masters's angry voice. "What in the hell . . . ?"

"I fell," Sarah Ann said proudly. "Just like Lisbeth."

Lisbeth's heart skittered around in her chest. No one had ever wanted to be like her. No one had ever looked at her with adoration.

Ben whirled around and faced her, his eyes glittering with anger. Barely contained violence radiated from him.

It was all she could do not to run, or melt right in front of him. Instead, summoning all her courage, she straightened her back and met his fury head-on with indignation of her own.

"She's not hurt. She was just learning to groom . . ."

But he wasn't listening. She saw that. Then she saw the leaves that clung to his coat. His dark trousers were stained with dirt and torn in one place.

"What happened?" she asked.

His blue eyes were cold, colder than she'd ever seen them. "Someone took a shot at me," he said, his voice little more than a growl.

"An accident?" she whispered, her eyes widening in shock.

"No," Ben said, tired of pretending. His enemy—and Sarah Ann's—was becoming bolder. He'd hoped to smoke him or her out, but he was too angry now. One approach hadn't worked. It was time to try another. Especially since the culprit must now realize that the game was up. "There were several shots. One might have been an accident. Three close misses were not."

Lisbeth looked stunned. She started to reach for him, then she dropped her hand. Understanding suddenly filled her eyes, along with a kind of pain he'd never seen before. She stepped away from him as if he'd hit her.

There was a small gasp from behind him and Ben silently cursed. He should have been aware that Sarah Ann was listening. He forced his eyes from Lisbeth's and swung around, picking Sarah Ann up and holding her close.

"It's all right, Sugarplum. You're safe."

"Don't go away." Her face, so proud just minutes ago, was crumpling. Her lips puckered, and the big green eyes swam with tears. "Please." The little voice wavered with fear.

"Dear God," he whispered, the words choking him. "I won't, Sugarplum. I promise. No one will ever hurt you, and I won't let anything happen to me."

"Promise?"

"I promise," he said solemnly. With several careless, angry words he had destroyed what little security he'd been able to build for her. Damn, he was a hell of a father.

Her arms were around his neck. He closed his eyes for a moment, holding her as securely as he could, trying to make her feel safe.

He heard a sob from behind him, then a bark—sharp and scolding. When he opened his eyes again and turned, Lisbeth was disappearing out the door, seeming to fly despite her bad ankle. Henry looked at him with accusing eyes, then with another bark he dashed after his mistress.

Ben closed his eyes again, leaning against the stall, murmuring soothing noises to Sarah Ann. But no amount of soothing could quiet the storm inside him, or the growing belief that he'd just made more than one terrible mistake.

❖❖❖

Lisbeth fled for the house, for the quiet of her room.

There had been no spoken accusation, but there might as well have been. Ben thought she'd had something to do with the shooting. The pain struck so deep, so sharply, that she had to bite down the cry that wanted to leap from her throat.

How could he possibly think she would try to harm him, or be part of an attempt to do so? And how could he believe she'd ever try to harm Sarah Ann? Because that accusation had been present, too, hovering between them. She recalled him telling her about the accident in Edinburgh. Had he been suspicious then? That he would think her capable of hurting a child was beyond bearing.

Lisbeth sank down onto her bed, the one on which she'd made love with Ben. She'd thought it had been love. She'd felt bewitched and beautiful. She'd felt wanted, really wanted for the first time in her life.

And now?

A huge paw tentatively appeared on the bed, then a

head. A tongue reached out for her face, and she felt its sympathetic swipe. And then the tears came. She hadn't cried for years, not even when Jamie had died. Shock had protected her then. Disbelief. Then a numbness.

Ben Masters had cut through that numbness, had made her feel alive again, maybe even alive for the first time. Now she felt her heart being cut from her breast.

Lisbeth lost track of time, didn't know how long she'd been lying there. She heard noises and knew the hunters had returned and were having lunch before the race. After the race, the guests would start returning home. Perhaps several, including Drew, would stay another day, but then she would be alone with Barbara, Hugh, and a man who thought her capable of murder. A man she had thought she could love.

Henry inched himself up onto the bed as he usually did, as if not quite sure he should be there, and lay close to her.

"What should I do, Henry?" she asked. He whined, obviously wishing to be of assistance but not quite knowing how.

Time inched by. The meal would be over. Bets would be made over the upcoming race. Horses would be readied.

Lisbeth wiped the last of the tears from her face. She wouldn't give Bennett Sebastian Masters the satisfaction of knowing he'd made her cry. She washed her face, then rang the bell for Effie.

❖❖❖

Ben took Sarah Ann to her room, helped her change into a dry gown, and distracted her with Annabelle for a while. He teased her and coaxed a smile, then extended his arm for her to join him for lunch. She always loved that; he knew it made her feel very grown-up, indeed.

They went down to eat and found the dining and drawing rooms full of milling guests, either talking about their morning success and the number of birds they'd shot, or placing bets on the five horses for the afternoon race. Excitement permeated the air, anticipation of what they hoped would be a rousing good race. Some had already watched Shadow in local races; others had heard about him.

But Lisbeth was nowhere to be seen. Barbara acted as hostess, reveling in the role, and Hugh seemed at ease at her side. Ben studied both, wondering if either of them had planned the ambush in the woods.

He still hadn't seen Drew Cameron. The devil in his head wondered whether he was with Lisbeth, or whether jealousy was impairing his objectivity.

He listened to the bets, to the gossip, as Sarah Ann clung to his hand, Suzanna clutched in her other hand. She brightened when someone spoke to her, especially when that person asked about the doll. "My mama gave her to me," she said proudly.

Her smile widened even more when she saw Drew come into the room. He made his way straight toward her.

"How's my favorite lady?" he asked.

"I fell," Sarah Ann said triumphantly.

Ben searched for guile in the man. He searched for ruthlessness. He searched for duplicity. He found nothing but concern for Sarah Ann.

Drew was dressed for riding. Not a strand of hair was out of place. No apprehension shone in his eyes. If he was anything but what he seemed at the moment, he was a damned fine actor. Most successful gamblers were.

"I didn't see you this morning," Ben said.

"I rode out to inspect the course." He turned his attention back to Sarah Ann. "What a pretty frock."

"Thank you," she said, preening enchantingly as only a child could.

"You're very welcome, love."

"Find me a coin again."

"Ah, you're just like all the other young ladies," he teased. "Always in search of a man's gold." But he reached up and plucked a coin from behind her ear. "That is for good luck," he said. "Mine and yours."

"Lady Lisbeth says you're going to ride Shadow," she said.

"Do you think I can have a favor?"

"What's a favor?" Sarah Ann asked.

"When the knights went into battle hundreds of years ago," he explained, "they took a token of their lady's favor. A scarf, or a handkerchief."

Ben watched Sarah Ann's face as she considered the request. "I don't have anything."

Her scarf was tucked into the neck of her dress. Effie had finally washed it, sneaking it out one evening when Sarah Ann had gone to sleep, replacing it before she'd awakened.

Drew reached out and touched it. "This would do very prettily."

Sarah Ann's eyes clouded. The smile disappeared, and she stood still.

Drew immediately responded to her mood. "It's all right, love. I think a kiss will do as well."

"Really?" she asked seriously.

"Better than well," he said solemnly.

Sarah Ann leaned over and kissed him, then she whispered something to him. Ben couldn't hear. He saw Andrew Cameron stiffen, glance up quickly at him, then whisper something back. Ben stood there, feeling alone. Anger burned like red coals in his gut.

Drew stood. "I'll do that for you, Lady Sarah Ann." He looked at Ben for a moment, his gaze troubled, and then he ambled away.

"What did you say to him?" Ben asked Sarah Ann.

"To take care of you," she said. "He said he would. He promised."

Ben felt as if the rug had been pulled out from under him. He sure couldn't quarrel with her intent, only with her choice of confidants.

Children are always wiser than we think, Mary May had

said when he'd first met Sarah Ann. *They are very good judges of character.*

Ben had been shocked at Sarah Ann's easy acceptance of him months ago. She had immediately asked whether he was her papa and had happily sat in his lap, which then and there showed her complete lack of judgment. He had been a killer. On the side of the law, yes, but a killer nonetheless.

No, Sarah Ann was a dreadful judge of character. So he dismissed her approval of Drew Cameron.

As he fixed her a plate of food, he couldn't help but notice the eyes of several young ladies on himself. Some he remembered from last night, others he did not.

He supposed most fathers would scoop up their daughters and run before considering a match with him. He had no title and little money of his own. For all they knew, he had nothing.

Dammit, he hated that image of himself. A guardian living off his daughter. Even more, he hated sitting here doing nothing when someone had just tried to kill him.

Barbara came over to where he and Sarah Ann had found seats. "Did you enjoy the hunt this morning?"

She looked particularly pretty. Clearly, she loved parties and being the center of attention.

Claire had been like that. And although he'd learned to be wary of that particular trait, he couldn't ignore Barbara's appeal, the sheer beauty of her black hair and violet eyes and laughing mouth. She appeared even more enchanting than usual, now that some of the petulance had gone from her face and her eyes were brighter. He noticed something else, too. Hugh was hovering around her, and she kept returning to his side. Partners in conspiracy?

Damn, but he felt boxed in. He didn't feel he could safely leave Sarah Ann with anyone. He wasn't sure whether he was the sole target, or whether he'd merely presented an opportunity to the murderer. And he couldn't do much investigating with a four-year-old in tow.

If only there was someone he could trust. But that, at the moment, was as remote a possibility as plucking a star from the heavens. Lisbeth. Hugh. Barbara. Drew. One of them was trying to kill him.

And at the moment, he couldn't believe it of any one of them.

Chapter Nineteen

Lisbeth was determined that nothing would interfere with today's triumph. Everything she and Jamie had worked toward—had risked—during the last five years would begin to be justified today. She tried not to think that Jamie had died before reaching this point. She tried not to think that one man could end it in a month.

This was to be Shadow's day.

She had selected a forest-green riding dress that she knew flattered her, and a matching green coat and jaunty hat. The dark colors would not offend those who thought she should still be in mourning.

Callum was in the stable, talking to Drew, who, Lisbeth knew, had ridden over the course earlier in the morning on another mount.

"Shadow may try to balk," Callum said. "Don't let him. Tell him who's in control."

Drew nodded. He swung around as he became aware of Lisbeth. "He's a fine horse."

"Jamie said he would be a champion," she said wistfully. "He should be riding him."

"Or you," Drew said fondly. "Damn shame you were born a woman. I would have liked to race you."

"You still can." She tilted her head challengingly.

"Maybe when that ankle improves," he replied, "though I think the new master of Calholm doesn't exactly approve of me. He's been glaring at me for two days now."

"He's not the new master," she countered. "Not yet."

"But everyone says the petition has been approved."

Callum gave a snort of disgust and stalked from the stall. "I'll get the other horse ready," he said and disappeared around the bend. Geordie would ride Torchfire, a six-year-old bay that was available for stud.

Lisbeth turned away from Drew, laying a hand on Shadow's side.

"You don't look happy," Drew said quietly.

She bit her lip. "Someone shot at Ben this morning."

"Devil you say," Drew said.

"And there was an accident in Edinburgh."

"Edinburgh?" His voice sharpened.

"Apparently after you left them, a carriage nearly ran them down."

He whistled. "There was also an accident in Liverpool." He was silent for a moment, and she turned around to look at him.

"You were there each time."

"Bloody hell," he exploded. "You don't think—?"

"Of course not," she said.

She saw a muscle working in his cheek. He was an attractive man with sandy hair and hazel eyes that reminded her a little of her own; in fact, she'd felt an odd familiarity the first time she'd met him. Almost as if she'd known him most of her life. She'd never felt that way about anyone before, had never felt comfortable with a man before, especially so quickly.

"And then there was Jamie," she said in a small voice.

"That *was* an accident." At her hesitation, he added, "Wasn't it?"

"He was such a good rider," she said.

"So are you, and you fell."

"Because I . . . became distracted."

"I don't think I'll ask you why," he said dryly. "But surely, Masters *can't* suspect you."

She lifted one shoulder in bewilderment.

"Bloody bastard," Drew swore. "I gave him more credit than that."

"But I can understand—"

"Well, I can't," he said, then stopped as he looked at her more closely. "You haven't, you aren't . . ."

She looked at him miserably.

Drew sighed heavily. "No wonder he's been glaring at me with such fury."

The infernal tears started again. She tried to blink them back. Drew brushed a tear away, then he pulled her to him.

"He's a bloody fool," Drew said.

She stayed in his embrace a moment, then pulled away. "Thank you for riding Shadow."

He nodded. "Anytime, love."

"Drew?"

"Yes?"

"Check the saddle well before you mount."

He had started to turn toward the horse, and he whirled back abruptly.

"Please, Drew."

"All right, m'lady," he said mischievously. "And I'll try not to fall."

She managed a small smile.

"And we'll win."

"I know," she replied.

He leaned over and kissed her forehead. "You can always come to America with me."

She shuddered.

He chuckled, though the smile didn't quite reach his eyes.

❖❖❖

Ben knew it would happen. He was even prepared for it, or he thought he was.

Sarah Ann made directly for Lisbeth as the guests gathered for the start of the race. He had to follow.

Lisbeth bent down and greeted his small charge, but her gaze avoided him.

"I missed you this morning, Lady Lisbeth," Sarah Ann said. "Papa and I both did. Annabelle, too."

"You'll have to tell Annabelle I'm sorry," Lisbeth said with that gentle smile that always took his breath away. It was much more potent than Barbara's dazzling smile, perhaps because it didn't come as often or as easily. It certainly wasn't coming his way at the moment.

He turned and watched the five riders. The spectators could see some of the jumps and part of the course, but not all. Ben felt the excitement build as the Scots carefully looked over Shadow and Torchfire.

Shadow was obviously nervous with a new rider on his back, but Ben grudgingly recognized that Drew Cameron was keeping him well under control. He was obviously an expert rider. What else did he do well?

"Look," Sarah Ann said as she pointed to Drew. "I gave him a favor."

"And what was that?" Lisbeth asked.

"He wanted my scarf, but I gave him a kiss instead. To help him win."

"I think that's much better," Lisbeth said. She cast Ben a quick glance, and he noted the coolness in her. Her face was tense, and he didn't know whether it came from apprehension about the race or his earlier veiled accusations. Her lips seemed to quiver a moment, but then she turned away, toward the horses, toward Callum, who was to announce the start.

"Hold me up," Sarah Ann demanded, and Ben swung her up onto his shoulder.

Lisbeth took several steps toward one of the Carmichael boys.

Ben couldn't blame her. He had hurt her, probably irreparably if she were innocent. He knew what distrust did to people, and he had torn to shreds that fragile beginning of trust—and intimacy—they'd shared.

He kept telling himself it was because of Sarah Ann. He couldn't take chances with her life. But he wasn't sure that was completely true. Distrusting was a hell of a lot easier than trusting.

"Look!" Sarah Ann exclaimed.

The horses were off, pounding across the ground. They reached the first jump, and suddenly appeared to be flying through the air as they all cleared it. He'd seldom seen better horsemanship than that of the riders in this race. On Shadow, Drew leaned close to the animal's neck, becoming as one with the horse, as he soared over a six-foot fence, then a brush hazard. Then the horses and riders disappeared from view and the crowd grew quiet, waiting.

Reluctant appreciation filled Ben. He looked at Lisbeth, wondering what he would see on her face. He found her looking at him, sad puzzlement marring her features. She should be feeling excitement, victory. And he had robbed her of it. He felt as if he'd destroyed something precious, and at that moment he hated himself.

Someone shouted, signaling that the horses were coming into the final furlong. Ben saw Lisbeth force a smile as Shadow lengthened his lead, flying over the last hazard with space to spare, Torchfire behind him, and the other three horses trailing.

And then it was over, and she was accepting congratulations.

"He's all ye said and more," Carmichael said, approaching her. "And I'll be going home poorer. Ye wouldn't be thinking of selling him, would you?"

Lisbeth shook her head. "But he has a brother—a yearling—that might be for sale. It will be up to Mr. Masters most likely." With her back stiff but a smile pasted on her face, she walked over to Shadow. And Drew Cameron. Both were surrounded quickly by a crowd of people.

Ben felt that he no longer existed for her.

"It was my kiss," Sarah Ann said to him.

He suddenly remembered she was still on his shoulder and set her down. "What, Sugarplum?"

"Drew won because of my kiss," she said, obviously annoyed that she had to remind him.

His fingers closed around hers. "Of course," he said. "Kisses are magic."

He remembered a particular few recent kisses. "Aye," he said. "They are." But all the magic was gone, and all he tasted were the bitter ashes of regret.

❖❖❖

The victory should have meant everything. It didn't mean anything.

Why did she keep caring?

Lisbeth accepted congratulations, giving the credit for the breeding to Jamie and the old Marquess, and the riding to Drew Cameron. She looked for Drew, but after dismounting he'd disappeared.

So had Ben.

She and Callum walked Shadow to the stables after the guests had left for the manor house.

Callum gave her as much of a smile as he ever quite managed. "We showed them, Lady Lisbeth."

"So we did," she said. "You'll be able to find a position anywhere now."

"What do you mean?"

She looked at his weathered face. "I'm not sure Mr. Masters will keep the horses. I heard his petition's been approved."

"It isn't right," he said. "These are Calholm horses. The old Marquess put his heart into them."

"So did Jamie," Lisbeth reminded him.

Callum muttered something under his breath, and Lisbeth looked at him quizzically.

"Lord Jamie dinna care," Callum said. "He planned to sell them."

"He never said anything to me about it."

"Because he knew ye would object. Lord Jamie never did like opposition. He would have gone ahead and sold them, like Lady Barbara wanted. Like the new master will do," he added bitterly, his mouth tightening.

The thudding in Lisbeth's heart almost drowned out everything else. "How do you know?"

"I heard yer Jamie talking to Lady Barbara." His voice was grim and his eyes cold. "I should not ha' said anything, but ye believe too easily."

He walked away, then, toward the stables, leaving her stunned. *Ye believe too easily.*

Jamie and Barbara. She wouldn't believe it. She *couldn't* believe it. She couldn't believe Jamie would sell his heritage, break his promise to his father, deceive her.

She'd lived with Jamie three years. She'd conceived a child with him.

But he never told you he loved you.

Her mind was going in circles, trying to remember fragments that might reveal truths. Jamie was a good horseman, a superb horseman. His father, he'd told her, put him on a horse before he could walk. John Hamilton valued that skill above all else.

But Jamie had never fed the horses tidbits of apples and carrots, had never stayed to talk to them, or curry them or cool them down. He'd always tossed the reins to the grooms and walked off.

She had been the one the Marquess spent hours with, talking about bloodlines and racing. Jamie had always found an excuse to leave.

Jamie. Always polite. Always proper. Always doing what his father wanted. And the Marquess had wanted his sons to have sons.

Lisbeth hadn't know what passion was, what desire was, until a few days ago. Jamie's lovemaking had been quick and efficient, though he had not been unkind, and she had believed their relations quite normal. She'd only been grateful that it hadn't been the onerous act her mother had described. She'd wanted to love Jamie, seeing in him what *she* wanted to see.

Had she done that again with Ben Masters?

Or could she believe Callum? Why would he lie about Jamie?

Lisbeth's head was swimming. She felt the earth moving under her, shaking her very foundation. She had to grab the door of a stall to keep her balance. Was her life all make-believe, as it had been when she was a child and she'd buried herself in books to escape the hatred in her home?

She had trusted Jamie. She had started to trust Ben Masters. She had given part of her soul to him. But he thought her capable of murder.

She couldn't go back to the manor. She couldn't face the departing guests, face Barbara who might have seduced her husband, face the man she had believed she loved.

A sense of urgency—even desperation—gave her the strength to handle the heavy tack, and she saddled a horse that hadn't raced. She found a stool and used it to mount, then galloped from the stables toward the castle ruins on the loch.

❖❖❖

Sarah Ann was the perfect lady as she said her goodbyes to the departing guests, and they responded in kind, clearly charmed.

Ben knew his own farewells were neither as charming nor well received. He sensed the continued wariness—and disapproval—of his new neighbors. He didn't blame them. Calholm belonged in the hands of the Hamiltons, not some upstart American pretender.

Several families were planning to stay the night, including Drew, whom he could have done without. But Drew lived in Edinburgh, at least a day's ride away, and Ben couldn't very well throw anyone from a house he didn't yet own. Would never own.

"Papa?"

Ben stooped down beside Sarah Ann in the now-empty hall. "Sugarplum?"

"Can I ride Pep'mint?"

"I think it might be better if you said hello to Annabelle," he said. "She must be very lonesome."

Sarah Ann immediately looked stricken, and he felt like a devil for manipulating her.

"Pep'mint's probably lonesome, too," Sarah Ann said.

"But he hasn't been locked up in your bedroom all alone this morning," he reminded her.

Sarah Ann thought about that for a moment, her desire obviously warring with responsibility, and he'd already discovered she had a stubborn streak where responsibility—or what she construed responsibility to be—was concerned.

"Poor Ann'belle," she said, slurring the word, and Ben knew she was sleepy. And that he'd won this particular skirmish. Once he got her to her room, she would play with Annabelle, then he would tell a story, and those eyes would close for an hour or so. Perhaps then he could get some answers from Drew Cameron.

❖❖❖

Drew wanted to punch the bloody hell out of Ben Masters.

Drew cared for few people, and Lisbeth was one of them. The first time he'd seen her he'd admired the spirit in her; mainly, he thought, because his own spirit had been all but beaten out of him.

He'd learned not to care for a bloody damn thing. He was the only child of an earl, who had all but bankrupted his own estate so Drew wouldn't inherit anything. He hadn't known why his father had hated him until he'd discovered he wasn't a Cameron in blood, only in name.

Bastard, his father had called him. The only reason he carried his father's name was because the earl had been too proud to publicly declare he couldn't father a child of his own, that his wife had been an adulteress.

Drew had paid for those two facts all his life.

It hadn't been until four years ago, though, that he'd discovered the details, when his father—on his death-bed—had called him a bastard and had made certain he'd never get a penny of his money.

By then, he hadn't cared. Or maybe he had. His father had made his mother's life hell, and she'd collapsed under it. She might have loved him once. He couldn't remember. But if she had, his father's hatred had drained her until she became only a shell, drinking to survive. Drew had been sent away to various schools, and greeted with invective on the few occasions when he returned home.

Rebellion had been his refuge. His revenge. He'd been dismissed from more schools than he could remember despite the fact that he had what most headmasters said was a brilliant mind. He'd gambled, stolen, and whored. His only interest was sports: riding, boxing, swordsmanship, shooting. He excelled at all of them. Violence became an outlet for the pain of rejection.

Then at one school, a teacher had taken an interest in him. He'd been a patient, gentle man who smiled at Drew's barbs, invited him to his room to talk, and treated him like a person of worth. Samuel Bascomb had briefly drawn the best from him.

But then Bascomb died, and he was alone again. He had learned one thing, though: that charm was more productive than bitterness. He learned to mask his uncertainty and hurt and anger with banter. He armed himself with indifference and made an art out of aimlessness.

He was one of the most worthless things in the world: a young titled gentleman with no money and no prospects. He could always marry wealth. There were numerous wealthy American misses on the marriage market, ready to trade fortunes for a British title. Some of his friends had already followed that course. He couldn't, though. He'd already sold most of his soul to the devil; he was going to preserve what little was left.

But he cared about Lisbeth. She had the strength he should have. Hell, he'd met her father, her oafish brothers. He didn't understand how she'd survived intact. But she had, and by God, no one was going to hurt her again.

Not if he had anything to do with it.

❖❖❖

One of the grooms told Ben that Lady Lisbeth had taken the road north to the loch. No one knew where Andrew Cameron had gone.

Ben wondered whether he would find them together.

Sarah Ann was sound asleep, and both Annabelle and Henry were with her. He'd asked Effie to stay with her, too, and had added two pound notes to secure the promise that she would not leave the child alone.

He saddled Bailey and led him from the stables, following the loch road in search of Lisbeth. He had to have answers. And he had to tell Lisbeth he and Sarah Ann would be leaving Scotland.

Ben saw her horse before he saw her. It was grazing just outside one of the walls. He dismounted, left his horse with the other, and walked to the chapel.

Lisbeth was on her knees, in front of the chapel. The sun shone down through the holes in the roof and seemed to shed a halo around her auburn hair, now wrapped around her head in braids. It was a severe style, but she looked lovely. But then she always looked lovely to him, even when she was wearing boy's trousers with a cap pushed down over her head.

He stood at the chapel entrance. Watching. Waiting. Strangely afraid.

As if she sensed his presence, she slowly rose and turned. No surprise flickered across her face.

He waited as she came toward him, pride stiffening her back, her eyes cool.

"I wanted to be alone," she said.

"I'm sorry."

"Are you?" Her voice trembled slightly.

He felt at a loss. "Lisbeth . . ."

"Aren't you worried I might stab you with the knife I have hidden in my dress? Or do you think I'm too cowardly for that? I have to get someone to do it for me?"

That was exactly what he'd implied earlier in the day, when he'd been so angry.

"Go away, Ben Masters," she said tiredly.

Going away was what he should do. But he couldn't move. And despite her words, the attraction was still strong between them. Tension reverberated in the air, heating it despite the cold wind. He saw her fighting it as he had fought it.

They both failed miserably.

"You shouldn't be on that ankle," he said stupidly.

"You shouldn't be on that leg," she retorted.

Their eyes were fastened on each other's.

But the hurt in her eyes was deep, deeper even than the attraction that flashed there. A small sound, almost like a sob, escaped her.

She turned to go, but his hand caught her, holding her, and she didn't try to break his grasp. She couldn't have if she had tried. He knew his strength, and he wasn't going to let her go. And she had too much innate dignity to fight him.

He wanted to apologize. Instead, he said the worst possible thing, and he knew it the moment he spoke the words. "Where's Cameron?"

Her face went white with anger. "We're having a tryst, of course. He's hiding behind that stone wall over there. Or maybe he's lurking in one of the wells. You're a bloody fool, Ben Masters. Now let me go."

Fury blazed in her eyes, and her body was stiff with indignation. She threw back her head with a contempt that ripped through him.

But he didn't let go. "Lisbeth, listen to me. He's been present every time there's been an . . . attempt on Sarah Ann and me."

"And you think we've been conspiring—"

"No," he said. "But Cameron—"

"Drew wouldn't," she cut in.

"How do you know?" His voice was harsher than he intended, but that damn jealousy kept pricking at him like the razor-sharp point of a steel blade.

"Are all American lawyers so suspicious?"

"Only those shot at, driven over, and smashed by crates."

Some of the anger left her eyes. "It wasn't me, and it couldn't have been Drew," she said.

"Why?"

"He has no reason."

"He has you."

Her eyes opened wide at that, and there was such surprise in them that Ben knew he'd been wrong. There was nothing between Lisbeth and Drew Cameron, at least not as far as she was concerned.

"He's a friend, nothing more," she said, her eyes still full of astonishment.

"Maybe he wants more."

"No." She shook her head. "His type runs more to actresses."

Ben felt a bitter taste in his mouth. Andrew Cameron was more than a friend to her, he felt it in his bones, but he didn't doubt that Lisbeth believed what she was saying.

"You didn't think—?" Lisbeth stopped in mid-sentence.

"I didn't know *what* to think," he said dryly. "I'm used to shooting back when I'm shot at. I tend to get angry when I'm ambushed." It was a partial explanation and he didn't realize what he'd revealed until she spoke.

"Are you shot at that much?"

Ben was silent. He owed her an explanation. But that meant even more explanations, and he didn't know whether he was ready to reveal his past or not.

"Keep your secrets," she said. "I don't want to hear them."

"Lisbeth." Her name was soft on his lips, almost pleading.

"I don't know who you are, or what you are," she said. "I thought I knew." He saw her swallow hard, then she continued. "You're a chameleon, Ben Masters. You slide in and out of roles. Well, now you have Calholm. Take joy in it." The anger in her voice startled him into letting go of her hand, and she backed off as if he were a rattlesnake. "The old Marquess gave me Shadow, and I hope you won't try to claim him. I'll be leaving Calholm as soon as possible."

"No," he said. "Calholm is your home."

"Not any longer. Perhaps it never was," she said. "It was a refuge, but never a home."

Ben moved forward, and she backed up.

"Don't," she said. "Don't come near me."

She was all defiance despite her trembling lips. Her hazel eyes were wide enough to swallow him. But she was against a wall, and when she tried to back up, she met its resistance. She looked like a fawn caught in the light of a torch.

A shiver shook her body, and he remembered her shivering at other times, in other ways, for other reasons. She had accepted him into her bed, into her life so totally and with such trust, and he'd thrown it all back at her today. He'd made a mockery of her trust.

Ben's hand came up, touching Lisbeth's face as lightly as he could.

She flinched as if his hand were a brand. "Don't," she whispered and her tongue licked her lips. "Don't," she said again, this time in a softer tone.

The very air sizzled between them. Her anger seemed

to fuel the heat rather than cool it. And when he heard her whisper his name—"Ben . . . please . . ."—he was lost.

His head bent, his lips came down on hers, and he kissed her. She resisted for a moment, then her lips yielded under his. He wrapped his arms around her, and her arms crept up around him, gingerly at first, reluctantly, but inevitably, as if some force compelled it. Currents of hot pleasure surged through him, though he still felt her resistance, her denial of what they both wanted.

A low moan rumbled through him as her mouth opened hesitantly in response to his subtle pressure. Her body trembled against his, and he felt every quiver, felt the jolt that streaked through her when his own arousal pressed against her.

He knew he should stop—she was still too hurt, too angry—but he couldn't. He wanted to convey something to her for which he had no words. The hell of it was he didn't even know what he was trying to say. Desire? Need? Love?

Another sob escaped her, and it went straight into his soul. He closed his eyes, and anguish coursed through him. Why did he hurt people he cared about? When had he stopped trusting so completely?

Despite the heat growing in his loins, Ben let Lisbeth go before he did anything even more despicable. He had made her want him, when he knew very well she didn't want any part of him.

He dropped his arms. "I'm sorry," he said for the second time that afternoon.

She stared at him with those enchanting eyes. "Don't you trust anyone?" she finally asked.

After another long silence, he replied, "I haven't for a long time."

"Because of Claire?"

He shrugged. "There are other reasons."

"Sarah Ann's mother? You've never talked about her."

He was silent for a moment, then said roughly, "She might be alive if she hadn't met me."

"Might?"

"Would be," he corrected. "I . . . stirred up something . . ."

Lisbeth was silent a moment, then her brows knitted together in concentration. "You blame yourself for her death?"

He didn't say anything, but the air was pregnant with his regret, with the sorrow he'd never fully admitted even to himself.

"Is that why . . . ?"

He didn't want to explain whys. He didn't even want to know the whys. What would it matter if he did? She had no reason to trust him again. And the only thing left for him to do was to leave. Go home to America, where he belonged. Make a decent life for himself and Sarah Ann, and do his best to forget Lisbeth Hamilton. A hopeless task.

Ben mumbled something about leaving her alone and being sorry, and he started to go.

She stopped him with a hand on his arm. "Ben . . . ?"

He turned back to her, and when he saw the look in her eyes, he could barely breathe. Her eyes—that startling hazel that continually seemed to change—were shining with hope, and the hope was laced with desire.

She said his name again, placing her hand flat against his chest in a soft caress. "Ben, I don't want you to go. I want . . ." Her words trailed off, her gaze searching his.

And in the next instant, she reached up, crooked a hand behind his neck to pull him down to her, and covered his mouth with hers.

Chapter Twenty

Before Lisbeth could catch a breath, Ben's arms were crushing her to him, he was lifting her off her feet, and his mouth was greedily devouring hers. She let him. And she let herself respond fully, without restraint. Not that he left her a choice.

It had been the doubt in his voice and in his eyes— the sadness, the remorse, the guilt—that had melted her heart. Suddenly, she had understood. He was afraid, even more afraid than she was, of losing yet another person he'd allowed himself to love. Either by betrayal or death, it seemed the women to whom he'd tried to give his heart had abandoned him. And he couldn't allow himself to trust that she wouldn't do the same thing.

It was a terrible thing not to trust. She knew. And she knew she had to show him that it could be different, that he could trust her. She had to show him, because she loved him and she always would. It terrified her, but she couldn't change it.

And so she gave herself over to his passion, and to him. She'd caught him off guard; he hadn't expected the kiss, and he hadn't been able to control his reaction to it. She didn't want him to control it. She wanted to know him. All of him. All the secrets he harbored, all the thoughts and feelings he rarely shared.

When he growled against her neck, trailing hot kisses down to her shoulder, she tilted her head to give him access. When his hands moved frantically over her, she helped him make his way through layers of clothing to find her breast. And when he lifted her skirts, his lips pressing hers against the wall, her body responded, seeking his.

Lisbeth felt herself sliding down the wall, until they were both on the ground, his jacket discarded, and his hand was fumbling at his trouser fastenings. She found herself assisting him, urgency pushing both of them. And then he was free.

"Lisbeth," he said raggedly, as his hands pulled down her pantalets and his hands caressed and seduced her body until she was raging with need for him. She pulled him down, unwilling to wait, and she felt his heated flesh against hers. His body was tense, almost rigid, but then he entered swiftly, his need filling her in a burst of desire.

She was lost, and she knew she would never be whole again without him. Desperation mixed with passion fueled her response as he moved deeper and deeper into her, becoming an integral part of her, reaching, it seemed, to her very soul.

She heard herself cry out as their bodies moved in a primitive rhythm which increased in intensity and speed, then the cry was buried in her throat as his lips crushed down on hers in fierce possession. The rhythm of their bodies became a primitive, erotic dance, an exploration into rapture, into ecstasy, into a world she'd never known or suspected existed. He drove and drove into her until she felt she would explode, and then rippling shudders ran through her body as she felt his warm seed spill inside her.

Burning need turned into satisfaction so exquisitely bliss-ful, so utterly joyful, she didn't know whether she could bear it.

She touched his cheek, and she felt the sweat of exer-tion there, despite the cool of the air. His breath came in heavy pants as his body gradually relaxed, though they remained joined. An incredible sweetness stole over her, complementing the deliciousness her body still felt. Her own breath came slower, though her body still quivered from the feel of him.

"Lisbeth," he said softly as he trailed a finger along her face, her cheek, her neck. She felt love in that touch, in its gentleness and tenderness. There was a kind of won-der in his face.

She smiled.

Her fingers caught his, and she touched his cheek with the back of her hand, holding it there, as she tried to contain the force and greatness of her love for him. She wanted to shout it out, to wrap him with it, but instead she contented herself with this small gesture of her trust and faith.

She would not, could not, force something he was not willing to give. She would wait until he realized, un-derstood that he loved her, too. Because she knew now that he did, even if he couldn't yet admit it.

He kissed her hand, and held it to his lips for a mo-ment longer, then he moved slightly, separating them.

"It's cold," he said.

"I hadn't noticed." She smiled against his neck. In-deed, the weather had been the last thing on her mind.

Disengaging slowly, he smoothed out her clothes, helping her with the pantalets that had been tossed to the side. With a few inches between them, Lisbeth felt the chill in the air. He must have seen her shiver because he took his coat and placed it over the riding jacket.

But she wasn't shivering from the cold. She was shivering from continuing quakes within her body, from the impact of their lovemaking.

She reached out her hand and grasped his. The love she felt, she knew, was shining in her eyes. His own expression was almost bewildered, but the reserve, the caution, had disappeared.

And he was smiling, that crooked smile she loved so much. She released his hand and touched his face, tracing a line that ran from his eyes to his cheekbone. "Do you let anyone get close to you?" she asked.

He shifted uncomfortably and started to say something.

"I don't mean Sarah Ann," she said. A child was easy to love, easy to trust. They hadn't learned deception.

A muscle in his cheek worked. "Do you?" he countered.

"I don't shove them away. Perhaps because I was . . . lonely as a child."

"Tell me about it," he prodded gently, his hand clasping hers. She moved closer to him, and his arm went around her.

"There's not much to tell. My father and mother hated each other. My brothers followed their example. They were all always fighting, always competing, always pitting one against the other. I can't ever remember hearing laughter in that house. Or feeling love. Only fighting. I hated that house, but my father didn't believe in education for girls. I learned to read with the help of a vicar's wife." She smiled suddenly. "She and one of my nannies were kind—extraordinarily so—but the nannie was fired, and the vicar died, and his wife moved away. And I was alone again."

She hesitated. "But I learned from them. I learned that people *could* love, that there could be warmth and kindness. But then . . . the loneliness grew worse when they left. So I turned to our horses. In the Highlands riding is a useful skill, and my father encouraged it, though I had to hide from him how much I loved it. That would have been a weakness. Animals were to be used. Those that stopped being useful were killed."

"And Jamie Hamilton?" Ben asked. "How did you meet him?"

"He was a school acquaintance of one of my brothers. My family was wealthy but didn't have a title, and they looked upon titles with awe. Jamie was invited to a hunt on our property. I had a sizable dowry, enough to make my family tolerable to his. My parents thought Jamie's title would give them . . . more respect."

"You loved him?" He had asked that question before, but had found her answer ambiguous. Now he really wanted to know. He had received mixed signals on the man, ranging from adoration to contempt.

Lisbeth hesitated. "He was kind. Undemanding. He was unlike my family in every way. I think I thought of him as a rescuing prince more than a man. Some of the other men my family tried to get me to accept were . . ." She shivered at the memory of those men who were like her father, brutal and crude, who thought a woman was made to be used. "I was eighteen, and I thought Jamie was wonderful."

"And was he?"

She hesitated again. "He was always considerate, and we shared an interest in horses. I was . . . content."

And she had been. She hadn't known anything else. She hadn't felt the joy and pain of passion, or the grief and ecstasy of love. She wondered whether she could ever be merely "content" again.

Ben's arm tightened around her shoulders as if he understood the words she hadn't spoken. There was a quiet comfort in the gesture, an understanding she hadn't quite expected. She wondered whether he still harbored suspicions.

"I couldn't hurt anyone," she said almost in a whisper, compelled to make him believe.

"I know," he said. "I think I always knew. I just . . ."

"You're frightened for Sarah Ann."

"I can't help feeling responsible for her mother's

death," he said. "I can't let anything else happen to her, and I feel so damned ineffective. It's like fighting a ghost. I know he's there, waiting, but I can't see him."

She sensed Ben didn't usually feel ineffective. From the beginning, he'd exuded the kind of control and confidence that marked men who were very good at what they did.

"Why do you feel responsible for Sarah Ann's mother?"

He sighed. "She got caught up in something I was involved in."

Those bloody allusions again. *What* something? She had given him her trust. She waited for him to do the same. She wanted it so badly, her breath was caught between her heart and her throat.

His hand went up to her face, fingers playing along its planes, hesitating at her mouth. "You've had your own losses, haven't you?" he said softly. "How did you stay so untouched?"

"I'm not untouched," she said.

"But you still believe . . . in magic, and love, and—"

"Trust," she finished for him.

"I want to," he said, his voice strained, aching. "But I've had to learn to forget all that."

"Why?"

He stopped caressing her face, and he turned her to face him. "Lisbeth, for the last four years, I've hunted men. That has a tendency to . . . sap a person of any feelings, especially trust."

Lisbeth felt her heart stop. "But you're a solicitor."

"I *used* to be a lawyer—a solicitor, if you like—but after the war I became a U.S. marshal."

"A marshal?"

"Like one of your constables," he explained. "I hunted outlaws."

"Why?" She was beginning to sound like Sarah Ann,

she thought, and evidently he agreed because the smallest smile twisted his mouth.

"After the war, I couldn't settle down in one place. There were . . . memories. And something I had to do. Marshaling seemed the best way to do it."

"The man you told me about? The one who saved your life?"

Ben looked at her with astonishment as if surprised she remembered, or made the connection.

"Yes," he said.

She'd always felt that man held a key to Ben Masters, and now she knew she'd been right.

"What happened?"

"I used him," he said curtly. "As cynically as one man can use another."

"I don't believe that."

"Believe it, Lisbeth," he insisted. "I used the life of his best friend as a pawn to make him do something completely abhorrent to him. I came damn close to destroying him. I did destroy Sarah Ann's mother."

"You thought you were doing the right thing," she guessed.

"I was arrogant," he said. "I thought I knew what was best for everyone."

"You said he was well today."

"Do you remember everything?" he asked, then continued softly. "If he's well, it isn't because of me."

She just looked at him. "Tell me about him." Anything to keep him talking, anything to plumb the depths she'd waited so long to discover.

Ben hesitated, and she took his hand and held it tightly. After a moment, he started his tale.

"He called himself Diablo, but his real name was Kane. After he was released from the Union prison where he was sent after helping me, he became an outlaw. He and his friend were sentenced to hang.

"As a marshal, I served warrants and hunted wanted men. They kept disappearing into a hideout in an area we called the Indian Territory, and we couldn't find that hideout. I was able to . . . persuade Diablo to find it for us in return for his friend's life.

"He hated me for it, but it was the only way he could save his friend from hanging. I made him befriend people, then betray them."

A moment of silence passed, then Lisbeth asked quietly, "And Sarah Ann's mother?" She kept going back to Mary May because, like Diablo, she seemed to be another key to the enigma that was Ben Masters. And, she admitted, she wanted to know about the woman who'd made such an impact on him. She feared part of her curiosity was sheer jealousy.

"Mary May knew where the hideout was," he continued. "A place called Sanctuary. She had . . . done some business with the man who ran it. After Diablo got in, he made enemies with one of the outlaws there, and the outlaw was thrown out of Sanctuary. All the 'guests' at Sanctuary were led in blindfolded; they didn't know where it was any more than the law did. But this man suspected Mary May knew the location. He tortured her to obtain the information so he could go back for Diablo. If I hadn't put everything in motion . . ."

Her hand was clutching his. "You can't blame yourself for doing what you thought was right."

"Oh, yes I can," he said. "I became very good at using people. At playing God."

She felt his pain, deep and ragged and raw.

"Now I know what it feels like to be hunted," he added dryly, "and I don't like it." He hesitated, then he continued after a moment. "That's why I struck out at you. But at least whoever is behind these attempts has decided to go after me and not Sarah Ann."

A shiver went up her spine and spread throughout her body. "Who's with Sarah Ann?"

"Effie." His brows knitted together at the concern in her voice. "Sarah Ann was tired. I told Effie not to leave her alone."

"Ben," Lisbeth said, rising to her feet, "don't you see? If *either one* of you is killed, the inheritance is in jeopardy. Without her, you have no claim. Without you, she has no guardian. Barbara or I, or even Hugh, would probably be appointed guardian."

"It keeps coming back to the only three who would benefit," he said, but this time there was no accusation in his voice. "Since it's not you—"

"There's only Barbara and Hugh," she finished. "But I still can't believe . . ."

But he wasn't listening any longer. He was on his feet and moving toward his horse. She was moving as quickly as she could behind him, disregarding the pain in her ankle.

Something was wrong. Very wrong. She felt it deep inside. The attempt on Ben's life that morning might well have been real. Then again, it might have been designed to relax his watch over Sarah Ann, make him think that he, not her, was the target—which was exactly what he had thought.

Hugh? Barbara?

She still couldn't believe it of either.

✧✧✧

As soon as Ben and Lisbeth reached Calholm, he saw Effie running toward the stable and he rode directly toward her.

"Where's Sarah Ann?" he asked, panic rising up in him.

Effie stuttered, tears streaming from her eyes. "I . . . I canna find her, sir. I left her . . . a minute only to get her some chocolate. I was just gone . . . hardly any time. I . . . I've looked everywhere in the manor."

"The stables?" he asked. "Have you been to the stables?"

"I . . . I was just going."

Swearing, Ben turned the horse toward the stable. She had to be there. She was probably currying Peppermint. He didn't wait for Bailey to stop before he was out of the saddle and opening the stable door.

"Sarah Ann," he yelled, then waited for her reply. There was none and his heart caught. "Sarah Ann," he tried again, as he strode down toward Peppermint's stall. He heard the fear in his own voice.

Callum Trapp appeared from the back. "Ye be scaring the horses to death—"

"Have you seen Sarah Ann?"

Trapp shook his head. "No, I took one of the 'orses out this afternoon and just returned. I've been putting the tack back. Is the lassie's pony in the stall? She might ha' come to visit him."

Ben, Trapp, and Lisbeth hurried toward Peppermint's stall. The pony was missing.

Ben shook his head. "She wouldn't have taken the pony alone. She can't saddle him."

Effie was sniffling behind them, and Ben turned to her. "Exactly when did you last see her?"

She looked frightened half out of her mind, and he wanted to shake her, but that would accomplish nothing. He gentled his voice. "Think back, Effie. Exactly when did you leave her room?"

"I do na' know," she replied, her voice quivering. "It's my fault. She were sleeping and I thought she might like something warm when she . . . and then Thad was downstairs talking about the race and . . ." Her voice trailed off, guilt written all over her face, and Ben realized she had been gone longer than "a minute."

"How long did you look for her?"

"I do na' know," Effie wailed. "I looked an' looked."

"An hour? Two?" He and Lisbeth had been gone about three hours. Making love while Sarah Ann awoke alone . . .

God, he would never forgive himself.

"I do na' know," Effie said again, backing away at his angry tone, bending her head in shame and regret, shying away as if expecting a blow.

He wanted to strike at something. God, how he needed to do that. But he was more to blame than anyone. Sarah Ann was *his* responsibility.

Trapp gave Effie a disgusted look. "Tears will no' help now. I'll see if any of the other horses are missing. You go to the manor and see if anyone saw her leave."

Ben looked at him questioningly.

"She probably just took a ride wi' one of the guests," he said.

Ben didn't believe it. Unless perhaps the guest was Drew Cameron. "I'll go with you," he told the trainer, then turned to Effie. She was still standing there as if glued to the ground. "Go find Duncan, and set all the servants looking for her. Search the house again. Go, dammit."

At that, she took off, stumbling from the stable. Then with Lisbeth at his side, he followed Trapp as the man checked each stall.

"One is gone," Trapp said. "Dragon Slayer."

"Have you seen Lord Kinloch around?" As Ben said the words, he heard Lisbeth's gasp.

"Not since the race," Callum replied.

Ben turned to Lisbeth. "Find him."

"He wouldn't have—"

"Someone did," he interrupted curtly. He couldn't trust Hugh and definitely not Cameron. And Lisbeth?

If he hadn't been so damn weak, so consumed by desire for her, he would be in his room right now, watching Sarah Ann play with Annabelle. Chills rocked him, along with raw anguish.

And fear, fear so deep he could hardly bear it.

But he had to. He had to think. Perhaps she was just lost. His gut said otherwise, though. Someone had probably taken her, and she was out there alone.

One of the Hamiltons. His enemy—and Sarah Ann's—was one of the Hamiltons.

"You can't go alone," she whispered. "You don't know the roads. I'll go with you."

"No," he said. "Look for Cameron."

She nodded, but doubt was in her eyes. "I'll get everyone looking. The grooms, the servants."

He turned away from her and looked to Callum Trapp. "If someone took her, where might they head?"

"The road leads to both Glasgow an' Edinburgh," Trapp said. "I would be bettin' on Edinburgh. It's closer and a good place to lose yerself in."

Ben nodded. Time was of the essence. If someone had taken her, they would be riding hard. He couldn't wait until the manor and grounds were searched. His gut told him she'd been kidnapped. And he'd seldom been wrong. "I'll search the road." He turned to Lisbeth. "Ask others to search the countryside."

She nodded. "Everyone will help," she whispered softly, but her eyes were bleak.

"I'll go wi' ye," Trapp said after a moment's silence. "I'll saddle the horses." He left, moving quicker than Ben had ever seen him.

Ben turned to Lisbeth, his heart torn to pieces.

"Ben . . ."

"It's my fault. I left her. I should have realized—"

She shook her head. "We'll find her. She's probably just searching for Annabelle someplace."

But he knew differently. "If we hadn't—"

"You couldn't watch her every moment." She reached out to him, but he stepped back. Part of him even blamed her, or at least his obsession with her. Even though he knew it was unfair. The fault was his. Totally.

He turned away.

"Ben . . ."

Her voice was pleading, but he couldn't answer. Instead, he moved away, meeting Callum who was now approaching with two horses. He took the reins to one and mounted.

Without looking back, he dug his heels into the flanks of his horse, and he and Trapp galloped away from Calholm.

Chapter Twenty-One

Sarah Ann had seemingly disappeared into thin air.

Ben and Callum galloped half the distance to Edinburgh, stopping the few travelers they saw. No one had seen a child on a pony. Ben wanted to go the other way, to Glasgow, but it was well past midnight, and a bare sliver of a moon disappeared behind the clouds, cutting visibility to nothing. Others, Callum also argued, were checking that route.

It was several hours past midnight when they returned to Calholm, hoping to find good news. There was none, although Cameron had been found—apparently in a female guest's bedroom.

Henry was also missing. Lisbeth guessed that he had followed Sarah Ann.

Hugh and the few remaining guests, as well as the household staff, had combed the countryside, including the castle ruins and the woods where the hunt had taken place.

Still, Ben bounded up the steps to Sarah Ann's room, hoping that some miracle had returned her. But it was empty except for Annabelle, who meowed piteously and prowled back and forth on the bed in her own search.

He felt sick at the thought of Sarah Ann's terror.

He hadn't been able to save Mary May, and now he'd failed to protect her daughter. He felt helpless, impotent. Damn whoever did this. Damn himself for allowing his preoccupation with Lisbeth to distract him.

Why hadn't he seen that Sarah Ann was still in danger? The attack on his own life had lulled him into thinking he was the sole target.

He didn't even know where to start looking. He was in a country he didn't know, among people he didn't trust. His years as a lawman didn't help now.

Only one clue had surfaced: a new groom was also missing. He'd been hired by Callum a few days ago and had had excellent references from a family in Edinburgh. No, Callum said, he had not checked the references. He'd had no reason to, after the man proved himself adept at handling horses. And now he too blamed himself.

Ben finally left Sarah Ann's room and went downstairs. Despite the early hour of the morning, all the searchers were still up, waiting for further instructions. Lisbeth and Barbara had scoured the house once again, then gone into the kitchen to see about providing food for the tired riders. Ben studied every face over and over again and found nothing but concern. His gaze lingered on Cameron and Hugh.

"I can't believe anyone would hurt Sarah Ann," Hugh said, collapsing into a chair with a glass of brandy.

Ben paced several times across the room. "I'm going out to look again."

"I'll go with you," offered Cameron, who was lounging wearily against a wall.

"So will I." Hugh jumped from his seat, spilling some of the brandy.

Callum hesitated. "Wait till morn. Ye canna see anything out there now."

"I'll take a lantern," Ben said. "I can't stand here and do nothing. God, I'll kill whoever did this." His eyes went around the room again. "No groom did it on his own."

Hugh spun around to face him. "What do you mean, Masters?"

"Exactly what I said. Only three people would benefit from my death or Sarah Ann's."

"Your death?" He looked puzzled.

"Someone took shots at me this morning during the grouse hunt."

Everyone looked stunned.

"When that didn't succeed," Ben continued tightly, "Sarah Ann apparently became the next target." *And I left her alone.* He would never forgive himself. And God help whoever had taken her.

Barbara entered then, followed by Lisbeth, both carrying trays of food. Duncan was behind them with a tray laden with two large decanters of spirits.

Hugh looked at them angrily. "You just missed being called murderers and kidnappers."

Barbara blinked several times as if trying to understand. Lisbeth's face went completely white.

"It seems Masters here doesn't think the child is merely lost. She's been kidnapped, or worse, and by one of us." He threw the glass he was holding against the fireplace and whirled around to face Ben.

"I've made no secret I believe Calholm should be mine," he said, "but I bloody well wouldn't hurt a child to get it." He strode out of the room, the heels of his boots echoing sharply down the hallway.

Ben glanced at Cameron, who straightened from the wall. "Am I a suspect, too? I have no interest in Calholm."

"Don't you?" Ben said with deadly softness.

The room was silent, ringing with silent accusations. Several of the guests shifted uncomfortably.

Cameron met his gaze steadily. "I think you can use this time more effectively," he challenged.

"What would you suggest?"

Cameron looked at the two women, and Ben's gaze followed that gaze. Lisbeth was like a statue, quiet and still and pale. Barbara's violet eyes were wide and wounded.

"Let's talk alone."

Ben hesitated. "All right," he finally said, leading the way from the room. He didn't know what Andrew Cameron wanted. He knew what he wanted at the moment: to commit an act of violence.

Cameron walked out to the yard. Several horses were still tethered to posts in front.

"What do you want?" Ben said sharply.

"I know what you think," Drew said. "Lisbeth told me. You're wrong. I have no intentions toward her."

Ben couldn't read the man's eyes in the dark, but he heard the sincerity in his voice. "You were in Glasgow when the crates fell, then Edinburgh when a carriage nearly ran us down."

"Our first meeting was a coincidence," Cameron said. "Edinburgh wasn't. I'd heard you were in the city. I arranged to meet you again. I *didn't* arrange for the carriage accident."

"You knew—"

"Only when Lisbeth told me today," he said. "You're right about one thing. I do care for Lisbeth. But you're wrong about why."

"Get to the point," Ben demanded.

Cameron hesitated, obviously reluctant to continue. Then he seemed to come to a decision. "Will you swear not to tell a living soul what I say?"

"If it has nothing to do with Sarah Ann."

"It doesn't."

"Then you have my word," Ben said, wanting this conversation over so he could be on his way.

"I believe Lisbeth is my sister. My half sister."

Nothing could have surprised Ben more. His silence prompted Cameron to continue.

"Her father . . . bedded my mother. I never understood why my father hated me as he did until he told me on his deathbed that I was not his son. He made sure I wouldn't get anything from him except the damn title, but he'd been too proud to admit he'd been cuckolded, particularly by a commoner."

"My mother's sister finally told me who the man was. My mother claimed he raped her, a charge I wasn't sure was accurate," he said bitterly. "But then I learned a great deal about my birth father, and it could well be true. Lisbeth was the only decent thing to come from that family."

"You've never told her?"

"That her father could be a rapist?" Cameron snorted. "I didn't want to add to her pain. But I did want to make sure nothing happened to her, so I arranged the meeting with Jamie, and insinuated myself into their circle. I had a title, meaningless as it is, so it wasn't difficult."

The implications began tumbling through Ben's head. "You have a reason to want to help her then."

"By killing you or hurting the child she obviously cares about deeply?" Cameron made an impatient sound. "You're a fool. I have eyes, Masters, even if you don't. She loves you, and she loves that child."

Ben let the words sink in. He knew Cameron was telling the truth. The story was too crazy *not* to be the truth, and everything fit, including the similarity of Lisbeth's and Cameron's eyes.

"You mentioned that a kidnapper might take Sarah Ann to Glasgow. Why?"

"It would have been easy enough to kill a child," Drew said. "A pillow over her head when she was sleeping, a fall from the pony. An accident would have been easy to arrange. I think whoever took her has no stomach for killing a little girl. The only alternative was to take her, perhaps sell her to a family who wanted a child."

"And ships sail from Glasgow," Ben said, continuing

the thought. "I should have thought about that, but Trapp said Edinburgh was more likely. It's closer and an easy place to disappear in."

"That's logical, too. But I would still bet on Glasgow. And there's no reason for you to think of it. You've been here only a little more than a month."

After suspecting him for so long, Ben found it hard to trust Cameron. After several moments, he voiced his question. "But who could be responsible?"

Cameron shrugged. "I have no idea. I don't particularly like Hugh, but I can't believe he would stoop this low."

Frustration clawed at Ben. Frustration and stark terror. "Tell Lisbeth I'm riding to Glasgow."

"I'm going with you."

Ben hesitated.

"Dammit, Masters, I know every tavern, every gambling hell, and every rogue in Glasgow," Drew said. "I stayed there often."

It wasn't the best of recommendations, Ben knew, but he had little choice. He didn't know Glasgow at all. And the hell of it was he believed Andrew Cameron. He didn't know why, but he did. "I'll inform Duncan—in case Sarah Ann is found, he can send someone after us—but I don't want anyone else to know where we're going," he finally said.

Drew nodded. "What about Lisbeth?"

Ben shook his head. "She's too trusting. I'll say we're going to search the woods again."

"I'll saddle the horses," Drew said.

Ben started back to the house when a faint whine stopped him. "Henry," he said and ran toward the barely visible figure at the gate. Drew was right behind him.

The dog was dragging himself, barely able to move, and Ben smelled the lingering odor of chloroform. The dog had been drugged, was barely conscious, and yet he had struggled home.

And Peppermint? Ben doubted that whoever had taken Sarah Ann had kept the pony.

Someone had planned this very well. That realization added to Ben's fury. Ruthlessly, he tamped it down. Rage interfered with his thinking.

Ben picked the dog up. Henry whined, his tongue lolling out of his gaping mouth. "I'll take him in to Lisbeth and talk to Duncan. You saddle the horses."

As soon as Ben entered the library, Lisbeth saw Henry and ran to him. The dog whined weakly.

"He's been chloroformed," Ben said. "He probably tried to follow whoever took Sarah Ann, and the kidnapper couldn't afford a shot."

Ben put the dog down, and Lisbeth knelt next to him.

"Brave Henry," she said as she saw blood on his mouth. "I think he might have taken a bite out of whoever—"

"Cameron and I are going out to look in the woods a while longer," he said. "The rest of you get some sleep and start looking again in the morning."

Lisbeth glanced up at him quickly, a question in her eyes. And worry. "Drew?"

"We've reached . . . an understanding."

Her face relaxed. "I'll go with you."

"I think Henry needs you," Ben said softly.

"But—"

He took her hand, and, ignoring curious stares from the others, he touched her face. "We'll be back . . . with Sarah Ann."

Callum Trapp stood near the door by himself. "I'll go with ye."

"No," Ben said flatly. "You need some rest so you can lead one of the search parties tomorrow."

Callum started to protest, but Ben didn't give him a chance. He started for the door, and Lisbeth put a hand on Callum's arm.

"He's right," Ben heard her say.

Moments later, he and Drew Cameron were galloping down the road toward Glasgow.

❖❖❖

Lisbeth nursed Henry, who had been taken to her room, through the night. The other guests had gone to bed, and Callum to his room in the back of the stables.

She left Henry only for a few moments to check on Annabelle, who immediately jumped down from Sarah Ann's bed and rubbed against her legs. It was, Lisbeth thought, as if the cat sensed something wrong, as if she felt a sense of loss. Lisbeth leaned down and picked her up, taking the cat back to her own room.

Annabelle immediately stalked over to a still groggy and sick Henry and licked him, meowing softly and flicking her tail in obvious distress.

Lisbeth wished she had gone with Ben and Drew. She desperately wanted to help, to do *something*. She tried to reason out Sarah Ann's disappearance; she still couldn't believe someone would take a child. Especially someone she knew. Someone in her family. The thought sickened her.

Only Henry saved her sanity. He needed her at the moment. And Ben would be back by daylight, hopefully with Sarah Ann. Ben was wrong; she hadn't been taken. Sarah Ann was simply lost. She had to be. Probably, the missing groom had simply quit after the heavy duties this weekend. Coincidence, that was all. She couldn't believe it was anything more.

They *would* find Sarah Ann.

❖❖❖

Ben and Drew reached Glasgow at noon, having ridden their horses nearly into the ground, stopping once to beg use of two fresh ones from a family Drew knew. Once explanations were made, the horses became readily available.

If the kidnapper had gone to Glasgow, he had a day's

head start, but he couldn't travel quickly with a sleeping child. At best, he probably made Glasgow in the early morning hours. Sometime during the long morning, Ben started calling his companion Drew, and the two of them developed an uneasy partnership formed by common purpose. Drew directed him straightaway to Broomielaw, where most of the ships docked. They soon discovered three ships were due to leave for America on the evening tide. Another twenty had Scottish destinations.

They had four hours until the first ship set sail, time to visit inns along the waterfront. No one had seen a child, or a man resembling the description of the missing groom. Ben began to doubt Drew's thinking. Perhaps the kidnapper *had* preferred Edinburgh and its numerous trains.

"The whisky dens," Drew said. "We'll try those next, then the captains of the ships."

Ben nodded. If the groom had been employed to take Sarah Ann from Scotland, he would wait until sailing time, then try to negotiate a last-minute passage, which would be unrecorded at the custom office. And a frightened man might well go to a whisky den for courage after the flight from Calholm.

"We'll separate," he said. Two could cover more area than one. If the man was drinking, he wouldn't take a child with him. Too many people would remember. That meant Sarah Ann could be tucked in a slum somewhere or lying unconscious in a vehicle of some type.

If the kidnapper had headed for Glasgow. It was still a big if. But Ben believed it was true. It made sense. The abduction had been well planned. Unless Sarah Ann had been killed—and he wouldn't let himself even think that—the kidnapper had to leave Scotland as quickly as possible. Sarah Ann was too bright not to ask for help or tell someone where she belonged. The only hope was a ship, and a private cabin, where Sarah Ann could be kept sedated.

Who? The question never left his mind. Nor did the

prospect of that person's slow demise. Ben was no longer a lawman. He was no longer bound by a code of conduct.

Drew, with only the slightest hesitation, agreed to his suggestion that they separate. Both remembered Callum's description of the groom: a small man no more than five feet tall, a sometimes jockey, with dark hair and pale blue eyes, and a nervous demeanor. Ben had seen him only once around the stables, but he knew he would recognize him. Drew didn't remember seeing him at all.

Glasgow had exploded as an industrial city during the 1800's, and its streets were dirty, its air clogged with smoke. The large number of working men, including those who worked in shipbuilding along the Clyde River, crowded numerous whisky dens. Ben visited three before wondering whether finding one man was an impossible task. He and Drew had given themselves one hour, then they would meet and visit each departing ship.

Ben found the man at the fourth drinking establishment. The moment he entered, a slender man kicked over a chair in his haste to leave and started at a run for a back hall.

Ben dove after him, catching him before he went more than a dozen feet. The groom crashed to the floor, yelling as he did. The whisky den was half full and the drinkers, some of them ugly drunk, surrounded the two men.

"He be tryin' to rob me," the groom cried out desperately in Scottish brogue. "A foreigner."

Mutters rippled through the room and two men approached.

"Let 'im go," one burly man said.

Ben had brought his pistol with him, tucking it into his belt. In one easy movement, his right hand pulled it from under his sheepskin coat as he dodged a fist. His other hand kept its grasp on his clawing, wriggling prisoner.

"Stay back," he ordered.

More than a little stunned, the mob moved back. But

the muttering grew louder, and Ben saw one man duck out the front, apparently going for help.

"Get up, Baxter," he told the groom. He put the man between himself and the crowd, pointing the barrel into the man's side. "Where's my little girl?"

"I don't know what you're talking about," the groom said sullenly.

"Then why did you leave Calholm suddenly?"

"Me and Trapp . . . we had a disagreement."

Trapp hadn't said anything about that.

"Ye don't see no kid, do you?" the groom said. He pleaded to the others. " 'E's a crazy American. Help me."

But one of the men had been listening. "What's tha' about a bairn?"

"My daughter," Ben said. "She was kidnapped yesterday, same time this man disappeared. She's four years old."

"I dinna do anything," the groom whined. "There's no lass here."

"What did you do with her?" Ben said, twisting the groom's arm until the man screamed. The den's customers moved in closer.

"I dinna do nothing," the groom repeated plaintively.

"Where is she?" Ben asked again, tightening his hold on the man's arm. In a moment, it would break. The groom realized it and started whimpering.

"I swear—"

"Where is she?" Ben said again, and this time his voice was like death. "Tell me now or I'll break your neck as well as your arm."

The groom screamed. The men started closing in again.

Ben turned the gun in their direction. "I'm very good with this, gentlemen," he said coldly. "There are six bullets, and I won't miss with any of them."

Tension radiated in the room, and Ben knew it was a matter of seconds before the mob rushed him. He cocked the pistol.

"Found the bloody piece of dung, did you?"

The question came from the doorway. Everyone turned toward the sound. Drew sauntered in with the self-assured arrogance of a true aristocrat. Resentment flashed across faces, but no one made a move toward him.

"And what has the bastard to say for himself?" Drew said with lazy insouciance.

"He's a bit reluctant to talk," Ben replied.

Drew turned his attention to the crowd. "Do any of you have use for baby snatchers?"

The mutters turned angrier. "Ye mean 'e really took a bairn?"

"Aye," Drew said.

" 'E said this American took 'is money."

"This American and I have been riding through the night to find him and the wee lass he took." Drew's hazel eyes were as hard as agates. "We think he was going to take her on a ship to America."

The leader who had demanded the groom's release stepped closer. "Ye give him to me and my fellows for a while. We'll get wha' ye want to know."

The groom looked around desperately, then slumped in Ben's hold. "My sister's keeping her. Two blocks away. I weren't going to hurt her."

"A Scot," one of the workers said disgustedly, swinging a fist into the groom's stomach.

Baxter sunk to the floor.

"The address," Ben said.

The man spat out something, and one of the workman stepped forward. "I know tha' place."

"We'll keep him fer you," another said. "You go see about the bairn."

Ben hesitated.

Drew nodded. "They'll keep him," he said. "I'll go with you."

Ben turned back to the groom. "Who planned this?"

Baxter whimpered. Drew stepped forward, putting the heel of his boot on the man's stomach. "Who?"

There was a hard promise to the voice, and the man trembled. "Trapp," he said finally.

"The trainer?" Drew asked.

"Aye," the groom said.

"Why?"

"I don't know. I just needed money."

Ben looked at Drew, then at the men surrounding the groom. He wanted to get to Sarah Ann. And then Callum Trapp.

"We'll keep him here for ye," one of the men assured him.

Drew looked at the man who said he knew the address. "Are you sure you know the way?"

"Aye," he answered. "Maeve Lackey lives there, entertains men occasionally. She said she had a brother who was a jockey. Jockey," he added jeeringly at the fallen man.

"Let's go," Ben told Drew and the other man, who introduced himself as Jack Dundee.

Dundee moved quickly through the dirty, smelly streets of the riverfront, followed by Drew and Ben. Ben kept thinking of Sarah Ann, her terror at waking in a strange place, at losing everything and everyone she'd come to know.

He wanted to kill Callum Trapp. He would kill him with his own hands. But what was the trainer after? Was he working for someone in the household?

They reached a dilapidated brick building. The street in front was swirling with slops hurled from windows. They ducked one such pail of contents. Cooking smells mixed with the other odors, and Ben felt he might be sick.

Dundee turned to him. "Maeve has a room on the first floor. To the left."

Ben led the way to the door, his hand on his pistol. He didn't know if anyone besides Baxter and Trapp were involved. He tried the door first, but it was locked and he pounded on it.

" 'Old your 'orses," said a woman's voice from within. "I'm comin'."

The door opened a crack, and Ben pushed it wide open, ignoring the indignant cries of a slatternly looking woman dressed only in a dirty, flimsy nightrobe.

"Where is she?" he said.

"Where is who? What right you got coming in here?"

"You have my daughter. That's my right," Ben said coldly. His eyes searched the room. He saw a door and went to it.

The woman sought to hold him back, but he easily shook off her hand as he opened the door to a tiny room. A small still form lay huddled on a dirty bed.

He reached the small lumpy bed in three strides and knelt next to it. Sarah Ann was sleeping deeply. A half-filled glass sat on a rickety chair next to the bed, and he sniffed it. Laudanum.

Ben lifted Sarah Ann, cradling her in his arms. He didn't know gratitude could be so painful. "Forgive me, Sugarplum, for leaving you alone." He leaned down and lightly kissed the dirty beloved face, closing his eyes against the force of emotion sweeping him. He saw a drop of water on her face; it took him a moment to realize it was a tear from his eyes.

"Is she all right?" Drew asked.

Ben nodded. "I think so."

"What should I do with her?" Drew indicated the woman who stood hunched against the wall, eyeing the door that was guarded by Jack Dundee.

"I dinna do nothing," the woman said. "My brother said the brat was orphaned. I wa' doing a kind deed, I was."

Ben looked down at Sarah Ann's dress, now dirty but still obviously of expensive cloth, and then back at the woman. "You're a liar."

"Ye ha' no right—"

Ben ignored her and turned back to Sarah Ann. "Sugarplum," he whispered. Her eyes remained closed.

"When did you last give her some of that?" he asked the woman, indicating the glass.

"I dinna gi' 'er anything."

"Then your brother?"

She shivered. "He'll kill me."

"Baxter isn't going to be in any position to kill anyone," Ben said. "When?" The question was like a shot.

"An 'our ago," she finally whined. "He arrived and told me to look after 'er for a while. That's all I know." Her bravado seem to fade with every word.

An hour ago.

That meant Sarah Ann would probably be asleep for several more hours. Ben wanted to see those blue eyes, to assure himself that no damage had been done. Damn Trapp.

Damn Scotland. He would never forgive the country, nor himself for bringing Sarah Ann here.

Ben stood. "I want to get her back to Calholm," he said. "I want to face Trapp."

"So do I," Drew said harshly. "What should we do with this woman?"

"Take her with us to her brother and call the constables. Let the law take care of them. We'll need their testimony against Trapp. If I don't kill him first," Ben said.

Drew smiled, a cold smile that surprised Ben. Drew Cameron seemed to make an art out of congeniality. Ben was seeing another side now, one that intrigued him. There was a recklessness that Ben recognized. He'd tried to tame his own; Cameron hadn't. He merely disguised it.

But none of that mattered. Ben wanted to take Sarah Ann home, to a place she knew and where she felt safe, even though he wondered whether she would ever feel safe again.

Annabelle was at Calholm, though. Annabelle and Henry and, he prayed fervently, Peppermint.

And Lisbeth.

Everyone and everything Sarah Ann loved.

And their enemy.

Chapter Twenty-Two

Lisbeth rose at dawn. She went to check on Sarah Ann's room, then Ben's. They were still empty.

Why weren't Ben and Drew back? They'd said they were going to search the woods again. They couldn't have been hurt. Or had they hurt each other? She remembered Ben's accusations, his suspicions about Drew. But she trusted Drew as she trusted herself and knew he would not hurt Sarah Ann.

Lisbeth found Duncan in the dining room and asked him if Ben had returned. The old man had obviously gotten no more sleep than she, and his eyes were dulled with fatigue.

The butler hesitated to answer her question, and Lisbeth realized he knew something that she did not. "Tell me, Duncan."

Distress filled his face.

"Duncan?" she prodded. "You must tell me."

He sighed heavily. "Mr. Masters told me he and Lord

Kinloch were going to Glasgow. He said no' to tell anyone unless the young miss was found, but I don't think he
meant ye, my lady."

Lisbeth wasn't so sure. Had his suspicions of her returned? She couldn't bear the thought, but then she knew
how hard Sarah Ann's disappearance had affected him.

But why Glasgow?

Ships. The thought occurred to her instantly. They
had gone to check the ships.

"Thank you, Duncan," Lisbeth called over her shoulder as she hurried from the room. Before she did anything
else, she would check the stables. Perhaps Callum had
seen the riders coming home.

To her surprise, Callum Trapp met her at the stable
door. He, too, looked weary.

"I've been out looking for the young lass," he said. "I
found her pony. He was tied in the woods south of here."

"Is he all right?" she asked.

"Aye. He ate several cups of oats."

"But did you . . . find anything else?"

Callum shook his head, and Lisbeth's hope died. Despite the missing groom, even the sick dog, she'd still
hoped that perhaps Sarah Ann had ridden out alone on
her pony, or perhaps had gone with the groom and then
had become separated. And the groom, fearing the wrath
of the family, had simply left. She'd frantically sought any
explanation other than the one Ben believed.

"No sign of the lass," Callum said. "And the American's horse is still gone."

"He and Drew have gone to Glasgow."

A frown creased his brow. "Glasgow? Why?"

Lisbeth shrugged. "I don't know. I thought you might
have talked to him about it yesterday when you searched
the road."

Callum shrugged. "No."

Lisbeth saw the deep worry in his eyes. "I know you
care for her, too," she said quickly. "We'll find her, and

she'll be so happy to see Peppermint. When Ben . . . Mr. Masters returns, please ask him to find me."

Callum turned around stiffly, going toward his room. Lisbeth knew he'd grown very fond of Sarah Ann. He'd helped teach her to ride and had been proud of how fast she'd learned. Under that glum exterior, Callum had more than one soft spot.

Lisbeth returned to the house and talked to the cook about breakfast. It was another gray Scottish dawn, with a light mist falling. She usually didn't mind these mornings, seeing a quiet beauty in them. But that morning seemed dreary and threatening. And sad.

Lisbeth kept her mind busy with seeing that the guests breakfasted, then started off on another search. Hugh went with them. Barbara, who didn't like horses, stayed at the house. She offered to look after the few remaining wives and daughters, as well as Henry and Annabelle, if Lisbeth wanted to join the other searchers. The offer stunned Lisbeth for a moment. Then she accepted.

She had not told Barbara or Hugh about Glasgow, but as the hours had crept by, she knew she had to do something or quietly go mad. She planned to ride toward Glasgow. There was but one road.

She didn't care now what the guests or family thought, what anyone thought. She dressed in her boy's trousers and shirt, and wool jacket. She tucked her hair under her cap and pulled the cap down over her face. Few would recognize her, and she could ride astride, making better time.

She slipped down the back steps and headed for the stable. It was empty. Apparently even Callum had returned to the woods. She looked in briefly on Peppermint, then saddled Shadow.

❖❖❖

Only the grace of God kept Ben awake as he and Drew rode toward Calholm with a sleeping Sarah Ann. Ben had finally relinquished her to his companion, for his arms had grown numb from holding his daughter.

A few more hours, Ben told himself, and they would be back at Calholm, and he would have Trapp's neck between his hands. The constables in Glasgow were holding Baxter and his sister, who were telling all in hopes of not being charged as accomplices. But neither seemed to have knowledge of anyone but Trapp engineering Sarah Ann's abduction.

Ben felt a prickling of unease. He'd accomplished his mission of rescuing Sarah Ann with little difficulty, and he'd never been happy with ease. Something always lay lurking behind a veneer of success.

Dusk was falling and as usual clouds filled the Scottish sky. The prickling along Ben's nerve ends increased as they approached a copse of trees protecting a turn of the road. His hand went instinctively toward the pistol tucked in the back of his trousers.

He didn't have time to reach it.

Suddenly, a figure appeared from the woods, a pistol already in his fist, and his finger on the trigger.

"Stand and hold," Callum Trapp said, not even trying to hide his identity.

Ben's hand kept moving toward the pistol.

"Raise your hands now, or ye'll taste a bullet."

"I think we'll taste it anyway," Ben said dryly, but he slowly raised his hands. His only hope now was to take the trainer by surprise. A deadly calm settled over him.

"Trapp," he acknowledged.

"Ye don't sound surprised."

Ben was careful. He didn't want to tell the man that he was through, that Baxter was telling everything to Glasgow authorities. Trapp wouldn't have anything to lose then.

"I was starting to figure it out," he said slowly, working his way through the lie. "Who had something to gain? Hugh and Lady Barbara, of course, and Lisbeth, but I didn't think any of them had the . . . steel to do it."

Ben shifted in his seat. He was aware of Drew next to him, his stillness as he held Sarah Ann against him.

"Even then," he continued, "I really didn't think you would harm a child. I thought you cared for her."

"I dinna harm her. Baxter would have found a good home for her. If you hadn't interfered—"

"And you were the one who shot at me, I suppose," Ben said lazily, stalling, looking for an advantage. "Why?"

"Ye have no right to Calholm," Trapp exclaimed. "Lady Lisbeth is the only one who cares about it, who cares about the horses, who cares about the Marquess's dream. We can win the Grand National with Shadow. The old Marquess promised me that when he hired me."

"Lisbeth doesn't know anything about this," Ben said, stating it as fact.

He snorted. "Lady Lisbeth? She's too soft in some ways, but when I make Shadow a champion, she'll be content."

"Her husband? Did you kill him, too?"

He shrugged. "He was going to sell the horses. I heard him telling that whore, Lady Barbara. He was sleeping wi' her, too. Lady Lisbeth was well rid of him."

So Callum Trapp *had* acted alone.

"And the accidents in Glasgow and Edinburgh?" Ben inquired with deceptive calm.

"I 'ave friends I asked to keep an eye out for an American and a little girl."

It made sense. Trapp had been to steeplechases and hurdle races throughout Scotland. It wouldn't have been difficult to find accomplices with so much at stake: a Grand National champion.

"What are you going to do now?"

"I have to kill you both."

"And Sarah Ann?"

Trapp shook his head. "I'll regret that. I never meant for the lass to be hurt, but now there's no 'elp for it."

"She's still sleeping from laudanum," Ben said. "She

knows nothing about you. You can say you found her. You can even be a hero," he added dryly.

He saw the flicker in Trapp's eyes, but it quickly disappeared and he shook his head again, regretfully. "She might have heard something. Now, get down from those horses," Trapp ordered, obviously tired of the conversation.

Ben hesitated, and then he saw a movement at the bend of the road. A rider. A second later, he recognized Lisbeth. The sound of hoofbeats alerted Trapp, too, and he moved his horse back so he could see the road, while still keeping his gun on Ben and Cameron.

Lisbeth started to canter up to them, and Ben saw her face, saw it change when she noticed the gun in Trapp's hand and where it was pointing.

"No!" she said, pulling hard on her reins.

Trapp's mouth worked for a moment, then turned hard. "Don't come any closer, Lady Lisbeth."

But she did, moving Shadow until he was nearly abreast of Trapp's horse. The two beasts sidestepped, each pawing the ground and snorting, and for an instant, Ben thought he might have a chance to reach for his gun while Trapp fought, one-handed, to control his mount. But the trainer got the animal to back off from Lisbeth's stallion without his gun hand wavering even once.

"I'm sorry, Lady Lisbeth," Trapp said slowly. "I dinna want ye to be involved."

"Involved in—"

Then comprehension flooded her face. And horror. "Not you," she whispered. "Please, not you."

"They have to die, Lady Lisbeth. We can still do it, you and I. We can still win the Grand National. We can make Shadow the greatest horse in Britain." His face took on a look of desperation.

"No," Lisbeth said. "You shoot them, and you'll have to shoot me."

"Don't say that, Lady Lisbeth," he pleaded. "It's always been the two of us, ever since ye came to Calholm. I

did everything for ye." Trapp gestured with his pistol
toward Ben. "He don't deserve Calholm."

Her voice had a frantic edge to it as she said, "But if
you kill him and Sarah Ann, Hugh will inherit, *not me*."

Trapp cursed. "If I had killed the American in the
woods, then ever'thing would ha' been right. Ye could
'ave adopted the lass, and managed Calholm. But I dinna
kill 'im, and I canna wait longer. He might sell the horses.
With the lass gone, your cousin could meet with another . . . mishap."

"No," she said. "You couldn't think I would—"

"It's right, Lady Lisbeth," Trapp insisted.

Ben watched Lisbeth's face pale. She looked at Sarah
Ann in Drew's arms, then back at Trapp. Then, with cal-
culated intent—Ben could almost see her make the decision—she relaxed her hold on Shadow's reins, and the
snorting, agitated stallion made straight for Trapp's horse.

"No!" Ben shouted.

Trapp saw, too, but with only one hand on the reins,
he could do little to keep his mount from rising to
Shadow's challenge. His attention on Ben wavered—and
so did the gun hand.

It was all Ben needed. He kicked his horse forward,
closing the few yards between himself and Trapp before
Lisbeth and her rearing stallion reached them. Then he
launched himself at the Scotsman. At the same time, the
pistol turned back toward him and discharged, and he felt
a bullet graze his side only a second before his body hit
Trapp's.

They both went tumbling to the ground. Trapp
landed beneath him, hitting the ground hard, but desperation gave the trainer strength. Twice, Trapp tried to kick
him, but Ben ploughed a fist into the twisted, angry
face—once, twice, three times, until the trainer lay still.

Ben sat up painfully and looked to see that Lisbeth
had tied Shadow to a tree at the side of the road. Trapp's
horse appeared to have lost interest with the challenge
now removed.

Drew had dismounted, laid Sarah Ann on the grass, and he and Lisbeth were both coming toward him. Lisbeth looked sick, her glance going from Ben to her longtime friend and trainer, who still lay, groaning, on the ground. Then, quickly, she hurried to where Sarah Ann lay.

"Is she . . . ?"

"She's been drugged for two days," Ben said. "She should be coming out of it soon."

Lisbeth leaned down and hugged Sarah Ann, listening to her breathe—as he too had done, Ben thought, to convince himself she was all right.

Then Lisbeth's gaze met his, her eyes full of grief. "I told him," she whispered. "I told Callum you'd gone to Glasgow. Duncan said he was not to tell anyone, but I didn't think . . ."

Ben climbed to his feet, stepped over to her, and pulled her into his arms. "You didn't know," he said.

But she looked up at him with eyes filled with guilt. "He said he did it for me."

"He did it for *himself*," Drew interrupted. "He wanted a Grand National champion, no matter the cost. You were his justification. But it was his need, not yours."

"Maybe it *was* my need," she said brokenly.

Ben felt her trembling, and his hold tightened. "Trapp did it, Lisbeth. Not you, for God's sake. He was obsessed."

The tremors in her seemed to increase, and he felt her heartbreak.

"He was going to hurt Sarah Ann."

"I think he tried to avoid that," Ben said gently. "His first hope was to get rid of me so you could adopt her. When that didn't work, he went ahead with plans to kidnap her. Baxter said he was to take her to America, sell her to a family who wanted a child."

Lisbeth's body was so rigid, he thought it might shatter.

"We might all be dead if you hadn't come when you

did," he said gently. "Damn, you were magnificent. Any other woman would have swooned. But you did everything just right—although you nearly gave me heart failure when I saw you were going to let those two stallions fight it out."

"Shadow and Firestorm hate each other," she said in a small voice. Then, suddenly, she wrenched away from him and stood alone, holding her arms with her hands as if she were freezing cold.

He tried to take her in his arms again, but she turned away, and the despairing look in her face kept him from trying again. She couldn't accept comforting now. Not yet. He knew exactly how she felt. He had felt that way when Mary May had died. His heart ached for the agony he knew she was suffering, and yet he knew no caress, no words would help at this moment. She needed time.

Trapp moved slightly, and Drew picked up the trainer's pistol, which lay in the road, then went and stood over the prisoner. Trapp sat up painfully, his gaze going to Lisbeth.

"Lady Lisbeth?" It was a plea for understanding. "Calholm should always have been yours."

"No," she said, her voice lifeless. "I'm not a Hamilton. Sarah Ann is. Dear God, Callum, how could you?"

"Shadow should have his chance," the trainer said. "He's a great horse. You believe it, too."

"Did you think I would condone murder and kidnapping?" she asked. "Did you know so little of me?"

Trapp's head bowed.

Ben watched as another thought struck her, and the horror on her face grew. "Jamie?" she whispered. "Not Jamie? It *was* an accident . . ." Her voice faded as she saw the truth on his face.

"He was going to sell the horses," Trapp said defensively. "He asked me to find buyers. Even for Shadow. The Marquess gave him to *you*. And he was bedding Lady Barbara," he said with mean satisfaction.

Ben knew that if Lisbeth's face could have gone

whiter, it would have. She swayed for a moment as if the revelation was the last blow she could withstand. He moved to her side, putting his hands around her waist, steadying her.

"Bastard," he said to Trapp. Then, softly, to Lisbeth, he added, "Don't believe anything he says."

She leaned against him as if her legs would no longer hold her. Her hands were clenched together in fists. His arms tightened around her, rocking her for a moment as he would Sarah Ann. After a moment, he felt her stiffen, and she broke away from him to walk to Sarah Ann and kneel down next to her.

"We'd best take her home," she said, tears glimmering in her eyes.

Ben's throat tightened. She had such gallantry and dignity, it made him hurt. From what she and Drew had both said, she'd had a joyless childhood, and yet she'd never lost her ability to trust, as he had. And now that instinctive tendency to trust was being challenged, and he saw her struggling with it.

"What are you going to do with him?" she asked.

Drew answered. "Take him back to Glasgow to face charges."

She nodded.

"Get him out of here," Ben said to Drew, "before I kill him."

"I need something to tie him with."

Lisbeth leaned down and tore a piece of cloth from Sarah Ann's petticoat. Silently, she handed it to Drew, who quickly tied Trapp's hands in front of him.

"I'll take him back to Glasgow now. I'll stop at my friend's for the night. They have a cellar room for Trapp here. You go back to Calholm and take care of the princess." He grinned. "You fight well for a solicitor."

Ben grinned. "You think like a lawman."

When Drew and Trapp were both mounted and he had the lead line from Trapp's horse in his hand, Drew said, "I'll see you in a day or two."

Ben nodded. "My thanks."

"A pleasure," Drew said. He turned to Lisbeth. "My lady," he said softly, "don't blame yourself for this. He had everyone fooled. And you saved all three of our lives by arriving as you did. I, for one, will be forever grateful." With that, he turned the horses and started back toward Glasgow.

"Make that two more grateful people," Ben added. "Now why don't you hand Sarah Ann to me, and let's get out of here."

As Lisbeth picked up the sleeping child, Sarah Ann's eyelids fluttered and she moaned softly. Ben took her in his arms, and she wriggled.

"Sugarplum?" he said softly.

Her eyes opened fully, and he could see them try to fasten on him and fail. "Papa?"

"Yes." He leaned over and kissed her cheek. "And Lady Lisbeth is here, too."

"I had bad dreams."

"We'll just have to kiss them away."

She snuggled up against him. "I dreamed you left me."

"I'll never leave you, Sugarplum. I promise." And he meant it. He couldn't imagine how he'd ever thought he might be able to leave her in Scotland, even if he had been assured she would have a loving family. She was as much a part of him as if she'd been his own child. She *was* his own child. The child of his heart.

"Want to go home," she demanded.

"Annabelle and Henry are anxious to see you," he said.

"And Peppermint," Lisbeth added quietly. There was no spirit to her voice, only an attempt to soothe.

Ben looked at her quickly, a question in his eyes.

"Callum said he found the pony this morning," she explained. "He's back in the stable."

"Pep'mint," Sarah Ann whispered. She smiled sleepily at Lisbeth. "I love you, Papa. And Lady Lisbeth . . . and An'belle and . . ." Her eyes closed again.

Ben's heart was caught in a vise so tight he could barely breathe. He had come too close to losing her to get over the fright as quickly as she probably would. He imagined he might be in for some nightmares of his own. "Let's get her back to Calholm," he said.

✧✧✧

It was late when they reached Calholm. Servants and guests alike, along with tenants who had aided in the search, surrounded the riders. Duncan reached Ben first and lifted his hands up for Sarah Ann, cradling her carefully in his arms, a tear running down his wrinkled face.

Barbara was there, too, and she smiled happily. Even Hugh's petulant mouth broke into a grin at seeing Sarah Ann.

But everyone quieted when Ben described what had happened and told them all that Callum Trapp and the groom, Baxter, had admitted to the kidnapping. He used few words, his delivery as concise and unemotional as a brief report in the newspaper. Lisbeth was astounded by his control. Questions came, but he ignored them, taking Sarah Ann from Duncan's arms and moving quickly into the manor and up the stairs to Sarah Ann's room.

Lisbeth dismounted slowly, and stammered out a few answers to questions, but then she simply couldn't say another word. Callum had been her friend for years, sometimes, it had seemed, her only friend. No matter what anyone said about Callum doing everything for himself, she knew the truth.

He had done it for her, too. And that made her as guilty as he.

Chapter Twenty-Three

Ben didn't leave Sarah Ann's side throughout the night, nor the next day. By the second day after their return from Glasgow, she was almost back to normal. He'd explained away the missing days by saying she'd had a fever and medicine.

She went riding on Peppermint, asking for Callum and being told only that he had resigned and gone to Glasgow. She remembered little of the time during which she'd been drugged. Still, the nightmares had returned.

While she was recovering, Ben wasn't able to think of much other than Sarah Ann, and he'd been hesitant to leave her with anyone. He knew he had to discard that all-encompassing fear for her; he couldn't stay with her every hour for the rest of his life. Though at the moment, he wanted to.

Everyone paid special attention to Sarah Ann. Barbara had brought her a small engraved locket. It had, Barbara said, once belonged to Sarah Ann's grandmother;

Barbara's husband, Hamish, had given it to her. Ben had been stunned at the gesture, at the genuineness of it. There was no guile in her voice, no hint of flirtation, only concern.

Hugh also stopped in and even tried a poor joke. He was awkward around children, although Ben recognized that he was trying in a bumbling way to apologize for his curtness of the past weeks.

Sarah Ann took it all in stride, giggling at Hugh's poor attempt at humor and expressing pleasure at Barbara's gift. Ben felt immense pride . . . and amazement at the recuperative powers the child seemed to posses. Now, if only her nightmares would end.

Lisbeth stopped in each day, too, though she was extraordinarily reserved, her eyes clouded by demons Ben recognized from his own past. He tried to put her at ease, but she wouldn't let him. She was like a block of ice, her body and face stiff, her words guarded. He read the guilt in her eyes, wanted to take her in his arms, and tell her none of it had been her fault, but he had no opportunity. Sarah Ann and often others were always with them.

Despite the help and concern that surrounded him at Calholm, Ben's need grew by the hour to return to the west, where he belonged. If he asked Lisbeth, would she come with him? She was used to the best of everything. There would be no manors, no servants, in Denver. He wanted to believe that she wouldn't care, that the Lisbeth he knew—*his* Lisbeth—was an independent woman with a pioneering spirit who would happily rise to the challenges presented by a half-tamed land. But he was uncertain—and afraid she would say no. If she did say yes, he was afraid that she wouldn't totally realize the sacrifices she would have to make, the hard work that might border on drudgery. If he couldn't adapt to wealth, how could she ever adapt to not having it?

Would she end up hating him?

All the guests left Calholm the morning after Sarah Ann's return. Drew returned from Glasgow, bringing news with him. Callum Trapp had committed suicide in his cell, cutting a vein with a knife he'd somehow obtained. Lisbeth went very pale, and disappeared for hours.

Drew had unexpectedly become a friend, and it had been a long time, Ben thought, since he had allowed himself one. Only now did he admit to himself how much he'd missed by shutting others out, by allowing the fear of loss to keep everyone at a distance. And the Scot was a godsend for Sarah Ann, with his quick wit and card tricks.

On the evening of Drew's return, after Sarah Ann's eyes had closed for the night, Ben invited Drew to his room for a drink.

"I received a communication from John Alistair yesterday," Ben said. "He will be here tomorrow for signatures and to discuss all the legal matters."

Drew's gaze sharpened. "It's official?"

Ben nodded.

Drew was silent for a moment. "Then what?"

"I have some ideas."

"You'll stay?"

Ben shook his head. "The life of a country gentleman doesn't appeal to me. I never intended to stay. I just wanted Sarah Ann to know her heritage, her family."

"And you ended up opening Pandora's box," Drew finished for him.

"Something like that. I can't simply walk off now, though, and negate the claim. It'll be Sarah Ann's decision when she's old enough. For now, I would like the Hamilton family to survive. I'm no farmer, but Hugh . . . well, he has possibilities, I think, if given the chance. I'm not fool enough, though, to hand it over to him to ruin. I want Alistair to continue as trustee, almost as a manager."

"And the horses?" Drew asked.

"The horses are draining Calholm," Ben said slowly. "Even if Shadow wins the Grand National, it will be years before there's enough money to support a stable this size—and Calholm doesn't have years."

Drew sighed. "It'll break Lisbeth's heart."

"Exactly," Ben said. "But the Hamiltons—and that includes Sarah Ann and Lisbeth—could lose everything unless those horses are sold. And the training course is taking up valuable pastureland."

"Shadow?"

"Shadow is hers. But the others have to go. Dammit, Drew, I know how much they mean to her."

Drew hesitated. "They did," he said finally. "I don't think they do now, not after what has happened."

Ben wished he believed it. But he'd listened to Lisbeth's hopes and dreams. He knew how hard she had fought for them.

Rather than pursue a dead end, Ben changed the subject. "I think you should tell her that you're her brother," he said abruptly.

"No." Drew shook his head. "She won't forgive me for not telling her sooner. She's already doubting herself, and the people she's trusted. I can't tell her that I've lied to her, at least by omission. Now now. Nor do I think she would appreciate learning her father is a rapist."

Ben swore.

"You're the only one who can help her now," Drew said.

"And how do I do that?" Ben asked bitterly. "By taking away every thing that's important to her?"

"*You're* important," Drew said.

Ben's mouth twisted in a cynical smile. "It's always been the horses, Drew. And I'm the original Jonah as far as women are concerned. Lisbeth won't want anything to do with me when I tell her about the stable."

"You underestimate her."

"No," Ben said. "I know she's strong. But everyone has disappointed her, including me. And I can't—"

"Can't what?"

Ben could only shrug his shoulders. Gulping his whisky, he stood in a gesture of dismissal. He saw anger flit through Drew's eyes but the Scotsman got the message. Lord Kinloch's gaze was cool as he set down his empty glass, rose from his chair and offered Ben a distinctly frosty "good night."

✧✧✧

John Alistair arrived at Calholm the following morning to officially deliver the news: the petition in Sarah Ann's behalf had been approved. The control of the estate was now in the hands of Sarah Ann's guardian, the title and lands entailed for Sarah Ann's son.

Hugh accepted the news with silence, Barbara with resignation, Lisbeth with the same icy calmness that she'd maintained since Trapp's confessions.

Afterward, Ben met with Alistair for an hour alone, asking questions and seeking advice. The solicitor was not happy with his plans, but he finally agreed to do what was necessary to implement them. Still, everything depended on unanimous family agreement, and as yet, Ben knew he had no agreement at all.

Ben went in search of Hugh, asking him to join him in the library Alistair had vacated.

Hugh looked at him with resignation, but followed him. He accepted a proffered drink, then said abruptly, "I'll be leaving tomorrow. I realize I no longer have a claim on Calholm. I'm grateful for your offer to settle my debts. It's more than I expected." His gaze dropped to the floor.

Ben paused a moment, then asked, "You still plan to go to America?"

"Why in the bloody hell do you care?"

Ben ignored the question. "And Barbara?"

Hugh shrugged. "Barbara will never leave Calholm. Especially for someone without a pence."

"Have you asked her?"

"I wouldn't do that," he said, anguish settling in his eyes. And pride.

Ben knew about pride. He knew way too much about it.

"I have a proposition for you," he said.

Hugh looked startled. "What?" His voice rang of suspicion.

Ben had to smile. He remembered the last man he'd made a proposition to. It had been met with the same degree of suspicion and lack of enthusiasm. But then, Diablo had been facing a noose.

Hugh looked as if his prospects were as gloomy.

"Can you run Calholm? Profitably?" Ben asked.

Hugh's stunned eyes stared at him. "Don't play with me, Masters."

"You've talked a good game. Could you really do it?"

He was baiting Hugh now, wanting to know exactly what the man was made of.

"Not with those bloody stables."

"If we were to sell the horses, all but Shadow?"

"The training field?"

"Put that into sheep pasture."

"The tenants?"

"They stay."

Hugh continued to stare at him, obviously trying to determine whether he was mad, or merely cruel. "Why?" he asked finally.

"Dammit, Hugh, can you?"

"It will take time, but I think, yes. Bloody hell, I know I can."

That was the answer Ben wanted. He didn't want fear, or bravado. He wanted commitment.

Hugh was eyeing him like a man might eye a tiger ready to pounce. "Why are you asking me this? Alistair was dead set against me having any part of Calholm."

"Alistair was afraid you might gamble Calholm away."

Hugh met his gaze straight on. "At one time, I might have. I've never had anything. I suppose you know that. Like Andrew Cameron, I had background and a noble family name and damn little else. But I have a talent for the land, and I finally realized I have no talent for cards."

"Some people never learn that."

Hugh snorted. "Like Ian?"

Ben nodded. "I want to return to America. I told Alistair I thought you could run Calholm for Sarah Ann. Sell the horses, but keep the tenant families. They can work with the additional sheep. You take half the profits you earn. The other half will be split three ways between Barbara, Lisbeth, and a trust fund for Sarah Ann until she comes of age."

"And then?"

Ben shrugged. "Then it will be up to her. I can't make promises, but I would hope she would sell at least part of it to you, whatever isn't entailed. In any event, you'll be doing what you want, and you should make money doing it. It would be a sight better than starting over in America with nothing."

A number of expressions had crossed Hugh's face: astonishment, cynicism, doubt, now hope.

"What about Lisbeth?" Hugh asked.

Ben sighed. "I haven't talked to her yet, and this agreement depends on her approval. I don't think she will object, though. She knows Calholm can't support the horses any longer, and she'd still have Shadow."

Hugh frowned. "I'm the last person to give advice, particularly where women are concerned, but you and Lisbeth . . ." He shook his head. "She and I have had our differences, but she deserves happiness, and I've never seen her . . . smile the way she has since you came."

Until recently, Ben silently amended. There had been no smiles of late. Still, hope shot through Ben like a warm ray of sun on a cold day. Maybe . . .

Holding the thought within, he changed the subject. "Barbara loves you."

Hugh's smile faltered. "I don't know."

"Don't underestimate her," Ben said. "I don't think very many people have given her a chance."

"Do you always go around saving souls?" Hugh asked, a muscle twitching in his cheek.

Ben chuckled. He had tried to help Diablo, but he'd

never thought he'd been saving a soul. Maybe he had, though Diablo certainly hadn't thought so at the time.

"So, what do you think? Will you do it?" he asked Hugh.

Hugh nodded. "Yes. And I won't disappoint you."

"I wouldn't have made the proposal if I thought you would."

"I'd by lying if I didn't tell you I think I should have had Calholm, but I also would be lying to myself if I believed I was ready. Going from nothing to everything is . . . well, it can be dangerous."

Ben knew in that moment he'd been right. Hugh's disappointment had made him strike out at everyone, but there was common sense under that exterior, and a growing awareness of his limitations. God knows, it had taken him long enough to find his own, Ben thought.

He held out his hand, and Hugh took it. "You'll have free rein for the most part, though I've asked Alistair to keep an eye on things."

"Fair enough," Hugh said, though he winced slightly. "When will you leave?"

Ben hesitated. He still had several matters to resolve, one very important one.

"I'm not sure," he replied.

"Thank you," Hugh said quietly. For the first time, they exchanged friendly smiles.

❖❖❖

Despite the successful meeting with Hugh, Ben felt only despair.

How was he going to tell Lisbeth?

He walked slowly up to Sarah Ann's room. Lisbeth was with her, sitting in a chair, a book lying facedown in her hands. Sarah Ann was asleep, a very pregnant Annabelle in her arms. She was clutching the scarf again, after having abandoned it for several days before the kidnapping.

His eyes went to Lisbeth, who rose and looked as if she were about to flee.

"I came to see how she was," Lisbeth said almost apologetically, and Ben knew that she felt guilt as strongly now as she had days ago.

How long had it taken him to rid himself of it? Days. Weeks. Months. Even now, he thought of Mary May—and the blood—and felt the burden on his conscience. He guessed he always would. But he'd had Sarah Ann to look after, and in every real way she had offered him salvation. He'd come to love her for herself, but taking care of her, raising her, being a good father to her, also had provided him a way to work off his debt to Mary May. He owed Mary May a life, and it was merely his incredible good fortune that giving his life to Sarah Ann had turned out to be the best thing he'd ever done for himself. But who did Lisbeth have to save her?

Ben held out his hand. "Lisbeth." It was a request, made softly.

She looked down at Sarah Ann, hesitant to leave.

"Duncan will keep watch over her," he said in a low voice. "I think I actually saw a tear in his eye when we brought her back."

"You did," she said. "She's won his heart, as well as everyone else's."

"Yes," he said, although they both knew Sarah Ann had not completely won Callum Trapp's heart.

The unspoken words seemed to hang in the room.

"Drew said he'll be leaving soon," she said nervously. "Sarah Ann will miss him."

"He's a good man," Ben said.

Her gaze finally met his. "How did you two—"

"Come to a truce?" he finished for her. He wanted to tell her who Drew was, but that was Drew's secret, not his. Instead, he shrugged. "He's a very capable man."

She looked at him strangely. "Not many people believe that."

"I believe that's his aim," Ben said. "The gambler's

greatest advantage. No one takes him seriously. That way he hears and sees things few others do."

His hand was still extended, still untaken. "Lisbeth, come take a ride with me."

She looked surprised. He hadn't left Sarah Ann's side except for the meeting with Alistair.

"Sarah Ann is safe now. I can't stay with her every moment until she's grown, although sometimes I'd like to. We'll leave Henry with her and I've already asked Duncan to keep an eye on her." He wanted Lisbeth away from the house, away from the others.

"Henry and Duncan—a peace-loving dog and an ancient retainer," Lisbeth said with the first trace of whimsy he'd seen in her in days. "A mighty combination." She hesitated a moment longer, then reluctantly agreed. "I'll change into a riding dress and meet you at the stables in a few minutes."

"I'll have the horses in front," he replied, leaving quickly. For years, he'd thought he had no emotions or that whatever he had were under control. But they whipped inside him now like a rawhide lash.

He was going to hurt her, and he didn't know how to avoid it. His only consolation was that she would never lose her home, that she would have the funds to live well, here or anyplace, if not to support a large stable of hungry horses.

Ben wanted Lisbeth to be with him. He couldn't imagine life without her now. Sarah Ann had lit one candle in an existence that had nothing but darkness; Lisbeth had lit another. But he could offer so little. At best, he and Sarah Ann would have a small house in Denver and he would engage in a struggling law practice, in what was little more than a boom town. He had a bad leg and would never be rich—for he wouldn't touch anything of Sarah Ann's. Lisbeth's opportunities were here. She was lovely enough to find someone else, someone of her own rank and social class.

But, God, he didn't want her to find anyone but him.

Ben saddled Bailey and Shadow, finishing as Lisbeth appeared in her moss-green riding dress. Her expression was wary, yet there was pride in her bearing, too. Pride despite having already endured so many kicks.

He wanted to take her face in his hands and kiss her.

Instead, he disciplined his expression and helped her into the sidesaddle. As she arranged her skirts, he thought of the first time he'd seen her, flying over a stone wall in boy's clothing. He would probably remember that as long as he lived.

"Where would you like to go?" he asked.

She hesitated. "The ruins."

It was the last place he wanted to go. But he nodded, and they cantered together down the road.

❖❖❖

The morning mist was gone, burned away by the sun, and the distant dark green hills were lovely.

Ordinarily, Lisbeth loved the hills on rare clear days like this one. But today she felt a heaviness and foreboding that created its own mist, one without magic but shrouded, instead, with dread.

Her heart was breaking, and she didn't know how to prevent it. Ben was going away. She knew it deep inside. She had known it for days. She'd seen that faraway look, the firming of resolution. The past few days had only confirmed a decision he'd already made.

She wished with all her soul that he would take her with him, but she hadn't a prayer that the thought had even crossed his mind. He had never said he loved her, not even when they'd made love so frantically just days ago. She'd thought she'd felt love in his touches, but then she'd been wrong about so much.

She wasn't sure what she would do after he left, whether she would stay or go. She felt lost, aimless, all her anchors swept away by Callum's treachery. She wanted nothing to do with the horses. They had cost too much in human terms: Jamie's life, almost Ben's and Sarah Ann's.

They had cost her everything. And for her, Calholm would be ever full of ghosts.

When they arrived at the ruins, Lisbeth allowed Ben to help her down, and they walked in to sit on what remained of the once-fortressed walls. The view was magnificent, the loch and the grassy hills beyond, dotted here and there with the white forms of sheep.

The scene seemed so peaceful, a stark contrast to the wracking pain inside her. Ben was silent beside her—trying to find the words, she guessed, to tell her what she already knew. She wanted to take his hand. She wanted to touch him. She wanted him to touch her. But Callum Trapp loomed between them like a wall. And so she sat there, as still as a statue.

"I'll miss this," he said softly, looking out over the Scottish hills.

She'd sensed his decision in every fiber of her body, and yet the words hurt more than she'd ever expected.

"Then don't leave." She hoped she didn't sound as desperate as she felt.

He took her hand, and a tingling reached upward through her arm and spread throughout her body.

He finally broke the strained silence, his voice low and hesitant. "I told you I used to be a lawyer . . . a solicitor. I used to be good at it before the war. I was in practice with my father, who'd pushed me toward it from the time I was very young. I would have done anything to please him. Anything."

Lisbeth heard the frustration and bitterness of having failed in his voice. "He told me the law was a noble profession, and I believed him," Ben continued. "Filled with that nobility, I went off to war, only to find there was nothing noble about killing people. And when I got home, my father had died, and I discovered that he'd represented war profiteers. Men who had sold shoddy goods to the army: shoes that fell apart, guns that backfired.

"After I discovered that, I wanted nothing to do with his practice," he said, "nor did I want to stay in Chicago where my former fiancée lived with her husband. I decided instead to find that Rebel who helped me. A quixotic quest, to be sure, but I needed some kind of . . . redemption, I suppose. Paying that debt was one way of getting it."

Lisbeth's hand had tightened around his. "But now you want to go back to the law?"

He nodded. "Diablo became an outlaw because of a corrupt government. And as a marshal I was an instrument of that government," he said slowly. "After his pardon, I realized I could do more to change the law in a courtroom than on horseback chasing wanted men back and forth across Indian Territory or evicting hardworking farmers from government land. And I was ready. Sarah Ann made it necessary, but I was looking forward to it."

The rare passion in his voice made Lisbeth realize then how much this trip had cost him. Ben had delayed his own dream for Sarah Ann. So many of his dreams had been smashed. She wouldn't detain him any longer. She would make it easy for him.

"I wanted Sarah Ann to have a family, to know her heritage," he added slowly. "It was never my intent to take anything away from those who belonged here." Slowly, he shook his head. "But now I can't turn my back on its future."

"Sarah Ann has always had the greatest claim," Lisbeth said. "It was what her grandfather would have wanted. Do whatever you feel you must do."

"I've got to go back, Lisbeth. I'm not a farmer. I never will be."

"I know," she whispered. "I always knew you would leave." *But the pain of the reality is so much greater than I expected.* She hesitated, then asked, "And Sarah Ann?"

"Sarah Ann belongs with me," he replied. "She's an American, though Scotland will always be a part of her life. We'll come back from time to time."

Lisbeth had never felt so empty. She wasn't going to cry, though. She wasn't.

"Lisbeth," he said, his fingers tightening briefly around hers, "I think Hugh can run Calholm with Alistair's help. I've talked to him, and he wants to do it. But I won't sign a contract with him if you don't agree. He knows that."

It took her a second or two to gather her composure. Then she said, "Of course I agree." She wanted to stand and walk away before he saw her grief. He would think it was for Calholm, the loss of the horses. But it wasn't. Her anguish was for the loss of him.

"Shadow is yours, of course," he was saying, "but—"

"But the other hunters must go," she finished for him, trying to sound nonchalant. "I know it. Perhaps I always knew it."

"I'm sorry, Lisbeth," he said. "I'm so sorry, but none of you will have any income if Calholm is bankrupt. Hugh has some good ideas, and he'll keep the tenants as long as they want to stay. But selling the horses is Calholm's only hope." He paused a moment, then said, "Alistair will hire an accountant to keep an eye on Hugh's management."

"And Barbara?"

"I think Barbara will be well taken care of," he said, with the barest hint of a smile in his voice. "Both you and she will get shares of the income from Calholm."

She swallowed. "That's very generous. It's my fault—"

"Dammit," he exploded. "Nothing is your fault. And you'll still have your chance to race Shadow. Enter him in the Grand National. Keep your dream."

Her dream was in ashes, as dead as her heart. What tiny, foolish part of her had hoped he would ask her to go with him?

Lisbeth untangled her hand from Ben's, fighting to keep back tears as she stood. "We'll miss you and Sarah Ann. And Annabelle." Could he tell how forced the lightness in her voice was?

She started toward Shadow. She wanted only to escape, but she felt Ben's presence next to her, then his hand.

"Dammit, Lisbeth."

She wouldn't look at him. She couldn't. "Let go of me," she said, but her voice held no authority.

His fingers were like iron around her arm and his warmth crept into her. She bit down on her lip to keep from burying herself in his embrace.

"Don't go yet," he whispered in her ear. His arms went around her, his hands pulling her close, so that her back leaned against his chest. She rested there in momentary surrender.

Ben felt Lisbeth relax, sensed the instant that she yielded to the attraction that always radiated between them, that was now greater than ever.

To hell with logic. To hell with reasoning. To hell with obstacles. They belonged together, and he simply couldn't let her go.

"Please, Ben . . ."

He heard her soft, broken request. And he ignored it.

He turned her so she was facing him. His gaze met hers directly. "What is it between us, Lisbeth?"

She went still, but her eyes were searching his face. They were that lovely hazel with flecks of gold, and they were so irresistible . . .

He leaned down and kissed her. They were worlds apart, even centuries apart in the way they lived. Yet he loved her.

His lips savored hers, caressed them slowly, then moved to do the same to every inch of her face, lingering around her eyes, then trailing toward the nape of her neck.

He tried to make the kisses undemanding, though he needed so much. He wanted to make her understand that it wasn't merely lust that he was feeling. When had he lost his ability to communicate? To say what was in his heart?

And then she leaned into him, her lips searching out

his, and when their lips met this time, the kiss was all warmth and yearning.

His hand went to her hair, pinned up with that little hat perched atop. He managed to pull off the hat, then the pins, then he ran his hands through her hair.

"Lisbeth," he breathed. "I want you too much."

"You can never want me too much," she replied. "Never . . ."

Her body was intertwined with his now; he couldn't tell where hers began and his ended. He couldn't tell a damn thing except that she had given him back his soul.

Her body trembled against his.

"Lisbeth?"

"Love me, Ben," she whispered. "Please . . ."

His lips came down on hers again. The kiss caught fire, and nothing mattered except the present.

Chapter Twenty-Four

Conflagration enveloped both of them.

Lisbeth was consumed by it. Melted in it. She felt like liquid heat. And when her eyes met his, she saw something there she'd never seen before: love. Solid. Real.

He wrapped his arms around her, his face touching hers. Their bodies touched, and she felt as if lightning was ripping through her.

In minutes, they were on the chapel floor, and his body merged with hers, possessing her, claiming her, yet there was a sweetness to the joining, a tender loving that radiated through her. Everything about him was tender, gentle. Yet a barely leashed passion made her own body surge with need, starting tremors that wouldn't stop.

She felt the wetness on her cheeks, and he kissed it away, murmuring to her as he did so. And then their bodies took over, saying what they had not. Loving. Caring. Giving.

They climbed together to a pinnacle, and when they

could stand no more, their bodies shared the triumph, sensations flowing from them as the sun bathed them with its brilliance.

Lisbeth snuggled against him, unwilling to move, unwilling to lose something so infinitely precious.

She felt safe now. And cherished in a way she'd never known before.

He leaned on one arm and looked at her through passion-clouded eyes. "Do you believe in magic?" he asked.

"I do now," she replied shyly, her fingers touching his nose, and then making circles near his eyes. "You're beautiful, you know."

"Lisbeth," he whispered. "Do you think you could ever leave Scotland?"

Lisbeth's heart jerked. The question was one she'd longed for, prayed for, hoped for. But was it because of the moment? Was it what he really wanted? He'd never said he loved her.

"You might like Colorado," he continued softly when she didn't answer. "I think it might be a little like your Highlands." He was silent for a moment, then added quickly, "Think about it," he said. He didn't give her a chance to answer, but rose, buttoning his trousers and helping her up.

She started to say something, but he put a finger on her mouth. "Think about it," he said again, and then he leaned over and kissed her.

He finally wrenched away, but Lisbeth felt warm and wanted and wonderful. He wanted her. He needed her. If only he loved her.

But she knew she would go with him, under any circumstances.

❖❖❖

Back at Calholm, Lisbeth went in search of Barbara. She had a question that had to be answered. Someday, perhaps, she could forgive herself for trusting Callum Trapp, for being blind to the truth of his motives. But for her own peace of mind right now, she had to know about Jamie, had to know if she'd truly misjudged everyone she'd ever trusted.

She simply couldn't go through the rest of her life second-guessing everything, doubting her own judgment at every turn. She couldn't live with the uncertainty.

She paused at Barbara's door, heard sobbing inside, and thought about going away. But she couldn't give Ben an answer without knowing about Jamie.

She knocked lightly.

There was silence. Then, "Who is it?"

"Lisbeth."

Another silence ensued, and then the door opened slowly.

Barbara's eyes were red, and there were telltale streaks down usually immaculate creamy cheeks. She looked totally miserable.

Barbara stood aside and allowed her to enter.

"Hugh's leaving," she said before Lisbeth could ask the cause.

"Why is he leaving and where?" Lisbeth asked as soon as she entered.

Barbara bit her lip. "He has no more claim on Calholm, nothing to do here. He said he won't stay any longer as . . . my guest. He plans to go to America."

So Hugh hadn't told her yet of Ben's offer. Probably because Ben had told Hugh that Lisbeth must first agree. She wanted to tell Barbara, but it was up to Hugh to do that.

"I offered to go with him," Barbara said, "but he—"

"Was too noble?"

Barbara nodded, swiping at her cheeks. "Sounds silly, doesn't it? Hugh being noble. But he has a stubborn streak."

Lisbeth knew only too well about stubborn streaks. "Perhaps it will work out," she said.

Barbara sniffed.

Lisbeth had never seen her sniff before. "And if you really love him, you'll find a way."

Barbara looked at her suspiciously. "Why are you being kind to me?"

Lisbeth shrugged, but she couldn't help smiling. "I think we both have the same problem."

"Ben?"

She nodded. "He's planning to leave, too."

"To go back to America? What about Calholm?"

"I'm not sure," Lisbeth replied, hating the lie but unable to break Ben's confidence.

Barbara stared at her. "Do you love him?"

Lisbeth nodded.

"What are you going to do?"

Lisbeth hesitated a moment, then drew a deep breath. "Callum Trapp said Jamie and you . . ."

Barbara looked stunned, then her face grew hard. "What did he say?"

"He said that Jamie was going to sell the horses, that you had convinced him, and that he . . . had bedded you."

Barbara snorted. "That little rat. I always—"

"Is it true?" Lisbeth said, a knot caught in her throat.

"Part of it," Barbara admitted. "Jamie did talk to me about the horses. He knew they had to be sold, but he also knew how much you wanted them."

"But *he* did, too. They were his father's—"

"He didn't love them the way you and his father did," Barbara said gently. "He was a realist, and he knew they were strangling the place. He wanted me to help convince you." She frowned in thought. "Callum must have heard that conversation. Jamie was killed just a few days later." She paused. "Jamie loved you, Lisbeth. That's why the decision was so hard for him. He never quite knew how to . . . express himself. His father, as you know, discouraged displays of affection as weakness. Hamish was the same. I didn't understand that until he'd died, and Jamie had the same problem. Everyone thought the Marquess was so wonderful, but his pride destroyed each of his sons," she said bitterly. "No, Lisbeth, Jamie never bedded me. Never tried to, though I . . . tried once to seduce him. I hated you because you had Jamie after Hamish died . . . and all you cared about were those bloody horses."

"I thought that was what he wanted, too," Lisbeth whispered.

"We've all been thinking at cross-purposes, haven't we?" Barbara said. "I imagine Callum Trapp played no little part in it."

Lisbeth turned away, tears blinding her. She had been so blind, so foolish.

"Lisbeth."

She caught her breath at Barbara's voice.

"I blamed myself for Hamish's death, too," her sister-in-law said. "He got into a stupid duel because I flirted with someone. Because of that, I despised myself, and I showed it by making myself a . . ."

Lisbeth whirled to face her, and saw all the misery she herself had been feeling. They suffered from the same problem; they'd just reacted differently. Barbara had rushed toward people; Lisbeth had avoided them and turned toward the horses. An empty dream.

"Don't let him go," Barbara said softly.

"And you shouldn't let Hugh go, either," Lisbeth said. "He does love you."

"I know," Barbara said.

Lisbeth stood there for a moment, bittersweet feelings rushing through her. She had tried so hard to make Jamie happy that she'd never looked below the surface. Perhaps because she'd been afraid to, afraid that he'd just wanted her dowry. They'd never talked about what was really important to each other, had merely made assumptions.

She vowed it would never happen again.

"Thank you," she said to Barbara.

The woman she'd thought was her enemy smiled back at her.

❖❖❖

Annabelle was missing!

One of the maids apparently had let her out when Ben and Sarah Ann went to the stables to see Peppermint. Sarah Ann became anxious when she wasn't found immediately, and that anxiety turned to wails when Annabelle still hadn't appeared by bedtime.

Annabelle never missed her nightly bowl of milk. Never.

The entire household started hunting for the cat.

Barbara and Hugh, who had appeared together at dinner with mysterious smiles, mussy hair, and even messier clothes, joined the search.

Lisbeth thought Henry might be able to sniff out the cat, but when she went to find him, she couldn't. It seemed he was missing, too.

The two animals had appeared to have a truce in effect—even a friendship of sorts—but . . .

With growing concern, everyone redoubled their efforts. Sarah Ann's tears turned into wooden stoicism. She sat on the bed, tearless, staring blankly at the wall, clutching her doll and her mother's scarf.

Ben stayed with her while others looked, but even he couldn't comfort her. Finally, Drew relieved him, and Ben rejoined the hunt. As he went to find Lisbeth, thinking they could search the house together, he thought that Drew would make one hell of an uncle, and he hoped the Scot would finally agree to tell Lisbeth of their relationship.

But first things first. That bloody damned cat!

Ben found Lisbeth on her way to search the stables, and together they made their way, stall by stall, toward the back where several stalls were empty. As they approached the last stall, they heard a frantic bark. Ben rushed toward the noise, but Lisbeth was faster. The bark had almost stopped his heart; if anything had happened to Annabelle . . .

Then he heard soft laughter and saw Lisbeth, her lantern held high, spreading light into the corner of the stall.

A growl warned him not to come any closer, and he looked to see Henry crouched protectively at the front of the stall. In back was Annabelle contentedly licking several tiny kittens. As Ben tried to move forward, Henry bared his teeth.

"You would almost believe he was the father," Lisbeth said, her laughter flowing like a warm current of air. Still chuckling, she leaned against him.

"I think he does believe it," Ben said. He took the lantern from her and hung it over the stall. Then he pulled her into his arms.

She melted into him, sinuously curving her body against his. As if she belonged there. And she did. Perhaps he'd always known it but had been afraid to commit himself again, afraid of the loss. But as he cradled Lisbeth in his arms and watched the cantankerous Annabelle, now so content with the life she'd produced, and he saw Henry sitting there, protecting her, Ben knew a quiet joy that was worth any price.

"I love you," he said, trying out the unfamiliar words. Then a little louder, his confidence deeper, he repeated, "I love you."

She tilted her head to look at him, her mouth forming a glorious smile. Her lips trembled slightly and he saw her swallow hard.

"I love you, too," she whispered. "So very much."

He held her tight. "I have to start from the beginning with my practice, and even then I'll be selective about the cases I take," he warned.

"Good," she replied, then she searched his face. "Are you sure you don't want to be a . . . what is it? . . . marshal?"

"No. But, Lisbeth, there won't be much money. I have enough to get us back and buy a small house. There won't be any servants."

"I always wanted to learn to cook," she said contentedly. "And I have some money of my own and—"

"That, like Sarah Ann's, will be yours," he interrupted. "If anything happens to me, I want you protected—"

"Aye," she said, but he thought the answer came
much too easily.

"Lisbeth—"

She stretched upward on tiptoes and stopped his
words with a kiss that went through him like a bolt of
lightning.

His lips caressed hers slowly, and then his mouth
moved to plant tender kisses all over her face. He felt her
tremors, and her breath blending with his, the beat of her
heart matching his own.

"Lisbeth." He said her name over and over again, as if
the word would make her his forever.

Slowly Ben ended the kiss and held Lisbeth away
from him a little, watching her carefully. There were, after
all, still a few formalities to observe.

"Will you marry me?" he asked.

"Oh, yes," she whispered.

"And come to America with me?"

Her eyes sparkled like a clear night sky. "Yes."

"I think I might need a whole ship all my own," he
murmured, not minding at all that a foolish grin was probably spreading over his face.

"A whole ship?"

"Well," he said, "there's you and me and Sarah Ann.
Annabelle, the kittens, Peppermint, Henry, Shadow,
maybe even Bailey."

"How on earth are we—?"

"We'll manage. Besides," he added wryly, "I don't
think I have a choice. Sarah Ann won't leave Peppermint
or Annabelle, Annabelle won't leave her kittens, Henry
won't leave Annabelle and her kittens. You should keep
Shadow and—"

"We'll need an ark at this rate." She laughed. "But what about Sarah Ann? Will she—"

"Approve?" he finished for her. "Oh, yes, she wants a family. I'm not sure she was ready for such a large one, but . . ."

"And sisters and brothers?"

"I think that would make her very, very happy."

"And you?"

"Yes," he said, knowing it was true. "A dozen at least."

She raised up to kiss him again. "I do love you."

"Will you marry me before we go?" he asked. "We would save on a cabin. Especially since—"

"We'll be taking half of Scotland with us."

"Aye," Ben replied, completing the bargain with a long kiss.

❖❖❖

Sarah Ann listlessly turned to look when the door to her room opened. Lisbeth entered with Ben right behind her, carrying a big box. Henry plodded behind, a paladin of the first order.

When Sarah Ann saw the kittens, her eyes grew large and a smile spread over her face. "Ann'belle's a mama!" she exclaimed.

"So she is," said Drew, who was sitting next to her.

"And Henry thinks he's the papa," Lisbeth added wryly.

"They're a fam'bly," Sarah Ann said.

Lisbeth felt Ben's arm circle her waist and she let him draw her against his side. "How would you like a family of your own?" he asked Sarah Ann. "A whole complete one with a mama as well as a papa. And a dog. Cat. Pony. Horse. Fleas. God knows what else." He looked at Drew. "Maybe even an uncle."

The latter was said almost under his breath, but Lisbeth heard. Her brows knitted together and Drew glared at him. Now, what was *that* all about? she wondered.

At the moment, she didn't much care. Her heart was doing flip-flops as she waited for Sarah Ann's answer. She loved the little girl, and Sarah Ann had said she loved her. But maybe she would be jealous of her papa taking a wife, maybe she wouldn't want her for a mama . . .

Lisbeth's last-minute fears evaporated when she saw the excited look Sarah Ann gave Ben.

"Fam'bly?" Sarah Ann said.

"I asked Lady Lisbeth to marry me," Ben told his daughter. "We want your approval."

Sarah Ann beamed. "I love Lady Lisbeth."

"And we'll go back to America."

Sarah Ann's smile broadened. "We're going home."

"I love you, Sugarplum."

Sarah Ann gave him a smile of complete contentment. Then she asked, "Can Drew go with us?"

"Hell, why not?" Ben said. "If he wants to. He'll be a bloody sight easier to tote than Shadow and that elephant of a dog." Then, as if it were an afterthought, he added, "I think."

Drew was staring at him. Lisbeth stared at Drew. What were these two men up to? No matter. The idea of Drew coming with them to America delighted her.

Lisbeth felt Ben's arms around her tighten.

"You're sure you want all this?" he asked softly, his lips near her ear.

She turned enough so that her mouth was only a fraction away from his. "That's what fam'blies are for," she said. "I can't wait."

Annabelle meowed. Henry barked. Drew disappeared out the door.

And the kiss that followed promised a very large fam'bly, indeed.

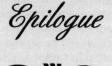

Epilogue

Denver

The biscuits were burning again, and never had Ben smelled anything sweeter.

After numerous attempts, Lisbeth had finally learned to use the wood stove. Except when her mind wasn't occupied with other matters.

He loved those other matters.

Drew Cameron had taken Sarah Ann and Henry to town, and Ben and Lisbeth used the opportunity to engage in building their family—and taking great pleasure in doing so. After a delightfully sensual romp in bed—in the middle of the day—she lay naked, snuggled in his arms, nibbling on the back of his hand. But then she started sniffing the air, too, and suddenly she sprang from their double bed.

"God's toothache," she uttered in dismay as he looked on contentedly.

He would give up biscuits any day in return for a rare lazy afternoon with her. Their small ranch lay outside the growing city, a perfect spot for raising Sarah Ann's swelling company of animals, and breeding a few horses. Lisbeth's Shadow was in demand, and while they couldn't command Grand National winner fees, stud fees were welcome to help build their small stable.

Ben had hung his shingle in Denver six months ago, and he had a growing list of clients. He had just finished a trial that had proved very rewarding, winning back a mining claim for a man dispossessed by a large mining company. And he'd had a few other small successes, too. He wrote wills, checked claims, and represented only those defendants he believed in. He'd even saved one innocent man from hanging.

Diablo, now a struggling rancher in North Texas, had written to him. His first child had been born and named Ben. The gesture had been both unexpected and touching. Ben had held the letter in his hand for a long time before relinquishing it to a curious Lisbeth.

He'd never been so content. Though he couldn't save the whole world as he'd once wanted to do, perhaps he could help just a little bit of it.

And Lisbeth and Sarah Ann gave color and joy to everything he did. As did Annabelle with all her children, Henry who still looked after them all, and Peppermint, Shadow, and Bailey, and his old horse from his marshaling days. There were more animals now: chickens and pigs and an elderly mule that had been abandoned. A new refugee seemed to appear every day.

And Drew. Drew had come to America with them, had helped restore the dilapidated ranch they'd purchased. He would be leaving in a couple of days, though, and Ben would regret it. They had become good friends. Drew had finally told Lisbeth that they were brother and sister, and it was almost as if she'd known.

Now Drew planned to seek his own fortune. He wouldn't tell Ben or Lisbeth how or where, but Ben knew his brother-in-law was a chameleon who could fit in nearly everywhere.

Lisbeth returned from the kitchen. "The biscuits are burned," she said happily enough, landing down on top of him. "Are you sure you aren't disappointed ye dinna marry Fiona?"

"Aye," he answered. "I'll take you over biscuits any day."

"Will you take two of us?" she asked with a twinkle in her eyes.

It took a moment for her meaning to register.

"Two?"

"Two," she confirmed.

He seemed puzzled at first, then he grinned. "Ah, well, what's another mouth to feed?" And his lips spread into a wide smile.

"Think about a trip back to Scotland," she said with an impish grin.

He had promised one every three years. Ben closed his eyes. Just remembering the logistics of the last trip made him tired. It had been no easy matter, and he didn't want to think about doing it again. Or maybe he did. It had been the finest trip he'd ever had, having married Lisbeth two days before they left in a double ceremony with Hugh and Barbara.

"I love you, little Scot," he said.

Lisbeth touched his face with a gentleness that always humbled him. "Thank you," she said, "for loving me."

It was the other way around, but they could have argued that point for years. Instead, Ben kissed her slowly, still bewildered by the good fortune that had come his way.

Then they heard a bark. A very loud bark.

And a meow from under their bed.

They both grabbed for their clothes.

Ben and Lisbeth smiled at each other. The fam'bly was back.

And they were about to hear some news.

About the Author

PATRICIA POTTER has become one of the most highly praised writers of historical romance since her impressive debut in 1988, when she won the Maggie Award and a Reviewer's Choice Award from *Romantic Times* for her first novel. She received the *Romantic Times* Career Achievement Award for Storyteller of the Year for 1992 and most recently was nominated for another Career Achievement Award, this time for Best Western Historical Romance of 1995. She has worked as a newspaper reporter in Atlanta and was president of the Georgia Romance Writers Association.

A penniless Scottish lord and a beautiful woman
disguised as a boy join a cattle drive
in Patricia Potter's next historical romance

The
Scotsman
Wore Spurs

Available in spring 1997
from Bantam Books

TURN THE PAGE FOR A SNEAK PEEK
AT THIS THRILLING NOVEL

Drew ignored the hooting from the two cowboys riding with him as he gingerly—very gingerly—picked himself up from the ground.

The fall was ignominious. He couldn't ever remember falling from a horse before. Horsemanship was one of the few accomplishments he claimed—that and gaming.

Kirby had warned him that cutting horses were unlike any other animal, their movements quick and sometimes unexpected when they saw a cow wandering off. The pinto Drew was riding had done just that, moving sharply when he'd just relaxed after a very long day in the saddle.

"Uncle Kirby said you could ride," Damien Kingsley said nastily. "What other tall tales did you hand him?"

Drew forced a wry smile to his face. He had been the butt of unending razing since he'd first gone on the Kingsley payroll a week earlier. His Scottish accent and unfamiliarity with cattle hadn't helped the image of tenderfoot.

"What do they have for horses in Scotland?" another man scoffed.

Damien, sitting a small roan, snickered. "You ain't going to be any use at all."

Drew tested his limbs. They seemed whole, if sore. He eyed the pinto with more than a little asperity, and the bloody beast bared its teeth as if laughing. Damn, but every bone in his body ached. He had raced horses, had ridden them long distances, but sitting in a saddle eighteen hours a day for a week strained even his experienced muscles. The thought of three months of this shriveled his soul.

Learn cow. That's what Kirby called learning the cattle business. In some strange ungrammatical way, the expression fit. But Drew was beginning to think he'd just as soon jump off the edge of the earth. He'd had no experience with cattle in Scotland, and his enthusiasm for being a cattle baron now had dimmed to the faint flicker of a dying candle.

Yet he'd never been a quitter, and he didn't much like the idea of starting now, nor did he want to see the triumph spreading across Damien's and his brother's faces. Even less did he want to disappoint Kirby.

He started for the pinto.

"Well, lookit that, will ya!" The exclamation came from a drover called Shorty, and all looked out in the direction the man pointed. Drew's own gaze followed the pointing arm.

Drew saw the most moth-eaten, woebegone, and decrepit beast he'd ever had the misfortune to see. Perched precariously on its bony back sat a small figure whose hat was as decrepit as the horse he rode.

"Mebbe Scotty could ride that," one of the men said, laughing uproariously at his own joke and using the name the other drovers had given Drew.

Drew would have loved to cram that laughter down his throat, along with his hat, but that would just make trouble for Kirby. He wondered how long he could curb a temper that had never been known for its temperance.

Then he watched, with the others, the slow approach of the rider, already feeling a measure of sympathy as he heard the men behind him continue to joke. He wondered whether he would ever fit in, or even, in truth, whether he wanted to. His first impression of the Kingsley hands was about as poor as theirs of him. They seemed uniformly loud, crude, even cruel. They seemed to have no real concern for the animals they rode or herded, and their sense of humor entirely escaped him, especially when he was the butt of it.

The rider and horse were just feet away now. The boy was enveloped by a coat much too big for him, and only a portion of his face was visible. Under the dirty slouch hat, a pair of dark blue eyes seemed to study him before they lowered and moved on to the other riders before going blank.

"I'm looking for the foreman," he mumbled in a voice that seemed to be changing.

"What for?" one of the men said, using his elbow to nudge a companion. "Want to sell that fine horse of yours? The fellow near the pinto may be interested."

Guffaws broke out again, and the boy's eyes went back to Drew, resting there for a moment. "Lookin' for a job," he said, ignoring the jibe. "Heard they might be hirin' here."

"Pint-size cowboys?" Damien said. "You heard wrong. We're full hired. More than full hired," he added, tossing a disagreeable look at Drew.

"Read about the drive in the newspaper," the boy said. "It said they be needing help. I want to see the foreman."

Drew admired the boy's persistence, especially in light of the snickers that had just been transferred from himself to the lad. But the drive *was* full hired. A number of much more promising looking cowboys had been turned down. He himself wouldn't have had a chance of hiring on, even at the miserly wage of fifty dollars and keep, had he not been Kirby's friend. It seemed every cowboy in the West wanted to ride with Kirby Kingsley on what was being called a historic drive.

"I'll take you," Drew said. "Follow me."

He took the reins of his horse and limped toward the corral where Kirby was making a final selection of horses to take. There would be ten horses per man, one hundred and eighty mounts in all, not including the sixteen mules designated for the two wagons that would accompany them.

"Mr. Kingsley?" He had stopped calling Kingsley by his first name when he went into his employ, especially around the other men. He had no wish to further aggravate their resentment toward the Scottish tenderfoot.

Kirby turned around, noticed his limp and gave him a grimace that passed for a smile. "Told you about those cutting horses."

"So you did," Drew said wryly. "I won't make the mistake of underestimating them again."

"Good. Nothing broken, I take it."

"Only my pride."

Kirby's lips twitched slightly, then his gaze went over to the boy. "That a horse, boy?"

The boy flushed, and the chin raised defiantly. "He has heart. Just 'cause no one ever took care of him . . ."

Kirby's smile disappeared. "You have a point. What's your name?"

"Gabe. Gabe Lewis."

"And what's your business?"

"I heard you was hiring."

"Men," Kirby said. "Not boys."

"I'm old enough."

"What? Fourteen? Fifteen?"

"Sixteen," the boy said angrily, "and I've been making my own way these past three years."

"You ever been on a drive?"

The boy hesitated, and Drew could almost see the wheels turning inside his head. He wanted to lie. He would have lied if he hadn't thought he might be caught in it. "No, but I'm a real fast learner."

"We don't need any more hands," Kirby said, turning away. The easy dismissal brought a deeper flush to the boy's face.

"Mr. Kingsley?"

Kingsley swung back around, irritation deepening the lines in his face. He waited for the boy to continue.

The boy's voice became a plea. "I'll do anything, Mr. Kingsley. Maybe I'm not so big, but I'm a real hard worker."

Kirby shook his head.

"I need the job real bad," the boy said in one last desperate plea.

"By the looks of that horse, I'd agree," Drew said helpfully. Strangely enough, he sensed his help wasn't welcome. The boy's gaze cut to his only for a briefest second, but there was no missing the scowl in them.

Kirby looked thoughtful for a moment. "Pepper, our cook, was complaining yesterday about his rheumatism. Maybe we could use someone to help him out. You up to being a louse, boy?"

"A louse?" The boy's eyes widened, and Drew noticed again how very blue they were.

"A cook's helper," Kirby explained. "A swamper. Clean up dishes, hunt cow chips, grind coffee. You ever done any cooking?"

"Of course," the boy said airily. Drew sensed bravado, and another lie, but Kirby didn't seem to notice. From the moment the boy had mentioned he was desperate, the rancher had softened perceptibly. Drew saw it, noted it. And it surprised him. There was nothing soft about Kirby Kingsley.

He knew, despite the fact he had saved Kirby's life, that if he couldn't pull his own weight he would be gone. His job had been based on the fact that Kirby had seen him shoot—and ride—and believed the rest would come easily enough.

If painfully.

But this slip of a boy sat a horse like a beginner, and he obviously lied about his ability to cook. Those dark blue eyes darted around just enough to say so. And he didn't look strong enough to control a team of four mules. Drew's eyes went to the numerous—but odd—bits and pieces of clothing; it was too hot for so much clothing, which meant he was trying to conceal a thin frame or feared someone would take what little he had if he didn't keep them close to his person.

But if Kirby had noted all these things, and Drew was sure he had because little escaped the man, he made no mention of them.

"My cook has to agree," Kirby was telling the boy. "If he does, I'll pay you twenty dollars and found."

The boy nodded.

"You can't cut it, you're gone," Kirby added. The boy nodded again.

"You don't have much to say, do you?" Kirby asked.

"Didn't know that was important." It was an impertinent reply, one Drew might have made himself, and he took another look at the boy's face.

There was no stubble, but the lad's skin was darkened by the sun and none too clean. But then the cook was none too fastidious himself, although Kirby proclaimed his food the best among cattle-drive cooks. That distinction appeared dubious at best—at least to Drew. Texas beef, he'd discovered, was tough and stringy, and the Kirbys' Mexican cook at home spiced it with hot peppers. He wondered if Pepper did the same, and he briefly longed for a piece of fresh salmon or good Scottish lamb.

He quickly discarded the thought. He doubted he would ever return to Scotland, where few of his memories were happy ones. If he had to suffer tough, tasteless beef to banish them, he would consider it more than a good trade.

"Drew?"

Kirby's sharp question broke his rambling thoughts and he turned his attention to the man next to him.

"Get the kid some food. I'll talk to Pepper."

"I need to take care of my horse," the boy said. "Give him some oats if you got any."

"Don't bother. He'll be mixed in with ours. Not that he looks like he'll last long."

"No," the boy said flatly.

Kirby, who had already turned to leave, stopped. "What did you say?"

"I'll take care of my own horse," the boy said stubbornly. "He's mine."

"If Pepper agrees to take you on, you'll ride on the hoodlum wagon," Kirby said. "You don't need a horse. Besides, all the hands put their horses in the remuda for common use. This one, though, won't be of any use. Might as well put him down."

The boy's eyes flew open in alarm. "No," the boy said stubbornly. "I'll take care of him."

"He won't last one day on the trail," Kirby said.

"No." The boy repeated as if it were the only word he knew.

"Then you can look for another job."

Drew couldn't help but admire the boy. His need—and desire—for the job was obvious, yet he wasn't going to give up the sorriest beast Drew had seen in a long time.

The kid's pluck appealed to Drew. "Maybe the horse has some potential," he said softly.

Kirby's eyes cut over to him. "That nag?"

"He's been mistreated, starved," the boy said defensively. "It ain't his fault."

Kirby looked at the boy. "How long you had him?"

"Just a week, Mr. Kingsley, but he's got grit. We rode all the way from Pickens."

Kirby looked from Drew to the kid, then back to Drew and shrugged his shoulders in surrender. "What the hell. But you're responsible," he told the kid. "If he can't keep up, I'll leave you both."

"He will. He's already getting stronger." The kid paused, then asked, "What's the hoodlum wagon?"

"Damn, don't you know anything?" Kirby's irritation was plain. "It's a second wagon. It carries bedrolls, extra saddles, tools. A chuck wagon for an outfit this size needs every inch for food and supplies.

The kid looked fascinated at this piece of information but said nothing.

Kingsley swore, frowned at Drew and turned his attention to the wrangler separating the horses. Drew smiled at the boy, who didn't smile back. He did slide down from the horse, somewhat painfully, Drew noticed.

"I'm Drew Cameron," he said.

The boy looked at him suspiciously and without warmth. "You talk funny."

"I'm from Scotland," Drew explained. "The other hands call me Scotty."

The boy didn't look satisfied, but didn't ask any more questions, either. Instead, still hunched in the coat, he followed Drew into the barn and then into a stall. Drew found some oats and poured them into a feed bucket. The horse looked at him with soft, grateful eyes, and he understood the boy's attachment. Hell, he'd had a horse he'd loved. Too much. Bile filled his throat as he remembered.

"I can take care of him alone," the boy said rudely.

"You got a name for this horse?"

"Billy, if it's any of your business."

"Hell of a name for a horse."

"It ain't your horse."

"No," Drew conceded as he watched the boy take off the bit, then the saddle. He struggled with it, and not just because the saddle was heavy. There was no deftness that comes with practice. His gaze went to the boy's hands. Gloves covered them. New gloves.

And the clothes were fairly new though some effort had been extended to hide that fact. Dirt was too uniform for it to have been accumulated naturally, and the denim trousers were still stiff, not soft and pliant. Something else didn't ring true. The "ain't," perhaps. Drew had an ear for nuances of sounds.

The natural skill had been invaluable in gaming; he could always detect a false note: desperation, bluffing, fear. He thought he detected all three now.

Why? Unless the boy had something to hide other than a need for a job. Could he be a runaway, or something else? Something more ominous?

Drew hadn't forgotten the ambush nor the

possibility that someone might try again. And he remembered the ambusher's words. *That little guy.* He very much doubted this slip of a boy could be involved, but he had seen danger and dynamite come in much smaller packages.

He immediately dismissed the idea as quickly as it flitted through his mind. Those last few months in Scotland had raised his caution. A man he'd never suspected—a trainer of horses—had proved to be a murderer and kidnapper. Many things, and people, had not been as they seemed.

"Where are you from?" he asked.

The boy's vivid blue gaze bore into his. "Places."

Drew grinned. It was an answer he'd given frequently. He merely nodded. The boy's business was his own until proved otherwise.

"The bunkhouse is the next building. Take any that doesn't look occupied," Drew said. He'd moved to the bunkhouse himself. There were several empty cots.

"When do we leave?"

Drew heard an anxious note in the boy's voice.

"In two days," Drew said.

"What do you do?" the boy asked unexpectedly, his eyes narrowing.

Drew shrugged. "Just a cowhand," he said, "and if I want to stay that way, I'd better get back to work." He turned, oddly discomfited by the hostility in the boy's vivid blue eyes.

What the bloody hell, anyway. The lad was none of his business.

❖❖❖

Gabe watched the tall figure leave the barn. She had almost swallowed her tongue when she'd first seen him. He was the same height as the man who'd killed her father. The same height and approximately the same weight.

Just a cowhand. He was a lot more than just a cowhand, if she was any judge of people. Nor did Kirby Kingsley treat him like another cowhand.

She hadn't expected a certain kindness, not from either man, but perhaps she had only imagined it. And Kingsley *had* been ready to kill her horse. She chalked that up to evidence of his cold-heartedness. As to the Scotsman, perhaps people had many facets to them.

Like her father. She never would have expected that he'd had a dark side, that he'd had secrets that someday would kill him.

The bunkhouse was the next building. She'd taken that into consideration. She'd tried to think of everything, but the reality of sleeping in the same room with a number of men was suddenly daunting. She wondered whether Drew Cameron slept there. And bless the Lord, but she was hot. She had to wear the layers of clothes to disguise her form, but the day seemed hotter than hell, and she knew the heat would only get worse during the drive.

To rid herself of that unhappy thought, her mind turned to the horse. He *was* a bag of bones, which is why she called him Billy. For Billy bones. She hadn't been about to tell the tall cowpoke with the Scottish accent that.

She ran her hand down the horse's neck and he trembled. She knew she would have risked losing the job—and her chance to prove Kingsley guilty of her father's murder—before she'd abandon Billy. The horse had stolen her heart the moment she'd seen its sad, hopeless eyes in the stable where she'd gone to purchase a mount. The liveryman had gone straight past Billy, but she'd hesitated.

"You don't want that one. He's done for. Cowpoke just left him here. Be best just to put him down."

"How much?" she'd asked.

"Hell, you can have him," the man said. "Five dollars for a saddle. But he won't last a day."

But Billy had lasted. She had purchased some oats and had ridden him slow and easy and the horse had looked at her with a kind of gratitude that made her heart break. He was hers, and she was going to make him well.

He nuzzled her hand. She put her cheek against his head, her thoughts returning to the Scottish cowboy. He didn't talk like a cowhand. Despite the Scottish lilt, he had the unmistakable mark of gentry about him. His voice was moderated, and he was well-spoken. And dear God, he was handsome.

His hair was a tawny light brown that shimmered in the sun, and his eyes were golden with flecks of brown and green and gray. Some would call them hazel, but that didn't quite fit their uniqueness. Like his hair, his eyes appeared to shimmer with gold, to flash, even dance, with amusement only he seemed to understand.

No matter what he'd said, he was no mere cowhand making fifty dollars a month.

She reluctantly picked up her saddlebags and bedroll with their meager contents. A second shirt, a second set of men's underwear, a shirt, soap, toothbrush. Her father's diary. She wasn't going to let that leave her hands. Nor the locket. It was pinned inside her shirt.

Gabe Lewis. She had to keep thinking of herself that way. Gabe Lewis had no family. He had no past, no future. He couldn't be seduced by a quick, empty grin.

With a heavy sigh, she made sure Billy had water. She added some more oats to his feed, then headed for the bunkhouse.